Published by:

I0615836

www.napsusa.org
NAPS
National Association for Public Safety

please visit us on the web at:
www.cafepress.com/manning
http://shermanmanning.blogspot.com/

or contact us at:
hallopeter@sunrise.ch

ISBN 978-0-9743260-1-6

Other Books by **Sherman Manning:**

KKK Kids Killing Kids - June 2010
Blue Eyed Blonde 2
Blue Eyed Blonde
Reach Beyond the Break and Hold On
Dream and Grow Rich
If It Doesn't Fit, You Must Acquit
Through the Valley of the Shadow of Death (Columbine High School)
Teens Are Dying/Parents Are Crying: Where Do We Go From Here?
American Dream, A Search for Justice Vol. 1 & 2
From Palace to Prison

G.B.G. Gang Bangers for God

"It is now May 2010, and I am excited about the special work which we are doing with and for the Face-Book Generation. Some awfully powerful (celebrated) folks have joined my G.B.G. /HEART team. The political stalwart John Burton has joined us. The brilliant, world renowned trial lawyer Robert D. Blasier (AKA "Bob") is the Attorney for G.B.G. (www.blasier.com)... I can't seem to get away (LOL) from Hanvard! President Obama went to Harvard and so did Bob. Dr. Franklin Curren heads my Advisory Board and he went to Harvard. Alvin Poussaint, M.D. is a G.B.G. supporter and he is an Associate Dean at Harvard... Everybody is waiting on my most controversial, powerful, sensational and bombshell dropping tome "K.K.K." (Kids Killing Kids); It is a book that is bigger than me. Every Kid will find "K.K.K." to be a spellbinding book. I could never have written it without the help of Dr. Lewis Yablonsky (of Harvard), C. Solis M.D., A. Duran, Ph.D., Dr. Gregg, Jimbo, Fred Schroeder, Daniel Bugriyev, A.W. Jeff Macomber, Warden (A) Tim Virga and Pat Kennedy etc. My arguments with, lectures from and guidance from these people has been an education per se... "K.K.K." will be published and in schools etc the second week of May 2010. Call 1-877-809-1659 or visit www.cafepress.com/manning to order "K.K.K." It will be available (to order) at every book store in the world and on Amazon.com. It will be worth the wait... Austin Sisneros, kids at McClatchy High School, Trona High School, Tanner (at Wharton High School) and young men around the world will be drawn to "K.K.K." like flies are drawn to defecation., I am aware that a few people are threatening to sue me for certain comments in "K.K.K." Enter Bob Blasier! Bob does not agree with my every word or thought; but he's qualihed to defend my constitutional right to free speech and artistic expression... Now I hope kids like Alex Bennett, David Schenirer (McClatchy), Jordan Simon, Kyle Evans, Aaron Maloney (and his brothers in Green Bay, Wisconsin), Michael Brewer, Jordan (at Rocketown), John Hackett, Will Rains, Joseph Rocha, Jason Zysman and Daniel Coverston will peruse this (Creating Monsters) tome, which I wrote in 2004. By popular demand my G.B.G. office in Zürich Switzerland decided to re-release "Creating Monsters" in preparation for the biggest, baddest and the most awesome youth book of the 21st Century. I stole (LOL) from Drew Pinsky, Dr. Phil, Dr. Janet Taylor, Dr. Jeff Gardere, Bishop T. D; Jakes, Bishop Eddie Long (my homeboy) and President Obama, etc, and used their "stuff" in "K.K.K." Students (i.e. Mike Corsetto, Cody Sheldon, Tyler Grady, C. J. Sheron,

Austin Sisneros, Paul Hauser, Joe Hanson, Tadd Carr, Alex Weinberg, Austin Paul, Ben Honeycutt (Ft. Oglethorpe, Ga.) Michael Castro, Tim Urban, Alex Lambert, Robert Graham (C.S.U. Sac), Alex Chivescu, Nicholas Labarbara etc) can still get G.B.G. clothing (i.e. T-shirts and caps etc) and take photos in them etc. And we will use your photos in the second printing of "K.K.K." (e-mail your photos in G.B.G. attire to Hallopeter@sunrise.ch and/or snail-mail photos to Sherman D. Manning J-98796, G.B.G./HEART President, CSP-Sacramento, P.O. Box 290066, Represa, Ca. 95671- 0066)... I wanna thank my supporters in Washington Township, Ohio. Ryan Macconnell, Heather Green, Penny and all of my law students at U.S. Mint Green, LTD etc. Y'all read "Creating Monsters" and as T. D. Jakes would say, "Get Ready! Get Ready!" for "K.K.K." coming soon! With a baby faced 15 year-old Wayne Treasy using the internet to text rage and assault, with Michael Wilson (Laguna Beach) using the internet as a tool of rage. With teen bullying and kiddie porn (via the internet) at an all time high etc. Bob Blasier is correct, we need "K.K.K."

Sherman D. Manning
President G.B.G./Heart

Status Update: I am now writing a smaller companion tome for "K.K.K."... "Bad Boys" will publish in September 2010. I'm writing it because kids can read "K.K.K." right before they get out of school for the summer and then peruse "Bad Boys" as soon as school starts after summer break. Bob Blasier and John Burton are providing informational infrastructure for "Bad Boys." And I am "High" off the (spiritual) dopamine, and emotional "High" which I get from writing tomes for Face-book teens. Van Hansis, Mick Hazen, Aaron Kelly, Justin Bieber and boys (and girls) around the world will be stoked by Bad Boys... "Poke" somebody and tell em...

O. J. SIMPSON'S LAWYER DEFENDS "K.K.K."
By Peter Andrist

Peter Andrist resides in Zurich Switzerland. He is an entrepreneur, philanthropist and the chairman of NAPS. He writes this special report from his Zurich office...

I'm Peter Andrist. Attorney Robert (A.K.A. "Bob") Blasier was on the O. J. Simpson Dream Team with Johnnie Cochran. Bob represented the Unabomber and hundreds of other high profile clients.

Bob has defended persons accused of white-collar crime, drug offenses, homicides and juvenile crimes etc.

Bob is considered "one of the best DNA experts in the world," states noted Attorney Daniel Broderick. Bob is also a personal injury expert. He's an expert on juvenile offenses and on 3-strikes. Bob Blasier is also a graduate of Harvard Law School...

So how do we explain one of the most powerful lawyers in the world writing to a prison inmate these words: "Sherman, (D. Manning) I hope that young people all over the world will be moved, inspired and enlightened by your book-"K.K.K." (Kids Killing Kids)". . .I've known Sherman a long time. He took me to the home of Ambassador Andrew Young (in Atlanta) and introduced me to "Uncle Andy". Rev. Hosea Williams stood on the balcony of Lorraine Motel with Dr. Martin Luther King Jr. when king was assassinated. Sherman took me to personally meet Rev. Williams in 1995. I've leamed not to doubt G.B.G./HEART President Sherman D. Manning. But -~ when he called a few weeks ago to say, "We have a Blue-Chip endorsement for our tome "K.K.K." from Bob," I was taken aback. But on March 24th at 10:45 pm Swiss time Bob Blasier called me. "To put together a team of inmates, counselors, guards and wardens...is indeed a great accomplishment. I commend Sherman," Bob says...and then on March 23, 2010, here comes the most powerful politician in California (State Senate President (Ret.) Chairman of the Ca. Democratic Party and longtime Willie Brown friend) Attomey John Burton into the mix. "I certainly hope that youngsters around the world will take a look at K.K.K and. . ." Chairman Burton states. Sherman is a pioneer, a trailblazer and an expert on kids in prison. But 'God' is the only way I can explain how a man locked up in jail and accused of some "Bad" stuff, etc. can convince the Dean of Psychiatry at Harvard to read "K.K.K."... The Director of Sherman's Advisory Board (Franklin Curren, M.D.) is a Harvard graduate. Dr. Alvin Poussaint (Dean of Psychiatry at Harvard) corresponds with Sherman. And now Bob Blasier? I believe that God has shown Sherman favor.

Curtis Lee served more than 20 years at Folsom Prison. Curtis is now in East Oakland Ca. transforming the lives of young gang-bangers by telling his story. We will get the book ("K.K.K.") to Curtis, Tony Dungy, Bishop Eddie Long, Bishop T. D. Jakes and Reverend Otis Moss etc, and I predict that kids across the world will be transfixed and transformed by this powerful book (we publish in less than 30 days)... A few public officials have threatened to sue Sherman due to some of his comments in the book.

But (although Bob may not agree with all of Sherman's statements etc.) Bob, Burton and others will vigorously defend Sherman's constitutional free speech rights. The very first published copy of "K.K.K." will go to Attorney Bob Blasier and I predict that in spite of all the controversies etc, Bob will be on Tyra Banks, The View, Larry King, Tavis Smiley and the Charlie Rose shows talking about this humongous book "K.K.K."... Ipso Facto (for the record) Sherman issued a presidential edict stating that "Bob Blasier (www.blasier.com) is the only lawyer in the world authorized to officially speak for G.B.G./HEART, NAPS, and for Sherman D. Manning!" Call l-877-809-1659 or visit www.cafepress.com/manning to reserve a copy of "K.K.K." The tome will be on Amazoncom and an E-Book. You may also order "K.K.K." at any bookstore in the world. I promise parents and students that the reason such powerful men (i.e. Chairman Burton and 'Bob') have endorsed such a sensationally titled ("K.K.K.") tome by a prisoner etc. The reason is it is an awesome book. No kid or youth will ever read another book like "K.K.K." The book needs to be in every home... "K.K.K." is bigger (and better) than Carl Rove's new memoir. And it was written in a dark (maximum security prison) place. But powerful photos are developed in dark rooms.

And in Sherman's dark room, a bright snapshot and psychological portrait of prisons has been developed.

Read the book. .

Peter Andrist
CHAIRMAN ~ NAPS

STATUS UPDATE: Joseph Latham V-70462, Jai Breisch, C. J. Sheron and Austin Sisneros should contact Sherman about the book forthwith.

Table of Contents

Dedications

Dedication: Honorable President Nelson Mandela

"A nation should not be judged by how it treats its highest citizens, but its lowest ones," stated the Honorable Mr. President Nelson Mandela. Mr. Mandela also stated, "I did not see the face or hear the voice of another prisoner. I was locked up for twenty-three hours a day . . . And every hour seemed like a year . . . I had nothing to read, nothing to write on or with and no one to talk to. The mind begins to turn in on itself and one desperately wants something outside oneself on which to fix one's attention. After a time in solitary confinement, I relished the company even of the insects in my cell and found myself on the verge of initiating conversations with a cockroach. Nothing is more dehumanizing than the absence of human contact." - "Long Walk To Freedom".

I seriously suggest and strongly recommend that every person who is reading my words right now, get a copy of "Long Walk To Freedom". That book is for the rich and the poor, the incarcerated and the liberated. It will move, inspire, enlighten, encourage and educate you. I've read Zig Zigler, Dennis Kimbro, Tony Robbins, John Grisham, William Bernhardt and even Tom Clancy. I've perused fiction, fantasy, non-fiction, psychology and politics. I am a Bibliophile of sorts and I love good books. But (hands down) one of the most moving, interesting and inspiring books I've ever put my hands on is, was and perhaps always will be "Long Walk To Freedom".

Mr. Mandela had a law degree, but he never stopped dreaming about those with no degree. He had a nice house of his own, but he never forgot those who had no house. Mr. Mandela stood up and fought for justice, the downtrodden, the neglected and the unprotected. He fought for the locked out, the left out and those who were forgotten about. They locked Mr. Mandela up for treason, but he continued to dream. For the first five years in prison, he could not receive visits, but he continued to fight. After five years in prison, he could only get a visit from his wife, Winnie Mandela, once every six months. For the first seventeen years in prison, Mr. Mandela could not receive newspapers, but he pressed on. For the first twenty-two years in prison, they wouldn't allow him to see a television, but he pressed forward. Mr. Mandela continued to yearn, to dream, to visualize, hope and pray. After spending twenty-seven years in prison, he kicked the prison cell wide open and the stone of apartheid was rolled away. Mr.

Mandela walked out holding the hand of his prison guard. And now, the Mandela whom was once called Mr. Prisoner is now called Mr. President. Attorney, Former President/Humanitarian Nelson Mandela seemed to know that once an individual has rid him herself of the fear of the oppressor and his prisons, his army and no police, there is nothing they can do.

You are completely liberated and not simply emancipated. You never wish to be assaulted, you never want to be hurt and you still feel humiliation and pain. But nevertheless, you feel that this is the price you must pay in order to assert your views, your ideas and your paradigm of justice. President Mandela successfully suppressed his emotions, maintained his sanity, rationality and his self-discipline in the face of the most dangerous and dehumanizing circumstances. "When one is faced with such situations, you want to think clearly and obviously you think more clearly if you are cool, you are steady and you are not rattled. Once you become rattled, you can make serious mistakes," Mr. Mandela often said. Mr. Mandela's prison ordeal transmogrified him into a much more reflective and influential kind of leader. He was cut off from mass audiences, public images and television cameras. Stripped down to man-to-man leadership and to the essentials of human relationship, away from the glitzy trappings of power. He learned about human sensitivities and how to deal with the fears and insecurities of others, including his Afrikaner wardens (guards). He was sensitized by his own sense of guilt, both about his family and about friends he had used during his political career, but he was acquiring a deeper confidence, feeling himself "master of my fate", like a classical hero. Unlike most politicians, in mid-career, he had time to become much more thoughtful and questioning, reading biographies and histories. And he deepened his interest in the law, which, though it had put him in prison, he realized provided the only possible basis for a lasting settlement. The law, not war, was the basis of his hopes for his country's future. Mr. Mandela's concentration emerged from his personal development. He had learned how to control his aggression, to "think with his brains, not his blood" and to channel or direct his energy into the goal of a negotiated victory. "Hope is the horse on which you travel to your destination to reach the winning post", Mr. Mandel wrote in a missive. "There is often a collective public amnesia about guys in jail," he had stated. "During the harsh days of the early 1970s, when the ANC seemed to sink into the shadows we had to force ourselves not to give in to despair," he states.

When his wife, Winnie went to jail on a false charge, Mr. Mandela wrote to her from his prison cell and helped her to see jail as perhaps a blessing in disguise.

"You may find that the cell is an ideal place to learn to know yourself, to search realistically and regularly the processes of your own mind and feelings. In judging our progress as individuals, we tend to concentrate on external factors such as one's social position, influence and popularity, wealth and standard of education . . . But internal factors may be even more crucial in assessing one's development as a human being: honesty, sincerity, simplicity, humility, purity, generosity, absence of vanity, readiness to serve your fellowmen qualities within the reach of every soul - are the foundation of one's spiritual life. At least, if for nothing else, the cell gives you the opportunity to look daily into your entire conduct to overcome the bad and develop whatever is good in you. Regular meditation say of about fifteen minutes a day before you turn in, can be very fruitful in this regard. You may find it difficult at first to pinpoint the negative factors in your life, but the tenth attempt may reap rich rewards. Never forget that a saint is a sinner that keeps on trying."

I would hope that Dr. Firpo Carr, Raymone Baine or Attorney Tom Mesereau would suggest to Michael Jackson (see "American Dream/A Search for Justice" for specifics on Michael's case) that he should read "Mandela" an autobiography and "Long Walk To Freedom" as Michael faces the toughest battle of his life. I hope Kobe will take the time to read those books.

Books were the fuel and the ammunition in the battle of ideas. "If we laid our hands on any book, however thick, said Mbeki, it was copied out and distributed to our membership throughout the prison." Malcolm X turned his prison cell into a classroom and read the entire dictionary. Dr. Martin Luther King, Jr. wrote his famous "Letter From A Birmingham Jail" in a cell. Mr. Mandela and that brilliant brother named Tokyo Sexuale actually turned Robben Island into a University of higher learning. They demanded that prisoners, read, tutor, lecture and study. During the long years in which they were denied the right to read, they smuggled books. Newspapers were like gold. And this is a strange contrast to what I see in prisons in America. First of all I would be remiss not to mention that America's prison system is designed to fail. And that by and large reading, studying and self-help are discouraged by prison authorities. Yet, I am also cognizant of the fact that the system is succeeding in creating failed humans. It's a rare thing in some prisons to find inmates interested in reading. Inmates are often intimidated by big books, education and politics for a variety of reasons. They have the prison subculture, which reinforces the belief that books are for boys and nerds but bullies use bullets, knives and sticks. Also the fact that the draconian laws, which have been passed in many states, make it impossible for many to even get out of prison. The inmate develops the attitude that, "I'm never going to get out anyway so why should I read". And so this barbaric system of locking people up and throwing away the keys has created an atmosphere and a subculture which makes it dangerous to be in prison, dangerous to work in prisons and even dangerous to get out of prison. For once the inmate gets out of prison he has often been injected with the mentality of the monster and infected with a venom, which will express itself via violence, rapes, age and murder. . .

So I have dedicated my writing to Mr. Mandela because he never gave up and because of the hundreds of celebrities, politicians and civil rights leaders whom I've written. The Honorable President Nelson Mandela is one of the few who writes back. On Oprah, I saw teenage boys reaching out to shake Mr. Mandela's hand who just wept uncontrollably. Canadian, "Free The Children", youth Craig Kielburger said, "I've met Bill Clinton, Liz Taylor, Mother Teresa, Hollywood movie stars, etc., but of them all I was most impressed with Mother Teresa and Mr. Nelson Mandela. I honor, salute, love, support and pray for the life, the legacy and the foundation of Mr. Nelson Mandela, Tokyo Sexuale and all of those who fought with, prayed for and supported the Honorable Nelson Mandela in South Africa and across the world . . ."

It seems that perhaps Supreme Court Justice Anthony Kennedy has read Mr. Mandela's writings. Justice Kennedy awed lawyers as he spoke at an ABA annual meeting in 2003 and expressed concern and compassion for the two million people in American prisons. A sentiment which is rarely voiced by government officials. "When someone is judged guilty and the appellate and the review process has ended, the legal profession seems to lose all interest. When the prisoner is taken away, our attention turns to the next case. When the door is locked against the prisoner, we do not think about what is behind it. We have a greater responsibility as a profession and as a people, we should know what happens after the prisoner is taken away. To be sure, the prisoner has violated the social contract: To be sure he must be punished to vindicate the law, to acknowledge the suffering of the victim, and to deter future crimes. Still, the prisoner is a person; still, he or she is part of the family of humankind." Justice Kennedy must have read the autobiography, "Mandela". He went on to tell the lawyers that a decent and free society, founded in respect for the individual, ought not to run a system with a sign at the entrance for inmates saying "Abandon Hope, All Ye Who Enter Here". Justice Kennedy has come to realize that a people confident of its laws should not be ashamed of mercy. Justice Kennedy encouraged Dennis Archer and the ABA to consider plans to breathe life into the clemency process and encourage lawyers to seek clemency for those who have served long enough. He even urged his listeners to confront the reality of the racial disparity in our nation's prisons and to examine the economic choices we make as a people to spend more money on housing prisoners than educating our children. He urged the ABA to create a public dialogue about America's prison system saying it is the "duty of the American people to begin that discussion at once". It should be noted that Justice Kennedy is not a liberal and was nominated by Former President Reagan.

Because of great men such as Mr. Mandela and great women such as Julie Stewart, people like George Soros and Paul Wright - it seems America is beginning to want to listen. I salute again - The Honorable Nelson Mandela.

* * *

Dedication: The Fortune Society

I also dedicate this book to Attorney Joanne Page and The Fortune Society in New York. I applaud Darcy Hirsh, Brian Robinson, Natalie Bimel, Carl Johnson, Jr. Stephan Likosky, Nora McCarthy, Anthony Papa, Edmond Taylor, Russ Luncsfond, David Schofield, William Teves, Jonathan Grassi, Brenda Ann Kenneally, Channie Byrd and all the good people who volunteer and support The Fortune Society.

Fortune news is their publication, a not-for-profit community based organization dedicated to educating the public about prisons, criminal justice issues and the root causes of crime, and to helping ex-offenders and at-risk youth break the cycle of incarceration and crime through a broad range of services. I encourage every person reading this book to call 212/691-7554 or log onto www.fortunesociety.org and find out more about this great group. I encourage great, rich and successful men such as Willie Gary, P. Diddy, Frank Tyson, George Soros, Tokyo and Mr. Bezos to write a check to help the Fortune Society. When we support groups such as The Fortune Society, FAMM, PLN and the Youth Media Council, we are really helping to protect public safety. (More on The Fortune Society and JoAnne Page in other chapters of this book). The Fortune Society news is a pipeline to the free world for prison inmates across America. It is also one of the few publications, which routinely features prison writers. It embraces free speech and artistic expression. It encourages inmates to use their communication skills to transcend the places, which hold them. I applaud The Fortune Society and (again) I am not opposed to The Fortune Society, PLN and The Western Prison Project using this tome and any of my work to raise money for their efforts. It has always been my goal to see these groups working together and if this book needs to be discounted for these groups so that they can use it as a vehicle to raise funds; I'm supportive. God Bless "The Fortune Society".

* * *

Dedication: Mr. Felix Dennis

I have learned a lot about the publishing brilliance and talents of Dennis Publications Co. the past week. I salute, exalt and applaud Mr. Felix Dennis. He publishes Blender, Maxim, Stuff and several other magazines that interest people all over the world, including guys in juvenile facilities, jails and prisons. Books, magazines and photos have a way of taking the prisoner, the lonely older lady, the aspiring college student as well as the professor into a whole new world. Photos stimulate and entertain the mind. And reading informs, inspires and can educate the mind. Mr. Felix Dennis has the uncanny ability to produce and publish magazines, which appeal to people from diverse walks of life.

I have perused Maxim, Stuff and Blender sporadically over the past year, but recently I began subscriptions. And on April 26th of this year, I received a notice indicating that my first issue of Stuff magazine was disallowed by C.D.C. because of an article on "A Prison Break". Then on April 29th, I received another notice indicating that my Maxim was being disallowed by C.D.C. because of an "article that threatens security and safety of inmates". I'm not certain as to what the Maxim article is about because I have not seen it. (By the time you're reading this tome, I'll know the specifics because I've asked Mr. Dennis to tell me what the article was about. Perhaps we can detail it more in a revised edition of this book). My thinking, however, is that the Stuff article is perhaps about the prison hostage situation and escape etc. in Arizona. If I'm correct, then disallowing this magazine is preposterous. Millions of inmates across the U.S.A. including me, saw this prison break on television. We saw it on the local news, on the national news and we read about it in newspapers. C.D.C. did not disallow the Sacramento Bee, New York Times or the LA Times newspapers when they did stories on this prison break. In fact, we see movies on prison escapes, guard beatings, etc. all the time. In fact, we were not disallowed to see the news a couple of weeks ago when prison guards beat an inmate maliciously at C.Y.A. Why were we allowed to see it? Why were we allowed to see those LAPD Cops beating Rodney King years ago in LA? The answer should be simple - This is the United States of America. And in this great country, we do have what we call free speech and artistic expression. I believe that disallowing Maxim and Stuff constitutes prior restraint, illegal censorship and illegal bias against Dennis Inc.

I'm aware of the fact that Prison Legal News has successfully sued prison authorities across this country for disallowing PLN into certain state prisons. Prison officials in Florida, Washington and a few other states utilized draconian, arbitrary and capricious policies to attempt to keep PLN out. But Paul Wright succeeded in getting fine litigators to take them to court and in each case PLN won. I have informed Mr. Felix Dennis, Amy Carpenter, Keith Blanchard and David Hilton that I intend to exhaust the appeals process as an inmate and upon exhausting that process, I'd like to sue and I would hope Dennis Publications will sue with me. I'm certain Larry Flynt, Robert Guccione, Floyd Abrams, Barry Keenan and Gerald Uelman will be interested in this case. In my book "American Dream/A Search For Justice" I outlined C.D.C.s violation of my rights as an author. I explained how they manipulate the rules and attempt to stifle, rape and trample free speech and artistic expression. I would hope that since the First Lady of California (Maria Shriver) is a reporter, she would motivate Arnold to enforce free speech and artistic expression in prisons in California. The disallowing of a magazine because of an article they don't like is random, arbitrary and unconstitutional on its face.

I hope that Mr. Felix Dennis will tell the world about this violation of his company's rights. This is Taliban Justice. This is the kind of censorship Mr. Mandela was subjected to on Robben Island in South Africa. Prison guards censored his mail, disallowed magazines and newspapers, etc. But the last time I checked this was the United States of America.

And reading an article is not going to cause an inmate to attempt to escape. Hustler first, Stuff second, Maxim was third - what's next on the CCPOA hit list? Are they going to begin to disallow the Sacramento Bee, New York Times, LA Times, etc? When they have an article C.D.C. does not like? Will books be next? Books by Malcolm X, Rubin "Hurricane" Carter? How about Mr. Mandela's "Long Walk To Freedom"? When Davey Turner files his lawsuit against C.Y.A. will prison officials shut off television power, cut the cables and keep out newspapers?

My last book "American Dream/A Search For Justice" is sitting up in the litigation coordinator's office right now. Prison officials disallowed it. I can't have my own book. This is wrong. But since my book was disallowed and is sitting next to Mr. Dennis' Maxim and Stuff, I assume, I'm in good company. Stan Williams, Robyn Goldberg, Details Magazine, Men's Fitness, Elle, FHM, Rolling Stone Magazine, Source, King Magazine, PLN, The Fortune News, Legal Times, Law Journal etc., etc. I salute, applaud and honor you. And to Mr. Felix Dennis, I say please continue to inform, entertain, inspire, educate and fascinate the world with your publishing genius. (More on Rolling Stone, Felix Dennis, FHM, etc. in other parts of this book).

Sherman Manning
May 2004 / 2010

Prologue

His hair is blondish brown. His eyes are sort of hazel. He has nice, pink lips and not a speck of hair anywhere on his baby face. Nice little body with a big, juicy butt. Too much butt for a boy in prison. He looks like a boy toy. He has all the right physical features to belong on a street corner, late at night, in Boystown on Santa Monica Blvd. His face is the essence of innocence. Girls would call him cute, women would say he's fine and a predator would say, "He's mine." And as scared, nervous and as immature as he is, he will mind. Oh yes, he will obey. He, Gary, nineteen years old, Montano is prey. Since this boy (toy), Gary, is now in prison, not only is he prey, but he will pay. He will pay with his lips, tongue and his anus . . . Now that Gary has gone to New Folsom State Prison, he's called Huerro. Some guys call him "Harry Potter" since when he wears his glasses he slightly resembles Harry Potter.

Huerro walks the yard in the prison knowing that heads are turning and he is being watched by all. He does not really know how to process this mentally. On the one hand, he's embarrassed. On the other hand, he likes the attention. He knows he's not gay but . . . "All eyes are on me," he mumbles to himself as he strolls around the yard. Sometimes he says, "They're sick, watching another man's butt." But Huerro is soft, fragile and really, really afraid. If guys only knew how many times he has silently cried himself to sleep. If they only knew how much he misses home, high school, his mommy, his daddy and his sisters. If they knew how terrified and horrified Huerro felt; that lump in his throat, butterflies in his belly, the trauma he felt when the judge sentenced him to eight years in prison, if the guys on the yard knew, they would laugh. They would (literally) use these facts as weaknesses and as accelerated methods, strategies or cons to get Huerro in the sack.

"You got yacks, Huerro!" Casper yells at him. "Screw you," Huerro replies amicably. Gary is the youngest guy in the yard and in prison, there are two types of inmates: The predator and the prey. Huerro is prey . . . It was December 29, 2002 after the 11:00 p.m. count when Columbia (an a/k/a) raped Huerro. They were cellmates.

Columbia had moved Huerro in under the pretences of being an o.b., a cool celly with a TV and radio. He knew Huerro was young, afraid, impressionable and gullible. He fed Huerro, dressed him up in nice shoes and took care of him for a week without incident. Then came D-Day . . . On the 29th of December, after that count, Columbia pumped fear, terror and anxiety into Gary's ears as he explained that if Huerro did not give it up, he'd slice (stab) him. Fifteen minutes after

14

Columbia had began his mental rape; Huerro was on his stomach on Columbia's bed getting physically raped. It was painful and humiliating and devastating . . . The next day Huerro didn't know what to do. If he told the cops, he'd be labeled a rat, snitch, rape victim and a faggot. If he told, Columbia would get one of his boys (prison buddies) to attack Huerro. "If you move to another cell, I'll kill you," Columbia had also told him.

I can't tell it to an inmate or to staff, but I know what I can do. I'll write the governor. I'll write Mr. Gray Davis and tell him my celly is raping me. Since he's the governor, he can take care of it. They'll move me, protect me or just come and transfer Columbia. That's what Huerro decided on January 4, 2003. Now that he's told me, I've got to let him screw me every night. I'll just let them get a doctor to check my anus for sperm and once they see it's his DNA in me, they'll charge him. I'm gonna tell the governor to put a rush on this because I'm literally being raped every night." Huerro told himself and so he did it. On January 5, 2003, Huerro wrote a six page urgent, life or death letter to Gray Davis. Huerro felt a sense of relief when he dropped his letter in the mailbox. He knew it wouldn't be long now. Few more nights of this paid and it would all be over. Help was on the way. This letter was going to the CEO of California; a democrat . . . Forty days and nights later Huerro was still in the cell with and being raped by Columbia. It took a total of forty-seven days before Huerro got an envelope marked "Office of the Gov. State of CA". He wondered why Gray Davis had written him. "I don't want a letter, I want help" Gary said as he opened the letter. The Governor's Office will not be able to take any action on your concerns at this time. However, this office has forwarded a copy of your letter to the Director of CA Prisons, Mr. Alameida. Thirty-six days after that forty-seven day wait (for a total of eighty-three days) Huerro got a letter from David Tristan in Alameida's office stating, "You should address your issues within the prison and file an inmate appeal or talk with your counselor." It took only twelve additional days (for a grand total of ninety-five days and nights of being raped) for counselor Janice Mayfield to call Huerro into her office. "You're trying to cause problems in this prison when you should be doing your time. Act like a man. If your celly was raping you, you would not be still in the cell with him. Now, if I hear of you trying to write the governor again, I'll have you on the first thing smoking to Pelican Bay. Now get out of my office."

Huerro got up and decided, "Screw it they'll just have to call me a rat, dude ain't gonna rape me tonight. Screw that counselor, I'm going to see the captain. Huerro went to see the captain and told him everything including the harsh and indifferent way he had been treated by counselor Janet Mayfield.

The captain looked at him and stated, "Kid, let me explain something to you. Janice Mayfield is my wife. My wife, now get up, turn around and put your hands behind your back." Captain Billy Mayfield called for Officer Blackburn and Greg Wolfe and told them to write him up for threatening staff and put him in the hole.

Everything I wrote beginning with the sentence, "his hair is blondish", was/is fiction. It was fiction based upon factual, actual happening inside the walls of prisons across America everyday.

It was the only fiction, which you'll find in this book. The fact that you thought a book was fiction was (I'll admit) subterfuge. I needed you to think it was fiction in order to get you to read the sad fact and reality is that fiction readers outnumber non-fiction readers ten to one in America. So I don't want to preach to the chair. I am attempting to start a revolution and it will take youth, students, lawyers, mothers, fathers, sisters and brothers to fight this revolution. We cannot fight the powers that be with the powers that be. If we're gonna subdue the subterranean justice being meted out here in America, we must reach out to real people who are ready to deal with real issues.

I am ready to fight. I want George Bush out of the White House. I respect the office of the president. Ipso facto my respect for the office, which he occupies, causes an automatic kind of respect to him.

But (i.e.) an unclean man by any other name is still an unclean man (continuing with the i.e.). If a man refuses to shower and brush his teeth for two weeks, he will stink and you can put an Armani, Hugo Boss or any kind of suit on that man that you can find. And from a distance that man might look like Don Novey, Ed Alameida, Gray Davis, etc., he might look good in that sharp suit. But the closer you get to him the more you'll dislike him. And once you get up close and personal, you'll smell the stench. You'll realize that what you saw on TV, in the newspaper, in a photograph or from a distance has deceived you. You thought you were looking at a clean man, but when you got up close your nose explained to you that what you had observed was a dirty man who was dressed up.

Now Mr. Bush may not be a dirty man and I understand that many consider him a good man. Maybe he is a good man, but I can't see it and his presidency does not pass the smell test. I smell a rat . . .

Likewise, when I look at the rapes (such as the real, true to life fiction about Gary in this book) murders, gangs and violence in prisons across America, I also smell a rat.

"Follow the money trail", I say to Governor Arnold in California. "Follow the money trail", I say to every governor in every state in North America. Once we discover who's getting the money, we will then understand how to clean up the bureaucracy in the prison hierarchy. In California, we'll have to look at Jim Brulte.

And many others, once we find out who's accepting money from prison guard unions then we'll understand why rapes, beatings and abuse are excused by the legislators, senators and governors in these states. For example (and remember this book is non-fiction) it was obvious to inmates in California years ago that the CCPOA owned Gray Davis. CA prison guards could do no wrong in the eyes of Mr. Davis' administration. And my only fear with the "terminators" administration is his (Arnold's) association with Pete Wilson and that crowd. Arnold is not corrupt. Arnold is basically a good man. But Arnold seems to be surrounding himself with the same crowd, which screwed up the prisons and the budget in California in the first place.

I hope Arnold will not follow all the advice given to him by guys like Pete Wilson. Pragmatically, I am troubled and anxious about the fact that it appears that Arnold wants to pursue higher office. He hinted that if laws are changed to allow immigrant citizens to run for president, he'd consider running. In all candor, most folks who plan to eventually run for president don't want anyone to have an excuse to call them soft on crime. And some of the things which Arnold will need to do in the Golden State in order to clean up the mess, which Gray, Pete and others made would have the potential to initially cause folks to claim he's soft on crime. For that reason alone, it is somewhat doubtful that Arnold will do what needs to be done to transform crime and punishment, clean up the subterranean, subterfuge running rampant in California's thirty-three prisons, which is propelled and prognosticated by the monopolistic, abusive, exclusive and corrupted advocacy of the CCPOA.

The fictional tale, which I told earlier, was based specifically on reality. It was more realistic than one would wish to imagine. The awful truth is that boys are raped on a daily, almost hourly basis in prisons across North America. California especially has a rape crisis in its prisons. Texas and New York are not far behind. Authors (and brothers) Mark and David Dow can corroborate this truth. I spoke with mark Dow via telephonic communications in early April (2004) and we discussed the horrible conditions of jails and prisons across America. "Sherman, I can imagine prison authorities give you hell for writing books in prison," Mark stated. "If you only knew. These people despise prison scribes. I'm like a cancer. They treat me as if I'm so much worse than the scum of the earth. If I smoked dope, gambled, fought or drank pruno, I'd be one of the fellas. As cool as could/can be. But the fact that I sit alone every single day of the week and write, write, write, makes me the problem," I told Mark. "But write on, write on," Mark indicated. Get Mark's book, "Machinery of Death".

I hope that guys such as Vinnie Faso, Nick Bentley and Alan Rafferty will get involved in the political process. I think that if folks like Alan, Nick and Vinnie were to write to the Governator/Terminator and say - Dear Arnold: I suggest that you realize it takes drastic, unique, creative and innovative measures to solve crucial, critical and emergency problems. Ipso facto, since our prisons are busting at the seams with violence, rage and hatred, I'd like to see you go inside every prison in California and give motivational speeches to staff as well as inmates. Challenge them to transform the prisons. Give them incentives to stop the violence and rehabilitate themselves. You (Mr. Arnold) are a celebrity and in a unique position to impress prisoners in ways others could not. I challenge you to exercise your star power and challenge prisoners to transmogrify their (emotional) scars into stars.

I think if Mr. Rafferty would get twenty of his friends, Vinnie gets twenty pals and Nick got twenty of his friends, etc. to all duplicate those missives and send them to the State Capitol, Arnold would take notice. We have got to get young folks back involved with politics. I want to see youngsters running for the city council, mayors, governors, the senate, the congress and even for the highest office in our land; the president.

I would argue with anybody who claims sixteen, seventeen and eighteen-year-old guys and gals are not mature enough to handle public office. If you can sign up for the military (deferred enlistment) at sixteen, fight in the war at seventeen, then you are mature enough to have a voice in the politics of our nation. Presently, we have a nation, which will allow seventeen and eighteen-year-old kids to handle machine guns, bombs and other explosives in wars in Fallujah, but won't let them buy a beer in America. If a kid is eleven or twelve years old in Florida and commits a crime, we try him/her in a court of law as an adult. "If he was mature enough to pull that trigger then he is mature enough to face the consequences as an adult as prosecutor Mary Hanlon Stone would argue. But what if a twelve year old wanted to run for governor? "He does not have the life experience, maturity or mental apparatus to run for public office. That's absolutely preposterous. He ought to be in school or out playing with his toys. Public office is no place for girls and boys", would come the argument from Mrs. M. H. Stone.

But I'll tell you that I believe we need to involve our youth in the process of dealing with the very serious issues our society is faced with. Who better to come to with solutions to youth violence, the violence in CYA, youth drug abuse, prison violence and teenage pregnancy than young people? The Bible says a child shall lead the world and without vision, the people perish. Some of our elderly statesmen have lost all of their vision.

I want to see Kevin Shelton, Michael Holtz, Alan Rafferty and Vinnie working with Gloria Romero and helping to devise strategies to implement programs to keep youth from going to juvenile facilities. They should also help us to come up with strategies that will help the kids who are already in juvenile facilities to learn skills which will help them stay out once they get out. A few weeks ago Gloria Romero exposed a secret C.D.C. video, which showed prison guards beating up a kid at C.Y.A. in Stockton. The guard beat the youth inmate a total of twenty-eight (licks with his fist) times as the kid lay face down in the floor. Guards Delwin Brown and Marcel Berry clearly utilized extensive force. KCRA aired it on the local news, but then Dan Rather aired it for the entire nation to see. And (believe it or not) a spokesman for the CCPOA (CA Prison thugs union) was foolish enough to defend this gladiator beating by saying, "Well the video does not show what happened in the office prior to the beating." His point? Perhaps he was attempting to imply that the kid could have said or done something bad enough to deserve getting his butt kicked. Not so, C.D.C. trains its officers to restrain inmates and wards (youth offenders). I researched the issue with a prison lieutenant. "If I jumped up and stabbed you right now and then laid face down on the floor what does C.D.C. policy and training say responding officers must do?" I asked. "They're required to handcuff you," the lieutenant made it clear that some officers (C.O. Mansky? Greg Wolfe? Sgt. Blackburn? Captain Martel? C. D. W. Stratton?) would beat the hell out of me. But that would be a violation of the rules. There is no justification for a sworn peace officer beating up an inmate. These are not supposed to be tit for tat type street brawls. Nevertheless, whatever the youth had done didn't hurt the officer too badly. It definitely didn't disable him or diminish his punching owner. He was clearly seen beating a kid with twenty-eight punches while the kid lay face down on the floor. And his partner kicked the kid. He should have kicked his partner and pulled him off that child.

Our state attorney general basically said it was probably excessive force, but he (I wonder how much money the CCPOA has given Bill Lockyer) would need to see what happened before the guard beat the kid in order to file charges on the guard. The local DA has refused to charge the guard. Why? Most local DAs are as afraid of the wrath of the CCPOA as was the Jews of Hitler. The CCPOA allegedly ran Richard Polanco out of town and out of office. I'd like to know if Mr. Polanco is still alive. According to guys like Lance Corcoran (due to the fact that we're rushing to press, I've been unable to determine if this is the Lance I know. If Mr. Corcoran is from the state of Georgia, I know him. And I'd like to talk to Lance). And Don Novey, C.D.C. guards can do no wrong. They claim to walk the toughest beat in the state. And they are the states finest.

I want to see the U.S. Attorney prosecute these guards for beating this kid. And since we have empirical data which proves California's Youth Authority has the most violent prisons in the nation; since there is a violent assault every eleven minutes in C.Y.A., we must get Federal Marshals to take over C.Y.A. as well as C.D.C. I submit that promoting Jeannie Woodford to C.D.C. Director was a great move. Arnold and Rod Hickman get an "A" for promoting Jeannie. She is proactive and she is not corrupted. But we can't put new wine into old or germ-filled bottles. We need new bottles. You can't teach ethics to a forty-year-old prison guard who has been lying, beating and drug smuggling for nineteen years. You have to fire him. And there are simply too many prison guards who have been corrupted for too long and a class in ethics ain't gonna change them!

Bring in the new blood! I suggest that undercover Federal agents infiltrate the prison system. We need a mandate from the president to let undercover Feds come into prisons for both inmates and guards. That's the only way to clean up the system. And if Lance Corcoran and Don Novey really believe in truth and justice; if they really believe there is no code of silence; if they really are not hiding any subterranean methods, they ought to welcome the feds into the prisons. Mr. Corcoran: Would you support a plan to allow undercover federal agents to come into the prisons as officers and as inmates?? Inquiring minds want to know.

I have seen too many men behind these walls who can't think properly, can't function clearly and who don't know what's wrong with their lives. They are suffering from arrested development, incarcerated spirits and locked up minds. Their developmental processes were interrupted, hampered and stunted by the violence, abuse, trauma and horrors they endured in the juvenile facilities and youth jails across this nation. The early attacks on their minds, bodies and spirits have simply ruined them for life. While they were young, vulnerable, impressionable and at the most receptive stages of their lives, they were sent to the wolves and recruited into the gangs in C.Y.A. and youth prisons across North America. This early introduction to violence, rage, anger, hatred, racism, rape and murder has caused something inside them to snap, click and slick. This magnet for corruption and volatility has grown stronger and stronger inside them as the years moved on. They were groomed for violence and trained to fail. In places such as New York, Texas, Alabama, Mississippi, Washington, New Jersey and California- there juvenile stay was merely training ground. In C.Y.A. they were schooled in how to become rougher, tougher and meaner. They were taught how to block out feelings, numb their consciences and do evil without looking back. To graduate into the Big House. The Big House is the adult prison system. These kids became and are becoming monsters. And when I began writing this book, I was inclined to utilize the term monster, somewhat metaphorically. But on further contemplation, I have come to the conclusion that the title creating monsters is to be taken literally. I submit without question that the California Youth Authority, the CA Department of Corrections and numerous (broken, violent and abusive) prison systems across the nation are literally "creating monsters". What is a monster? A monster is not some green giant with smoke coming out of his/her ears that we may have seen in a Spielberg movie. A monster according to the dictionary is a very wicked person. When one can go out and blow up synagogues, killing innocent women and children, one is very wicked. When one can molest children, rape senior citizens and commit cannibalism, one is a very wicked monster. The gentleman (see my book, "American Dream/A Search For Justice") who dragged jimmy Lee Byrd to death by chaining him to his truck, was a monster. This perpetrator of this heinous crime (dragging Jimmy Lee Byrd until his head was actually separated from his shoulders) was indeed a monster. He was not a monster by nature! There are no natural monsters. His monsterism (if you will) was taught to him in the "Texas" prison system. He did not grow up violently, nor did he grow up a racist. Yet when he went to prison on a minor crime and was forced to join a prison gang, forced not to deal with Blacks, forced to participate in prison race riots, etc. he was transformed. And even his daddy said, "When he came home, he was a different person. He was made with the world." I am simply waiting to see a Davey Turner, a Gerry Spence or a Johnnie Cochran file a lawsuit against C.Y.A. and/or C.D.C. for creating monsters. I seriously believe that one of these guys (presently in or out of prison) are gonna wake up and realize that the reason they have wrecked their lives and ipso facto committed so many crimes is because they were the victim(s) of the making of a monster at the hands of prison guards. They ought to file class action lawsuits against any system, which had a hand in this creative/destructive process.

Perhaps Josef Griessae Muerscher, (brilliant attorney in Hamburg, Germany) Charles Ogletree, Skip Gates, David Cole and Noah Feldman will combine their legal expertise and help to develop this creative type lawsuit against C.D.C., C.Y.A. and prisons across this country. I suggest . . . But experience has taught me that many of us enjoy rhetoric. We like to talk about what should or could be done. But talk is cheap. And as it relates to the horrendous status and conditions of crime and punishment, laws and justice in America' all o us know that the conditions are critical. We all are cognizant of the fact that there are indeed men and women trapped behind these walls who are not guilty of the crimes for which they are doing time. Even the Honorable Judge Barry Loncke in Sacramento declared in a race and justice meeting (two years ago) that, "We need to put together a Blue Ribbon commission which is similar to the Truth Reconciliation Commission in South Africa. We need to look into these prisons and weed out those who don't belong there." I commend Judge Barry Loncke. Those were powerful words. And his heart was definitely in the right place. But we ain't done nothing about that (wrongful convictions) problem since that meeting. All too often our leaders will call meetings and give great press releases but do nothing proactive, creative or innovative after the meeting. If Judge Loncke, Judge Jane Ure (a great judge) and others want to start this Blue Ribbon commission, I'd like to apply for a review immediately! I'd like for the Governator to read my trial transcripts! After he and Maria read my transcripts, the governor would order my immediate release and save the taxpayers five hundred thousand dollars! We can put fifteen kids in private college for a year with the money the state would save by sending me home to Atlanta . . .

I spoke on the telephone with Rishi. Rishi is a brilliant little lady who works in Oakland at the Youth Media Council. This council is an outgrowth of the former, "We interrupt this message" which was/is a media advocacy group. (Read more about Kim Deterline and "We Interrupt This Message" in the best-selling tome, "American Dream/A Search for Justice").

Rishi was gregarious, affable, informed and highly intelligent. She logged on to my Website (www.cafeshops.com/manning) literally while we were talking. "I'm looking at your Website now and it looks great," Rishi told me. She sort of carried on a three-way conversation with a co-worker by the name of Jeff and me simultaneously. Rishi told me she is organizing a national campaign right now against clear channel. She updated me on the status of the two Mexican youths who sat in prison, wrongfully convicted before their group told the nation about the case. Deterline/We Interrupt/The media council got those boys out! Rishi also informed me that Malkia Cyril now heads the media council. I certainly hope and pray that we can work with the Youth Media Council, Rishi, Jeff and Malkia to put this book in the hands of every activist, pastor, youth leader, youth politician, college and high school student in California and across the country. (I encourage every prisoner, lawyer, politician and human being to support the Youth Media Council. They are an active, authentic, positive, non-profit organization. Send them a check today at 1611 Telegraph Avenue/ Suite 510/Oakland, California 94612. They cannot continue to right the good fight without money, volunteers, etc. If you are a civilian, you ought to call Rishi or Jeff and ask how can you volunteer. Call 510/444-0640. No collect calls! I hope the college kids at "Off" magazine, Third Eye Movement, Soulforce, etc. will come along with us and fight for justice. Rishi will be mailing me more data on her projects soon and I intend to tell the world about them in my next book . . .

I spoke with distinguished, esteemed and high profile Private Detective Jay Saltpeter a few days ago. "Got your new book! Great! Great!" Jay and I discussed his efforts to exonerate Marty (more on Marty later) in New York. I asked Jay for the address of a certain individual so this guy could help me. "You don't need him, you're better off with me," Jay told me. And I hope that meant Jay is considering helping me get freedom.

It is time for Maria Shriver to convince Arnold to allow the media to come back inside California prisons. It is time to reinstitute inmate's rights to correspond with the media confidentially. Prison guards don't want us to write the media confidentially. As a matter of fact, I saw where Gloria Romero and assemblyman Mark Leno are supporting my suggestion (via their own motion) to bring reporters back into the prison.

Upon viewing the press conference, I wrote Mark Leno an important missive. I took it to a counselor to have it mailed certified/return/receipt requested. I never got the receipt. I went back to the counselor and asked what happened and she claims, "I took care of it same day you gave it to me. Check with the mail room or trust office." The mail was stolen. It never left the prison. It was read by the counselor or somebody who decided, "Mark Leno will not get this letter". And a federal crime (mail theft) was committed! But it will go unpunished! If you write the warden, it's like Gary writing the governor (Davis). They just don't care. Ipso facto, as much as I respect, support and admire Jeannie Woodford, she'll have to do more than hold a few ethics classes if she's gonna save C.D.C.

It will require a catharsis! I've been redundantly reminding my readers (sometimes two or three times within the same paragraph) that serious, drastic and severe problems often require drastic solutions. No doctor ever desires to amputate a person's finger or toe, much less an arm or a leg. But if that limb is bleeding so profusely or is so severely damaged (i.e., infected) that it runs the risk of killing the person, the doctor removes the limb in order to save the body.

Roderick Q. Hickman, Jeannie Woodford, Walter Allen and Arnold will have to utilize the scalpel of justice and the scissors of truth and discipline and cut off/out some of the limbs of C.D.C. and C.Y.A. where treatment is effective and appropriate they ought to utilize it. Some C.D.C. officers have made a few mistakes in judgment or lied under pressure or out of fear (of retaliation and/or out of fear of the wrath of the CCPOA) and the can be saved. These officers often can be rehabilitated and kept working. Let's retrain them, teach them ethics, diversity, sensitivity and professionalism. Don't throw the baby out with the bath water. But in those instances where we find violence, abuse, drug smuggling, mail theft, racism and promotions scams, etc. cut off the limb. Get rid of those employees whoever they are. And very, very often it is those at the administrative level who's corrupt. Guards have told me for years, "Hell, I learned how to do beat downs and cover it up from captains and wardens. The boys downtown running the department are the one's who taught us the code of silence." On a transport a few months ago C.O. Zamudio indicated, "Rod Hickman is corrupted. He is a politician and he has a lot of dirt on him. But he's got sense and he won't buck against the CCPOA. The CCPOA is running the department not Rod." In December of 2003, when I told Captain Martel and George Stratton I was gonna write Rod about what they were doing to me, "I don't give a (expletive) about Rod Hickman. Rod knows me and he knows I don't play. I've got more power downtown than Rod will ever have. I have senators in my hip pocket," stated C.D.W. George Stratton.

This kind of blatant misuse of power must be checked. I'm calling on Mrs. Woodford and Mr. Hickman to check it. They must check it and correct it. Where there is no obvious evidence of wrongdoing, they must let it be known that they are suspicious and they should let it be known that if and when they get one scintilla of evidence of lying, retaliation against whistleblowers, retaliation against

24

inmates, promotions scams such as those by Terry L. Rosario, etc. they're gonna start at the head and begin firing people. If Mike Knowles is condoning misconduct by John Doe or Martel they need to fire Knowles. Then fire Stratton! Then fire Chastain. The way you break up cars, cliques and gangs is to begin with taking out the leader. Martel, Chastain and Stratton are corrupted, mean spirited, arrogant and pompous leaders. Everywhere Chastain goes, there is mess. Sexual misconduct, sexual assaults, rapes and abuse seem to follow Chastain like a shadow. Chastain learned his antics, tricks and cover-ups from the best (worst); his cousin Terry L. Rosario taught Chastain and others. Rosario was walked off prison grounds and suspended for ninety days because he was accused of being an accessory to murder by default. An inmate said he gave a note to Rosario and former Captain Timmy Lalker (pseudonym) and that John Doe was present. He told them his buddy was going to be hit (killed) the next day. They did nothing about it and the inmate was killed the next day. After the Attorney General refused (wish we'd had Gloria Romero as I believe she would have called on the U.S. Attorney to step in) to prosecute Lalker, Terry Rosario and company were brought back, given their full rank and back pay. Rosario retired in 2002. Even though he retired in 2002 with a ninety thousand dollar salary, he was allowed to return to the same prison (New Folsom) in the same position (Chief Deputy Warden) as Acting C.D.W. with full (at a rate of ninety thousand dollars annually) pay plus full (ninety grand) retirement. So for six months in 2002 Terry earned about fifteen thousand dollars per month for a total of ninety grand for six months. After earning fifteen grand monthly for six months, he was then kept on board as Acting Associate Warden (one step lower) for six months. For those six months, he earned about thirteen grand per month. Oh, by the way Terry L. Rosario only had a G.E.D. and we wonder why California has a budget deficit. I hope Mrs. Woodford, Mr. Hickman and the Governator will implement rules prohibiting this kind of double dipping. It's a taxpayer rip off, as Cesar Cruz would argue . . .

I'm begging Tavis Smiley, Tom Joyner and Doug Banks to talk about this. Tavis Smiley is a brilliant man. The mere way he handled the Farrakhan interview demonstrated his awesome mind. I know Tavis could expose C.D.C. corruption. We need Tavis, Jamie Foxx, Mike Farrell and Risni to tell America about the youth abuse, youth violence and the shameful conditions of juvenile facilities and youth prisons in the west coast. We must stop allowing crazed, abusive and egotistical prison guards to toughen our kids up and teach them violence.

And it takes action to create change. Those who are perusing this book and just want to read it as a novel and then do nothing, you'll not really who I'm looking to reach. I want to reach out and touch those students at Savannah State College who are in the classes of Professor Johnnie D. Myers. These students heard an activist named Sky Edeawo. Mrs. Edeawo is a South Georgia Coordinator for FAMM who distributes literature at town hall meetings on prison issues. Sky speaks eloquently at schools and colleges and is making a difference. I want that urban studies class professor and Professor Myers to get this book into the hands of their students. I want those students to ally themselves with Cathryn Ferrigno, Sky, Julie Stewart Lafonda Jones and James Muscoreil Jr. They can get with Peter Ninemire to organize, strategize and galvanize against mandatory minimums, harsh prison conditions. When we reach youth in high schools and colleges and get them involved, we will transform crime, law, the judicial system and society. Young people are innovative, creative, energetic and creative. If we impact them and equip them with the tools of change and respect their ability to implement those changes in policy and changes in crime and punishment - we will rebuild America. I love young people and I've always known that if they are involved in think tanks, blue ribbon committees, youth activist groups, etc. they are much less likely to be involved in committing crimes and using drugs.

It is going to require people to follow in the footsteps of Sky and go into these colleges, high schools and churches and recruit, inspire an involve the students if a change if gonna come.

We need to involve the youth, educate the youth, liberate the youth and protect the youth. On the note of pretension, I am quite frustrated with the way we treat pedophiles in this country. It is sickening! I can't understand how we can allow priests, teachers, scout leaders, etc. to moles children and get probation! I have watched judges impose light sentences of wicked men destroying our children's innocence on a daily basis.

I know that we have a justice crisis in this nation. Too many men go to prison for crimes they did not commit. There are many, many cases where folks are falsely accused of child molestation. We need to be careful and be certain that the person is guilty of the crime before we give him the time. I know of many wrongful convictions right here in California. And when a disgruntled mom coerces her child (for example) into falsely accusing a man of child rape - we ought to send the mother to prison! When anybody falsely accuses anybody of rape, we ought to send the false accuser to prison!

But when a person actually harms a child physically or sexually, I believe in the fabric of my being that person should never, ever receive probation. He needs to go to prison. Now I want him treated intensively while he's in prison. I don't want inmates or staff trying to be vigilantes and abusing him, etc. But I do want the person in prison for a very, very long time. And all too often we are being lenient on molesters and tough on weed smokers. We need to do better. Our children deserve better. Let's restructure laws as it relates to child molesters. Put some meant and muscle behind those laws.

I saw a guy get out the other day who claims he had over two hundred child victims. This guy was sick. He apparently got his conviction overturned. Now if he had been exonerated on a factual basis of innocence I'd be arguing for his rights to be left alone. But first of all, I knew the buy. He was (indeed) a pervert. Next - he admitted to having more than two hundred victims out there. His case was overturned purely on a technicality. One of his victims committed suicide because he feared having to testify against this guy again. So he walked out of Mule Creek Prison a few weeks ago and is already in jail in Oregon. He was driving a van around town with a mattress and kiddie porn in the van. Gimme a break. And I also blame the system in California! Why was this guy allowed to wallow around in prison farting his life away? I don't support hurting, beating or abusing any prisoner, but we should have been treating him. But C.D.C. does not have a single penologist working in this system. There should have been a sexual dysfunction therapist working with this guy. Can we be real? Any man sick enough to be attracted to a child needs punishment and treatment. And he ain't gonna stop being attracted to children just because we put him in prison. A pedophile must be treated! Not on probation! But treat him while he is (where he belongs - away from children) in prison!

I'm not interested in prison revolutionaries who want to show us how bad they are by stabbing or killing a molester. One wrong does not make another wrong, right. Society ain't gonna reward me or exonerate me because I beat up a molester! The injustice system will only reward me by striking me out, putting me in ad-seg and in some way diminishing my privileges. So I need not attempt to redeem myself by attaching a molester. I'm no judge, prosecutor or jury and I've seen too many wrongful convictions. I've watched innocent men like Rolando Cruz get falsely convicted of sexual crimes of which they're innocent. But if the pervert is guilty, he will be rewarded! God will punish (severely) anybody evil enough to harm a child. God is not blind nor is he asleep! God's arms are not so short that he won't reach out and grab a molester and punish him. Trust me, God will get vengeance. By the same token, we must not decide to use violence in the prisons as a mechanism of punishment against fellow inmates. No matter what their criminal convictions. I have absolutely no sympathy for any earthling who would harm a child. None whatsoever! But let's admit that they are sick. You gotta be real sick, real evil, real perverted and quite weird to receive stimulation and gratification from the physical abuse of or sexual contact with a child. So we need to become pragmatic, realistic and smart when dealing with molesters. Treatment must be intense and punishment must be severe. For more on the epidemic of child perverts go to www.cafeshops.com/manning and get my book "American Dream/A Search For Justice".

Today I received a missive from Ann Rose-Pierce, Editor of "After Seventeen Years" newspaper. It reads in part "I visited your web site and would very much like to read your book. I will review it in our newsletter . . . I will also review it on my weekly radio show . . . Membership in our organization is simple. There is only one requirement that you believe prisoners are human beings and deserve to be treated as such." I am thankful for Anne's willingness to review my book "American Dream/A Search For Justice" in the newsletter and willingness to discuss it on her show. (To receive Anne's newspaper, write to "After Seventeen Years" 3225 SE. Alder Ct. #1, Portland, Oregon 97214. Send tow or three dollars to help them keep up the good work).

I need my readers to call in to shows such as the Doug Banks Radio Show, Tom Joyner, Air America, Larry King and Ed Schultz and tell these hosts about this book. When you begin to write letters to editors, call radio shows and write to your political representatives about this book. They will read it and a change will come. I encourage you to send a donation to the Prison Legal News. They are the only national newspaper, which is consistently published and is at the forefront of prison and criminal justice issues. Call PLN in Seattle, Washington (or log on to their website at www.prisonlegalnews.org) and get their publications. Also send a donation to help them keep going. Even if it's only three or four dollars it will help out. And PLN needs volunteers. Other organizations I strenuously suggest you contact and support include the following: ACLU National Prison Project, Washington D.C., Florida Prison, Legal Perspectives in Chuluota, Florida, November Coalition in Colville, Washington, Stop Prisoner Rape in Los Angeles, CA, Justice Denied in Coquille, Oregon. FAMM in D.C., Children of Incarcerate Parents in Eagle Rock, CA,

Western Prison Project in Portland, Oregon. For addresses on the aforementioned call 206/781-6524.

I want to strenuously encourage each man, woman and teen who is reading this page right now to (please) go to www.cafeshops.com/manning and order a copy of this book (and "American Dream/A Search For Justice") and send it to your local pastor or state legislator. Cafeshops will mail it wherever you want it to go (including to prisoners, prison wardens and prison directors) if you request it. I am sick and tired of people writing me to ask, "What can I do to help"? Here is the answer: get another copy of this book and send it to somebody else. If your local book store doesn't carry it tell them to get it. If your mayor, local press, etc. does not have it, get it for them. Some of you can afford to buy three or four copies and you ought to help students! Buy a copy or two and have it mailed to Criminal Law, Urban Studies and Political Professors at Yale, Morehouse College, U. C. Davis, U. C. Berkeley and colleges across this country. I receive letter after letter from professors and college bookstores asking me to donate a copy to their schools. I can't do it all. So you the reader must invest to help our students. Just call information and get the address to a college in your area and then have cafeshops or amazon.com to mail them a copy of this book. I'll repeat: (once more) you can help us to change the world if you will stop what you're doing right now and order another copy of this book. You folks out at the NAACP, ABA, pastors and leaders who have received gratis copies of this book; you must give back by ordering a copy for a prisoner. If you don't know anyone in prison just order a copy and send it to Anne Rose-Pierce (after seventeen years) and Anne will get it to a prisoner! There are thousands of indigent inmates who never get a letter or a book in the mail. You don't need to like them to help them. If you don't get some books to them and help them get better who will? They will rot and get bitter and angrier. And nearly six hundred and twenty thousand of them will be released this year and they're coming to your neighborhood. You ought to want them to get better. You should want them to read something inspirational, motivational and transformational. And it's gonna take books, not bars to turn their scars into stars. Some pedophile will read this book and decide to get help! Some vicious thug, murderer or robber will read this book and decide to transform themselves from the inside out. The guy whom I believe will try to hurt or kill President George Bush may read this book and decide to see a psychiatrist. I'm concerned that this guy will get out and be stupid enough to try to hurt the President. We must reach inside these walls and transform men and women. You can call

Professor Nai'm Akbar in Tallahassee at Sound/Mind Productions and he has a long list of inmates begging for books. Get this book to them. The politicians, the pastors, the students and the media need to read this book. I wrote it from my heart and not just my head. Get involved! Make a difference. Help make America better . . . www.cafeshops.com/manning - Barnes&Noble.com. E-mail - hallopeter@freesurf.ch

Oprah

Many guys in prison are anti Oprah. They dislike the fact that she does a lot of shows on victim's rights and they allege that she does not like prisoners. They're upset that she never has guys like Cornel West, Henry Gates or Dr. Na'im Akbar on her show. And it would be very convenient for this writer to join the chorus of Oprah haters. But I love myself some Oprah Winfrey. She has received a gratis copy of every book I've written. I've gotten thank you notes and photos, etc. from people such as President Nelson Mandela. But I've never received one single note from Oprah. I asked her staff for just a photo of her (I love pictures. In dungeons of despair pictures can light up a dark spot) but no reply. Even still, I celebrate the live, love, altruism and generosity of Oprah. I told y'all in "American Dream/A Search For Justice" about the case of Marcus Dixon in my home state of Georgia. I also wrote in that book that the Georgia Supreme Court needed to let Marcus out of prison. On May 11, 2004 Oprah gave a special update and told the world that the Georgia Supreme Court had released Marcus Dixon. My celly stated, "You helped get hi out because of what you wrote in your book." I replied, "I hope I helped, but more than likely, Oprah got him out." I shouted Hallelujah, I cried, I prayed and I thought about my mother. Marcus should have never been in prison. And the world should know his story, the whole story. It is about good vs. evil. It's about truth vs. lies, false accusations, racism and prosecutorial misconduct. It is also about love and the willingness to rise above race and hatred. Marcus was adopted by a White family (Ken and Perry Dixon) in a small city in Rome, Georgia. I spoke numerous times at the Pine Hill Baptist Church in Rose so I'm very familiar with the city. And there are some very good White and Black folks in Rome. But as with many rural towns, there is still a group of people who maintain hillbilly and backwoods beliefs. So the fact that Ken and Perry Adopted little Black Marcus Dixon makes me proud to be an American. But White folks who adopt Black kids (and vice versa) and live happily ever after, don't make Time Magazine, Newsweek or the evening news. Matthew Hale and David Dukes are stories considered worthy of media attention. Situations involving race related crime, killings or church burning are media worthy. But Ken and Perry never made the news. And nobody had ever heard of Marcus until he was accused of raping a White girl in school. The fact that Marcus was an "A" student en route to Vanderbilt never made the news. But when he was arrested and tried and sent to prison somehow many of us heard all about it. You will have to get "American

Dream/A Search For Justice" to get the details of the accusations against Marcus. But by the Grace of Almighty God and because Oprah exposed the case to the world, Marcus is free at last, free at last, thank God Almighty, Marcus is free at last . . .

Oprah showed a White woman who was on the jury that convicted Marcus of a minor charge (a charge the jury was hoodwinked by the D.A. into believing would not send Marcus to prison) at Marcus' house, hugging him and crying. This woman told Marcus, "I'm sorry. You don't know how many nights I lay awake worrying about you. I'm so sorry." Marcus told this White sister, "It's okay." But she replied, "No, it's not okay." This woman risked her life status in the community of Rome, Georgia, etc. to stand up and say, "This was wrong. Marcus spent fourteen months of his life in prison and he was innocent." God Bless this juror. And I would hope that Al Franken, Chuck D., Randi Rhodes, Katherine Lanpher, Mr. Vonkaenel, Joey Gluvers, D. J. Hubka and Roberta Franklin will tell the world about the courage, honor and remarkable open-mindedness of this White juror and Marcus' White parents. And God is going to bless Oprah for what she did on her show.

Oprah was methodical, uncanny and when Oprah didn't cry while interviewing the alleged victim that spoke volumes, we all know Oprah is a big ole crybaby! And when the girl cried with no tears even my cell partner said, "How is she crying? Ain't no tears coming out." It spoke volumes. And when Oprah walked up in the Georgia prison and sat down with the accused rapist (Marcus Dixon) and she fought tears while interviewing him, nothing else needed to be said.

Marcus is free now and if Marcus is reading this, I need to tell Marcus to never let it happen to somebody else. Marcus, you are free to live your life. You don't have to become an activist. You don't have to become a lawyer. You are not required to become a pen pal to a prisoner, etc. You can live your life as you want to. But don't ever forget what happened to you. And never take a day, an hour or even a second for granted. A lot of guys in prison may try to reach you and play guilt trips on you, etc., but I am in prison and I too am wrongly convicted. And I am your "homeboy", but I am telling you that you owe me nothing! And you don't owe anybody in prison anything. The only person you owe is the universe and you owe it to yourself and the human race to be the best that you can be at whatever you do. I want you to study, pray, meditate, deprogram yourself and just open your heart to the Universe and God will lead you to where you are supposed to go.

You were allowed to go into dirt (prison) because you are a seed. And a seed cannot grow unless it's in dirt and in darkness. You have been brought up out of the darkness and you've grown. Now connect with your spirit and God will lead you. It ain't gonna be easy, but you can succeed. If I can be biased and manipulative, I will tell you go to Morehouse, Lil Brother. Ain't but four houses! My house, your house, the White House and Mo' House! I love you Marcus, Perry, Ken and Casey. God knew exactly what he was doing.

It has now come to light that twenty-six year old Nick Berg was decapitated in Iraq as retaliation against America for the abuse of Iraqi prisoners. My soul ached as I shed tears for Nick's mother, Suzanne and his father, Michael. I know his little brother is also hurting and I was glad to see (a Black man . . . As I point out the fact that Bruce is Black only because Sean Hannity, Rush Limbaugh and Armstrong and Getty ain't gonna tell ya this. They only mention race when it is Blacks against Whites or Hispanics, etc. But Edward James almost said it right, "It's time for us to realize that there is not but one race - the human race.") Bruce Hauser stated, "I loved Nick like he was my own son. He was a great young man." Michael Perry pointed out that perhaps Nick's blood is on the Bush Administration's hands. Nick was in Iraq teaching communication and helping with computer literacy. He tried to come back to America more than a month before he was beheaded by those wicked thugs. But he was detained by American Bush Administrators because they claimed there was a question about his identity. FBI agents in America visited Nick's parents in Pennsylvania to verify his identity. When U. S. officials in Iraq finally released Nick in Iraq to come back to America, he was captured by Iraqis. Shouldn't Bush's powerful military folks have at least saw to it that Nick made his journey to the airport safely? They did not. After being captured in Iraq, the photos of our military soldiers raping, sodomizing and dehumanizing Iraqi prisoners came out and these thugs decided to behead this twenty-six year old young man to get back at the U. S. Nick would have been home if he had not been falsely arrested and detained in Iraq by his own (U. S.) people. He probably would not have been beheaded if our soldiers had not abused Iraq's prisoners. Make no mistake about it, I love America. I honor, respect and celebrate all of the thousands of U.S. military soldiers who have risked their lives going to fight in Iraq. I believe most U.S. soldiers are great soldiers who do their jobs well. And I still don't buy the allegation that it was only six soldiers involved. On the Iraqi prison rapes, abuse and killing by U. S. soldiers in the prison Mr. Bush says, "That's not the way we do things in America." Mr. Bush is mistaken.

That (I'm sorry to tell you) is exactly how we do things in America. Prison guards in American prisons abuse, mistreat, rape, sodomize and kill inmates every month in the year right here in Texas, California, New York and Arizona. Mr. Bush must not be reading the local newspapers. Many prison guards are also military reservists. (I wish Seymour Hirsh at The New Yorker would investigate to find out the percentage) and these same guards in American prisons are over in Iraq fighting the war. (I want my readers to pray for me because I'm out there right now.) And prison authorities in America do the same thing Rumsfeld and Bush did. They learn about the abuse, they hide it from the media for as long as possible. They cover it up if they can. And if it gets out, they claim these were isolated events and do not respect the last majority of prison guards. It happened when Captain Doug Pieper (see my book "American Dream/A Search For Justice") told the warden at Folsom about abuse and violence fomenting. Administrator Max Lemon told the California Senate. Our media found out and now C.D.C. is reacting and trying to convince America that by and large, they have the best guards in the country. And they imply that, "Hey, why y'all complaining? Most of the guys in prison are murderers anyway." They don't tell the public that more than (a low estimate) ten thousand inmates were falsely accused and wrongly convicted right here in the U.S. as of last year alone. They don't tell us that Amnesty International estimates that more than seventy percent of those we have imprisoned in Iraq committed no crimes at all. They're just Iraqis! We loved them so much that we went over to liberate them (not to occupy according to Mr. Bush). They were great people in need of U.S. Liberation, but now that we've raped, sodomized, beat and killed them in prison, they "were vicious thugs anyway"! There is a strong powerful correlation in American justice and the justice we've exploited to Iraq. There is a cord of abusive continuity in false arrests, abuse in prisons by guards, cover-ups, damage control and the writing off of misconduct at isolate incidents, which reaches all the way from the false arrest of Marcus Dixon in Rome, Georgia to the torture center at Abu Ghurayb.

Right here at Mule Creek Prison in Ione, California, we have to beg for books. Prison authorities will not allow books (not religious books, self-help books, etc.) to come in routinely through regular mail. They must be processed through R&R as it delays our receipt of them. If Jeff Bezos sent me "Democracy Matters" by Cornel West today, it would be a month before I actually received it through R&R. But we can get drugs, alcohol and weapons (from their guards any day of the week at any prison in the state of California) anytime. And their guards often set us up, beat us, rape us and sometimes kill us. So I sadly must inform Mr. Bush this is how we do it right here in America!

Let us remember that in California, tuition of college kids is being heightened. Teachers and professors are getting laid off. There are no colleges or schools being built. But C.D.C. officers are getting pay raises and Delano II is being built at a cost of $700 million, even though the inmate population is decreasing and California has a $415 billion budget deficit.

To respond to criticism of mismanaged money and C.D.C.s costs overruns - management is asking staff to "cut off lights when not in use" . . .

Google founders Sergey Brin and Larry Page are brilliant, altruistic young geniuses. And I hope Mr. Hickman, Mrs. Woodford and the Bush administration will learn from these young men. "A management team distracted by a series of short term targets is as pointless as a dieter stepping on a scale every half hour" Sergey says. Mr. Bush, Mr. Hickman, are you reading? Google's company motto is "Don't Be Evil". And this is what should have been told to that prosecutor who took Marcus' freedom - Don't Be Evil!

Those soldiers sodomizing people we claimed to be liberating must be told, don't be evil. These thugs who beheaded Nick Berg; don't be evil. And every prison guard right here in America need to be required to not be evil. If Mr. Bush really thinks that's not how we do it in America, I challenge him to issue an executive order vetoing the ban on cameras and media in prisons in America. Let the prison system in America become transparent, held accountable and let the world see how we do it in Angola, Pelican Bay, Reidsville, Rikers Island, C.Y.A. and the prisons in Texas, etc. In the meantime, I ask The New Yorker, College Newspapers, the Street Breeze, CN&R, SN&R, Alternative Weeklies, Frontline, Al Franken, etc. to do stories on exactly how we do it in prisons in America. In California, Texas, New York, etc., etc., they'll find wardens unqualified to be wardens. Wardens and captains with false college degrees from places like Lexington University, Columbia State College, etc. They'll find, promotion scams, drug smuggling, rape, sodomy, sensory deprivation, starvation, psychological abuse, torture, inmates forced to wear hoods, murders all right here in our prisons in America.

The same prison subculture, which creates the monsters, which wreak havoc in our communities, molest our children and kill our elderly. That same system created the monsters, which abused and tortured the prisoners at Abu Ghurayb. And the taking of the photos were actually a trophy of sorts just as Americans took of lynching in the '40s, '50s and '60s right here in America. Remember Emmett Till? Ask Stanley Nelson or William Greaves or Mr. Beauchamp. Remember the college student/prison guard experiment in the '70s? Ask professor Zimbardo at Stanford, Peter Sussman, Cornel West at Princeton or Professor Gates at Harvard. If Mr. Bush really, really wants to know how we do it in America, he should call S.P.R. in Los Angeles, Human Rights Watch, P.L.N. or Amnesty International. They will tell him that what we saw on television takes place in the prisons in this country. What we need is homeland security and a catharsis in our prisons.

We need to release, exonerate and vindicate more Marcus Dixons (I.e. Mumia Abu Jamal, Pedro Armando Quant, David Wong, etc., etc.) And if Bush thinks all of "them" in prison belong "there", he should call Rubin "Hurricane" Carter, Rolando Cruz, David Quindt, Anthony Porter, Joe Salvati, Kenny Waters, Barry Scheck, Retired Judge Rudolph Loncke, Supreme court Justice Anthony Kennedy or Julie Stewart. Everyday of my life I pray for our President and I pray for our soldiers who are risking and losing their lives in war everyday. But I would be remiss if I didn't state here that I also pray for Mumia, Kevin Cooper and for me. I pray that the word will finally get out that we are literally, methodically, sadistically, creating monsters in the greatest country on the face of the planet . . .

Creating Monsters

Judges, prosecutors and even politicians in America have gone crazy. There used to be a time when politicians represented the collective wishes of their constituents. In a democracy, we assume that our government is made up of the people, run by the people and operates for the people. Here in North America, we proudly proclaim to be "one nation", indivisible, under God. We are indeed the richest nation on the face of the planet. We who live, move and have our being in America are residing in the most powerful country on the planet. It is a country, which is proud of her history, freedom and prosperity. Without question, America is a great country. America is also a country in which the people, who make up the country, need to take "a closer look". If we take a very close, meticulous and analytical look at laws and justice, we might find ourselves amazed. If we take "a closer look" at prosecutors, judges, juvenile facilities, jails and prisons, we will surely begin to question the wisdom and judgment of those who write, enforce and apply the laws of our land.

There are some strange, unique and troubling things taking place in police agencies, prosecutors' offices and in courtrooms in America. The juvenile facilities, jails and prisons are a reflection of the bungled and jumbled justice being metered out in courtrooms across America. The defendants who are on trial in those courtrooms are a reflection of the selective, often biased and classicist police departments who are charged with enforcing our laws every day. The police officer has power.

The police officer is the first link in the chain of the judicial system. He or she has the power to arrest a politician, pastor, parishioner or the Pope. Ipso facto, the police officer can be and very often is, a dangerous, renegade and a rogue. What do we do when the police need policing? Where do we turn when police officers are criminals? Every day of the week, police officers set up, frame up, falsely arrest, beat up and in some cases, kill citizens in inner/urban cities across America.

One can review news clippings covering the past five years in Cincinnati, Ohio and one will find that the police there have declared a war on poor people. They beat, brutalize and kill innocent, poor and uneducated people in Ohio very often. And sadly, they get away with it. No matter how compelling the evidence or how many credible eyewitnesses there are to police killings and misconduct, prosecutors are extremely reluctant to file charges against a police officer. "DAs consider cops one of them. It's like a family affair. And they'll do anything to protect one of their own," stated Sacramento Defense Lawyer Paul Comiskey.

When they "are," charged, very often judges discover (miraculously) strange technicalities in the case(s), which they utilize as a reason to dismiss the case(s). In the rare case that actually goes to trial - judges and juries are extremely reluctant to convict a police officer of a crime. And so the beatings, corruption, false arrests and the cover-ups continue.

We Americans have a hard time believing our police officers are often corrupt. We want to believe in our police. We "need" to believe in our police. And this want and need causes some of us to put police officers on pedestals and to forget that they (too) are human beings.

Just as we have good and bad in all people, good doctors and bad doctors, good lawyers and bad lawyers, etc., there are good police officers and bad cops as well. First of all, we should "pay police" officers more. They deserve good wages and great benefits. Good officers risk their lives every hour and every second they're on the job. It is foolish for us to pay them as little as we pay them.

I can recall a funeral, which was held at Salem Baptist Church in Atlanta, Georgia. This was the going home celebration for Sergeant Turner. Sgt. Turner had been an Atlanta police officer for more than twenty-five years. Sgt. Turner was a full time officer, father, husband and a good man. He worked three jobs to put his kids through college. While he was working at his third job as a security guard in West End Mall (while a full-time Atlanta police sergeant), Sgt. Turner was shot down by a vicious thug. His death alone was tragic, but the fact that a man, who had given the city more than twenty-five years of his life, still didn't earn enough money (as a police sergeant) to go home at the end of the day is sad . . .

Jasper Williams looked over at Andy Young (who was mayor at that time) and Governor Joe Frank Harris and told them, "We don't mind paying a few more pennies in taxes to ensure that police officers earn decent wages. We need to pay our police more money. If we paid them right, Sgt. Turner wouldn't be laying in this coffin right now. He would have had no need to be a part-time security guard." What we pay city cops across this nation is absolutely pathetic. This needs to change . . .

But there are some police officers in every police department across the country who are thugs. They themselves are "Bad Boys". And we do need to ask ourselves what are we going to do when they come for us. What do you do when a criminal comes to arrest you?

What do you do when you're a poor White man on a lonely highway and you are stopped by a racist Black cop? (There are some racist Black people too). What does the Brown or Black man do when he's stopped at two o'clock in the morning on a rural road by a racist "Bad Boy" (police officer)? Who can we call on when the cops we call on are corrupted? Make no mistake about the fact that some of them are badge wearing, gun toting gangsters. When they want you, they'll find a way to get you. When they get you, it's almost impossible to prove that they got you, wrongly. But - it happens everyday . . .

We see it in the media, now more than ever before. Some of us assumed the Rodney King beating was an anomaly or an aberration . . . Yet, we saw Amadou Diallo; we saw a Haitian man beat by the police. They sodomized this man with a plunger! These were not street thugs. These were New York's finest. They wore badges and committed these heinous crimes at the police headquarters!

It seems strange that we forget that police officers are not saints or angels. They are a microcosm of society-at-large. They are a reflection of us. Some of us are mean. Some of us are bitter, racist, bigots, vicious, liars and brutal. They are us. The only difference in them and us is that they have not been "convicted" of a felony. That's it and that's all.

So perhaps if we were to make an attempt to rectify the problems of police corruption, police brutality, frame ups and false arrests; we have to begin with analyzing how we "hire" police officers. We would need to weed and seed. Weed out (via discovery . . . by investigating, etc.) the Bad Boys and seed in (plant) the good boys. We would need to screen applicants better. The question is, "Why do you want to become a police officer"? That is a powerful question and it is a telling question. But as it is today, we have rogue and renegade cops hiring other cops. We should require potential officers to undergo extensive psychological examinations. They should undergo stress tests and examinations to determine their views on race, homosexuality, lesbianism, patriotism and religion. We must get into the minds of our future police officers. How did Mark Fuhrman ever become a policeman?

Mark is a racist! Mark is homophobic and an atheist. Who in their right mind would hire him? As we know, the Los Angeles Police Department did hire Mr. Fuhrman. And had it not been for the tenacious and skillful investigation launched by Johnnie Cochran and his "Dream Team", Mark would still be a policeman right now.

Mark is not an aberration. Go to Louisville, Kentucky - Macon and Summerville, Georgia - Albany, New York - Chattanooga,

Tennessee and Chesterfield, Virginia . . . stop in Henrico County, Virginia and in rural towns all over America and you will discover a few Fuhrmans in every police department.

And so the corruption begins with the arrest, the arrest leads to jail and jail is hell. When a guilty man goes to jail, it's hell. It is a filthy, nasty, dirty and scary place to be. It is gut-wrenching and dehumanizing to be in jail. You sleep on floors, fear for your safety, sexuality and even for your very life in jail. It is a horrible, evil, awful, low and terrifying place to be. Prison is hell . . .

Just today, I called home and I talked to my grandmother, Dollie Manning (whom I love with all my heart. We call her "Cat". She is the greatest woman I know. She and James Manning have been better to me than I've been to myself. I thank God for them). She told me that they buried my cousin, Trina, Saturday. Just that simple. Trina is no more. Last time I saw her, she was fine. She was a funny, gregarious and affable human being. She always lit up a room and brought humor and joy to any situation. And now, while held captive in prison for a crime I did not commit; she dies. I won't even attempt to explain to you the pain, sorrow and hurt, which I feel at this very moment. But I will use my present pain as a power to try to elucidate to you the foolishness of the prison subculture. As I hung up the telephone today, I was wiping my eyes and battling the tears. I didn't want my fellow convicts to see me crying, but Cortez noticed my tears (God always sends a bit of humanity in the midst of insanity). Cortez came over and asked, "What's wrong, brother?" He got my cell door opened for me and then brought this manuscript (the tome you're reading right now) up to me. He gave me a lunch sack (a great big sacrifice because Bradford Cortez is a great big ole brother) and he said, "God bless you, man. I hope you feel better. I'll come up later and check on you." But by an large, if I were to yell out on the tier that I just had death in my family, most guys would not give a darn and the few who cared would be afraid to show it. If they put their arms around me and prayed for me, somebody might think we're weak or gay or crazy. So my suffering, pain and hurt must be private. I must grieve alone. I have to cry alone. I have to reminisce alone. In prison, you're basically "alone". I feel bad that I was not there to put my arms around my aunt (we call her "Aunt Boot") and comfort her and tell her that it will be all right. My heart is absolutely broken. I feel sick. I'm torn up on the inside and I don't know which way to turn and I am all - "alone". Guys in prison are quick to say, "I got a me number and not a we number. I came in by myself and I'm gonna leave by myself." A number?

In prison you are known more by your number than you are by your name (i.e. my prison identification number is J98796). If I got mail with the name "Sherman D. Manning", but that number was not on it, I may not receive the mail. But, if that number was on it and no name - I'd get the mail.

So here I sit, all torn up and hurt on the inside and what shall I do? I'll move on and "deal with it". That's what the prison subculture requires of me. Tupac said, "it's me against the world." And he (Shakur) also said, "it ain't easy."

It is absolutely important for society-at-large to get an adequate and realistic picture, a bird's eye view of what prison is really like. This tome is an inside view. It is also a view of a judicial system, which all too often sends babies, boys and girls to prison when there are more constructive options. My opinion is that when most men go to prison (prisons as they are today), they will never be the same again. Prison is a rattlesnake. Prison is a place, which basically destroys any and everybody, which comes in contact with it.

There is a heightened "noise" level in prison, horrible sanitation and extreme idleness. "Noise", per se, often traumatizes people. Various experiments have proven that people subjected to higher levels of noise, display higher incidences of anxiety and other emotional symptoms. The prisoner has little or no control over his/her movements and/or over the noise level. The inability to control or modify the noise level, confronts the convict with his vulnerability and powerlessness and this helps explain the increased incidences of depression, rage and other mental illnesses in prisons.

Hygiene is also a problem in prisons. In most prisons, toilets are hooked up in a way that one inmate's flushed waste often backs up into his neighbor's toilet or sink. Hot water quite often is unavailable for showers and for washing trays in the kitchen. Prison is a breeding place for roaches and rats. Most kitchens in prisons are gross and disgusting.

In all segregation units and quite often in general populations, food is served in cells and this adds to the roach problem (i.e. New Folsom Prison in California). In many high-security units, men can be observed lying in darkened cells with roaches crawling over them. Thousand of prisons across the nation have pigeon waste inside prison cellblocks, where broken and disrepaired windows served as entry ports for birds. Because of the lack of adequate sanitation, combined with poor ventilation and inadequate heating, inmates are repulsed by the ever-present stench of animal and human waste and endangered by a heightened risk of infection and infestation.

41

In prisons, rape, violence and idleness are pervasive. Gyms are no more as they have been converted into dormitories due to prison overcrowding. This crowding leads to depression, anger, fights, stabbings, rapes and murder. This increased violence leads to more frequent and longer lockdowns. (Prison guards receive time and a half anytime inmates are on lockdown). States such as California paid more than $300 million extra; in taxpayer dollars to prison guards for their lockdowns. Numerous states, including California, have removed all weights from prisons. Certainly, with fewer meaningful prison jobs, rehabilitation or counseling, more idleness and less hope prevails.

Gumption tells us that all prisoners tolerate their time in prison better and are less likely to re-offend after release if, during the sentences they serve, the juvenile facilities and prisons have adequate space, the prisoners are given some privacy as well as some control over the noise level, and a certain amount of meaningful programs and activities are available.

Severe prison overcrowding and the discontinuation of educational and rehabilitation programs lead to a heightened level of anxiety and stress in American prisons. Yet, rather than attempting to remedy the crowding and violence, corrections officials opt to build state-of-the-art "max: - max:" or "super-maximum control units" or "SHUs" where prisoners who can't conform or who speak out too vehemently (and write tomes) are kept in cells twenty-three or more hours per day, often for years. Forty-three states and the Federal Prison System now has super-maximum control units. Experts in psychiatry such as Dr. Terry Kupers, MD stated, "The forced idleness and isolation in these units cause many previously stable men and women to exhibit signs of serious mental illness. But for people who already suffer from mental disorders, the segregation environment is totally intolerable."

Corrections, as a profession, have a duty it cannot ethnically ignore. It is bad enough for prison not to reform offenders (this goal has become unfashionable to pursue) and even worse for prisons not to provide for basic needs, fail to protect the vulnerable and to needlessly circumscribe, etc. And now prisons are almost routinely driving sane or mostly sane prisoners over the brink into horror, insanity and madness.

In the typical American prison today, prisoners become irritable, racial tensions mount, tempers flare, the abuse of the weak intensifies, there are many rapes, staff assaults and the rage keeps building and building and building.

42

Juvenile facilities, jails and prisons constitute toughness and meanness training; the tougher and more violent a convict becomes, the better chance he or she has for survival in the "monster factory". Due to public apathy, the meanness goes unabated and proliferates and the violence escalates.

In late January of 2004, a report was released on juveniles and the youth prison facilities in California, which was scathing. This report indicated that these facilities are a horrible, miserable and torturous failure. Kids, our babies, boys and girls go there and get abused, brutalized, mistreated and neglected. The report came on the heels of two youths who were found dead in their cells. Authorities have ruled the two cellmate's deaths as suicides. Yet, the parents of one of the boys believe they were murdered because they refused to join gangs. If they were murdered, that speaks to the problem of violence, gangs and meanness, which is epidemic in jails, juvenile facilities and prisons. If they committed suicide, that speaks of the lack of adequate counseling, mental health staff and psychological intervention in youth facilities nationwide. (Governor Arnold Schwarzenegger recently appointed Walter Allen, III as C.Y.A. Director in California. Mr. Allen is the first African-American C.Y.A. Director in California. Rod Q. Hickman is also the first youth and adult correctional agency head who is Black. I've met Rod and I hope he does well).

We need to allocate adequate funding for serious counselors, psychiatric social workers, community organizers and mentors to intervene in our juvenile facilities to reduce gang violence, drug abuse and idleness. When we allow our kids to basically be raised and reared in the juvenile facilities, etc. and they become educated in how to commit more crimes and how to become more violent; this is a recipe for failure.

I want to do more than paint a vivid picture of the horrors inside juvenile facilities, jails and prisons. I'd also like to write in terms of pragmatic solutions. If we're lucky, somebody will send Mr. Allen, Mr. Hickman, Governator/Terminator Arnold and wardens (across our nation) this tome and perhaps they will use it as a tool for transformation (at minimum). I hope that the parents, families, pastors and friends of those who are incarcerated, will send this book behind the walls, gates and barbed wires of the prisons. When we get this book into the prisons, I believe some inmates will use their own initiative to transmogrify their own lives from the inside out.

I have pointed out repeatedly that juvenile facilities, jails and prisons house many inmates who consistently commit vicious crimes

43

and who deserve to remain behind bars for long periods of time. Some of the folks in prison are right where they belong and society has understandable fears about many of these hard-core thugs that we can't ignore. These are quite often the convicts who became predators in the prison domination hierarchy, preying on younger, smaller, less hardened offenders. They make life a living hell for the less violent prisoners. And contrary to the erroneous fears, which are generated by the media's concentration on the most vicious and depraved, well over half (about sixty-eight percent) of today's prisoners have never been convicted of a violent crime. If we tally new admissions to prison instead of the present composition of the entire prison population, the figure for violent convictions drops to nearly twenty percent, because violent offenders serve longer sentences and accumulate in the system, whereas the large majority of inmates are convicted of nonviolent crimes such as drug possession and other victimless offenses and then let out after a few years. So the fact is three-quarters of those entering prisons today have been convicted of minor, nonviolent crimes!

A large majority of prisoners ran into problems with the law because of drug and alcohol abuse and evidence disputes the notion that locking people up in prison makes them less prone to substance abuse after they are released. Throwing drug addicts into these hellish and violent institutions makes them angrier, meaner and less caring of others upon their release. Putting them in prison causes them to become sicker, slicker and they get out and return (to prison) quicker. While they are in prison, the violence, hatred, abuse, drugs, rapes and murders they see "creates monsters". The subculture running rampart in those prisons almost forces them to become monsters, animals, thugs and predators. The average prisoner (contrary to erroneous assumptions) "will be released in less than five years". Ninety-five percent of all prisoners will eventually get out of prison, in spite of the harsher sentences.

The vast majority of rough, tough, hardcore, violent offenders are ultimately sentenced to life in prison. So the bigger problem, in terms of public safety, is the much larger number of inmates who are locked up for nonviolent offenses. After spending a couple of years in the madhouse (prison), where they must be tough/violent to survive, they have severe difficulty containing their anger and behaving in an appropriate manner in a social setting when they get out. Nonviolent prisoners tend to come out of jails, juvenile facilities and prisons full of resentment, rage and in ruins.

The rate of second arrests (re-arrests for inmates who've served one prison term) rose dramatically between 1985 and 1995, the same years we saw the demise of rehabilitation, education and counseling in prisons. These were the same years we saw the rise in prison overcrowding and the advent of super-maximum control prisons. This rising second-arrest rate and the booming proportion of parolees who are re-incarcerated suggest that the imprisonment binge of recent years really fosters crime and destroys ex-cons' chances of "going clean".

Some would argue that an analytical, meticulous and pragmatic look ought to be taken at crime and punishment in America. Scholars have argued for years in favor of the restoration of education and rehabilitation in the prisons. Yet, I am saying that there is a paralysis, which comes from too much analysis. We don't need any presidential, senate, congressional or state studies on crime and punishment. We don't need critical thinkers to conduct more, long, boring and expensive studies on prisons.

What we must do is protect public safety! And in order to protect the safety and security of our brothers, sisters, fathers and mothers, we must take massive action to correct corrections. We must take massive action to treat drug offenders and prevent them from ever going to prison in the first place. We must discontinue this wild theory that we have about being able to incarcerate our way out of crime. We must stop sending eight, nine and ten-year-old children to juvenile facilities so quickly. We must stop sending teenagers to adult prisons. It has been said that it takes a village to raise a child. I think it takes a nation to save that child if he grows up in poverty. It is almost unbelievable to note that America still refuses to recognize the direct correlation between poverty and crime. Yet, statistics and empirical data prove conclusively that poverty breeds crime. Ghettos and slums are havens for drugs, alcohol, shootings and killings. And you will find a liquor store, pawnshop (which specializes in gun and knife sales) and a check-cashing store in every slum project. Who owns the stores? Whose idea was it to make certain that guns, knives and alcohol are infiltrated into poor neighborhoods? The girls and boys born into these slums have no way out. They didn't make a mistake. They were born into a mistake. They didn't commit crimes. They were born into crime. For years and years, we have tried desperately to avoid, ignore and get around the fact that poverty is a basic cause of crime. We can argue day and night around it. Rush Limbaugh can do all the talk shows he wants pointing out scenarios in which some poor people have gotten out of poverty without ever having committed a crime. Amen to those people. And I concur strenuously with the opinion that one can and sporadically does get out of the projects, ghettoes and slums

45

without committing crimes. The fact still remains that poverty breeds crime. It is indisputable. So if we are to look meticulously inside the "monster factory" (juvenile facilities, jails and prisons) then we must also gaze (at least casually) at how and why they got there . . . Poverty is a part of the equation. For certain reasons, we have a government, which can never find the funding to feed our hungry, clothe our naked, house and educate our homeless and illiterate. But we located $100 billion (with a B not an M) to wage a war in Iraq for "weapons of mass destruction", which did not exist. I submit boldly that prisons are "weapons of mass destruction"! And poverty is a "weapon of mass destruction". And illiteracy is a "weapon of mass destruction". It would behoove John Kerry, Joe Biden, George Bush, Colin Powell and Condoleeza Rice to wage a "war" on the "weapons" (P.P.I.: poverty, prisons and illiteracy) of "mass destruction" right here in America . . . Prisons are filled with poor people. (I've not conducted a recent research on this statistic; however, I would tend to believe that more than eighty-five percent of the "American monster factory" population are/were poor. And nearly eighty percent are functionally illiterate).

A rich man who is called in by police officers, or who ever suspects he may be under investigation, will consult his lawyer. A guy from Oak Park, (CA), Perry Homes, (GA), Harlem, (NY) or Watts cannot consult a public defender and seek advice. Former President Reagan, for example, spent almost six hundred thousand dollars on legal advice to respond to an investigation concerning his actions in connection with the Iran-Contra affair and the investigation never led to criminal charges being filed against him. And advice prior to indictment is critical to protecting rights, particularly since police are not required to inform you of your rights. Basically, courts have ruled an arrestee has no right to an appointed counsel until after adversary proceedings have been formally initiated. In many instances, evidence has been tainted and tampered with and witnesses have been coached into misidentification, etc. Before the poor defendant gets an appointed lawyer, the court treats lineups and the initiation of criminal investigations as "non" critical stages. As a practical matter, the rich are not dependent upon the state for legal help. So when an individual has the money to hire his own defense team, he/she will be able to have counsel at his/her side during all encounters with law enforcement agents. Ipso facto, he/she will never see the inside of a prison. If there is a bail of millions of dollars, he will make bail. The poor languish in jail, unable to make even a few thousand dollars bail. The deck is stacked against the poor. Equal protection under the law? It's a myth . . .

The poor will plead out to prison time, often at the suggestion or coercion of their public defender. Public defenders often just want to "keep the line moving" . . . If the poor person goes to trial, chances are likely he or she will be convicted. And in rare cases where a wealthy individual gets convicted at trial, there are nine levels of appeal that can be challenged. The rich will and can afford to appeal at each and every level on each and every issue. The poor are provided appellate public defenders through only the first level of appeal. If they try to challenge their conviction through the other eight levels, they must do so in propria (representing themselves) as their own lawyer. Now you have a poor, illiterate man or woman trying to comprehend the law. In ninety-eight percent of the cases, they fail . . . It should be noted that the rich are out on bail and not in jail during these lengthy appeals. The poor person sits incarcerated, unable to make bail, while they await their denials from the Appellate Courts.

The courts have also ruled that poor defendants have no right to counsel at any stage of post-conviction proceedings even while facing the death penalty . . . When a rich person hires an attorney, he does not hire the first lawyer who comes along. He interviews the people and gets recommendations and referrals. Chances are, P. Diddy and Johnnie Cochran, Jr. told Michael Jackson what a great lawyer Ben Brafman is. I would easily recommend Gerry Spence, Barry Tarlow, Willie Gary or Donald Marks. But poor people are not given any vote in the matter. The person entrusted to protect their life and liberty is appointed by the courts. There are personality conflicts, biases and prejudices, which often stymie the attorney-client relationship. A defendant can file a Marsden motion, which is a motion to dismiss his/her attorney. But he will receive no help from the courts in preparing this motion. If the judge dismisses his/her lawyer, the judge won't replace the attorney. "You're on your own," is what the judge will tell the defendant. So given the option of representing himself before a jury, the defendant often keeps a Donald Dorfman type lawyer as his lawyer. Guys like Mr. Dorfman seemingly don't give a darn about their clients. But a good lawyer must care. "Caring about your client means everything," stated noted Defense Lawyer Murray J. Janus. "If you don't care, you can't win," stated Gerry Spence. "I may not be the best lawyer in town, but I really do care about my clients," stated Paul Comiskey. "This is O. J. Simpson's one day in court . . . You hold his very life in your hands. Be fair," argued Johnnie before that jury in 1995. You can't make that kind of argument unless you care. "With everything inside me, I ask you to find Beverly Ann Monroe not guilty of this horrible crime," argued Janus before a jury in

Richmond, Virginia. Willie Gary won one of the largest civil settlements in Florida for families, which had been cheated by a large funeral home chain. Because he tried the case with passion, care, concern and soul power. "They robbed these poor people. They just didn't care. The love of money is the root of all evil" . . .

But these overworked, underpaid and often-undereducated public defenders have been known to send their clients up the river. And often a poor defendant gets a lawyer fresh out of law school who has never tried a case in their lifetime, even in death penalty cases. Often, representation by counsel for the poor is like getting brain surgery from a podiatrist or heart surgery from a proctologist.

So basically, the "war on crime" is a "war on the poor". The rich man's law says you're "innocent 'til proven guilty". Yet, the poor man's law says, "You're innocent 'til proven indigent". But America, this great, beautiful, powerful and prosperous country, refuses to pragmatically fight the "war on crime", which can't ever succeed until there is a "war on poverty"!

Based on extensive research and correspondence with noted criminologists abroad and in America, it is evident that most of the civilized world considers the U.S. decision to use prisons to fight crime - a decision which flies in the face of logic. Empirical data suggests that incarceration rates have little or no influence over crime rates. The low opinion of our justice system comes from the pragmatic understanding that poverty is the most potent factor in determining who is most likely to end up in the "monster factory". Ipso facto, it is preposterous, ridiculous and nonsensical to withdraw money from the few programs, which fight poverty or help people rise above its influence to pay for more prison cells. Prison cells cost fifty to eighty-five thousand dollars per jail cell to build. This foolish fiscal maneuvering plays a crucial role in one of the most significant human migrations in America's history - a migration which has seen millions of poor Americans uprooted from urban communities and relocated into monster factories.

America's juvenile facilities, jail and prison population is being harvested from our booming fields of urban and inner-city poverty. Certainly these fields are overwhelmingly composed of Black and Brown citizens and so too is the new jail and juvenile population. In Washington, DC and Baltimore, more than fifty percent of Black men between the ages of eighteen and thirty-five are now under the watchful eyes of the justice system; i.e. in prison, on probation or parole. Eighty percent of those being sent to prison nowadays are Black or Hispanic, although statistics tell us that these minorities are not committing anywhere near eighty percent of America's crimes. "No Whites allowed", seems to be the hidden sign standing over the gates of America's prison system. The above-referenced statistics are a result of a race-biased law enforcement system. It is also indicative of the fact that more than ninety percent of America's prosecutors (both state and federal) are White, 94.6 percent of the judges nationwide are also White and these guys often take their biases and prejudices into the courtroom and up on the bench.

At the rate of the current prison expansion, we will eventually consume every dollar of every state budget in the union. There will be no public education, no infrastructure, nothing but prisons, jails and juvenile facilities. This is devastating the lives and families of those who live in low-income communities.

The monster factory shall never, ever be disabled by those who built it - the media, the politicians, those who make up the prison industrial complex, and the shareholders of the corporations who build, design, supply and repair prisons. For them, crime has become a gold mine.

I will repeat, poverty breeds crime and politicians have known it for decades. The fact that law enforcement authorities and the courts are often biased against all poor defendants, causes the prisons to be filled with our underclass. So in a real sense, the poor are helping make the rich richer every day. The more arrests, the more convictions. Prosecutors are paid to prosecute and judges are paid to judge (not to mention stenographers, interpreters, bailiffs, etc.). So the prisoner basically ensures the salaries of every courthouse employee, every police officer, prison guard and prison warden. And when we expand our research, we find that entire communities and companies have gotten rich off the poor prisoner.

When northern New York lost dairy and mining industries, politicians turned to prisons as an "economic salvation". Towns such as Dannemora, which houses Clinton correctional facility, have become totally dependent on the prison business for their survival. Clinton's two thousand jobs pour more than $2 million in pay into the local economy every week. And Clinton is only a drop in the large bucket for a region floating in prison dollars. Northern New York went from housing two prisons in the '70s to nineteen today and those new prisons have accounted for a $1.7 billion construction boom. Also creating an annual, astronomical windfall of about $440 million a year in salaries and operating expenses for that vicinity.

With billions of dollars and thousands of jobs at stake, it must come as no surprise that most of these rural towns now employ lobbyists and pay campaign money to politicians to ensure that the war on crime does not end anytime soon.

Dealing with juvenile offenders at the local, state and national level has become a $3 billion a year market, and this is small compared to the $50 billion being spent annually for programs for incarcerated at-risk youths.

Prison labor is another area where the private and public sector are cashing in on America's more than 2-1/2 billion prisoners. Unicorp, a government entity, which manufactures products by prison labor, now has yearly sales of more than $600 million a year. By 1998, there were over twenty-six hundred jail and prison industries operating in the U.S., a figure that reflects a more than five hundred percent increase in such industries in the past decade. Industries in (the monster factory) prison include everything from accounting, to sewing, to the manufacturing of false teeth, to telemarketing, parts for Boeing aircraft and logos for luxurious cars (i.e. Lexus). So politicians are lying when they claim only a few obscure companies are utilizing prisoners to reduce their labor costs.

Major billion dollar companies such as Spalding, Microsoft, IBM, Texas Instruments, Compaq, AT&T, Eddie Bauer, Victoria's Secret, TWA and Chevron are all utilizing prisoners as a portion of their workforce.

Of the billions of dollars being earned off the captive, slave labor of prisoners; the inmates are basically paid twenty cents an hour. Not twenty dollars - twenty cents. One company in Maquiladora, Mexico closed down its data processing operation in favor of a prison labor force in San Quentin State Prison. Many companies have laid off their entire work force and replaced them with a "monster factory" work force.

Filmmaker Michael Moore (who is also an activist) should join forces with Spike Lee and make a movie about secret, backroom, questionable bids and tactics being worked out between prison officials and corporate America in order to unemploy civilians and employ prisoners.

Disney, General Electric, Corrections Corporation of America, American Express, Wackenhut and Proctor and Gamble all profit from crime.

The media? Crime shows? Advertisement being sold/bought during those shows? Even the evening news profits tremendously from crime. America watches people being arrested, cuffed and led away to jail so often that we are numbed by it. We have lost our innocence and become immune to what we see. The pain of those we see on TV en-route to jail has become the gain to corporate America and the media. Shareholders of AT&T, Proctor and Gamble, TWA, etc. own shares in each person entering the criminal injustice system. Crime has become a positive thing in economic terms for many.

Millions of us here in North America have tapped into this cash crop of profit, which increases each time a poor homeless person steals food, or a drug addict steals drugs to make his/her pain disappear. Wall Street now watches the crime figures calculated by the FBI and the Justice Department just as they monitor unemployment and quarterly profit/loss statements.

Forty-six percent of all U.S. households or 71 million people own stock in more than two thousand mutual funds, which profit on crime and prisons. Most people are not aware of these facts. I repeat that many people are uninformed and have absolutely no idea that their money is being used to promote, condone, support and produce crime! Case in point: the teacher's union on the west coast has been outspoken in criticizing hard-on-crime policies such as California's harsh three-strikes law, yet the teacher's pension fund invests in private-prison companies, which owe most of their success to hard-on-crime sentencing measures such as the three-strikes law. It's safe to assume that the teachers' union members have no idea where their funds are going and they (like many others of us) have turned their money over to fund and investment gurus.

One would tend to surmise that prison, jail and juvenile facility expansion would reflect crime growth and/or population growth. But wait, according to American crime victimization surveys, our nation's overall crime rates from 1972 'til 1982 was relatively flat; a bit up in one area one year, a bit down the next. Between 1983 and 1999 the number of persons being victimized by crime actually went down! Certainly these statistics don't substantiate, explain or corroborate a one thousand percent increase in incarceration rates!

Less than eight percent of the prison population growth can be attributed to the overall growth of the population of America. Since the early 80s, when right wing Republican Ronald Reagan declared the current "war on (the poor) crime" by telling a TV audience that to win this war on the poor (crime?) requires the same amount of commitment it took to win World War II, crime has been near the top of every poll of the public's stated concerns. We have truly become convinced that we are living in a war zone. Even though many other industrialized nations have higher crime rates than we do in America, by 1992, forty-one percent of Americans felt unsafe walking the streets in their own neighborhood. None of the other nations with crime rates as high as ours feel as unsafe as we do.

Even more troubling, this crime anxiety appeared at a time when statistics proved that Americans are safer now than they were in the 1970s with the exception of our people trapped in urban pockets of poverty.

The same forces which have helped to create the chosen between the real danger of crime and our impression of crime and the resultant diverging trends in crime rates and incarceration rates are controlled by the entities that have the most to gain by fighting a war on (the poor) crime and increasing the (monster factory) prison population, namely, politicians, law enforcement agencies and those who run the Prison Industrial Complex.

The defense industry did the same thing in the late '50s and '60s leading President Dwight Eisenhower to warn Americans that the Military Industrial Complex had gained a dangerous amount of influence over our political system and its defense policies. "In the councils of government, we must guard against the acquisition of unwarranted influence, whether sought or unsought, by the Military Industrial Complex. The potential for the disastrous rise of misplaced power exists and will persist . . . we should take nothing for granted".

Eisenhower was concerned that the defense industry was manipulating Capitol Hill to put forth the perception that there was a service "missile gap" between America and the Soviet Union. The idea being that Soviet military capabilities were far greater than our own and that we needed to spend much more money on defense to restore the balance of power and thereby "keep" America safe. America's response to the fear created by the "missile gap" propaganda - the public enthusiastically supported the government's massive increases in defense spending at the beginning of the cold war.

President Eisenhower was a former military general who has privy to information, which proved there was "not" a missile gap, and it was a ploy being played up in the media by politicians and corporations.

History has a tendency of repeating itself and the "missile gap" ploy of the '60s is the "crime gap" ploy for the '80s, '90s and now. These ploys had been the backbone of the Prison Industrial Complex.

Donald Trump, Don King and Bill Gates would say, "Follow the money trail". We are pouring hundreds of billions of dollars into the bank accounts of the shareholders of the Prison Industrial Complex. And this spending cannot be backed up, substantiated or corroborated by crime statistics. I'm not a conspiracy theorist! But obviously somebody, somewhere had/has a plan and the plan is working!

Did you know that Federal Crime Control Acts, over the past ten years, have based their fund allocation to law enforcement on crime rates. Does this give the FBI and local police incentives to up their crime rate reports?

"The more dangerous the streets are perceived to be by the public, the easier it is for source organizations to justify additional spending and budgetary and personnel increases," stated Steven Chermak of Indiana University at Bloomington's Department of Criminal Justice.

When the public began to question whether or not the war on (crime) the poor was working - statistics were manipulated to prove crime was going down. This convenient logic is explained by Steven Donziger of the NCJC (National Criminal Justice Commission) in this way: "If crime is going up, then we need to 'build more prisons' and if crime is going down, it's because we 'built more prisons' - and building even more prisons will therefore drive crime down even lower."

Gil Kerlikowske, former police commissioner of Buffalo, NY, told the New York Post that new pressure on police agencies to prove that it is winning the war on crime (the poor) through lower crime figures, "creates a new area for police corruption and ethics". Kerlikowske went on to explain that the pay raises and promotions, which were connected to escalating crime rates have, in the '90s, become increasingly tied to statistics showing that crime has been reduced. As a result of this new need to demonstrate that crime-way spending was justified, one police department after another has been caught fabricating lower crime rates.

In Boca Raton, Florida, a police chief gave his permission to a captain on his force to systematically downgrade property crimes such as burglaries. That bogus reporting allowed the city to report an eleven percent drop in crime in 1998. Boca Raton was not the only one. Figures in Atlanta, New York, Philadelphia and other cities were all found to have been underreported in 1998.

Because of the major incentives for law enforcement to exaggerate the crime statistics, either down or up depending upon its needs, most experts are warning that politicians and the media should not rely on UCR (Uniform Crime Report, which is the main statistical source used by NBC, ABC and CBS newsgroups) when it comes to informing the public on determining crime justice policies. This warning has not been heeded.

We must also realize that when we "create new laws", we "create more crime" and we are creating new laws every day! If you put two hundred thousand new police officers on the streets (in mostly inner city areas), they will find more crime. When you weaken and dilute the rights of our citizenry in such a way as to allow random searches without sufficient probable cause, you will uncover and discover more crimes. When you allow racial profiling, driving while Black, Brown or poor, etc., you will arrest more minorities. Aaron Goodwin of Oakland, California is a multi-millionaire sports agent who happens to be Black. He was pulled over and forced to lay on the ground because he was driving a luxury vehicle in 2003.

Case after case has proven that if you're Black or Brown, you are pulled over more than Whites are when you drive a nice car. Johnnie Cochran was pulled over and abused by police because he was driving a Rolls Royce. Oprah was refused service (Oprah!) in an expensive jewelry store because she had on no makeup and wasn't recognized by the sales clerks. They figured she was a poor Black woman. Had she protested, she would have been arrested. If you put twenty-five squad cars in a ghetto, which is contained within a two-mile radius, you will make more arrests than you will in the same sized suburbs, which has only ten police cars in the area.

Empirical and statistical data proves that the rich in Hollywood smoke more dope, use more acid, drink more liquor and snort more cocaine than the poor in Watts, Compton and Inglewood do, combined!

Yet, most of the arrests are in Watts, Nickerson Gardens and the Oak Parks of America because that's where the police are! Ipso facto, the number of poor folks being arrested for drug-related crimes has been on the rise since the 1980s.

So the UCR is putting out false data. They keep claiming crime is down for this purpose and up for another purpose. Presently, the UCR says crime is up and they refuse to take the other variables into account. Look at it this way: If there was a particular highway where the speed limit was seventy-five miles an hour in 2003 and in 2004, we changed that speed limit to fifty-five miles an hour and if we used UCR methodologies, police agencies could allege that people are driving faster than ever before on this highway because more speeding violations are being issued than before.

John Ashcroft: "I've ordered all federal and state agencies to get tough on speeders! We must wage a war on crime. And speeding is a crime! These speeders are violating the law and they are risking the lives of others. Just imagine a truck going seventy-five miles an hour on a narrow road where the speed limit is only fifty-five. He's risking our children's lives. What if he hits a pedestrian, a senior citizen or a handicapped person?"

Mr. Ashcroft could (hypothetically) give that speech and the media would hype it. We would all be upset about those people over in Idaho who have absolutely no respect for the law and speed limits and we would be absolutely glad that Mr. Ashcroft was putting their speeders in jail, etc. But nobody would take the time to explain to us that the law was recently changed. Likewise, the increase in crime reflected in the UCR in the 80s and early 90s didn't come from an actual increase in crimes.

If we are actually waiting on politicians to warn us that the war on crime is actually a war on the poor, we will be waiting. If we are waiting on judges, prosecutors or the CEO's of AT&T or Walkenhorst or MCI-WorldCom, to tell us that prisons are not working, we will be waiting, waiting, waiting and waiting.

The "monster factory" is alive and well and here to stay as long as they can earn billions of dollars doing it. If it is to be rectified and dealt with pragmatically, it will have to come from the people. The taxpayers will have to demand the truth and a better return on their investment.

The day has come for Americans to stand up and demand the truth from our leaders. As long as we sit by and automatically assume the media is telling us the facts, just the facts, we will be hoodwinked. We may as well give our checkbooks to our politicians and exclaim, "Here's my money. You spend it however you want to spend it".

Barry Krisberg, former president of the National Council on crime and delinquency said, "No one thinks that California is safer today than it was ten years ago, even though we have twice as many people locked up." Al Blumstein (Dean of the school of Urban and Public Affairs at Carnegie Mellon University) and Frank Zimring (Earl Warren Legal Justice Institute at the University of California) both concur with that opinion.

How can any of us believe that building more juvenile facilities, jails and prisons are working when we still don't feel safe at home? When we accept the fact that for every one school, which is built in America, nineteen jails, juvenile facilities or prisons have been built; we as a nation are in trouble. Apparently and obviously, we need to slow down, look analytically and pragmatically beneath the hype and begin to pose the ultimate question: What's really going on? And when we are capable of getting real answers to these real questions concerning public safety, taxpayer money and expenditures; then we will be able to make some necessary, sensible and money saving changes. The time to look at law enforcement, the economics of our police forces, the soundness of our courts and the effectiveness of our prisons are long past due.

Any working class, middle class or even wealthy taxpayer (without a vested interest in the Prison Industrial Complex) would be wise to demand to know "where their money is going".

And for a long time, now I have been awestruck, amazed and befuddled by our lackadaisical attitude toward the costs and (so-called) rewards of justice in America! It is absolutely horrible, ridiculous and preposterous to sit back and allow our politicians to spend our money any way they choose! For decades, we have been guilty of allowing politicians to spend our money wildly (wisely?). And while we allow the mismanagement, misuse and abuse of our tax dollars, we have children going to bed at night hungry and homeless people sleeping outside on the streets.

"It ain't easy being me, will I see the penitentiary or will I stay free?" These were the words sung by Tupac Shakur. This has become the battle cry of almost every homeless, minority and poor person in America. But then it's not, nor has it ever been, easy.

President Bush and his Republican colleagues had/have $100 million in the bank! $100 million - for what? Television ads that are going to be run to try to help Mr. Bush get re-elected next November. My stomach turns when I consider all the good, positive and kind things, which could be done with $100 million. We could feed every homeless child or send almost three thousand poor kids with high grades, but low funds to Ivy League colleges with $100 million. But big money politics control the country and politicians nowadays must have nearly a quarter of a "billion" dollars in order to run an effective campaign for the President of the U.S.A.

April 16, 2003, George W. Bush visited the shop floor at the Boeing plant in St. Louis. His two-hour appearance drew several hundred people who assist in making the military's $49 million F-18 Hornet Fighters. About forty of them were deployed during the war in Iraq. The mission of his visit was twofold: to give thanks to blue-collar workers who equipped soldiers for their foreign adventures and to provide reassurance in the atmosphere of elevating unemployment. A week before Bush's visit, this same plant announced the layoffs of about two hundred and sixty people. Already in 2003, Boeing had cut five thousand positions nationwide, in addition to the thirty thousand jobs the company cut in 2002. During his tour, when he rarely mentioned domestic issues at home, there were F-18s in the background.

Yet this "Hardware in the Heartland" tour skipped numerous locales where thousands of hardworking men were contributing a large share to the war effort. Just fifty miles to the northeast of Boeing there were two hundred and sixty-five workers in the apparel factory in Greenville, Illinois. These workers averaged more than one thousand desert-tan camouflage shirts per day, 194,950 of which were bought in 2002 by the Department of Defense and worn by the U. S. Infantry in the Middle East. There were also three hundred workers at the Kevlar Helmet Factory in Beaumont, Texas, who fill one hundred percent of the U.S. Military's demands for battlefield headgear. Also there is a factory in Marion, Illinois, which solders millions of dollars worth of cables for the Pentagon's tow and patriot missiles. Neither governmental nor presidential plaudits were forthcoming for these workers - all of whom are "federal" and "state prisoners".

This captive labor force, which enables the U.S. Military to cheaply meet its needs ranging from weapons production, apparel manufacturing, to transportation servicing and communication infrastructure is located in the "monster factory". The American military is equipped with guns to shoot, radios to call and maps to navigate, thanks to the twenty-two thousand prisoners working for the state and federal prison industries, a quasi-public, for-profit corporation run by the Bureau of Prisons. In 2002, this company sold $679.8 million worth of goods and services to the U.S. government, over $425 million of which went to the Department of Defense.

During the 1990-91 Persian Gulf conflict, prisoners produced camouflage battle-dress uniforms, belts, sandbags, lighting systems, blankets, chemical gas detection devises, night vision eyewear and bomb components.

After the September 11th attacks, prisoners took a key role in relief work; prisoner's labor supplied all the protective goggles worn by recovery workers at the Pentagon and at the New York site. Yet, we saw no prisoners being lauded or praised by the Bush administration. Nor did these prisoners get feature stories on any major network news program.

Did you know that the Federal Prison Industries now ranks as the government's thirty-ninth largest contractor? What else do I need to tell you after the previous sentence? Will you re-read it or shall I re-write it? Call your senator, e-mail your congressman, call talk shows and the Associated Press and ask them why didn't they tell you (the reader of this tome) that the "Monster Factory Industrial Complex" is the thirty-ninth largest contractor for the government of the United States of America? Its (F.P.I.) Labor Force has no union. Its workers cannot ever vote. They are second and third class citizens, but they toil daily to produce products for our military.

Prisoners manufacture and supply many of the weapons and essential components of those weapons (i.e., hardware and components for weapons ranging in size from 30mm to 300mm battleship guns. Practice targets, devices used to simulate battle conditions, cable assemblies for patriot missiles, the remote control panels and the launchers for the tow and other guided missile systems) for the U.S. Department of Defense.

In a single year (2002) "monster factory" workers crafted $30 million worth of the wire assemblies, which go into all types of land, sea and airborne communication systems.

From the manufacture of millions of dollars worth of electrical cords to Humvee Reptir for the marines, FPI offers a large array of goods and services. FPI enjoys a "mandatory source status". (Yet our Federal Government sued Bill Gates for operating a monopoly?) This MSS requires federal agencies to purchase its products even if the same items can be bought cheaper at another company. I could not get a single defense-purchasing representative to comment on the record!

Can you imagine the fact that out of 1.3 million pairs of desert-tan battle trousers worn by our troops in Iraq and other parts of the Middle East, all but three hundred thousand were produced by prisoners? Three out of four active-duty soldiers in the Middle East wear pants made by prisoners of the FPI factories in Atlanta or Beaumont or Seagoville, Texas. Monster factory competitors, such as Propper International, point out that they use free labor to make the exact same trousers for the government at $2.39 cheaper per pair. So organized labor questions why the government should buy from a company depending solely upon prison workers, simultaneously paying sub-minimum wages (from fifteen cents to $1.10 per hour), skirting workplace safety standards and exploiting its full exemption from payroll and social security taxes, which free world employers are required to pay.

Prisoners are often involved in highly sensitive work, which involves the physical safety of our soldiers in the field. In 2001, FPI earned twelve million dollars in sales of "body armor" to the Defense Department, and in 1999 prisoners patched holes in thirty-two thousand dollars worth of malfunctioning parachutes. There is absolutely no screening (security) to work in FPI factories. As an experiment,

"Middle East Report" contacted three of the men who were convicted for bombing the World Trade Center in 1993. Two of them had not only worked in FPI factories, but they reported being compelled to do so. Mohammad A. Salamen waged a long legal battle before being excused from working for the prison company. He pointed out that since he, along with thirty percent of the federal prison population, were not even legal residents of the U.S., he should not be permitted legally - much less forced - to work for the company. Potential incentives for sabotage of FPI's military products are high. Imagine a paratrooper jumping out of a plane knowing his parachute was restored by a terrorist, robber, hit man, rapist or molester who is in prison? Wow!

Also note that when prison authorities can turn a profit on prisoners, there is less incentive to invest in more expensive ways to fill prisoner's time, such as drug treatment, counseling and literacy programs. More than four hundred prison teachers were fired as a direct result of the booming Prison Industrial Complex in the state of California. And think of guys in prison writing or calling home and telling their brothers and sisters what they did at work today. The brother or sister who is the recipient of that call describes their day at the unemployment office because their job was cut or they were laid off!!

As the U.S. occupation of Iraq marches on with nary an "exit" strategy in sight, however, the politics of prison labor are "nowhere in sight" . . . The twenty-two thousand (some claim more) prisoner employees of FPI, in spite of their vital importance to the "Bush war effort" remain underpaid, locked up, locked out and forgotten about. Bush never mentions them and the press never interviews them.

Keep in mind there are tens of thousands of other inmates working in state prisons (not really a part per se of "FPI") who also do billions of dollars worth of work for the U.S. Government and the private corporations, which I referred to earlier. Maybe somebody ought to ask Rush Limbaugh about the P.I.C. and F.P.I. . . . .

Let me be clear: These prisons, which are being built everyday at the expense of the American taxpayer, are a rip off. And there are various forces, which ultimately profit from crime and become extremely wealthy on the backs of the (poor) broken, busted and disgusted prisoners who are forced to work for slave wages. For the reader who thinks this forced slave labor translates into jobs for inmates upon their release - wrong! Statistics show that eighty-nine percent of private companies refuse to hire ex-cons. Even more, many of the jobs in prison are not available outside of prison. It stands to reason that since companies are downsizing, laying off and firing workers - and replacing those workers with prison labor forces; there will be no jobs for those prisoners once they become ex-prisoners.

I am not anti-Bush! Nor am I anti-republican! I am anti-exploitation and anti-devastation. It has become quite clear to me that poverty is a weapon of mass destruction. The victims of this weaponry end up addicted, afflicted, in jail or dead. If America is to truly wage a war, it ought to be a "war for the poor". A "war" must be waged "for" the illiterate because those who are poor, who can't read, write or count need food and housing just as badly as those we fed in Afghanistan when we dropped "bread" and "bombs" simultaneously from military planes.

Although I am not necessarily opposed to reparations being paid to the great, great grandchildren of slaves, etc., this is "not" an argument for reparations. Rather it is an argument for preparation. To be sure, if America would invest in preparing poor kids (Black, White, Indian and Hispanic) for life and teaching them life-coping skills while they are young; we would not need to pay to house them in prisons when they get older . . . There is no argument about the fact that kids in "Perry" Homes (in Atlanta, GA) can't, don't and won't get the kind of education, which the kids in "Merry" Homes (Buckhead, Bel Air, Beverly Hills, etc.) will receive. When African Queen and best-selling author Toni Morrison was asked by Tavis Smiley what she would do to save America's schools, she replied candidly, "I would pour tons and tons and tons of money into public schools." She went on to say, " The worse mistake America ever made was cutting public school budgets and using that money to build prisons." Mrs. Morrison also stated that parents ought to go into those public schools and "sit down". If kids are acting out and not learning, etc. then parents, neighbors, pastors, deacons, retired or unemployed relatives ought to go into those classrooms and sit! Education has lost its glamour in the ghettos. Black folks used to consider education an "act of defiance". Indeed it is! Yet, many kids today think it's corny to be smart. So we must fight that erroneous thinking and make the learning process an exciting one. Learning is an adventure. Toni Morrison reminds us that the brain was designed to learn. A good education is freedom and the appetite for learning is non-stop. So we must "demand" that our president, our senate and our congress put money (billions of dollars) back into our public school system and give those teachers the tools and equipment they need to do the most important job on the planet - to teach.

I suggest every public school in America, every prison warden, all community leaders, etc. provide their students, prisoners and followers with a copy of "Vernon Can Read" by Mr. Vernon Jordan. Reading is a powerful tool. One chess master in New York City admitted that the inability to win a chess game led him to the world of books. He happened to see a book and he opened it. When he opened the book, he read a strategy, which instructed him on how to win a chess game. He has gone on to become one of the top five chess players in the entire world. Now he reads voraciously because he says a book will take you anywhere in the world that you want to go. Just a hundred years ago in Georgia, if you could read and were Black, you went to jail or died! I am not only encouraging Blacks to read books, but I encourage "all" to read. Brilliant people read and people who want to become brilliant "must" read. You can read Shakespeare, James Baldwin, W.E.B. Dubois, etc., that's necessary, but you should also read Zig Zigler, Les Brown, Tony Robbins, Steve Covey, Dr. Na'im Akbar and Joel Dyer. The more you read, the more informed you are. And a lack of information leads to devastation and degradation. Read! Read!! Read!!! . . .

If you have never read one of my books before, I guess I should take this opportunity to remind you that not only am I a consultant, entrepreneur, CEO, etc., I am also a motivational speaker, peak performance coach and a "gospel preacher". And so my books are, in a sense, an argument. An argument for justice! And so it is obvious that I am prone to digressing sporadically and changing subjects without warning. But please rest assured you are still reading "Creating Monsters" and this tome is absolutely "non-fiction".

I am a multi-dimensional thinker, a multi-directional writer and perhaps the manner in which I read affects the way I write. At times, I read twelve to sixteen hours per day and on any given day, I will read "A Lawyers Life" for four hours, "How To Argue And Win Every Case" for four hours and "Awaken The Giant Within" for four hours. Ipso facto, there is an argument for justice, profiles on great lawyers, "wrongful convictions", self help for the poor and arguments against political corruption in every book, which I write. If you need to dilute the potency of emotions, power and fervency, which is in my books, I would suggest you take a break every hour or so and read a bit of poetry. I'm not being sarcastic at all. I've just found that mixing up books works for me. Many times if I'm reading a book that makes me angry, I'll take sporadic respites and go entertain myself awhile; then I come back to the book. I would hope that after you finish the last page of this book, you are moved to "take action". Armchair revolutionaries won't disband the "monster factory". Rhetoric alone does not transform prison cells into classrooms, this book is a "call to action". It is a call for Americans and all people across the world who wants to leave the world a little bit better than they found it. So, I must encourage each of you who is reading, to tell your friends about this book. And once they read it, I would hope it speaks for itself . . . Mass imprisonment is a direct outgrowth of social and legal policies, which have, for the past two decades, firmly favored incarceration over rehabilitation, treatment and alternate forms of sentencing. Let us remember that there are four hundred and fifty-five thousand people sent to prison every year - and two million Black men now under various forms of correctional supervision. Mass incarceration pays! "Crime does pay"! Crime pays billions, as I've already shown. Yet, mass imprisonment has taken a heavy and deadly toll on the poor in the form of collateral damage. This collateral damage is bleeding ferociously over into the very fabric of American society. Mass incarceration is consistently destabilizing entire families, barrios and communities.

This destabilization, as it were, is horrible in lower-income urban centers, and within communities of color as a whole. The residual impact is now being felt across our country. Mass imprisonment has exacerbated mental illnesses and poverty; denied citizens the right to vote through felony disenfranchisement laws; left drug and alcohol problems untreated and contributed to outbreaks of serious infectious diseases ranging from tuberculosis to hepatitis C. Mass incarceration has created and is "creating monsters", murderers, molesters, rapists and robbers. How do you make a monster? . . .

We must first understand that prior to planting a garden, etc., the ground must be loosened up. One cannot plant corn seeds in concrete. The ground must be broken. The soil must be loosened. Once the ground is broken or loosened then it's ripe for planting . . . Kids who grow up in the suburbs and in middle class neighborhoods are reared on solid (concrete) foundations. These foundations protect against incarceration, poverty and violence. Yet, the foundations of our young Blacks, Browns and poor White have been loosened by hopelessness . . . (again). These people didn't (initially) "make mistakes", but they were "born into mistakes". Their lives are ripe for failure. Ripe for dope instead of hope, ripe for jail and not Yale. Their foundations are weak, watered and withering and integration actually contributed to their devastation. Please understand that I believe White folks, Mexicans and Black folks can and should live amongst each other in peace. I am "not" opposed to racial integration at all. However, one of the beauties of (if not the only beauty of) segregation was that back in the day all Black folks (rich and poor) lived together.

Ipso facto, a Black doctor would live next door to a Black lawyer and right across the street from them lived a janitor and a maid. So the sons and daughters of the maid and janitor saw success right in front of their very eyes each and every day. The poor Black boy would see the middle class Black doctor pull his Cadillac in and out of the driveway every day. The poor Black girl would see the successful Black lawyer pull his Lincoln in and out day and night. The neighbor's kids would play together. Through a process of some form of association, in many cases, there was assimilation. Often the poor would mentally envision themselves becoming a doctor, lawyer, teacher, preacher, entrepreneur or realtor. But what happened is (I'm being a bit redundant, but since they show the same commercials over and over all day long on TV to program us; why not remake the same point I made earlier in this book. If this were fiction you could complain. In fiction, we look for plot, characters, scenery and style. In non-fiction: Look for power! Look for facts and sometimes repetition!) as soon as they allowed us to live in the suburbs all the successful, middle class and professional Black folks moved out of the ghettos and left the poor behind. Who would the poor look up to then? The dope dealers, pimps and prostitutes were the only ones left in the hood who had the symbols of success. So our kids began to look up to thugs, thieves and "crime", which became the only way to succeed and grow rich. I am not criticizing middle class Blacks for moving to the suburbs. That's not a sin. There is no sin in getting in where you fit in. The sin however, is in not going back to help, school, tutor, educate, liberate and encourage those they left behind. I understand what led to many of them not going back. It's easier to "talk" it than it is to "walk" it and many a Black professional was so damned glad to get out that they said, "I'll never go back". It wasn't necessarily a conscious abandonment of these people for some successful Blacks. It was (for some of them) a sense of relief and a hidden fear that going back could somehow bring them back.

For example, how many people get out of the hospital and never go back? Many, if not most! But when we're "in" that hospital bed, we wish we could get a visit. We are isolated, lonely and depressed while we are in that hospital room. So why is it that when we get discharged from the hospital most of us never go back? "I remember how lonely I was so I'm going to go back and just visit the sick. Even people I don't know and people who are not in my family. I'm just going back because it is the right thing to do." Did you say that or do that after you got out of the hospital? The answer is probably no. And it is not because you are a bad person. It is not (necessarily) because you think you are better than the people who are in the hospital either. You just got out and got caught up in living your life as if nobody (else) was in the hospital and in need of a visit. I have to believe that if somebody came by your house and reminded you of how lonely, depressed and stressed you felt in the hospital and that person asked you to go with them to visit a sick person, etc., you would go back. Ipso facto, let this tome remind all of the brothers and sisters who have made it out of the hoods to go back into the hoods. All of the basketball, baseball and football superstars who are Black, came out of the ghetto and they should consider this book a "reminder". A friendly reminder. We need not only to go back one day a year to pass out food on Thanksgiving. I know we're busy. I know we are living large and we paid a lot of dues to enable ourselves to get in a position to be prospering as we are. But let us consider going back at least once or twice per month to do workshops, seminars and teach-ins in the hood. After we lecture, encourage, inspire and educate our people then we can pass out turkeys and ham.

Pragmatically, it would also be wise (financially) for our White brothers and sisters (also) to go into these hoods. Let us consider not using fear as a reason not to go back. I am cognizant of the fact that many preppy White kids from the suburbs drive into the ghettos to buy drugs. Are they afraid? Hell yes, they are, but they overcome their fears in order to go get what they want. If we don't invest in our youth in the inner cities "now", we will (I promise you) pay for our troubled youth "later". We will pay thirty-five and forty dollars per year to send and keep them in jail. Why not (instead) invest (one or two days per week "now") to prepare them to go to Yale. We can (I repeat) invest now or later . . . and I must remind us that we cannot blame all of the horrors of our jails, prison or even society on the politicians. Who elected them? How many eligible voters don't vote? I saw Mr. Bush yesterday on Meet The Press attempting to justify the war on Iraq. I must state here that George W. Bush is our president. And as such, I respect the position he holds. I am also praying for Mr. Bush

and from what I saw yesterday, we need to pray for Mr. Bush. I'm very, very serious. I fear that this man is subconsciously (perhaps) becoming a warmonger. And one of the problems I had with his platform on Meet The Press was the fact that his statements contradicted themselves every few minutes . . . i.e., when asked by Tim Russert, "Are you prepared to lose (the office of the presidency)? "I'm not gonna lose," replied Mr. Bush appearing (according to citizens polled) very over-confident and arrogant! Yet, about four minutes later that same person (Mr. Bush) stated, "And if I'm given the privilege to serve as president again . . ." Apparently the politician kicked in and perhaps he remember his coaching and decided to try to appear humble. Mr. Bush went on to make statements such as: "I sit here behind this desk and make decisions with war on my mind." He also stated, "I want to lead the world." And, "I know where I want to lead the world." Now to my readers who are Bush supporters, I must ask, doesn't this sound a bit like a dictator or a man who is possessed?? I'm concerned about the mentality of our president. He is beginning to sound sort of like some of the dictators, which we adamantly oppose in this great country. I will not disrespect our president by calling him a Hitler or Hussein, etc., like some people do, but I shall indicate that A. We must pray for George W. Bush and B. Perhaps we should consider electing John Kerry, Howard Dean or Mr. Edwards, in the upcoming election.

By the time you have this book in your hands, the final hour will have come and perhaps gone for Kevin Cooper who is on death row. Kevin is scheduled to die tonight at the hands of our government this very moment (as I write this). Lawyers Greg Evans, Mrs. Eggers, Lanny Davis and David Alexander are writing vigorously to try to save Kevin's life. Apparently there seems to be exculpatory evidence such as blond hairs found in the victim's hands that could not have belonged to Kevin (he is Black), which makes his conviction seem suspect. A decade ago I would have believed he was guilty! "There is no way prosecutors, police and a judge will kill an innocent man," I would have argued. But Barry Scheck, Gerry Spence, Johnnie Cochran, Rubin "Hurricane" Carter, Governor George Ryan, Honorable President Nelson Mandela, Anthony Porter and Denzel Washington have educated me. Now I know that law enforcement can be corrupted, evil and cold-blooded at times. Actor Mike Farrell went to San Quentin yesterday and said he believes Kevin Cooper is innocent and was set up by the police and D.A. Denzel, Robert Dreyfuss, Hurricane Carter, Jesse Jackson, and many others have come to Sacramento pleading for justice on Kevin's behalf. The terminator (I was personally let down because I believe Arnold is a good man. I know Maria Shriver is an excellent woman and I had hoped she could influence Arnold on this one) denied the appeal. So did the Federal and Supreme Court. So before I finish writing this book, I'll tell you whether or not he was/is executed. Keep reading . . . It's not looking good right now. I hope and pray that Arnold will (in the future) do justice, have mercy and walk humbly with God. I also hope he has not allowed Mr. Peter Wilson to dictate to him and that Arnold is his own man. Whether they kill (I hope not) Kevin Cooper or not, the other challenge is for Jesse, Farrell, Alexander, Gerry Spence, Denzel, Comiskey and the rest of us to stand up and organize to outlaw the death (murder) penalty in America! We must meet the real challenge and work, organize, strategize and galvanize to get it "outlawed". Upon completion of reading this book, I would surmise that most crime victims and/or the families of victims of crime would rather a person be sentenced to life without parole (in the monster factory) than be sentenced to death. I know for a fact that if (God forbid) someone kills a member of my family I would want that person sentenced to "live" in prison 'til they die in prison. I want them to think about it each and every day for a very long time. Death (for a murderer) is the easy way out. And I need to elucidate and describe for you what the monster factory is like. It is not a county club. Prisoners are not cuddled and coddled. It is a horrible place. It is awful, evil and wicked. It is a warehouse and a mechanism, which is being utilized to create monsters!

It is Monday morning and the rattlesnake is alive and operating. My day began with a potential breach of institutional security and a possible threat to my safety. My subconscious mind just woke me up. My cell door was wide open and they were "running chow" (serving breakfast). There are two hundred men housed in my building. Two hundred! Some are rapists, child molesters, murderers, serial killers and perverts. I am not as popular as some of my supporters would surmise. To my captors (C.D.C. authorities) I am viewed as a threat. The pen is mightier than the sword, so my voluminous writing, publishing, analyzing and the fact that I try to be a thinker is a problem for them. Norman Mailer and the Honorable Nelson Mandela both said, "The most dangerous inmate in prison is the writer." To my peers (fellow inmates) I'm a square. I don't fit in. I don't smoke weed, I shoot no heroin, I drink no hooch, (pruno, prison made wine) I don't gamble and I spend little time socializing. To some of the brothers who share my pigmentation, I am viewed as one who thinks he's better than them. A few of them even assume I am an Uncle Tom. Some think I'm fabulously wealthy, so I don't appreciate their personal story or struggles. To some of my peers who don't share my complexion, I am a racist. Some of them actually think I hate White people. Rarely will you find three inmates in a row who share the same opinion of Sherman Diahric Manning. So with this mixed bag of opinions shared amongst my fellow prisoners and with my noticeable unpopularity in prison, it should come as no surprise that I was a bit perturbed to wake up to an open cell door. Anyone or any ten (or twenty) of the two hundred men housed in this building could have run into my cell and killed me. In a secure prison where there was an appreciation for safety and security, there would be rules on door opening (i.e., an announcement: "Any inmate, who is going to breakfast, turn on your bright light and put a piece of paper in your cell door window"). This way if a person didn't want or plan to go to breakfast (or imagine being threatened, "When we go to breakfast, I'll kill you . . ." perhaps the inmate is afraid and is waiting to speak to an officer, etc. Maybe he has no plan to leave his cell. Yet, they will open the cell door anyway; even if you're sound asleep) his door would not be opened.

After breakfast, at around 7:35 a.m., the control officer announced, "Porters come to work" and began opening the doors of the building porters. My door did not open although I am a porter. I waited a while. I would have been glad not to go to work, but C.D.C. purposely keeps you on edge. "If I take off my clothes and get back in bed; then my door will open," I thought to myself. So I yelled out the door to Officer O'Ware (pseudonym) and said, "Manning 240". He relayed the message to the control cop, Officer Bingam (pseudonym) told O'Ware, "He's off today." She was incorrect and it really should not have mattered anyway. They allow most prisoners to come to work (play) on their days off all the time. Those guys come out and congregate at a table to gamble. On my days off, if I come out, I isolate myself at a table to write. Ipso facto, I'm at a table this very minute writing the book, which you are reading.

Officer Bingam is a good soul. She has a good spirit and she means well, but like so many of us, she tries to fit in. Her efforts to fit in causes her to use a lot of profanity. (I hate to hear women cuss. I always have. I surmise it is because the "Queen", Dollie Manning, who raised me, didn't cuss). Also Officer Bingham is very, very moody. Nevertheless, I've come to the point in my prison stay where I'm too busy to get into the officers and their characters. I spend as little time as possible dealing with them. I basically act as if they don't exist.

At the moment, I'm looking at Carlton (pseudonym) who is an inmate prison clerk. He's a rat (snitch) and allegedly an undercover homosexual. He's presently asking the control cop to let him out of the building. Carlton has his boom box in his left hand and a green folder in his right hand and is apparently trying to go up to the program office (the nerve center for the facility) to make copies of something. The captain, lieutenants and sergeants, etc. have their offices in the program building. Carlton could actually be using the green folder as a "cap" (decoy, subterfuge or cover) to make it appear that he's going to make copies. He could actually be going to check in. "Tom has heroin in cell 000. Mike has pruno in cell 1000, Manning is writing another book, etc., etc." It happens every day. I would guesstimate there are at least one hundred rats in this building alone. Perhaps sixty percent of them routinely and consistently report to the officer anything, which they can find out.

Two inmates and one civilian employee just drove an "upright" (scissor lift) into our building. It is utilized to reach the ceiling lights and ventilation covers, etc. in the buildings. I would say the ceiling in this building is twenty-four feet high. They are here today to change the ventilation cover. Both inmates are up on top of the lift. The civilian employee is standing beneath them with his hands in his pockets. He's wearing brown khaki-like trousers and a white shirt. The two inmates are in blue jeans and blue shirts. They're doing the work and he's doing nothing. The state is paying them (the inmates) the astronomical sum of eight cents per hour. The motionless civilian employee (who has now found a spot on the floor, which he appears to be staring at) is being paid only twenty-five dollars per hour. Officer Bingam is now reading the newspaper. Usually she sits in the dayroom and watches the television. There are only about five inmates presently milling around the dayroom. Yard was released a while ago and most guys went outside. The ones who are still inside their cells will get a dayroom release at 10:00 a.m. This will be the time they can shower, wash clothes, use the telephone, play cards, etc.

The yard is full. Men are working out on the bars. Men are jogging, playing hand ball, basketball or just walking around and around the track. The yard is about the size of a high school football field. There are five housing units, which are located on the outer perimeter of the yard, buildings one through five. I am housed in building two. There is always a lot of yelling, cussing, obstreperous and belligerent chatter on the yard and in dayrooms. The average conversation is about dope, women, getting out (of prison), violence, gangbanging, former fights, former assaults, gossip, rumors, innuendo and propaganda. Political discussions and constructive conversations geared toward a positive outcome are an aberration or anomaly in prison. There is an enormous fixation with pornography and cartoons in prisons. Perhaps seventy percent of the men in prison (nationwide) watch at least two hours of cartoons every day. The news, talk shows, etc. are viewed as taboo and uncool.

Books are banned (in a sense) via a self-imposed ban. Basically most of the little reading that goes on in prisons takes place in the hole (ad-seg) only when an inmate can't get to a TV or radio.

That reading is usually fiction. By and large most inmates spend their days (if they don't have jobs) listening to rap music, rock, heavy metal, playing cards, drinking, doing drugs and telling "war stories" (embellished stories about so-called fights they were in before). Basically, there is little to do in prison. Rehabilitation, classes, courses and/or self-help type programs were eliminated years and years ago. So we have a large group of boys who never grew up and never matured. Most grew up in fatherless homes. Most didn't finish (many didn't even start) high school. Most are violent, volatile, vicious, illiterate and scared. The macho walk and hard core talk are disguises . . . They mask the fear, the pain, the strain and void. There is a lot of hopelessness, trauma and hurt beneath the masks. Those who have mastered the art of the façade are usually the more dangerous and volatile. There are hardcore predators and naïve victims. When a man enters prison, he will hunt other men or be hunted. To be or not to be . . . On a daily basis, I see seventeen and eighteen-year-old babies come into this place. Deep inside (in spite of my own anger at the injustice, which I am a recipient of), I actually feel sorry for them. And in prison you're not supposed to feel sorry for anybody. "Take your feelings and mail them home to your family," I was told by an ignorant, institutionalized programmed, prison born, prison bred, prison fed (and when he dies he'll be prison dead) inmate a couple of days ago. He "was" (emphasis on the word "was") my celly. I insisted that he move. I'm very careful about who lives in the cell with me. The poison, venom, evil and wickedness rub off easily. Association brings about assimilation. One never finds a perfect cell partner because it is unnatural for two adult males to cohabitate in the same cell. That is mentally, psychologically, physically and emotionally against nature. Yet, I try to pick and choose the lesser of evils. I try to get a guy who has a job working hours opposite my job hours. Unfortunately (but truthfully) sometimes, I prefer a cell partner who watches a lot of television (with headphones) or is a music fanatic or who sleeps a lot to keep him out of my way.

Just in!! The Federal Court of Appeals has granted Kevin Cooper a stay of execution! Praise God! I don't know all of the details at this juncture, but I just heard K.C.R.A. television news host announce it. I jumped up from the table and yelled, "Praise God!" There is a God! Jesse Jackson, Hurricane, Mike Farrell, James Cromwell, Greg Evans, David Alexander, Attorney Eggers, the people who protested in front of the governor's house; they did it. By the Grace of Almighty God. More to come . . .

Some would ask why I don't try to help a celly, etc. I have tried many times! I try now sometimes and I will continue to try in the future. Some accept help. Some reject help. You win some, lose some and some are rained out. I am just being authentic and probitistic in this tome. The bottom line is I am on a mission. My days are filled with writing and this book will save lives. I am humbled by the fact that God uses me to write. I respect, realize and recognize the power of a book. This book will be read by kids in South Africa, boys and girls in the ghettos of Chicago, pastors, prisoners, saints and sinners all over the world. When I'm dead and gone somebody will "read this book". Therefore, I need all the time, peace, serenity and silence I can get, so if my celly won't shut up, get out of my way and let me write, he must go. If my celly asks for advice, books to read or wants to sporadically converse with me, I am affable and even gregarious. I want to help somebody. Yet, my situation is complex and change does not come easily in prison. The pressure is on to keep up the front, false image and the façade of masculinity and machoism. It's a helluva place.

The day (my day in prison), which I was telling you about earlier, ended with me writing, writing, writing. Sporadically (on that day) I was interrupted by a variety of characters. One guy was an armchair revolutionary who talks a good game: "Atlanta," he said to me. "I think somebody ought to just sit in the dayroom like you do (he thinks I'm doing legal work) and write a book about all these people in here. I'm the only one who ever thought about that, man, but somebody ought to do it."

On a slower day, had I not been submerged in writing you (the reader), I would have challenged him on it. I would have asked him why he didn't write it. I would have attempted to motivate him and inspire him. Yet I politely told him, "That's a good idea man and one day we must discuss it. But I gotta get back to this work I'm doing, man. I'll holler at you." He got up and said, "Stay with your legal work, Atlanta, cause that's what's gonna end up getting you outta here. Alright, I'm going to find me some weed, dog."

Before I get deep into the heart of creating monsters, I'd like to engage in a bit of rambling tautology and redundancy. Allow me please . . . Arnold Schwarzenegger let me down! The fact that he would not temporarily stall an execution where a man's "life" was at stake is cold! I don't dislike Arnold. In fact, I have expressed confidence in a lot of the things he seems to be trying to do for California. But he blew "this" one. It would appear that he has not shaken his advisors. If Arnold continues to listen to Pete Wilson, he will not leave the kind of special legacy, which I feel he is capable of leaving. What if Kevin Cooper is really innocent? What if they had gone ahead and executed him the other day and tested the evidence "after" murdering him and then found out he was/is innocent? It has happened before; I could not live with blood on my (hands) conscience. But Arnold had the audacity, the unmitigated gall and disrespect to refuse to meet with Jesse Jackson. How dare he refuse to meet with a man who has met with presidents, princesses, kings, queens and leaders of the world? How dare Arnold refuse to meet with a man who has rescued hostages from Syria and Iraq? Margita Thompson, Dick Riordin and Maria need to have a talk with Arnold.

"When you're Black or Brown and you're arrested, you have no money and you get a public defender and you go to prison, you're fodder for the system and you often die. If you're White, have money and you get first class lawyers, then rarely do you go to death row." Jesse was right although KCRA TV and several other local news stations are displaying false and misleading statistical data about the percentages of Whites vs. Blacks on death row. It was absolutely irresponsible for KCRA not to point out the fact that Black people as a whole, make up less than fourteen percent of the U.S. population. If KCRA had been interested in telling the entire truth, they would have shown that (per capita) Blacks and Browns outnumber Whites in death row. By an astronomical, unfair and unequal number. But KCRA did what mass media does; they eviscerated the truth with inadequate statistics. It was their way of saying, "There are more Whites than Blacks on death row so what is Jesse talking about?" Now the question is how many of you (readers) are willing to write, e-mail or call KCRA and challenge them on their story and false reporting? If you want authentic death row statistics, contact Mike Farrell, James Cromwell or Rubin "Hurricane" Carter . . .

"The arrogance of White men has made me a rich man!" stated entrepreneur, hip hop mogul and multimillionaire Russell Simmons. "Arrogant, rich and closed-minded White men refused to be open-minded enough to invest in hip hop twenty years ago. They told me no and I thank God everyday that they told me no. They refused to be open-minded enough to see a future in hip hop. But their children couldn't resist hip hop. White kids couldn't get enough of it." Russell used to sell dope on the street corners in Hollis. He got high, drunk and slang dope. Now he's slinging hope. He has a thirty-five thousand square foot mansion in the Hamptons. He is a friend to Donald Trump and says he learned a lot from the "Donald". Ipso facto, Sean P. Diddy Combs said, "I have stalked the life of Russell Simmons. I go into whatever verve Russell goes into. I model him." When asked about the hypocrisy of promoting gangster rap, Russell replied, "Gangsta Rap? We don't need to talk about Gangster Rap. Let's talk about our gangster government. George Bush worships a gun, but we don't want to talk about that. Fifty Cents watched his mother get killed. His mother was a drug dealer. He has been shot a lot of times. On one of those times, he was hit nine times in one shooting, but he survived it. So his poetry is his reality. They rap about what they see. What about the poverty and suffering that people endure in Hollis (Perry Homes, Watts, Oak Park, Bankhead Courts) every day? Nobody wants to talk about that ignorance. Nobody wants to deal with poverty, illiteracy and hunger right here in America. We just want to make an issue out of the lyrics of Black rappers."

Russell changed my own paradigm. I still don't like the "N" word and I am absolutely opposed to referring to women as bitches, but I understand his point completely. If we are ever gonna stop "creating monsters", we are going to have to deal with the basic, elemental problems which causes crime; poverty! When will we deal with it? I am not opposed to wealth. I don't support punishing the wealthy! Instead, I propose that we help to show others how to create wealth. I'm down for entrepreneurs! I support business, self-help and people coming up! But those of us able to come up must reach back and bring somebody with us.

I'll reiterate that we need Donald Trump, Don King, P. Diddy, Bill Gates, etc. to help us begin a war on poverty. Foundations are great! Giving to charity is wonderful, but we are gonna need to do more than that! Mr. President, there can be no war on crime without a war on the conditions which lead to the commission of crimes! Mr. President let's wage a "war on poverty"! Now I'm not naïve enough to assume those few sentences are going to motivate Mr. Bush to change. But I am hopeful that Bill Gates, John Johnson, Oprah, Russell, P. Diddy and others will read this and decide to take more action. They could (for instance) bring cameras into their offices and show our youth what they do. Why don't we get Bill Gates, Chris Gardner, Willie Gary and Andrew Goodwin to make a one-hour video (each) "message to our youth" about how to get out of poverty? Why can't we infiltrate the hoods and ghettos with these videos just like we infiltrate them with drugs and guns?

Mr. Limbaugh claims to be a person with talent on loan from God? He talks about self-reliance and education, etc. and says he's not racist or classicist? Fine, let's go with that claim. Let's not call Rush a liar, liar, big fat liar. Let's challenge Rush to help us teach self-reliance. Rush: (Are you reading, buddy?) I want you to replicate your success via video. You (Rush) already have video and audio equipment; make a one-hour video motivating our youth! Then make fifty-one thousand copies and send it to every public school in America! That way we can save this country you say you love so much . . . In case Rush did not read the words above, I must challenge every reader to call his show and tell him about it.

Now I want every politician, pastor, professor, teacher and citizen in this country to know that we are responsible (collectively) for the murders, rapes, molestations and drug abuse that are destroying our country. We did it. It's not "them" and "their" problem. It's "us" and "our" problem. We (even if indirectly) created every serial killer, serial rapist and predator in this country. There are no natural born killers. Violence is not innate and one of the main ways we have created monsters is by allowing our prisons to become havens of hopelessness, shame and violence. When we began to allow houses of rehabilitation to transform into homes of devastation, we exacerbated the problems, which had already begun in the womb of poverty. The cradle of small crimes is in the ghettos. The juvenile facilities, jails and prisons are undergraduate schools for monsters.

What are our prisons like today? Mayors give an address called "the state of the city". Governors tell us "the state of the state". The President? - "The state of the union"! My assignment is to give you "the state of the prison"!

It is dank, horrible, ruthless, cynical, evil, cruel, unusual, perverted and a simple bastion of wickedness. Prisons? I need to somehow convey to you the atmosphere and sensations of what it is and feels like to be in prison . . . Some people have been in prison so long that it is difficult for them to even remember specifically how they got there. Some have been in for so long that their fantasies of the free world are no longer distinguishable from what they "know" the free world is really like. They've been locked up for so long that being free is exactly like a free man's dreams of heaven. To die and go to the free world.

The person who is state-raised-reared in the juvenile facilities and prisons from an early age learns over and over that people in society can do anything to him and not be penalized by law enforcement. He learns they can do anything to him with the full force of the state behind them. The juvenile must march in lock-step to his meals in huge mess halls. The child in the juvenile facility begins early on to become programmed. Programmed to fail. In fact, it is ironic that the word "program" is used and spoken into the ears of juveniles and prison inmates numerous times each day. "You need to learn how

73

to program. We will throw you into the hole if you don't program. If you don't do what you're told, we will interrupt your program . . ." In penological institutions, the word program takes on an entire "new" meaning. To program in prison means to abide by the rules and if you (program) abide by the rules, you will be allowed to do your own "program" (second meaning: i.e., having your TV, radio, canteen, and telephone privileges, etc., those are considered "your own program". And if you don't "program" they will take your program) uninterrupted. But in process of this programming, subconsciously there begins to be a kind of deterioration of life coping skills. The ability to make decisions and think for yourself begins to dissipate in the prisons.

Self-help, initiative and a positive mental attitude becomes "arrested" (by prison guards) and apprehended while learning to cope and survive in the prisons. For the youth who is incarcerated; his creative and rational mental skills are arrested. Ipso facto, his ability to develop into an authentic man and decent human being is stunted. The "officials teach" inmates not to think, decide, choose, create and study. Analytical thinking, the ability to deduce, scrutinize and meditate or contemplate are also arrested through the process of programming. Prisoners are told when to get up (out of bed), when to go to sleep, when to shower, when to eat and what to eat. The prisoner has no voice in even how long (given an average of five minutes) he eats. The effects of all decisions being made for any individual has the potential and strong probability of affecting the remainder of that individual's life. After spending several years being told what to do, when to do it, how to do it and asked how long you can do it; the ability to think, create, decide and choose are lost.

Prison guards routinely abuse the inmates under their auspices verbally, mentally, physically and even sexually. Female prisoners are raped on a daily basis by prison guards and these rapes often go unreported for fear of retaliation by (often) the administration (more on rape later).

The mind of the prisoner becomes jaded, polluted and corrupted quickly. Every thing the prisoner experiences at the hands of the authorities serves as a reminder and a reinforcement to the fact that he or she does not matter, is unimportant and is a nobody. The prisoner often becomes antisocial. The inter-developmental social skills that are sharpened and fertilized in grade, middle and high school - are stunted, blunted and blocked in the penal institution. The juvenile or prisoner begins to doubt himself and has no belief in his/her ability to communicate verbally or associate socially. So he draws within himself or becomes a part of a group, clique or gang. The group gives him a sense of belonging and becomes his big brother, his daddy, sister or mother. The gang is the family, which was disrupted when he was sentenced to go to jail. He believes his stress, lashes out at the system, which sent him to prison, and gains some semblance of self-esteem in, by and through his gang. Often he begins to work out. He focuses on pushups, burpees, sit-ups and running. He fine tunes and builds up his body. Simultaneously, he neglects and forgets his mind. He reads no books or newspapers. If he peruses a newspaper, it is the sports or entertainment sections he's looking for. If he seeks out a magazine, it is porn he's seeking. If he watches television, it is cartoons, soap operas or comedy he's watching. Slowly but certainly, he begins to tune the outside world out and to build a new world within. His "new world" has orders and the orders are to be cool, masculine and strong by any means necessary. If he has to pretend to be a Muslim, Christian or Buddhist to fit in, he will. If he has to pretend to be racist, vicious or cold to fit in, he will. If he has to pretend to like rap when he really likes rock or country, when he really likes classical, he will. Whatever it takes to survive, he will do it. Whatever needs to be said or done to thrive, he will say or do it. He's not really losing his identity. Quite often, he's never developed or established an identity. And since repetition is the mother of skill, his repeated protestations about being a racist, hating Whites, Blacks or Browns, etc. becomes who he is. He loses his humanity in the midst of the insanity. He has become a fool for ignorance and a tool for the system . . . There are some who at some point in their lives, serve a few years in prison, get out and never go back. And some, who do come back, serve a short-term get out again and then never return. But the convict who is "state raised", who grows up from boyhood to manhood in the prison's hood is wrecked for life. He is (to put it lightly) unstable (emotionally and psychologically) and this instability is caused by a lifetime of incarceration. More often than not; when one spends long years with their bodies locked up, they then begin to suffer from what I called a locked up mind and an incarcerated spirit. There is absolutely nothing more sad, more damaging, more dangerous or strange than an incarcerated mind and an incarcerated spirit. When it gets to the point that the "mind" and/or "spirit" is incarcerated, institutionalized and poisoned there is often no turning back. The man or woman whose minds and spirits are incarcerated is a "monster"!

The American society provides us with the prerogatives of women and men, of adults. Men are afforded their dues. After eighteen, you are regarded as a man by society. Nobody interferes with your life, slaps you on the hands or disrespects you. The American society is solicitous in general and serves you. Eventually your own judgment is tempered as you gradually see that it has real effects; it impinges on the society, the whole world. Life's experience mellows your emotions because you are free to go and come at will, work and play as you choose. You may pursue any object of love, danger, pleasure, profit, etc. You are taught by the very terms of your social existence, by the nature of your own emotions, etc. You learn about yourself, your potential, your likes, dislikes, strengths and weaknesses. You mature emotionally and you grow up mentally.

For the state-raised convict, it is a different kinda party! A mere boy in reform school, he is punished for being a "boy". In prison, he is penalized for attempting to be a man. He is treated like an adolescent in jail and prison. In civilian life (the streets/the free world) an adolescent is denied use of the telephone or television for any disobedience, any screw up. The prisoner will be thrown in the hole (administrative segregation . . .syn. solitary confinement) for any disobedience or screw up. The convict will go to the hole for murder as well as for stealing an orange out of the mess (chow . . .dining) hall. He will get out of the hole in either case, and the length of his stay for either offense (often) is no different. Prison regimes have convicts making extreme decisions concerning moderate questions, decisions which only fit the logical choices of either or. Absolute no contradiction is allowed openly. The prisoner is not allowed to change. He/she is only allowed to submit; "agreement" does not exist (agreement implies equality). The prisoner is the rebellious adolescent who must obey and submit to the judgment of "grown-ups" - "tyrants".

The prisoner who is not raised by the state, tolerates the situation because of his social maturity obtained prior to incarceration. He/she knows things are different outside the "monster factory". Yet, on the contrary, the state-raised convict has no conception of any difference. He lacks real life (free world) experience and, therefore, maturity. His judgments are untemperate, rash; his emotions, actions, are impulsive, raw, and uneven.

There are emotions - an entire spectrum of emotions - that he (the state-raised prisoner) knows of only through words, through reading (if he reads or can read) and his childish imagination. He can "imagine" he feels those emotions (or therefore knows what they are), but he does not. His passions, even in his thirty's and forty's, are those of a boy.

These things called emotions are one of the hidden, deep, dark sides of the state-raised inmate. This is the foul and evil underbelly, which everyone hides from everyone else. The other half concerns judgment, reason (ethical, moral, cultural). This is the mantle of pride, integrity and honor. It is the high importance he naturally places on force and violence. It is what he feels that makes him effective, a man whose judgment impinges on others, on the world: Dangerous killers, rapists who act alone and without emotion, who act with principles and calculation, to avenge themselves, establish and defend their own principles with acts of murder and madness, which usually evade prosecution by law! This is the state-raised prisoner's true conception of manhood, in the highest sense . . .

On February 13, 2004, a twenty-one-year-old young man was interviewed by Mike Teselle on KCRA TV news about the horrors of life behind bars in C.Y.A. (California Youth Authority). His identity was disguised, as was that of his mother for fear of retaliation by the youth prison guards. This young man experienced a desire to educate the American public about what's really going on in the youth prisons.

He had been housed at Preston Youth Facility in Ione, CA near where I am. "I was sentenced to serve three years when I was seventeen years old. I was arrested for basically being involved in consensual sex with a minor. I pled out to lascivious acts with a minor," stated the young man. He went on to explain that prison guards would stage fights. "They will take a youngster under their wings and bring him in weed, crank, speed, prescription drugs and food from the free world, etc. and anybody they (the prison guards) didn't like they would get their boy(s) (the youth inmate to whom the guard had been smuggling drugs and food) to beat him down. Guards told everybody I was a sex offender," the young man stated. "They'd call me Chester, Rapo or Baby Raper. I thought I was supposed to be there for punishment and rehabilitation. That place was a hellhole. I was taught how older criminals live. I was taught hatred, rage, anger and racism. It is out of control. It is more violent than any movie I have ever seen in my life time."

This young man reinforces my argument that we are "creating monsters"! His life will never be the same again. Living everyday under the threat of death, rape and assault, damages the mind in ways one could never imagine. When one is a teenager, the fear is magnified and multiplied. You go there thinking you can just report it to your keepers (guards). Yet, you find that (all too often) the keepers are contriving and conspiring with the kept. How can you live like that for years and not transform into a monster, a killer and an animal? I've often argued that the media risks the life of the arrested when they tell the world a man is charged with a sex crime. Prisoners watch the news and when he gets to prison, they will be waiting to attack and kill him. But I've discovered that even when cases involving sexual allegations don't make the news, we still learn about them from prison guards. They are glad to tell us, "He's in here for rape." I have no love for a sexual predator. Just as I have no love for a mental predator. I have no love for killers, drug dealers, etc. either. But no matter how unpopular it may sound, I must say it is not my place, my job or my duty to assault a man because he was convicted of a certain crime. I will not be used as a tool (fool) for the system and go around assaulting people because the media tells me they committed certain crimes.

What if he didn't do it? What if she's innocent? All too often guys in prisons rant, rave and rail about how corrupted the system is. So-called prison revolutionaries are quick to talk about "he lied on me" or "officer so and so set me up with a dope case", etc. But seemingly we don't want to accept the fact that there is also a possibility that the dude we heard was a Chester, molester or rapist might have (also) been lied on, set up and convicted of a crime he did not commit. My mind goes back to Rolando Cruz in Illinois. This Mexican brother was convicted of a heinous crime. Rolando was convicted of raping, molesting, sodomizing and killing an eight or nine-year-old White girl. After numerous failed appeals and years in prison - Rubin "Hurricane" Carter and others proved Rolando "did not commit" the crime. He was innocent! But what if some fellow con had killed Rolando in prison because "I heard dude is a Chester"? They'd have killed an innocent man! We cannot depend on the media to run our lives for us. Members of the media sensationalize, yellow journalize (if you will) and embellish stories everyday. But they are not going to tell a man how to get out of prison. Media hype will just tell a man who is lucky enough to get out of prison, how to "get prison out of him". (If Mike Teselle is perusing this tome, I want Mike to share this book with the former C.Y.A. Ward; maybe it can help him). Senator Gloria Romero and Jackie Speier have called the conditions of C.Y.A. "Barbaric, horrifying, cruel, unusual, violent" and "worse than I could have imagined". I applaud the seeming determination of Mrs. Romero and Speier to "expose" the viciousness and failings of the youth and adult prison system in California. I personally believe both Mrs. Romero and Spier are authentic and sincere in their concern and intentions. What I am not so certain about is whether or not they know the magnitude of their endeavors. I'm not certain they can even fathom what it is going to require to fix this broken system. C.D.C. and C.Y.A. have routinely gotten bad press and negative publicity and they are also known for pulling publicity stunts via putting band-aids on bleeding wounds. They will give the system a pseudo transformation via a cosmetic makeover. Prisons nationwide routinely sells these makeovers to lawmakers. But what C.D.C., C.Y.A. (and every Department of Corrections and Youth Facilities nationwide) needs is not a cosmetic makeover. They need major surgery via a total face-lift. We cannot simply cover up these blemishes. We've been covering up the lack of rehabilitation, covering up prison guard abuse, prison guard drug smuggling, etc. for far too long. It's time now for Rod Hickman and Arnold to act as a terminator! They need to pull out the knife and prepare for "major surgery". The system is in critical condition, so we must start cutting. We must cut out the good ole boys, captains, lieutenants, wardens and directors, etc., anybody who is corrupted, racist or wicked. They must be cut out, removed from the system and replaced.

In prison R&R means Receiving and Release Department. R&R handles incoming packages, etc. and it's also the place where parolees are released from prison. R&R for Arnold and Rod Hickman ought to take on a new definition. R&R should mean remove and replace. We must remove (cut out as does the plastic surgeon) the Bunnells, Martels, Strattons and Billy Maxfields of the system and replace them with the Max Lemons and Jacksons, Mrs. Romero and Schwarzenegger, etc. All of us must approach corrections with pragmatism and realism. We must be sensible.

Rod Q. Hickman seems to be a good man. I think he means well, but Rod can't do it alone. As head of C.Y.A. and C.D.C., he's the general practitioner! The catharsis needed within these walls requires a surgeon. We need a specialist. We need a czar. We need to sweep the dirt out and bring in new blood. The staff are broken, busted and disgusted. The inmates are also in critical condition. Make no mistake: I blame inmates (also) for the problems. We must punish criminal conduct when it is perpetuated by inmates as well as when it is perpetuated by staff. Inmates should not be allowed to run out of control! I accept the fact that even though I am innocent and I should not be here - I am in prison. Ipso facto, some of my privileges are diminished. I don't argue that prison should be a walk in the park. I do argue that the public is mislead into thinking it is when it definitely is "not". Yet, my dignity and my humanity were not diminished because I came to prison. As such, I should be treated with professionalism, respect and tact by staff. I should not live in fear of being set up, abused or lied on by "staff". These arbitrary and capricious transfers, ad-seg placements, etc. should not be allowed, ignored or condoned by Mr. Hickman. Likewise inmate on inmate violence should not be

79

tolerated. The elements, which breed this violence (i.e., drugs, alcohol and gambling) must be swept out of the system.

Search prison guards entering prison everyday. Strip-search them for drugs and weapons daily. If this is done, we'd eliminate eighty percent of the drug trafficking in prisons nationwide. You can bet your bottom dollar that the guards' unions, the Lance Corcorans, etc. would fight tooth and nail in opposition of this idea. But let us remind them that this is a critical situation and it comes with the territory of working in the prisons. Tell them that since the public is paying hundreds of billions of dollars to keep people in prisons; and are also paying the salaries of all prison guards, etc., the public has the ultimate last word and our citizens want a better return on their tax investments. Our public, which has been hoodwinked into believing that prisoners were being coddled, etc. and that "that" was the problem, this public now knows that prison guard corruption is one of the major components of the problem and that locking men in a zoo, a monster factory and still allowing them to use, abuse and deal drugs is a threat to the safety of the public. Ipso facto, if you are going to work in a prison, you are going to submit daily to strip searches! Mr. Bush, John Ashcroft and Mr. Rumsfeld tell us that "we are at war" and certain civil rights must be diminished in the interest of security when you're in a war. Well, Rod, Arnold, Gloria (Romero), Jackie, Burton, Joe Biden and Senator Kennedy . . . "we are in a war". Our children are being molested! Our elderly are being abused, raped and murdered. We are spending billions on prisons and they are breeding more prisons. There is a state of emergency. We must operate and activate emergency procedures in order to deal with and rectify the massive problems that Mrs. Romero, Max Lemon, Judge Steve White, Critical Resistance, CA Prison Focus, Prison Law Offices, Jesse Jackson, Al Sharpton and others have exposed. The barbaric, tragic and horrible conditions of our juvenile facilities, jails and prisons (nationwide) are in require a "code red" mentality. Strip-search the guards! Fire the wardens! Dismiss the rednecks! Get the Black power, White power, Brown power advocates off the prison payrolls. Bring in newly trained, clean cut, professional and disciplined staff members ready to fight corruption, protect the public by keeping the peace, enforcing the rules and guaranteeing security in the prisons.

Rod Hickman and governors nationwide must be creative and innovative in this new war. Let's use operation prison storm and shock and awe. Let's force our politicians to open the doors to the prisons and allow the media to storm them and show the public what's really going on! We should shock corrupted staff and awe violent inmates.

Let's bring education, self-help and counseling back into the prisons. Let's require inmates to get an education! Let's provide incentives for success in the prisons. Let us seek outside help and volunteers. C.D.C. does not employ a single penologist, in any of its thirty-three prisons! That is unheard of. We need penologists, pastors, scholars and volunteers on staff at every prison. Wardens must be forced to enact the recommendations, which are made by their specialists. C.D.C. has a history of refusing to follow the recommendations of specialists.

"This man cannot handle ad-seg. He should be placed on C.T.Q. in his cell, but don't put him in the hole. He will decompensate, I assure you," Dr. Tom Heddleblad (pseudonym) told a captain (M. Martel) at New Folsom in 2001! "Screw him. His Black ass is going to ad-seg," Martel said. They found him hanging nine hours later. He committed suicide and Martel did not get punished. Martel should have been "fired that day".

For years and years, The Little Hoover Commission had made numerous suggestions to C.D.C. The Little Hoover Commission is comprised of a Blue Ribbon Task Force of scholars, specialists and professionals. It was sanctioned by governors. Yet, when they supply report after report - those reports go unheeded! The Little Hoover Commission is "useless" in California because C.D.C. does not abide by or follow their recommendations. I'd love to get William Greaves, Spike Lee and John Singleton in here to film these prisons. Let's place undercover officers from the F.B.I. in the prisons. Let's plant undercover cameras in the prisons to document guard brutality, cruel and unusual punishment, etc. Why not? Remember this is a new kind of war. Rights are diminished as Mr. Bush will tell you . . .

Another point of focus must be disbanding the severe gang problems in prisons. From the local jails, to juvenile facilities, youth authority and in the prisons all across America, gangs are running the programs. I am not writing philosophically or metaphorically when I say that these places are infested with gangs. When a gang member comes to prison he may lose his colors, but he does not lose the color of this thinking. Nor does he lose his connections. He is usually a person who is state-raised. His daddy or his brothers and cousins are all in gangs. Growing up, he was taught that the gang was his family. It gives him a sense of belonging and makes him feel accepted, respected and important. He becomes addicted to the adrenaline rush, the hype, the excitement and the violence, which comes from being in the gang. He actually thinks it's cool to go to jail! Getting locked up adds credence to his status, reputation and power as a gang member. He has a kick butt now and take names later mentality. When he goes to jail or juvenile facilities or prison, he still takes his orders from other, older gang leaders who are already in the prisons. Those gang leaders coordinate, orchestrate and operate the gangs in prison in collusion with the gang leaders outside the prisons. Hits are ordered from the free world and carried out in the prisons. If a gang member testifies against another gang member in court, etc. to reduce his sentence, he is a dead man. The orders to assault, rape or murder him are already in play by the time he arrives in the joint (juvenile facility, jail or prison).

Also he will get his gang symbols tattooed all over his body in the prison (see my book "America Dream/A Search For Justice - 2004 edition . . .) and he naturally cherishes and treasures these symbols. He fears being alone, but with these symbols, he is immediately recognized by other homeys as one of their own. This is more important to him than his children, family or friends. He is committed to the structure.

Prison authorities have done very little to disband and disarm the gangs in prisons. In fact, the guards have their gangs and those guards who are not a part of the guards' gang are a part of the inmates' gangs - literally! I.e., C.O. Acosta was a member of C.D.C.'s elite S&I (Special Investigations) unit. He was stationed at New Folsom State Prison. He got caught bringing in hits for the Mexican Mafia. He was caught and (finally) fired! But Sgt. R. N. Saunders and Sgt. Scarcella wreaked havoc on Black and Brown inmates for twenty plus years as members of the Aryan Brotherhood. At the time they were in power, the wardens were afraid to discipline them. Afraid for their lives.

I filed several complaints on R. N. Saunders as well as Mr. Scarcella, which were routinely dismissed out of hand in the late 90s. Finally, Sgt. Elsberry stepped up to the plate and admitted that she witnessed Sgt. Scarcella and R.N. Saunders beat a Black inmate mercilessly. Sgt. Scarcella was fired and Saunders is on leave. I would not be surprised if both Saunders and Scarcella end up back on the job with promotions. We must understand that in a free society, such as America with the drug problems and poverty running rampart in the inner cities - gangs are pretty much expected. We almost take gangs as a given in the urban poverty zone. And how to tackle the gang problems in the free world is not an issue we will deal with in this particular tome. But I mention the gang problem in civilian life to point out that there should be no gang problem in the prisons. Prisons are supposed to be controlled environments. Prisons are supposed to be run and operated by set rules and regulations and enforced by staff! The gang problems in the streets should not run rampant in the prisons.

There must be a reason that gangs are (allowed/encouraged?) able to infiltrate places of incarceration. But until or unless those reasons are examined, explored and dealt with, the "creation" of "monsters", vicious, dastardly and violent human specimens, "shall march on".

Let there be no doubt that one of the main reasons the media is not allowed to come into the prisons and interview inmates in places such as California is because somebody is hiding something.

I am perhaps considered an authority on gangs and an expert on how to neutralize and disband them, not because I was in a gang; I was not. But rather because I have spent the past eight years dealing with gang and ex-gang members. I have analyzed, scrutinized and rationalized their structure, organization and been privy to confidential information pertaining to gangs. I know a lot about the Bulldogs, Breeds, Crips, Mexican Mafia, Northerners, Southerners, Northern Structure, Black Gorilla Family, 415, etc., etc., etc., because I have dealt with them. A.B., Skinheads, Nazi Low Rider, Pecker Woods, etc. - I have lived with them. (As bold and courageous as I am, there are still some things even I can't write; yet).

It actually amazes me at how these guys light up Christmas trees when they are discussing their gangs. I literally can see the lights come on and their eyes begin to gleam and glow with ebullience when they describe (although it is usually an embellished version of the true life story) their banging, dope slinging, hits (murders), shootings and even their rapes. I have been blessed with a gift to get people to open up and drop the facades and tell me the truth about their lives and pasts and hopes and dreams. It amazes even me at how many bullies and violent gang members have told me, "I've never told anybody this, but I was molested when I was seven years old and . . ." I guess one of the reasons is that they know I won't repeat it. Ipso facto, you will never, ever read the real names of gang members in any of my books if the subject or revelations involve their past crimes or ties or data, which could get them (or me) killed. I will not violate that trust or bond by snitching or ratting them out.

I will inform you that when a man in prison looks at me and admits he was molested and that he has molested, there is absolutely no question in my mind that he is telling the truth. I've heard lots and lots of war stories and many are told with the teller always coming out as the victor. I discount most of those tales. Yet, when I am told, "I was afraid. I was scared and he beat me down," etc. that's when my ears perk up. They have my full attention! I listen and I listen closely. My mentor, my hero and my leader, (may he rest in the heavens) the late Rev. Hosea Williams used to tell me, "Rev. Manning, God gave you one mouth and two ears. You oughta listen twice as much as you talk." So I've read, I've studied, I've looked, listened, experienced and learned. I know beyond all doubt that dealing with gangs in general and gangs in the prisons will require skillful, pragmatic and disciplined action. We can't throw words at the problems. You can't talk "at" gang members. You can't talk down to gangsters. Simultaneously, you can't pander or cater to them . . . The fact remains that once you lock a guy up, take away his freedom and have control over his every movement - there is no way his gang should control and/or maintain an active status in the prisons. The only way the gang can keep its power and be active and operational in a controlled environment, is if the controllers have lost control. And certainly our argument is that the controllers (prison guards) have lost or don't desire (to have) control. The fact that the gangs in the prisons are as potent as the gangs in the streets, speaks volumes about the lack of a grip on the prisons by the "keepers of the gates". I have been surprised at the lack of written data on gangs in the prisons. It would appear that somebody is afraid or uninterested in dealing with the root causes of violence, killings, and drugs in the prisons as well as in the street. When groups such as "Critical Resistance", "California Prison Focus", etc. attempt to educate the public about these elemental problems, which ultimately serve to increase the wealth of the masterminds in charge of the Prison Industrial Complex, they are often ignored. Since we have been incapable of infusing these effective, grassroot groups with adequate funding to help them to fight the good fight, their power is diluted and their message is ignored. We need Michael Jackson, Chris Gardner, Andrew Goodwin, Kobe, Donald Trump, Jayson Williams and others to help find these groups. If Russell Simmons, P. Diddy, Snoop, M&M, Fifty Cents and others who have come up through the struggle in the streets would help these groups out, we would begin to be able to resolve the problems.

If we could motivate great ministries such as T. D. Jakes, Eddie Long, World Changers, etc. to put money into the focus of the prisons, the Resistance (against P.I.C.), which is critical, etc., we would transform the streets and change the prisons.

But the fact remains that no major, wealthy individuals are dealing with the problems of gangs in the streets or gangs in the prisons. When I began writing this tome less than two weeks ago, I reported that Mr. Bush had more than $100 million in the bank for his re-election. I've just learned that he has raised another $100 million. Mr. Bush now has nearly $200 million in the bank to wage a war via the media; to apparently get back in office and wage another war! He stated the other day, "I'm a war president!!" That speaks volumes. I don't have the time or space to adequately write about the hypocrisy, foolishness and the evils of anybody being willing to give nearly a quarter of a billion dollars just to get a man re-elected. Yet, we have homeless men and women and children sleeping outside four blocks away from the Whitehouse. Four blocks away from the House where Mr. Bush sleeps comfortably with two hundred million dollars in the bank. There are (literally) mothers with children quivering outside on park benches on Dupont Circle. This is wrong. It is going to take George Soros, William R. Johnson, Peter and Harry Morton, Chris Andrew Heinz and all of us to change this. This is our America. These are our people and these are our problems.   What will we do about it? You can read this book and do nothing! Or you can read this book as if it is a manual on how to make America better. Ipso facto, you can log on to cafeshops.com/Manning and order more copies of this book and have them mailed to your senator, your congressman, your governor, the local editor of your newspaper, etc. Just one book can change the world if the reader takes action. You can and should call your local jail and juvenile facility and ask who is the chaplain and send him this book and ask him to give it to an inmate. You can come up with innovative and creative ways to get this book into the hands of prisoners, wardens, legislators, pastors, prosecutors and the press. It is as simple as stopping right now and punching in cafeshops.com/manning.html and ordering this book! (I.e., I'd like you to send one copy of "American Dream/A Search For Justice" and "Creating Monsters" to Governor Arnold Schwarzenegger at the State Capitol, Sacramento, CA 95814). How difficult could that be? It is not. If you have no computer access or don't want to use your credit card, you can call 877/809-1659 from 8-5 p.m., Monday through Friday, U.S.A. time. "Books can change your whole life," stated former Ambassador Andrew Young. I'll tell you here and now that many of the gangsters in prison who don't read, don't write and don't study would (indeed) definitely "read this book" if you sent it to them! Prisoners love mail! Mail is the central avenue or chain that a prisoner has to the free world. If inmate so and so got a book in the mail from somebody he or she doesn't even know; I assure you they would be surprised, mesmerized and they would read it. How do you get their address? If you have a name, you simply call prison headquarters (i.e. C.D.C. Headquarters in Sacramento, G.D.C. Headquarters in Atlanta, GA) and give them the name and C.D.C. number and they will give you the inmate's mailing address.

Another way is to log on to the World Wide Web. There are tons of inmate listings, i.e. thepamperedprisoner.com, outlawsonline.com, inmateclassified.com . . .

On these websites, there are names and addresses for tens of thousands of prisoners world wide - "begging for mail". If you don't want to be a pen pal to a prisoner or don't want him or her writing you, etc., simply instruct cafeshop's publishers not to give your name or address (i.e. I want "Creating Monsters" mailed to inmate John Doe #J98796 at M.C.S.P., A-2-240, P. O. Box 409099, Ione, CA 95640-9099. Please do not put my name or address on the billing or shipping information. The tome is an anonymous gift). Voila, the prisoner gets a book in the mail and never knows who sent it. It starts with you and me. What will you do? Will you help? . . . You will . . .

I am not a prophet of doom or a cynical person. I believe that a positive mental attitude is the right mental attitude. Yet, as it relates to the problems of the prisons and the problems in the prisons, I am a realist. If there is an authentic transformation, it's probably not gonna come from the national or local governments.

With all due respect, what does Mr. Schwarzenegger know about operating prisons? Nothing! He's a movie actor turned politician. He has absolutely "no clue" about the inner workings of a prison. Clueless, clueless, clueless. We may recall that Mr. Reagan was also a movie actor turned politician. He too was a "governor" in the state of California. This might be a clue as to how/why the California prison system is (by far) the most violent system in the nation. I am not implying that Mr. Reagan did something crooked or sinister as governor. I am stating emphatically that Reagan didn't know a darn thing about how to run a prison system! How many of you who are reading my words this very moment (those of you who are not lawyers, judges, government workers, etc.) would know how to run thirty-three state prisons with one hundred and sixty-three thousand inmates beginning tomorrow? Think of it: You are an actor, or janitor or computer programmer, etc. and you ran for governor and are elected! Then tomorrow "you" (although your masters degree is in business administration or technology, etc) must figure out how to fix thirty-three broken prisons. You would be lost! It could be argued that the answer is to hire advisors to show you how to run them. But the prisons went bad under Reagan's watch and Pete Wilson's administration exacerbated the corruption, violence and hatred. Now, unfortunately, Pete Wilson is a trusted advisor to Arnold! What does that tell us? I'll be positive and rather than merely criticize Arnold, I'll state clearly that the best thing Mr. Schwarzenegger can do is to get better advisors! It appears that he has a good YACA Director in the person of Rod Q. Hickman, but Rod can't do it alone. As I stated, Rod is a "General Practitioner". We need some specialists. Arnold needs a diverse (meaning not just old White men) group of experts to help him and Rod straighten out C.D.C. If Arnold would get Dr. Na'im Akbar, Professor David Cole, Professor Ogletree, Professor Cornel West, Donald Specter, Leland Linahan, a few penologists, criminologists and Joe (Batman) Clark and call a summit meeting with these people, they could/would show him how to turn the prisons around. I know I'm right. Will Arnold take my advice? Another key would be to get input from the prisoners. Nobody knows more about the prison subculture than prisoners. (This is way too innovative and I know Peter Wilson would oppose this idea; but what the hell! Why doesn't one of you e-mail Pete and tell him I mention him a lot in this book and he should read it. If Mr. Wilson wishes to criticize or scrutinize my tome, I will publish his full reply in my next book. I challenge Mr. Wilson to show me where I'm wrong).

Arnold should make time twice per month (at least) to visit the prisons! Arnold is in a unique position because he's big, he's bad, he's tough, and he's the terminator. I have personally asked hardcore, belligerent gangsters, "Would you go to the chapel or the gym if you knew Arnold was coming here to speak?" One by one came the unanimous reply, "Hell yes!!" I am certain that some of them would want his autograph. But I would persuade Arnold to use autographed photos, etc. as incentives and motivating mechanisms to clean up C.D.C. "I am Governor Arnold Schwarzenegger. I have come here to San Quentin State Prison as has no other governor before me. I have come to join with the staff and the inmates at this prison to turn this place around. I want the violence to stop! I want the gangs disbanded. I want staff abuse and corruption stopped. I want this prison to be a conducive environment for transformation. We can do it . . . I'll Be Back!"

I could draw up a twelve-step plan that Mr. Schwarzenegger could present in the prison that would instantly begin to create change. The challenge is how do you get the Arnold who refused to even meet with "Rev. Jesse Jackson" to meet with prisoners? I don't even know that we could get Rod Q. Hickman to meet with us. I am also quite cognizant of the fact that a governor speaking in the prisons is almost unheard of. But the recall election of Brother Gray Davis was unheard of! The terminator's journey from a poor boy in Austria to becoming Mr. Olympia and a successful movie star in America is unheard of. If Arnold really loves California the way he says he does, he can write his name farther in history by transmogrifying the prisons and juvenile facilities. But he can't be too arrogant or busy to meet with the people who know. Arnold would be very wise to call up the Honorable Nelson Mandela and seek the advice of that great, brilliant man on how to turn the prisons around. If Mr. Mandela will meet with Arnold - it would be a blessing, a miracle and a warming experience for Arnold. I am hopeful that Margita Thompson, Mr. Stutzman, Mr. Bustamente and you will make certain that Arnold and governors across the nation get this book. But if only one or two of them take action on what they read; we will see a great change.

In the monster factory, what the human model prisoners will emulate is a fanatically defiant and alienated individual who cannot fathom what forgiveness is, or mercy or tolerance, because he does not have any experience with such values. Such values are foreign to his emotions and he imagines them as "weaknesses" specifically because the unprincipled prisoner appears to escape punishment through such "weaknesses" on the part of society.

Yet, if you act like a man (a man such as yourself) you are doomed; you are hated and feared. You are "crazy" by the authorities standards - but they are prejudiced against prison behavior you feel.

Can you imagine how the prisoner feels - to be treated like a little boy and not a man? When he was a boy, he was treated as a man. He no doubt grew up in a fatherless home and when he got into trouble the juvenile authorities constantly said to him, "Quit crying! Quit acting like a kid". Now he is a man and prison guards treat him like a boy. Do you know what this does psychologically to a human being?

So the guard frowns at him and says, "Why are you not at work?" or "Put your shirttail in!" Do that and do this. He speaks to the convict as if the convict is a kid. This is an attitude that prisoners deal with for years and when their anger, resentment and hatred build up, they explode. When they explode, they hurt themselves by behaving like a contrite and unruly boy. So often, in order to avoid that deeper humiliation, the prisoner develops a method of turning the tables. He reviews the entire situation - and he becomes the man chastising the little boy and it costs him dearly in terms of going to the hole and extending his prison stay.

Many guys never adjust to daily prison life. Some cannot go a month in prison without incurring a rules violation. Does that mean he cannot "adjust" to society outside prison? The prison authorities say yes - but the prisoner remembers society and it is not like prison. They feel that if they ever did adjust to prison, they could by that fact alone, never adjust to society. They'd be back in the "monster factory" within months. Prison they feel is only mutiny and revolt.

The prisoner is told to accept that he did it all to himself. Even the Rubin "Hurricane" Carters, Rolando Cruzes, Anthony Porters and David Quindts, etc. Guys who are innocent, wrongly convicted and trapped in prison are still expected to believe that their suffering, their pain, their hurt and sorrow is their own fault. In prison, every minute for years you are forced to believe that your suffering is a result of your "offensive behavior" and that it is self-inflicted. Even if you're innocent, I repeat. If a guard like Captain Martel, C.O. Mansky or C.O. M. Todd beats you down, your indoctrination is supposed to force you to believe you did it to yourself. If a prisoner is thrown into solitary confinement for talking back to an officer, he should believe he brought this upon himself! This belief is forced by indoctrination! And (on a personal note) I might have become indoctrinated were it not for the ignorant and evil quality of people who are employed in the prisons!!

The inmate is taught (programmed) that what is expected of him is to never ever resist and never ever question orders. A prisoner is programmed to plead with the guards and to accept guilt for even things, which he did not do. It is not unheard of for a prisoner to be written up for making threats against and arguing with guards they've never even seen or met. Prisoners are routinely thrown in the hole for things the guards know they never did and there is nothing the prisoner can do about it! In California, if you write to members of the senate, you often get no reply. If you get a reply, you can see from the contents of the missive that the senator never read your letter.

The prison regime has so much power over the inmate's life (not enough power to disband the gangs??) that they can commit any crime or atrocity against the inmate and the prisoner's status or "record" will acquit the authorities.

In the few cases where the inmate has the intelligence to sue; judges dismiss the cases because of (diplomatic??) prisoncratic immunity . . . The judge is shown the violent past of the prisoner and the judge is prejudiced against the prisoner. The prisoner is fodder for the system. No one seems to care . . .

Former Chief Deputy Warden Terry L. Rosario once told me, "You are the most dangerous inmate in this prison!" When I asked why would he think that. He replied, "The most dangerous prisoners and I do mean that in a physical sense also, are readers and writers."

Books! Books! Books! They have always been my friends thanks to Brenda Smith, Dollie and James Manning and Uncle Melvin

Jackson and tomes are dangerous where injustice is epidemic and systemic. Books are limited in every prison in California. Book reading is frowned upon. "Stop reading because you might grow. And if you grow you'll know that we are transferring you into a monster, a madman, an animal," is what prison authorities want to say!

No federal prison has a prison library! Federal authorities claim inmates misuse their knowledge if they are allowed to educate themselves. They claim inmates misuse the Britannica Encyclopedias to learn to make guns, bombs, acids and explosives. They claim that Akbar and Marx lies to them about their conditions and makes them craven, immoral and desperate. Ipso facto, perhaps it explains why the federal prisons began "education programs" in their prison, i.e., so they learn only what they want them to learn. This is really called training and programming - not educating. (See "Natural Psychology & Human Transformation" by Na'im Akbar).

Ambassador Andy Young asked me why books are such a touchy subject to prison authorities. Andy as well as you (outside prison) had/have a problem comprehending this subject because you and he are free. But men who are caged, oppressed men know the "value of books", (if they are not caught up shooting dope and drinking wine) because if they ever become enamored of, curious about or interested in, a single idea - and pursue it - they are on the highway to transformation!

In the seventies and eighties, they (prison authorities) only beat you down physically. Now they go for your "mind" in prison today. The stakes are much, much higher. Prisons today are like a gladiator prison ("school") in Ancient Rome during the suppression and oppression of Christians and slaves. Prisoners are naturally pitted against each other through prison regime manipulation!

The American public needs to know that many (and I do mean tens of thousands) prisoners are enduring torture, beatings, forced injections of dangerous drugs, starvation and often solitary confinement in dark, damp, dank and cold cells. The cells they put guys in are often awash in urine and feces and they are treated worse than wild animals. Our penal institutions, as they are today, force prisoners to become either a broken, cringing animal, bowing before all authority and power, or a rebel, holding on to human dignity through defiance and animalistic belligerence.

Prisons are monster factories and houses of destruction, madness and rage. They are crime schools. They are absolutely not the "country clubs" that our politicians tell us they are. If you were to all of a sudden be thrown into prison tomorrow where you did not know a single person; would this be your story?:

"I was in bed when six inmates came to my bunk, pulled off the blankets and told me to pull my pants down. I said, 'No' and they punched me in the face. They said they'd kill me if I didn't get on the floor and lay on my stomach. I got on the floor and they ripped off my pants and underwear. Two guys spread my legs apart while two more held my hands in front of me. While I was being screwed from behind another guy would make me suck his penis. This went on until all the inmates had raped me and one of them said it was 1:30 a.m. so let's go to bed. They threw me on my bed, covered me with a blanket and one guy said, 'Good boy, we'll see you again tomorrow night.'" Would that be your story? . . .

As free people go about their daily lives, young White guys are being raped inside juvenile facilities, jails and prisons by the thousands on a daily basis. After perusing this tome, it may not be so difficult to comprehend a prisoner's hatred and meanness. The depth of the convict's daily insane brutality drives him and forces him to become brutal and wicked.

There have been times that I have felt that convicts nationwide should "tear the fucking walls down" and disallow anyone to dehumanize us in the ways that they do. At times, I sense a terrible tearing wound in my heart when I think about what they do to us. I have felt helplessly encaged by powers I can't vanquish or control. I have become ensnared in a web of memories about what Mary Hanlon Stone, Ricardo Calvaris, Russell Camosky, Judge Robert Altman and Dave Winkler did to me. I think of how they willfully, deliberately and consciously lied on me and stole my freedom. I get bewildered, shocked, weak and fatigued at times. On the streets, you can cry freely, but in prison, tears lead to challenges and deep, embittered stares. Prison is a dead land, filled with threats, where there is no appeal from the death sentences meted out for infractions of the convict code. If you will imagine being chased and hunted through the jungles of Nam everyday for twenty-five years, then you'll know what prison is like. Everything about the "monster factory" life distorts reality, beginning with the elemental assumption that incarceration can alter criminal behavior, when the truth is that it entrenches it more firmly. Confinement perverts and destroys and assassinates every skill a human needs to live productively in free society.

In the free world, convicts have families and friends, etc. But in prison, in this monster factory, we have nothing but the speed of our fists and the sharpness of a shank! We have only this one weapon of rebelling against the oppression and suppression of our brain-dead keepers who represent an American whose judicial standards let rich guilty men go free and sends poor innocent men to prison.

Many men in prison cannot really look at themselves in the mirror for fear of what they will see. "How did I become this monster?" In an authentic sense he no longer knows who he is. We are forced to relinquish every vestige of dignity, strip searched with anal inspections on a whim, cussed, beaten, deprived of any privacy, forced to cell with another man and pressed into madness. It takes a toll on us. A man's sensibilities are progressively eroded by prison programming. Prison is dank. Prison is lonely! Prison is scary. Prison is cold. Prison is a failure. What shocks me is not that some have been able to survive prison. Rather, I am shocked that the prisons are still standing and that the cruelty of this life is still going on. In New Folsom, five thousand men endure cruelty, discrimination, arbitrary ad-seg placement, deprivation and devastation daily and the system is growing stronger. Most of my fellow Americans are completely ignorant of the fact that prisons are producing killers. No one has bothered to tell them. We are more interested in whether or not Bill Clinton got fellatio from Monica Lewinsky than whether or not the man we are killing on death row might be innocent.

I'm not advocating the liberation of violent murderers, rapists or sociopaths. They should remain in prison. But the vast majority of prisoners are imprisoned for petty crimes that have more to do with bad judgment and poverty than serious criminal intent or character defect. They are not yet confirmed in criminality and monsterism, but the system makes them criminals. America needs to know we have a system of so-called justice, which is unjust, unfair, biased, racists and classicists. That system of injustice is at minimum facilitating, enhancing and contributing to the murder, rapes, molestations and perversions that we see on the streets everyday. Show me a man who was eighteen and sentenced to prison for some minor offense . . . sentenced to serve five years with eighty percent . . . By the time he gets out, I "assure you" that he will be a monster! He will not be able to function in society again. Percentage wise, I will assure you that between eighty-five and ninety percent of teenage boys who spend more than two years in prison will become violent predators. They enter the gates of the big house (prison) with peach fuzz on their face, innocence in their hearts and fear in their minds. By the time the prison regime (with its belittling, dehumanizing and brutal mistreatment) gets finished with them and by the time the older cons finish raping, assaulting, conditioning and schooling him - you have a "monster"!

The making of a "monster" is not that difficult! Prison authorities and convicts have it down to a science. They've mastered it! If you are caught reading books, they better be smut (pornography) books! If you're caught watching TV, it had better be cartoons or sports! You can be shamed, abandoned, disowned or attacked by fellow convicts for reading non-fiction. You can be set up written up or thrown in ad-seg by the regime for reading.

In prisons in the state of Georgia, inmates are not allowed TVs in their cells, but there is one in the dayroom. Warden Garrison Parker stated (via telephonic interview) that sports overrule anything else on TV in Georgia prisons! Why?

Most states disallow conjugal visiting and even California has just about eliminated all conjugal visitation. All totally nude female photos were banned in 2003 in California prisons; however, inmates in California prisons are still allowed to receive photos (totally nude) of anyone's posterior anatomy! Understand me clearly: Photos of a woman's frontal private parts (including breast and vagina) are now disallowed in California! Yet, photos of a man or woman's naked buttocks are (indeed) allowed!

Visitation? You may hug and kiss your wife just before the end of your visit. Then you return to your cell and find your celly walking around in his boxers. It would appear that C.D.C. is also attempting to create homosexual, raging and raping monsters!

It is now 11:31 a.m. in the monster factory (Mule Creek State Prison in Ione, CA). I am sitting in the zoo at an iron table in the middle of the dayroom. I see approximately eighty men mingling around living in this (our so-called society) place. To my right there is an old White guy with silver hair and glasses. He is sitting at a table about six feet away from me. His table is filled with lunchmeat, cigarettes and tootsie rolls. He sells them as if he were a grocer. The problem is that all of his items he sells came from the garbage. He literally rummages through the trashcans and pulls out discarded lunchmeats, cookies and bread and he sells them. He picks up cigarette butts from the floor and the ground outside and re-rolls them and puts them on the market. I had been feeling sorry for him and thinking he was a frail, weak old man who can barely move around until one morning outside the dining hall, I saw him (literally) leap over a four-foot guardrail. I thought perhaps he saw some cash money or a watch or had dropped something and felt it was important to immediately retrieve it. To my utter amazement, he was jumping over the rail to get a cigarette butt. I didn't know he could jump so high or move so fast.

On initial observation, I thought it strange to see a man pulling food out of the trashcans that people spit in. But a closer scrutiny, it's even stranger that people actually buy this stuff from him.

I see about twenty people gambling. About fifteen men are intoxicated; perhaps twenty are high on heroin, cocaine or weed. To my left hang two telephones on the wall. Both telephones are empty. Nobody is calling home today. Six guys are watching a karate flick on TV and a few guys are wrestling and horse playing. Two Muslims are discussing their celly problems and appear to be a bit perturbed. I see men with hearts that have been broken, dreams that have been busted, and hopes that have been crushed into an awful despair. I see pain, misery and woe.

I see ignorance, a sense of pain, tension and a denseness, which leads ultimately to institutionalization and de-socialization. I see a horrible tragic, evil gruesome thing that is happening, which is a prisonization and a dehumanization transpiring right before my very eyes.

It's now 1:00 p.m. . . . I stopped writing yesterday initially because there was an incident on the yard. Apparently an inmate refused to obey a direct order rapidly enough, so eight officers pepper-sprayed him, beat him down and then booked him for resisting. As a result, we were locked down and our program (that word again) was suspended. Never mind the fact that many guys had parents, children, friends and lawyers expecting telephone calls from us, etc. None of this is/was important to the prison regime. The only thing which mattered to them was the fact that an inmate had supposedly resisted them! And boys never say "no" to their daddies! So all programs were cancelled. I returned to my cell and opened up "Long Walk to Freedom" by President Mandela. I am always amazed by the fact that regardless of how many times one peruses a great tome, one can always come back to it and gain something new. Quite frankly, "Long Walk to Freedom" is simply one of the most powerful, impactful and inspiring books I have ever read. I needed it yesterday because writing takes a lot out of you. I love to write. In prison, writing has probably served to keep me sane. Writing has been my own private therapist. But at times, I must renew my spirit and rejuice my own mind if I am to oil the wheels of my own mental apparatus. At times writing can become disenchanting. (Yet, it's a frustration, which I enjoy).

As a public speaker, I am a sensitive speaker. Preparation, voice pitch, diction, articulation and even eloquence are weapons or tools, which I've learned to successfully employ when giving a speech. Yet, as an author, I sometimes feel that you don't feel what I'm saying (writing). I feel like I did when I was in Paris with Sabine, Lillian and Peter. I had to give a motivational speech to about five or six hundred Frenchmen and Peter was the only one in our group who spoke fluent French. So Peter had one microphone and I had the other and he interpreted my speech in French as I gave it in English. Now we got a lot of smiles, applause and even a standing ovation when I was finished, but I felt cheated and I felt as if I cheated them. There are some words, which don't translate easily, but Peter is smart enough to improvise and exchange, but it still felt like I was not really connecting the way I like to connect with an audience. I like to take the pulse of the people. I know by their faces and their eyes whether or not I'm communicating my message effectively. I know when/how to educate, elevate, encourage, entertain and inform. All of these things (when speaking live) require a sense of timing and a sense of reading people.

Writing is wonderful and a great tool to effect in change. Yet, I wish I could see you right now. I wish I knew how you felt about justice, injustice, prison, freedom, equality and equal protection. I wish I could speak to you as well as listen. That is my forte. I'm always afraid I'm not going to reach the right person or I'm afraid my writing style (my false starts and subject changes) will offend you. That is my fear, but I press on knowing that this is still a major instrument for change that I can use and I do so as best I can. I hope you will reach down inside of you and do all that you can do to just make the world better. Yes, I am very cognizant of the fact that this is mid 2004 and everybody is busy doing their things. We have our own agendas and we're too busy to concern ourselves with others. But America got a warning with the World Trade Center - the Twin Towers! I am not suggesting that God did it! God did not fly those planes into the Twin Towers! Not the God that I worship. Jehovah God, through his son Jesus Christ does not work like that. But God allowed it. America was brought to her knees! And ninety days later, we were back to normal! What a shame and a pity. What must God allow next in order to gather America back together? If the gut-wrenching sight of burning bodies and buildings, if more than three thousand people burning and jumping to their deaths is not enough to bring people back together - what is? For the life of me, I cannot understand how we can forget about nearly three million people trapped in prisons all across America as if they don't matter. And many of the folks who forget are people who go to church every Sunday of every month. Some way, some how, Matthew - Chapter 25 is dead, void and mute to them. "I was in prison and you

95

visited me not," stated Jesus Christ. You don't need a strong concordance, biblical illustrator, biblical encyclopedia or Josh McDowell to understand those words. "In as much as you have done it unto the least of these my brethren, you've done it also unto me," Jesus said. But I don't see many church folks bombarding the prisons. I don't see many pastors in the prisons. When was the last time any pastor stood in a protest and demanded that the least of these be treated with respect? I'm still looking for Robert Schuller, Benny Hinn, Billy Graham and Jerry Falwell to tell their members to think success, make positive confessions as they go into the prisons to visit, restore and bring back to life the Josephs, Pauls and Silases who are trapped in the prisons. I love God, I respect church and I love preachers, but I must be clear; by and large as it pertains to the least of these our brothers, pastors, evangelists and churches are missing in action.

Peter (Andrist) told me, "When we get you out of prison, your church shall have three million members minimum. All the prisoners shall join your church and then their families will join also. We will win. We will get Rubin 'Hurricane', Denzel Washington, Mike Farrell, Rolando Cruz, Andrew Goodwin, Steve Soboroff, John Gardner, Dwayne Hall, Paul and Jan Crouch, Deion Sanders, Michael Irving, Jr., Kevin Cooper, etc. to all become honorary members of 'the least of these Baptist Church'. We must believe God did not allow this horrific, tragic, evil wrongful conviction to happen to you for nothing. There shall come from this suffering a new move, a stronger, kinder and even more powerful Sherman Manning. I believe that with all of my heart." God bless Peter Andrist . . .

I wanna pause or digress a moment and talk (write) directly to guys in juvenile facilities, jails and prisons across our country. To you politicians, pundits, media people, lawyers, judges and other civilian readers, I'll get back to you shortly.

To the incarcerated bodies all across this nation, I wanna tell you don't allow them to incarcerate your spirit. Unlock your mind. I know your spirit has been broken. Your dreams and visions busted. You've had to see your grapes of hope, crushed into the raisins of despair, but it is time for you to be a man. If you did the crime, do the time. Do not allow the time to do you. I don't need to give you a twelve-step program on how to survive or how to get out of prison. You don't need me to count for you; hell you invented mathematics. If you have really forgotten how to be a man, write to Dr. Na'im Akbar out in Tallahassee, Florida and tell him to send you, "From Maleness to Manhood". Read "Breaking the Psychological Chains of Slavery" and "Mis-education to Education" also by Dr. Akbar. Get your ass in gear and quit bull crapping around. Life is tough and you're in a tough place. You can't get out until you start seeing out. You've got to have a dream, a vision, a goal and a hope. Stop wasting your time. You have caroused around, gotten high and drunk. You've tried everything you know how to try to escape the misery and tragedy and pain of your life. You feel like a miserable, horrible, lonely failure. That gal left you! Family and friends stop writing to you. Homeboys testified and some testilied against you. You are down, down, down! Down so low that you gotta look up just to see your shoe heel! But let me remind you that when they are going to build a building real high, they dig the ditch (foundation) real low and you can go (at least) as "high up" as you went low down. We fall down, but we can "get back up" again! Donnie McClurkin can tell you that a saint ain't nothing but a sinner who fell down, but they got back up. At this particular junction in your life it is feasible for me to inform you that you are ripe for a miracle. For some of you who are serving life sentences; who are trapped in mental darkness and simultaneously cutting your own lights off - "you need a miracle". Quite frankly, I am cognizant of the fact that there are Muslims, Buddhists, Atheists, Agnostics, Jewish and other brothers "reading" this tome right now. In prison it has become cool to claim not to believe in "God", but I gotta tell you that as messed up as you are right now, "you need to take your case to Jesus". I'm gonna say it again - "you need to take your case to Jesus"! The only way you are ever going to get out of prison, out of the gang, out of your misery, woe, addition, etc. is to "take your case to Jesus".

He can deliver you! He will change your walk and talk. He will pick you up when you're down and give you liberty while you're trapped and bound. He'll change you and rearrange you. "Take your case to Jesus".

Get off that dope. Just put it down. There are creative forces which are innate with mankind that can assist you in your endeavors. But you must call on them. Call on the force of hope, will power, strength of character and imagination. Stop the violence. End the self-destruction and choose to go another way. Your oppressor wants you to remain oppressed, and as long as you are doped up, coked up, shuffling, grinning and jiving you are the typical prisoner. You are the prison guard's job security. But when you start dreaming and striving and yearning, when you start reading, writing and learning, when you apply mental force and spiritual creativity, you begin to drop the seals from your very eyes. Your ability to think, to create, to build, to organize and strategize becomes (per se) an act of defiance. We must learn how true power operates. Blaming all our problems on White people, the wrong people or the right people is a waste of time. Don't nobody want to hear you (or my) sob story. Get over it. Rise above it. All of us have been through the mother fire of suffering. We have all had people to desert, abandon and betray us on the highest levels of our lives. But get over it. Move past it. You can cry about it later, but a man in a burning house can't waste time. You've got to get out of dodge. I bring experience to the table! I bring a now-ness to the table. Because I am right here with you.

I am in Mule Creek State Prison for a crime I did not commit. Thus far, I have not convinced Johnnie Cochran, Gerry Spence, Gerald Uelmen, Donald Marks or Tom Messereau to get me out either. I ain't heard nothing from Al Sharpton or Jesse Jackson. I've gotten letters from "Mr. Mandela" and still heard nothing from civil and human rights legends right here in America. If Rev. Hosea Williams were alive right now he'd be fighting for me. I don't have the help I need. I have not convinced Doug Banks, Tavis Smiley, Tom Joyner, Tony Brown, Oprah or Montel that I need them! I don't know what to do either. But this one thing I do know is "I won't quit"! Quitting is not an option. Failure is not a possibility. I'll journey on! One day, someway, somehow a Maya Angelou, Toni Morrison, a John Johnson, Bill Gates, Donald Trump, Russell Simmons or somebody is gonna "get me out of here"!

In the meantime, I am "practicing my gifts". The Holy Bible says that your "gift" will make room for you! Joseph was in prison for attempted rape. He was innocent, but his "gift" brought him out. I'm in the prison, reading books, a prolific author in the prison, advising businesses in the prison, meditating and educating in the prison. I know they can lock me in prison, but they can't lock God out of the prison! Our God is an awesome God! He goes in jails, juvenile facilities, prison camps, in the hood, the suites as well as the streets. God - He will penetrate a slave tent, He will tear up heaven to get His child out. God is an awesome God. He is right there where you are. He (too) has weapons of mass destruction. God unleashed His weapons of mass destruction against Pharaoh in Egypt. God went out and talked frog talk, fly talk and even gnats as he unleashed his wrath on Pharaoh. When Moses found himself trapped at the Red Sea. God stepped in. Can't you hear God telling Moses, "Get up off your knees. Wipe those tears out of your eyes. Don't you know that I am! I am that I am! I am a way out of no way. I am a bridge over troubled waters. I am the God of Abraham, Isaac and Jacob. I got your back. Don't you know who I am. Your answer is in your hand. Take that rod in your hand - stretch it out and speak to the people. Tell them to stand still and see my salvation." God began to speak in a liquid language. He spoke a language the waters understood. God grabbed the tail of the east wind and fanned the bottom of the Red Sea dry. The waters congealed like Jell-O on the right and left hand side and Moses and Israel walked across on dry-shod. When Pharaoh and his army tried to cross, the waters reverted and Pharaoh and his army drowned in the Red Sea. I hear the people singing, "Oh, Mary don't you weep. Tell your little sista Martha not to moan. Pharaoh and his army got drowned in the sea one day."

I need to tell you in the prison. I want to tell you. I've got to tell you not to quit. Don't give up! You may rest a minute, but don't quit. You may have to cry, but don't give up. You might have to fast and meditate and do breathing exercises, "but don't quit". You may have to block the windows in your cell with paper or cardboard, cut all the lights out and blast your music to camouflage your crying and hide your tears, but "don't give up". I want you to know that all things work together for good for them that love and obey God. All things don't look good. All things don't feel good or seem good, but they are working together. And God is working it out! I said God is working it out! Don't hang yourself, don't slit your wrist, and don't overdose on drugs. Don't drink yourself to death. Don't get violent. Don't physically attack the prison regime. Don't stick anybody, but stick it out. Tough times never last, but tough people do. Take a licking and keep on ticking. Hold on a little while longer. You're in too deep to quit now. God is not finished with you. The darkest hour of the night is just before dawn. "Morning will come". My brother and sister, behind every dark cloud there is a silver lining. Weeping may endure for a night, but joy cometh in the morning. You're too close to your destiny to be hindered by your history. A miracle is right around the corner. Destiny is inside of you. Don't give up! Don't you quit. When things go wrong as they sometimes will, when the road you're traveling seems all up hill, rest just a bit, but don't you quit because quitters never win and winners never quit. I want some brothers in the jails, juvenile facilities and in the prisons to get ready to take a five-minute break. I want you to put the book down a minute and walk around in the dayroom and tell another brother not to quit. Tell him! He needs to hear it from you. He is just as lonely as you are. He has thought about suicide too. He's got pain, issues, hurts and fears. He's tired too. Just look him in the eyes and tell him "it's me too". Tell him not to quit. Don't let him give up. Look at him and tell him, "You can lean on me." Tell that brother, "I got your back." Don't let him quit. Don't let him give up. He needs you. I'm serious. I want you (even if you're not in prison - just call somebody over the telephone or e-mail somebody right now and tell them) to go tell somebody don't quit! Don't give up!!!

I want a prison guard to tell another prison guard not to quit. You wardens who are reading this, call another warden and tell them not to quit. There are some great human beings working in corrections. Not all of them are evil, mean and vicious. I know many professional, upstanding, caring and concerned prison guards. And God Bless them! Some of them such as Patricia Kennedy (New Folsom), Lt. Lincoln, Buffy, Lt. Jimmy Garon, Purdie, etc. are fair, by the book and decent. Were it not for the Pat Kennedys, Lincolns and Clarence Joneses (GA Dept. of Corrections) the prisons would literally bust open at the seams. They would explode and we would see the walls come down. The prisons would explode, burn and fall, if there were not some tremendously dedicated law abiding citizens risking their lives coming into these walls of torture and keeping the peace everyday. I salute, applaud, compliment and commend Pat Kennedy, Clarence Jones, Lt. Percy Massey, Sergeant Burnette, Lt. Gaton, C.O. Alexander, O'Neal Claiborney, Sgt. D. Farmon and thousands of others (the good guys) who uphold and enforce the rule of law in an evenhanded, fair and professional manner in prisons everyday. We need more of them . . .

As for the bad guys - we need a catharsis. Those vicious staff members who feed off of the evil of the kept (those inmates who are evil, destructive and violent; and there are many) need to be retired and fired! Mr. Howard Dean dropped out of the race for president (the media ran him out by playing and replaying his hoorah over and over. The media can make or break you). The other day, Bush said he wants his "grassroots" movement to continue. He said he wants to change the country with his six hundred and forty thousand supporters. Well I know a way those six hundred and forty thousand can change the country. The can join with "The Justice Lobby", CA Prison Focus, Critical Resistance and raise money to expose how politicians profit from crime! I want Howard Dean and his movement-minded young army to join with us and fight wrongful convictions, fight poverty and illiteracy, put America back to work and expose every politician who's taking money from these shyster prison guards' unions. Let's tell America that Mr. George W. Bush accepted six hundred thousand dollars from "Enron"!

The scandal ridden, fraud stricken, infamous Enron Corporation gave our president over half a million bucks. Let's tell America the truth about crime and punishment. Dr. Dean we need you and we need your people. Let us start a revolution over the Internet,

100

wage a war, organize, galvanize and strategize. We can do it. Dean may not be the king, but he can be a kingmaker. If we transform the "monster factory", the "halls of torture" and get out of the business of "creating monsters" - we will affect and effect and protect the public's safety.

We need to correct corrections. As Gloria Romero stated that we'll either change the prisons or let's just declare it the Department of Warehousing. I have watched correctional officers, doctor paperwork, falsify reports, etc. in order to prevent a parole or a probation or to justify a murder.

They make (knowingly) false accusations and threaten anyone who seeks to expose them. Those type actions constitute a despicable and flagrant abuse of power in the severest fashion. Ask former Sgt. Scarcella and R. N. Saunders about Jack McLamb, Bo Gritz and Sponge!

I've seen many brutalized and abused by this process of systemic vindictiveness. Many of the things the prison regime does to us are a series of retaliatory measures and kneejerk snaps to judgment. Convicts are suffering cruel and unusual punishment needlessly because of harassment by prison officials. I have become a target of reprisal and retaliation because of my outspoken advocacy of integration, civil rights and rehabilitation. It is clear what is transpiring. All these punitive acts (i.e. by Captain M. Martel, C.D.W. Stratton, Billy and Janice Mayfield) are retaliatory because they occurred after I published my books and demanded justice. There is a violent, hostile racial climate as well as severe discrimination against minority staff and inmates rampant within C.D.C. and prisons nationwide. Just as we face down foreign weapons of mass destruction, so too must we face down homegrown domestic prison policies of mass destruction. Many of the exclusionary, corrupted C.D.C. policies are anti-reform, anti-peace and they are divisive. They seek to drive a wedge between us rather than bringing us together.

And America (calling Dr. Dean, Jesse, Al, the church, the grassroots, foot soldiers) must wake up. We are throwing hundreds of billions of dollars into new jails to lock our youth up instead of investing money in new schools, libraries and colleges to lift our youth up. We must wake up.

Prison regimes have a vested interest in inmate race and gang warfare in order to keep inmates fighting and increase the justification for the need to keep them locked up.

California prison staff racism (and in states nationwide) is a disaster of titanic proportions. C.D.C. has made a veritable orgy of

101

false and misleading statements to the media in order to "cover up" their code of silence, the brotherhood and their corrupting. They are "master liars"! Some of them at the top are cunningly smart, extremely dishonest, vindictive, unfailingly violent and wicked people. Their self-defense case presented to the senate in January was like cotton candy. When you'd bite into it, there was nothing there. It's a sham, a shame and a cover-up . . .

I've personally suffered at the vicious hands of these people. But no man has ever risen without being purified through the fire of suffering. A mother suffers so that her child may live. The condition of wheat growing is that the seed grain should perish. Life comes out of death. I am alive today . . .

This tome aims to comfort the afflicted and afflict the comfortable. Writing is one of the few tools remaining through which I can convey realities and chip away at the monstrous image the public has about all prisoners. It's not all of us, but they (the prison regime) would have us all become what they tell you we are. I have remade myself while coming to terms with the challenges of my wrongful conviction. So I challenge prisoners to transcend their tragic mistakes, their personal vices and the pain of their life situation in search of something better in life.

The "monster factory", the "hall of torture", the "prison" is a place where everything is an assault upon your self-worth, self-esteem and your dignity. As I've mentioned, the daily routines are designed (skillfully and willfully) to kill any desire to make decisions. The mind becomes paralyzed by the process. You become like an old pair of scissors; you become rusty and slow. You have to find (and unfortunately most don't have that kind of initiative) a way out of this madness! You must out think your keepers. Supreme Court Justice Thurgood Marshall said, "When the prison gates slam behind an inmate, he does not lose his human quality; his mind does not become closed to ideas; his intellect does not cease to feed on a free and open interchange of opinions whether an O. Henry writing his short stories in a jail cell or a frightened young inmate writing his family, a prisoner needs a medium for self-expression." Yet most prison regimes in New York, California, Texas, Alabama, etc., fight strategic wars against inmate self-expression. They impose vicious sanctions on he who would choose to express himself. Limiting prisoners' freedom of speech is suicidal. In the confines of our fetid prisons, entire generations of boys are being schooled in life-shaping lessons antithetical to democracy and liberty. Someday these prisoners will be free again. I challenge every judge, D.A., politician and prison guard to remember that the gates of prisons and jails swing both ways. Most guys here today are going back to society to sit beside you on the buses and trains and planes. They shall sit next to your children and families at the theaters, with no bars or fences between you. If you don't build within them a wall of moral integrity, self-respect and a respect for others, you have not protected society - which is you! Whether prisoners deserve it or not, you owe it to yourselves as citizens of an enlightened and humane society to proceed more intelligently in your treatment of the inmate. I should end the book right there! You can take that and run with it. If you really think about it, that's all you need to know!

Creating monsters? A report in early 1997 by the Human Rights Watch found that sexual abuse is endemic to prisons across our country. Respected researcher and physician, Dr. James Gilligan reported in his book "Violence" that approximately eighteen rapes per minute occur in prison. In California, it's estimated that twenty-five rapes per minute occur. That's one hundred and sixty-eight thousand sexual assaults in prison every week or about nine million per year!

Sadly, sexual assault are just one of the many dangers waiting to twist the minds of the folks sentenced to serve time in our prisons. Extortion, race wars behind bars, rival gang conflicts, guard abuse, random, rampant violence, and the demand for absolute loyalty to fellow prisoners - loyalty which very often requires committing rapes, assaults and (yes) murders behind walls, etc. That's what the real deal prison is about.

In an interview, which appeared in December 1998 in "Vanity Fair", Chris Stone, head of New York's Vera Institute of Justice, described prisons and jails as "factories for crime" where the strong rule the weak. He noted that even though most inmates entering prison will spend only two years behind bars, it is those two years which will "shape their future actions" forever. This was obviously the case with Tom William (Bill) King.

February 25, 1999, Judge Joe Bob Golden sentenced Bill King to death for the racially motivated murder of forty-nine-year-old James (Jimmy) Byrd, Jr., a Black man who lived in King's hometown of Jasper, Texas. Bill King and two other men chained Jimmy to the bumper of their pickup truck. They dragged him down an asphalt road until his arm, shoulder and head were severed from his body. Why? Because Byrd was Black is the easy answer, but the prison/monster factory and the effects of the prison structure's creation of his monsterism is the more accurate answer.

Bill's dad, Ronald, said that his son was not a murdering racist "before" he went to prison. In fact, Ronald said his son was an average kid with Black childhood friends until he had a minor run-in with Texas Law Enforcement, which sent him to the "monster factory" for two years. Ronald said his son went into prison as a normal White kid who had made a mistake and came out of prison a dangerous, hyper and angry man who hated Blacks, Mexicans and Jews. Attorney C. Haden "Sonny" Cribbs, Jr. (King's lawyer) told jurors, "What happened in prison? I don't know. What I do know is he was not a racist or a killer when he went into prison, but he was when he came out of prison."

While in prison, King tattooed racist hatred type symbols up and down both arms. He had joined a White supremacist prison gang.

Elaborating about King's initial prison experience, Brian Levin, former professor of Criminal Justice and Director of the Center on Hate and Extremism at Richard Stockton College, told NBC Nightly news in 1999 that Bill's racist murder of James Byrd was exactly the kind of thing that should be expected when you dump a young kid in prison where racist gangs are a way of life. Levin continued by stating, "Prison is a crash course in hate." Much like the tattoos on King's arms are a permanent fixture, so too was the transformation that had transpired in his mind in just two years in prison. A "monster" had been "created" and was unleashed. Byrd was as much killed by the Texas Department of Corrections as he was by Bill King. Gerry Spence, Willie Gary or Isaac Byrd should have sued T.D.C. for being an accessory to murder. In an effort to survive the day-to-day horrors of prison life in his earlier life, this small five-foot-seven inch man fell prey to the affects of the madness of the monster factory.

Bill King's experience is not an aberration. As I've pointed out in efforts to remain safe in prison, inmates have little choice but to seek protection of prison gangs like the Mexican Mafia, Aryan Brotherhood, Sacramaniacs or Nazi Lowriders. Sometimes joining violent anti-Semitic, anti-Black, etc. organizations are the only alternative for Whites in prison who don't want to become rape victims.

The gang, for the inmate, becomes his family, friend, protection, support and teacher. You are thrown into prison tomorrow for a non-violent, drug-related offense and forced to choose between being a victim of rape, beatings, murder or extortion or becoming a rapist, batterer, murderer or extortionist; what will you choose? More often than not, the instinct to survive makes becoming the "victor" the choice rather than becoming the victim.

Today's prisons are a blueprint for rage. Not everyone who gets out will become a Bill King, but many will exhibit behaviors resulting from the scars of fear, anger and prison devastation - such as alcohol and drug abuse, child abuse, wife beating and an escalation in their willingness to utilize violence as a first resort.

"The internal prison culture is a far more powerful influence than any attempts at rehabilitation," wrote Thomas Mathiesen, Professor of Sociology of Law at the University of Oslo in Norway. "In more popular terms, the prison in a cultural sense, first of all functions as a crime school." He went on to say, "I will respectfully disagree with the professor on the issue of rehabilitation simply because American prisons stopped really investing in rehabilitation two decades ago and the lack of adequate funding for education, counseling and therapy in prisons is the exact reason(s) the prison subculture has fortified and become explosive.

If one is not inclined to worry about the guys who will get out tomorrow, one should be concerned about the guys who will be getting out when your children and your children's children grow up - make no mistake about it America is violent right now. But in 2024 (when I'm 53) yours and my children will be living in a war zone if we don't turn this nation around now. The violence in the inner city will filter over into the outer city. The wars being fought in the hoods will be fought in the suburbs. We will experience the after-effects of the shock and awe warfare being taught in the prisons right now if we don't turn prisons around right now!

"We have embarked on a great social experiment no other society in human history has ever imprisoned so many of its own citizens for the purpose of crime control," stated Marc Mauer in Atlantic Monthly in 1999.

The view from the prison cell is a helluva view, I must admit. Some of the best people I've ever met in my lifetime (staff and inmate alike) I've met them here in the "monster factory". Some of the worse most despicable and evil folks I've ever encountered have also been here in the prisons. I've met bright, skillful and brilliant folks, right behind these barbed wire fences. I've met folks who did not (staff and inmate alike) know how to say their ABCs behind these walls. I could also literally write a twelve-volume tome on cellies I've had. Just my cellies alone have been an interesting experience . . . My absolute refusal to bow to the California prison regime's segregation (by race) rules has landed me (fortunately) on two of California's (there are only three) P.C. (protective custody) or sensitive housing yards. Ipso facto, I've had White, Mexican, Indian and other cellies. If a White guy celled with me on a mainline (general population - non P.C. any of the other thirty prisons in CA) he would be (without question) stabbed, raped (for certain) and perhaps even murdered by Whites on that yard and the guards would instigate it. And "yours truly" would be stabbed, assaulted and perhaps murdered by Black folks.

Celling with another race is a serious, major violation in the CA Prison system. Very interesting to me is the fact that in the state of Georgia, it is the absolute opposite! If you were arrested and sentenced to prison in Atlanta, Decatur, Fayetteville, Savannah, etc. today, you'd more than likely be housed in the cell with a person who didn't look like you tonight. Even at the most notoriously violent prison in Georgia, Reidsville State Prison (The Pelican Bay of Georgia) Whites and Blacks routinely cell together without incident. Celling by race is unheard of in the Georgia prison system, i.e., Alto, Phillips C.I., Valdosta C.I., etc., and one would think that perhaps the great state of California should/would study the Georgia State Prison system to see how they were able to integrate their prisons and then model what they did. A. That is wishful thinking. B. That would be unnecessary because C.D.C. already knows how to integrate its prison cells. They did it at New Folsom State Prison on Facility A! They did/do it at Mule Creek etc., everyday! So racially motivated incidents on Facility A in New Folsom are far and few between. I was there for "seven years". I just left there four months ago. A few Blacks did not like it, as well as a few Mexicans and Whites, but the fact remains I was never assaulted for having a White, Mexican or Indian cell partner and neither were they. As a matter of fact, we had more anger directed toward us by old school prison guards who would work overtime and come over from other yards (B&C Facility) than we did from fellow inmates. I used to laugh when a prison guard from another facility would work in our building and come over to do the 9:30 p.m. count and look in to see Brandon Martinez and me, Jeffrey G. Howell and me or Adam Delgadillo and me in our cell(s). You'd see the guard do a double take! He or she would look back in the cell with utter amazement on their faces. Some such as C.O. Mansky, C.O. M. Todd and C.O. Teurs would look in with utter hate in their eyes. I've had Teurs, Todd, Mansky and Stratton to literally catch my White celly alone and say, "Why are you selling your racial pride out by living with this nigger." An attempt to incite my cell partners against me. But I've had some unique, interesting and strange cellies. A celly is a very serious matter. C.D.C. takes it as if it were a joke. I've noticed at Mule Creek it is extremely difficult to get a cell change. Some of them almost come out and tell you to attack your celly and they will move you both to the hole. But if you go to staff and attempt to explain you were trying to prevent a fight or alleviate a problem prior to its developing into an explosive situation, they usually don't take action. "Deal with it. You have two options: A. Take off on each other and we'll put you both in ad-seg. B. Work it out." I've been told. It is as if they want you to fight so they can pepper spray you, rough you up and then get the right to throw you into ad-seg.

I once had a celly named Michael. Michael was a White guy with a receding hair line. He was twenty-six years old. When I met him he had a Bible in his hands and said he was a Christian. He moved in with me and told me he had kids, etc. He seemed to be okay. On his third day in the cell, I came in and he was acting a bit strange. I got a vibe that something was out of order. We engaged in small talk and idle chatter for a while. He had no TV or radio, etc. and so I shared my appliances with him. He wanted to watch Stargate or Star Trek or something that evening, so I put on my headphones and put in a sermon by Bishop Jakes. I listened to a message while I allowed this gentleman to utilize my TV . . . Out of the blue, he jumped up and yelled that he was a Satanist! I didn't immediately reply. After all this was a guy who presented himself to me as a Bible toting child of God. Now he was yelling that he was a Satanist. Yelling this, mind you, while he was watching my TV. I waited and about twenty minutes later, he once again imposed on my sermon listening by yelling to me that he had power. He said he'd sold out to the devil, etc. I removed my headphones and asked him what was his reason for telling me this at this time. He didn't respond. I then told him, "Michael, you can have any faith you want to have, but don't attempt to impose any of your beliefs on me." He said okay . . .The next day, I returned to the cell from work and this former Bible totter, now devil worshiper was strutting around in the cell with a see-through net bag on his body, no underwear and he had on makeshift lipstick. The net bag was actually a laundry bag, which he had manipulated and improvised to make it appear as a one-piece bathing suit. The lipstick was actually cherry kool-aid he'd somehow gotten on his lips. "I'm really a queen," he told me. I was a bit perturbed. "Man, you better get that crap off and put some clothes on. I'm telling you, you're pushing me. Get your clothes on and tomorrow you will find you another cell," I told Mr. Michael. He went over and put on his male clothing. He began to ramble on a bit about his life, etc. and I'd like to be able to report that I prayed for him and rebuked his demons, etc., but I didn't. I was livid and he began to oppose my demand that he must move. I didn't sleep that night. Every time he moved, my eyes were open! The next day I reminded him en-route to yard, "Find you a cell - you've got to get out of here."

When I returned to the cell, he had the cell door blocked and locked from the inside! He had all of my property packed up! He had my radio blasting heavy metal and the guy who was dressed as a queen the night before - now had on jeans, no shirt and a bandana tied around his head. I yelled to control to open the cell door. "He's got it jammed from the inside," The cop told me. He sent C.O. Brandon in to inspect. My concern was not only that I had a nut in the cell, but I was also worried that he was going to break my TV, radio, hot pot, etc. Wow! Another day in the prison. Brandon talked him into unlocking the cell and coming out. They told me, "Your property is not broken. He didn't break anything, but dude is a nut. You can't be in here when we bring him out because we don't want a fight." I left out. They pulled him out and threw him into ad-seg.

I had another celly who presented himself as an intelligent and decent person. "Hi, my name is Paul (pseudonym) and I am looking for a celly. You seem to be a very studious and intelligent guy. Every time I see you, you are reading or writing and that's all I do," he said. He was very articulate and noticeably bright. Two days later, I moved in with Paul. We hit it off pretty good. We both had C.D.C. corruption on our minds. He had been set up by prison guards. They had (literally) lied on him and put out a false rumor that Paul was a child molester. He was stabbed by the Skinheads. I read the incident reports. Paul almost died. He explained to me how they methodically assaulted and tried to kill him. Our rapport was quite good and then . . . I cut off my television . . . and then . . . came . . . a towel . . . He placed a towel over the face (screen) of my TV. "You're an intelligent guy," he stated. "So I'm sure you know they monitor us through the TV when you cut them off. That's when they can see and hear us . . ." To make a very long story concise, he was not acting, nor was he embellishing his beliefs. This guy genuinely thought we were being monitored via the TV. A few days later, he showed me a bump on his knee - "That's where I believe they put the chip in me." He was absolutely serious, congruent and he totally believes what he was saying. I began to investigate: I asked how, when and why he thought "they" would put an implant in him. I don't have the time to detail the specifics of his ramblings.

I will report to you that this intelligent, well spoken and articulate young White man (who is a computer genius) absolutely hates President George W. Bush! He despises Mr. Bush. It perhaps would not take much for this guy to attempt to kill Mr. Bush. "I wish I could blow him away! Burn him up from head to toe. He is an animal!" stated this guy. I explained to him that violence is never the answer and violence should be avoided at all costs. I also told him he'd better watch who he makes those presidential threatening-type statements to because - "You'll look around and be grabbed up by the secret service," I said. Let me be clear: A. I like this guy. B. I don't think he means any harm. C. If he got the correct medication, I think he could live a successful, productive and non-violent life. D. To be candid, I think if pushed and given some type of once in a lifetime opportunity - he would explode and certainly try to kill Mr. George W. Bush!

I think that nobody, under any circumstances should ever try to do harm to our President. I don't agree with a lot of the Bush policies and I would love to debate him any day of the week on domestic issues, the war in Iraq or criminal justice. But at the end of the debate, I'd shake his hand and call him "Mr. President".

Back to my ex-celly. Sadly, his mother also has issues. Perhaps it runs in the family. He put me on the telephone with his mother one night and she (a free, civilian professional) began to tell me about her implant!! I was mesmerized. I'm telling you it astonishes me to meet, greet and speak with people who are articulate, intelligent and educated, but simultaneously crazier than hell. This woman believes an implant was placed in her after a car accident. Furthermore, the government (she believes) set up the car accident. When she was hospitalized, she was sedated and "That's when they got me," she said. Weekly she sends her imprisoned son all kinds of data she downloads from the Internet on mind control, etc., etc. That was my celly. He goes home in less than a year.

I cannot name all of the cell partners I've had who were going home in less than a year and their plan was to sell drugs, get high, et revenge on somebody who testified against them, etc., etc. They are absolutely lost! They are absolutely confused! Their minds have been damaged and diseased. Ninety percent of their mental damage was incurred "in the prisons".

I cannot over emphasize, nor is there ever a need to embellish mental illnesses in the prisons. Most guys in prison who have spent more than, say then years are suffering from some sort (i.e., SHU syndrome, P.T.S.S., antisocial disability, personality disorder, paranoia, rage, etc.) of mental illness. Those illnesses are exacerbated by long-term solitary confinement, prison guard abuse, wrongful convictions, racism, etc. At this very moment, I've just completed a ten-minute (literally) rambling, meandering conversation with a gentleman whom I

109

was celled with for nine days. He is literally one of the brightest guys I've met in prison and his heart is in the right place. He's well versed and well read in politics, current affairs, Black history, etc. and he's crazy. He suffers from a bi-polar disorder that's the underlining mental illness he has, but there are a series of other mental problems from which he is suffering. If there is any up side to his story, it is the fact that deep within he does know he has a problem. "Tell me the truth, does my breath stink?" he asked me on day two in the cell. The same, exact question was asked of me on days three, four, five, six, seven and eight . . . After I moved out with him (from nut to nut) and in with the gentleman who basically (almost seriously and I am genuinely concerned) wants to kill President Bush, etc. I was telling him (bi-polar cell partner) about some of the unique (to say the least) beliefs that my new celly has/had and this guy said, "He's crazy, he really believes that?" Then I told him, "And dude absolutely believes they are monitoring us through our TVs." As these words rolled off of my lips, his body language transformed before my very eyes and his eyes lit up. "Wait a minute, you're not lying to me are you? Dude does have some problems, but he's right about the TV and I wouldn't doubt it if they do have a chip inside of him, because . . ." Need I say (write) more?

I submit to you my fellow Americans that it is extremely difficult to find three convicts in a straight row in prison who are not mentally challenged. The other exacerbating attribute is drugs such as heroin, bad weed, acid, pruno mixed with psychotropic drugs and cocaine. These prisons (I repeat) are full of drugs. The harsh treatment of vicious prison guards, along with the refusal of legislators to allocate funding for treatment, counseling and self-help programs in juvenile facilities and prisons are literally "creating monsters". I want John Ashcroft, U.S. Civil Rights leaders, Gloria Romero, Jackie Spier, Mark Leno, Larry King, pastors, leaders and grand juries to come into these prisons and they will see (eyewitness) the making of the monsters in the monster factory. They need to come unannounced. Don't warn prison authorities that you're coming. (See my book "American Dream/A Search For Justice") David Kelly, Mark Burnette and Tony Brown ought to do shows about it, pastors ought to preach about it and professors ought to sing about how we are (literally) "creating monsters", who will be released into the community to wreak havoc.

I wanna say here and now that if after reading this book you are not inclined to write a letter to the editor, call a talk show, e-mail your governors and senators and tell them (to also get this book) to clean up these prisons, then you deserve the crime that is in your neighborhoods and cities. I'm fed up with the complaints and Monday morning quarterbacking after the killings, after the rapes and after the molestations. We must file some preemptive strikes. When we find laws such as three-strikes, which are not working, we must modify, amend and change them. Even Joe Klaas (Polly Klan's grandfather) admits that three-strikes as it is, ain't working. We're filling up the juvenile facilities, jails and prisons and emptying the schools and colleges. The folks we are sending to prisons and jails are very often non-violent. Once prison guards get their hands on them, once hardcore criminals get their influence on them, once they get acclimated to the survival tactics and mechanisms of the prison subculture, they will become monsters! The only way to break this vicious cycle is to transform the way we "prevent crime", the way we "punish" criminals and the prisons we send them to be punished in.

Prisons ought to be detox units. They ought to be halls of transformation and rehabilitation. But as they exist, they are busting at the seams with violence, drugs, rapes, abuse and racism. Gangs are alive and well. Hell, hits are called from the inside out now. There are gang members in prison who can have you killed within eight hours! If you think I'm lying, call the Modesto Police Department and speak to Officer Delgado. When Delgado wants to know why youths are getting shot and killed for wearing the wrong colors in Modesto City, he calls and visits prison gang members! This should not be. Prison gangs must be terminated. I know you've read this fact (about the power of gang members in here to order killings out there) in your local newspaper because they don't know like I know.

Now that you know, you ought to call your governor and tell him you won't take it any more! You're not paying your tax dollars to contribute to prison viciousness and public violence. You pay way too much money in taxes in California, New York, Texas, Washington, Georgia, Alabama, Florida and Oregon to try to protect public safety. You pay too much money into failing justice systems, which are producing killers and sociopath. Follow the money. The schools are emptying and the prisons are filling. And all the guys in prisons today, will be in your city tomorrow and your money is being used to make them worse and not better, damn!!! How can this be? You must insist upon a change. You must demand a change. Your family members who have loved ones in prisons, parents with kids in juvenile facilities, etc., your pastors with members who are incarcerated . . . here and now you can make a "difference". Join with us and let us unite our efforts. Let us demand that rehabilitation and restoration be brought back into the prisons. Let us demand that prison guards at C.Y.A. and juveniles all over America "stop beating" our children!

Let us organize, strategize and galvanize our efforts jointly! Call 206/781-6524 and tell Paul Wright you're ready to fight for the safety of the public by demanding a change in crime and punishment. Call WLS Radio Station in Chicago and tell Carl Jeffers you'd like him to do a few shows every month on wrongful convictions and the prison system. Ask Mr. Jeffers to have New York Private Investigator, Jay Salpeter, on his show. Ask him to have Paul Wright, Rubin "Hurricane" Carter and Arianna Huffington on his show. Call Larry King, Tom Joyner, Montel and ask them to get Jay, Paul and David Quindt on their shows. (Don't just read my words . . . Take action . . . Do it! Get on your computer, the Internet, use your telephone, typewriter and the U.S. mail to put these issues out there). We can do it, but it will take "all" of us working together to make a change.

If you want a scientific recipe for the process of "creating monsters", I must submit (with non-fiction authenticity and probity) that the recipe is in the hands of every prison guard in America. Wardens such as Mike Knowles, George Stratton and Mike Bunnell have the blueprints for how to erect, manufacture, construct and build a "monster factory" in their hands. The ingredients to this process of producing clones, predators, rapists, pedophiles, murderers and wife-beating sociopaths have been tried, tested and proven effective. Prison directors, parole board members and state governors have methodically, systematically and stealthily rocked the media to sleep and numbed the public's sense of outrage as they methodically take babies and boys and transform them into belligerent, obstreperous, bellicose, non-thinking disgraces to the human race. When the public wakes up, they will have to follow the money!! They will discover that their tax dollars have funded billion dollar delivery rooms for the creation of monsters. They will discover that in states such as California, politicians have gotten filthy rich off of crime and punishment. They will discover that the CCPOA pays politicians bonuses, kickbacks and basically insulates its members from oversight and corrections. The American taxpayer should demand an investigation into racketeering, money laundering and illegal bribery, which is transpiring in state prison systems across our nation.

Where is the money? How much money is Jim Brulte worth? How much money does Jim Brulte earn? How much money does former Governor Gray Davis have? Does he have a Swiss or offshore bank account? Did any of that money come from the CCPOA,

Walkenhorst, Access, MCI, Don Novey and other special interest groups?

The public is going to have to demand a full-scale investigation, audit and inspection of the very finances of prison systems across this nation. (If I die in prison, it won't be suicide. It won't be an inmate killing. The U.S. Justice Department, the FBI, Jesse Jackson, George Soros, Tavis Smiley, Oprah, Don King, Bill Gates, Ed Schultz, Mrs. A. Huffington, the Sacramento News and Review, the Associated Press, Larry King, Farrakhan, Joe and Michael Jackson, Johnnie Cochran, Barry Scheck, Harvey Levin and Judge Greg Mathis must investigate C.D.C. and the CCPOA. I was fine at New Folsom and they retaliated against me by throwing me into ad-seg and transferring me. I'm fine where I am now and have made it clear to Mr. Hickman, Mr. Brady, Mrs. Jeannie Woodford and Mr. Schwarzenegger that I'm okay right here. But the few corrupted officials have the power to order a transfer, ad-seg, a SHU program, etc., any day of the week. Their favorite line is "for the safety and security of the institution". Next favorite? "For the inmate's own safety ". Please don't let them do me again . . .).

Hell must be raised over the radio waves, television stations, college campuses and in the churches across this nation. Guys in prison can do little to raise awareness. We are the victims of Taliban Justice. Our mail is sabotaged, delayed, screened censored and stolen . . . If C.D.C. does not like an article in the news, etc. they will withhold it if it's in print. The publishers of Stuff magazine, Hustler and Maxim ought to sue C.D.C. In the months of April and May, no C.D.C. inmate at Mule Creek Prison was allowed to receive Stuff or Maxim due to C.D.C.'s dislike of the contents of certain articles in those publications.

I would hope Paul Wright could get Floyd Abrams, Jay Alan Sekulow, Michael Ratner, David Coles and the ACLU to file Amicus Briefs for this violation of free speech, censorship and discrimination against the media. We watch the Arizona guard hostage taking story on ABC, CBS and NBC news on television. We see movie after movie about prison escapes, etc. Yet somebody downtown in Sacramento (Billy Mayfield? Jay Schievelbein? David Tristan? Don Novey? Lance Corcoran?) decided we shouldn't "read" about it in Stuff and Maxim. That is preposterous, prejudicial and discriminatory on its face. Every inmate in C.D.C. ought to be reimbursed for the missed issues. And Jackie Spier, Mark Leno, John Burton, Darrell Steinberg, Gloria Romero, The Youth Media Council, Van Jones, Paul Wright and media lawyers all across this country ought to sue C.D.C.

National Public Radio, Tavis, Montel, Ed Schultz, Al Franken, Larry King and Carl Jeffers ought to call C.D.C. managers, the CCPOA, Paul Wright, Anne Rice, Arianna Huffington and the Terminator on air and discuss this ludicrous and unconstitutional censorship.

By and large - inmates are "not" going to take prison guards hostage because they read about it in Stuff or Maxim. (And I certainly oppose any inmate doing anything violent to any staff member. Violence by inmates is never justified. I encourage inmates to have family members to call the media. Have family and friends to inundate congressmen, senators, governors, etc. with e-mails and telephone calls about prison guard abuse and the lack of rehabilitation. Family members en-masse ought to write letters to the editor at the local newspaper and ask church pastors, activists, etc. to help inundate the media about these issues of prison staff corruption/abuse etc. I will remind you reading now, whoever you are that you should call prison legal news, FAMM in D.C., The Fortune Society, Justice Lobby, The Quakers, FCL in Sacramento, etc and make donations to them "today". They need money to fight injustice! The Youth Media Council, California Prison Focus, November Coalition, Western Prison Project, Justice Denied Magazine, Children of Incarcerated Parents, Stop Prisoner Rape, etc. need money. Call them, e-mail them, visit their websites and tell all your church family about them. Help).

I will repeat: Prison politicians, prison guard unions, wardens and secret business moguls with vested (and invested) interests in crime, prison construction and the Prison Industrial Complex have methodically, strategically and stealthily numbed the public to the dastardly process of the making of the monsters. I'd like to see Dateline, NBC, 48 Hours, Primetime Live and Frontline do in depth studies on crimes committed by ex-offenders, etc. I promise the public that when a hard-nosed investigator digs beneath the surface and begins to pry underneath the camouflaged statistics and dig deeper and deeper into laws, crimes, criminals and justice, they will discover some startling realities. May I ask you (the reader) do you really (can we be real?) think Gloria Romero and Jackie Spier are the only two California state senators who see that C.Y.A. is a gladiator school for violence expertise? Do you really believe Gloria and Jackie are the only two who see the brutality, viciousness and corruption in the upper echelons of C.D.C.? Do you really think Pete Wilson, Gray Davis, Jim Brulte and Bill Lockyer couldn't/can't see it? Do you not find it strange that even crime victim's groups and conservative are now admitting that three-strikes ain't working? Do you not find it strange, shocking and weird that C.Y.A. is the most violent youth prison system in the nation? Do you find it shocking that there is a violent assault every eleven minutes in C.Y.A.? Do you find it strange that governors routinely cut grade through high school and community colleges' budgets, but never lay off prison staff and never cut prison budgets? Do you find it strange that three strikes in California and similar measures in New York, Kansas and Alabama have incarcerated (for life) more non-violent weed smokers, drug addicts and petty thieves than child molesters, rapists and murderers combined? If you want the statistics to prove this call Marc Mauer, Paul at PLN or Leslie at CA Prison Focus.

* * *

Attorney Murray J. Janus

Q.　　　　Governor Davis - why did you refuse to answer inmates' mail in California?

A.　　　　My administration cared deeply about our state's prisoners.

Q.　　　　The question was/is Mr. Davis - why did you refuse to answer inmates' mail?

A.　　　　I never stated that I refused to answer inmates' mail.

Q.　　　　No. You didn't state it, sir. I asked it; did you?

A.　　　　I had ample staff who always assured that we answered inmates' mail.

Q.　　　　Governor, with all due respect to you, I feel like we're playing semantic　　gymnastics here and I'm searching for the truth. The question is - did you ever　　　　answer inmates' mail?

A.　　　　I don't think I ever personally answered inmates' mail.

Q.　　　　Can you recall ever reading any letters from an inmate in your state's prisons?

A.　　　　Not really, sir.

Q.　　　　I have a statement here from your former Chief of Staff, which states that on average your office received five hundred and sixty letters per week from CA inmates complaining about abuse, killings, rapes and violence. Now I know you　　　can't　testify or speak to the content of these missives cause you didn't read　them, but does that number sound right, Mr. Governor?

A.　　　　Yes.

Q.　　　　Why didn't you ever read a single letter?

A.　　　　I was too busy dealing with other major issues in our state such as trying to fix　the budget, etc.

Q.   And since prisons received almost $6 billion of that very important budget, sir,   you didn't think it important to know what was going on in your prisons?

A.   I did.

Q.   And I also have affidavits stating that you took calls from the CCPOA almost   daily and that the CCPOA gave you $2 million in campaign contributions, sir. Is   that a fact?

A.   And to imply that taking calls from the guards' union had anything to do with   campaign contributions is simply ludicrous, Mr. Janus, and you know it.

Q.   And I also know that it is ludicrous to assume you would take daily calls from   any union in the state if they didn't contribute heavily to your campaign, sir.   Isn't that true?

A.   I took calls all the time, Attorney Janus.

Q.   Did you take daily calls from the teachers' union?

A.   Not that I recall.

Q.   But you do recall taking daily calls from the likes of Don Novey, Lance   Corcoran and David Tristan, correct, sir?

A.   David Tristan is not a CCPOA member.

Q.   The fact that you know David Tristan is not a member further proves you are in   bed or were in bed with the CCPOA.

Objection Your Honor . . . Mr. Janus' characterization of the Governor being in bed with the CCPOA is slanderous, prejudicial and assumes facts not in evidence.

Rebuttal - Janus: Your Honor, this is a cross-examination and a first year law student knows you're given broad latitude in cross-examination. Mr. Davis opened the door to the bed statement. The fact that the former governor of the largest state in North America would know who is not a member of a union with forty-six thousand members clearly shows he had an intimate - no pun intended - a close inside knowledge of the CCPOA.

Now I don't mind re-stating the question. In fact - if I may, I'll withdraw the question, Your Honor.

Q.   Governor Davis, how do you know David Tristan is not a member of the   CCPOA?

A.   Well, generally speaking, most top level administrators in C.D.C. are not   members of the CCPOA.

Q.   Why not?

A.   Well, due to sort of the structure of the union itself. For example, if a prison   guard gets in trouble, anything short of a felony conviction, etc., he will face being fired. So he needs the union

116

. . . I sort of didn't state that the way I   intended.   But what I
meant is, say a lieutenant in C.D.C., if he's charged or   accused
of misconduct etc., anything short of a felony - the worse that can
happen to him is a step down. He could/would (at worse) be
demoted to   sergeant. A captain would be demoted to lieutenant.
A prison guard step one - has nowhere to step down, but out of a job.
So by and large all step one guards are members of the CCPOA. And
one up through the ranks until about the rank   of captain.   But
when you get to, say, associate warden - most of them steer   clear of
the union and save themselves the seventy dollars monthly union fees.
       They've got a long ways down to step, if they get in trouble
you see.

       Q.   Governor - You just basically explained the structure
of the entire CCPOA and   answered three other questions before I ever
asked them. But how do you know   this?

       A.   Because I have to deal with the unions a lot.

       Q.   Unions. How many members are in the CA Teachers
Union?

       A.   I don't know the exact number.

       Q.   Can you just give me an estimate?

       A.   I'm not certain.

       Q.   What are the union fees of a CA high school teacher?

       A.   I don't have an exact figure, sir. I'm not the treasurer
or secretary or anything. I   was the governor of the entire state
- remember?

       Q.   I'm asking the questions here, Mr. Davis. But to
answer you, yes I do remember   and I also remember you just told
me the exact fee that prison guards pay into the CCPOA. Do you?

       A.   Well, I can explain . . .

       Q.   That's okay, Mr. Davis. I think this jury understands
clearly. They (too) remember that the CCPOA gave you more money
than any other union in the state. Nothing further, Mr. Davis. You're
excused.

       Gray Davis appeared shaken. He got up and hastily left the
halls of justice. Mr. Davis had the look on his face, which seemed to
say, "Thank God this is over. Let me get outta here".

       Now stood famed trial attorney of the century . . . Mr. Johnnie
L. Cochran. "Call Mr. Hurtle."

       Ombudsman Hurtle hustled down to the witness stand in what
appeared to be a fifty-dollar, brown, J.C. Penny suit, a tan tie and a K-
Mart blue light special off white shirt. "I thought only white boys got

117

dressed in the dark. This brother is not a brutha," Johnnie whispered to Attorney Willie Gary. Mr. Gary chuckled.

Johnnie then stood to give what everyone knew would be a long and tedious cross-examination of ombudsman Hurtle. This was a special circumstances type (if you will) witness. Hurtle had already given direct testimony for the state. Johnnie had asked the court to allow him to reserve cross-examination until later. Hurtle took his seat and immediately began perspiring. He appeared pensive and intimidated. He had no idea how many different ways Johnnie would attack, belittle, demean and badger him. All he did know was that in the mock trials, Chris Darden had imitated Cochran. And Chris had kept him on the stand for four hours. "Do you think Johnnie will cross me that long?" Hurtle had asked Chris Darden. "Longer," Darden had replied.

Well it was time, D-Day. Johnnie Cochran sat at the super lawyers table perusing what appeared to be at least two hundred documents in a cursory fashion. "Are you ready, Mr. Cochran?" the Judge asked.

Cochran: Yes, I am your Honor. Thank you so kindly.

Q.   Mr. Hurtle, how you doing?

A.   I'm fine, thank you.

Q.   Are you an Uncle Tom?

Attorney General: Objection! Objection! Objection!

Cochran: Withdrawn Your Honor.

The Court: Mr. Cochran, you know better than that. You will not use that kind of language in my courtroom. Now just who do you think you are?

Cochran: Don't you talk to me like that, Your Honor. I'm a man too. Now the term "Uncle Tom" is not profanity; nor is it vulgar language. It simply describes a sort of house Negro of sorts. And I have a right to go there. I've gotten reports that this man is working more for C.D.C. than he is for the state. He opened the door on it in his direct testimony when he stated that he was a go between, a mediator, unbiased and that he had no loyalty to C.D.C. Now we hear he does. He's always defending guards and the administrators. He makes false off the record promises to inmates and suckers them in to withdrawing complaints. This man is a disgrace!

The Court: You may continue your questions.

Cochran: Mr. Hurtle, thank you for coming in and you have a nice day. Good time for lunch, Your Honor?

Attorney General: He can't do that, Your Honor.

The Court: Do what?

Attorney General: Never mind, Judge.

Cochran looked at Gerry Spence and laughed. The jury also laughed. There was no doubt about the fact that this was Johnnie Cochran's jury.

At lunch, Barry Scheck was animated as he, Johnnie and twelve other lawyers sat at a long table at "The Palm" on Santa Monica Blvd. Barry told Johnnie, "You know we always say a D.A. can get a Grand Jury to indict a ham sandwich. Well, I think you can get this jury to exonerate Jeffrey Dahlmer even though he's dead. They love you."

Back in court, after lunch, Johnnie Cochran, Barry Scheck and Willie Gary prepared to give their triplicate closing arguments. First came Barry Scheck:

"It is unthinkable to know that in New York, Georgia, Florida, Alabama and right here in California, our prisons are in a state of emergency. We have a crisis in the prisons across our country. There are ten thousand innocent people convicted for crimes they did not commit every year. These people are charged, arrested, convicted and sentenced to prisons for crimes they did not commit. Many of them actually go to death row. We're killing people for crimes they did not commit. We remedy killings with punishments of murder. We kill those that we suspect of killing and then tell citizens not to kill. And they go to horrible prisons and are forced into gangs based on where they grew up and the color of their skin. And they are forced to become the predators or the prey. Prisons in California have the most powerful, notorious, violent and vicious gangs in the country. Gangs are a problem in prisons in general, but it is epidemic in prisons in California. We've got prison gangsters ordering murders. Street murders being ordered by inmates? I'm not here just to blame people. Perhaps Pete Wilson can legitimately be blamed. There is enough blame to go around to Gray Davis, legislators and our senators. But really it is all of us. We have let this prison thing get out of control. And I am appalled that the Terminator has not proven to be an exterminator and he has not visited or walked through a single prison in this state since he's been in office. Arnold, Arnold, Arnold where are you? You inherited a black hole; a nightmare. But it's your mess now. What will you do about prison guards maliciously beating up our boys in C.Y.A.? What will you do about satanic cults, blood and human sacrifices in C.D.C.? What will you do about Guard Greg Wolfe bringing in race, hate materials to inmates? What will you do about the fact that inmates are being raped, murdered, decapitated and in three cases in Pelican Bay; eaten by other inmates?

119

It is time to get innocent men out of prison. The wrongly convicted and factually innocent men in prison need to get out of there. We need to establish a committee to review all claims of innocence and release the innocent ones. We can't allow any person to languish in prison for a crime of which he's innocent.

We must open up C.D.C. to public scrutiny, oversight and correction. Mr. Schwarzenegger complains that state senators have too much time on their hands. He says this excess idle time leads to funny laws, etc. and that legislators ought to cut back and become part time workers. I agree that they do have too much time on their hands. And many senators and assemblymen, etc. are actually lawyers. Well, I think it's time we use their legal brilliance and give them something to do with their excess time. I suggest that Senators Romero, Speier, Burton, Darrell Steinberg, Mark Leno and Mrs. Midgen establish the truth and reconciliation committee with the power to release wrongly convicted inmates. Let's put Willie Brown, who also has a law degree and Barry Loncke in charge of this commission. Let's do it and let's do it now. These lawmakers can utilize their time by letting the wrong guys out of jail and making space to put the right guys in jail. We certainly can get law professors, etc. to serve as advisors to this task force . . ."

Barry argued for a total of seventy-four minutes climaxing with, "I say open up these prisons and let innocent men come home. We can't sweep innocence under the rug. We must let them come home. If you don't do the crime, you shouldn't do the time. Thank you."

Attorney Willie Gary:

"I have stood up in high schools and colleges from Stuart, Florida all the way to New York telling our youth that hard work, education and faith in God will pay off. I've told our kids to rise above racism, poverty, drugs, gangs and violence.

But now I have to try to figure out a way to rise above racial profiling by police officers. I have to try to tell them to not join a gang, but to travel in groups because they may have to produce alibi witnesses if they're ever falsely accused of rape, murder or kidnapping. I have to try to add cautionary warnings to youth in schools in places like Ohio, where cops kill Black teens everyday of the week. I must warn our youngsters in Nickerson Gardens, Hunters Point, Watts, in Oakland, etc. about the Riders, the Rampart Divisions, Sponge and the A.B. All of which are peace and police officers who are supposed to serve and protect, but instead they disturb and neglect.

120

Police frame-ups, falsely accusing people of crimes they didn't commit and sending our youth to adult jails and prisons is indefensible and inexcusable. Jesus Christ said, "Suffer the little children and let them come unto me." But instead, we abuse them; we beat them, mistreat them and arrest them. We spend more on incarceration than we do on education. We give them first class jail cells, but second class schoolhouses. If my son graduates high school tomorrow and wants a scholarship for college, the state won't pay; not for his higher education. But if my boy commits a crime, we'll pay thirty-five to fifty thousand dollars per year on his incarceration. And when he gets there, he'll get educated, by prison guards, in violence, abuse, profanity, inhumanity and he'll end up suffering from insanity. Prisons for our kids are a recipe for failure. We focus more on putting handcuffs on their wrists and shackles on their ankles than we do on putting books in their hands and shoes on their feet. This is awful. This is like a nightmare. How can we give up on our youth? I can't understand how any governor would cut college funding and not cut prison guard's salaries. How dare we spend more to house a non-violent offender in prison than we do on teaching kids to read, write and count. Have we really given up on young people in America - or is it only a California thing?

What's going on here? I see a bunch of thugs in uniform calling themselves counselors and prison guards raising our children in gladiator schools.

Bill Lockyer refused to prosecute C.Y.A. guards who clearly beat a young boy bloody while he lay prostate on the floor. We saw it on videotape and Bill basically says that whatever the boy did before the video came on, justified him getting assaulted by the grown man prison guard. The CCPOA paid Bill. Yes, they bribed him and threatened to ruin him if he prosecuted. 'I will ruin your professional and personal life if you prosecute my guards in this case,' Dan Novey told Bill. And on the 23rd of April, Bill took a walk on the case.

Gloria Romero was outraged. Where is the recall petition on Lockyer? If that had been a prisoner beating a guard or a citizen beating a police officer on video, what would Bill do? He'd prosecute to the full extent of the law.

This was an abuse of power and it causes hopelessness, anger and rage in the prisons. It makes prison guards feel above the law.

This was a child, a teen, a kid being maliciously beat by a prison guard and Bill Lockyer says it's okay. My motivational speeches are beginning to turn into lectures on how to avoid being beat up by peace officers. The children are our tomorrow. The children are our future. We are destroying a whole generation of children.

Walter Allen, Rod Hickman, Arnold, Judge, ladies and gentlemen of the jury, what's going on?"

Willie argued for two hours and twenty-nine minutes. Johnnie Cochran stood up and slowly looked at each juror. He put his notepad down on the podium. He slowly began to walk over to the jury box. Johnnie looked into the eyes of each juror. After sixty seconds, he spoke:

"This is America. This is the United States of America, the melting pot, the land of opportunity, home of the brave and the place where dreams become reality. This is the greatest country on the face of the planet. I love America. I love this land. Martin Luther King, Jr. also loved the United States of America. And even though he loved America, he still spoke out, marched and confronted her politicians when they erred. Dr. King stood in our nations capital with more than three hundred thousand people and talked about a dream he had. He eloquently, articulately and metaphorically described his dream of liberty, justice and brotherhood for all of us. And he also talked about a kind of promissory note or a check, which the country had given to poor Whites, Latinos and Blacks in America. He explained that this check had bounced and come back marked insufficient funds. But Dr. King refused to believe that the American Bank of Justice was broke. And I want to say to you today that I too have a dream. I have a dream for this great country. I grew up in Shreveport, Louisiana during the Great Depression. Jim Crow's iron heel remained tightly clenched around the throats of Louisiana's working Black folks. As I sat in Little Union Baptist Church every Sunday morning, listening to the choirs sing and the eloquent sermons preached by Rev. Dr. C. A. W. Clark, I had visions and hopes about the future of our America. Dr. Clark, through the breadth of his learning, the artfulness of his oratory and the depth of his conviction, stirred a fire in my belly and a passion for justice. Martin Luther King, Jr., Thurgood Marshall, Clarence Darrow and Dr. Clark taught me that mere eloquence without conviction is hollow; conviction, which does not find a voice, is impotent. I can remember Rev. Clark singing, praying and preaching about, 'the old rugged cross' and it seems to me that the notion of goodness and mercy transforming the worst imaginable 'suffering and shame' into an act of redemption is a powerful reproach to the mean-spirited, bitter direction our American justice system has taken. Dr. Clark's description of the horrible day that Jesus was crucified, how his own cross was placed on a hill between those two common thieves has transformed my life. The one thief mocked Christ, but the other - Dismas, "the good thief", repented of his former life and rebuked his partner in crime for reviling a blameless man. I still hear the breathless wonder in C. A. W. Clark's voice as he recited to us, from memory, our savior's reply, 'And Jesus said unto him, verily I say unto thee, today thou shalt be with me in paradise.' There he was, a repentant criminal, an offender, and his salvation had been announced at Calvary by the savior himself. Not another man in history can make that claim neither judge nor juror, nor prosecutor nor lawmaker, no matter how exalted their station in life. And when I listen to such people dismiss the very concept of rehabilitation as an absurdity, I find myself wishing that they had just one Sundays benefit of Dr. Clark's sermons. During my childhood, my mother, Hattie B. Cochran used to tell us that 'truth crushed to earth, will rise again'.

And so the truth, Dr. Clark's message teaching that Christ in Calvary still believed in rehabilitation and reconciliation has been a driving force of my life. It has enabled me to see that the biggest mistake we made in America and yes in California was to take rehabilitation out of prisons. Also, the fact that Christ was a blameless and innocent man, but was killed, murdered and crucified at Calvary has taught me to know that wrongful convictions and the incarceration of innocent men didn't start in California, with poverty or the color of a man's skin; it started with sin. It began with men who wanted to try to silence anybody who threatened the political structure, the ideals or the powers that be. Jesus was killed for a crime he didn't commit. So I was able to believe in Geronimo Pratt, Rolando Cruz, Rubin Carter, David Quindt, Anthony Porter and Sherman Manning when they were in jails, prisons and even in death row and they told me they were innocent.

The vile injustice inflicted on these men was/is approved by Governor George Bush, Governors Peter Wilson and Gray Davis. That's why I fight and that's why we're here. I am bigger than the O. J. Simpson case. My career is larger than defending Michael Jackson, P. Diddy Combs and even Geronimo. I want to use the law and skill and courage as an advocate to change society for the better. I want to make a difference for all of us, Black, White, Latino, Indian and all. I have worked my entire life to get here where I stand today. I went to college and struggled to go to law school to get here today. I was a prosecutor in the D.A.'s office because I believed in law and order. I was not always a defense lawyer. I served my country. I gave of my talent and time. I tried and now I'm struggling to see justice roll down like waters and righteousness like a mighty stream because injustice anywhere is a threat to justice everywhere. Listen to me." Johnnie Cochran was standing as erect as a five star General in the U. S. Army. "I love this country and so does Mumia Abu Jamal, so does Sherman Manning. So does Marty Tankleff and Jay Salpeter. But we have Mumia and Marty and Sherman in prison for crimes they did not commit. And David Lynn, Mike Rale, Jay Salpeter and Paul Ciollini are trying to get them out. And our governors won't pardon them, parole boards won't parole them, judges won't exonerate them and we have forgotten them. They will die in prison if we don't do justice, have mercy and walk humbly with our God.

It is absolutely unspeakable and unthinkable to disrupt families and destroy entire communities because of rushes to judgment, false accusations and judicial misconduct. It's time to come full circle and stop throwing lives away under the guise of draconian policies we call three-strikes and being tough on crime. We gotta be smart on crime.

Violent, vicious men who get fair trials and are proven guilty beyond a reasonable doubt to a moral certainty ought to be in prison. But we have nowhere to put them because Mumia, Manning, Marty and thousands of dope smokers and petty thieves are occupying bed space in the monster factory. They see the witching circle, satanic occults, gang rapes and unspeakable violence in these halls of despair. And it very often breaks their spirits, damages their minds and 'creates monsters'. Prisons are creating robot like, helpless and unthinking men because we refuse to reach them and teach them before they go to prison. My argument is being transcribed today and it will appear in a tome entitled, 'Creating Monsters'. But Sherman Manning, Mumia Abu Jamal and most prisoners shall never see it because they are in prison. And prison authorities right here in California make it difficult if not impossible for inmates to read books in prison. They devise inconsistent, incomprehensible and preposterous rules prohibiting the expression, protection, exercise of and studying of free speech in prison. This is ridiculous. I hope Gloria Romero, Jackie, Mark Leno, Van Jones, the ACLU, NAACP, ADL, SCLC, FAMM and the PLN will help us demand a change. We're fools for not demanding that inmates be allowed books in prison. I've contemplated dramatizing this travesty by getting the Youth Media Council, Books Not Bars, Churches and Human Rights Watch to send books en mass to prisons. Maybe we should collectively mail fifty thousand copies of 'Journey to Justice', 'Actual Innocence', 'Prison Legal News', 'Creating Monsters', 'Prison Madness' and 'American Dream/A Search for Justice' to the Governor's Office in California and inundate the

Governor's staff with books, mail and e-mails and demand that they be put in prison libraries across the state.

Arnold should think it's 'fantastic' to put transformational books in prisons and to straighten out the minds of our boys before we release them back into society. Think about it. Ed Stokes tried to assault Sherman Manning in prison a couple of months before Ed got out of Mule Creek on child molestation charges. Ed was a monster who should be in prison. Ed should have been analyzed, meticulously monitored and treated intensively before he ever saw the light of day. But instead, they let him out and C.D.C. then leaked reports into the press that he told a prison therapist that he had over two hundred victims in the streets. Ed went to Washington State, then Oregon, bought kiddie porn, a van with a mattress in it and an ambulance to lure kids into his sadistic ploys to molest them. Sherman moved into his cell, 240 in Building Two in Mule Creek after Ed was thrown into the hole for assaulting another inmate. Yet, Ed was released back into population and being the sociopath that he was he tried to assault Sherman because Sherman was in his cell. We are releasing monsters like Ed every day of the week. Marc Mauer, Mark Dow, Elliott Currie, Mike Farrell and Dennis Archer can tell you this. But we also incarcerate men who didn't do the crime. And we also lock up kids for petty crimes and dope dealing. And these wrongly convicted men and non-violent kids go to prisons and get contaminated and devastated by the prison subculture, which is as it is because prison bureaucracies designed it that way.

If we continue to lock 'em up and throw away the key - if we continue to punish them for reading and writing books - if we continue to refuse to educate them before they go to prison and refuse to rehabilitate them when/if they get to prison - if we continue to refuse to prosecute prosecutors for misconduct, refuse to prosecute guards for assault, etc., etc., then we deserve the damn monsters that we are creating!!

The doors to the prison swing both ways. Most of them will get out of prison. And they will maim, molest, murder, torture, attack, abuse and rob us. If Arnold, Rod, Jeannie, the Senate, the President, this Judge, you, me and the media don't demand a change right here, right now then we deserve the Stokes, Mansons, murder and mayhem, which we are creating in the monster factory. It's got to stop. It's gotta end today. I'm not implying that all police officers are racist or corrupt. We're not alleging that all prosecutors and judges are corrupt. We're not claiming all prison guards are abusive or violent. There are thousands upon thousands of police officers who serve and protect our communities. They serve with honor, valor and with courage. I know many prosecutors like David Hicks, Aubrey Davis and Mary Davis who are fair and unbiased and smart in crime. I know judges like Jane Ure who do the right thing. I know thousands of correctional officers who do a good job and go home. There are many good peace officers in California and in this country. God bless them. But we also have some ignorant thugs working in our prisons and they want us to believe they walk the toughest beat in the state. Police officers out in these inner cities are walking a tougher beat. There are no cells on the streets. And there are no inmates in prisons carrying machine guns. The guards own the gates in prison, but the toughest beat is being walked by our children who have to be afraid that a monster like Ed Stokes, Charles Manson, a pedophile or sociopath is going to steal their innocence and take their lives.

Joanne Page can tell you that taxpayers are paying a hundred thousand dollars per cage, per cell to warehouse the monster. And then fifty thousand dollars per year, per inmate to keep him there. That is extortion and bureaucratic betrayal at the highest levels of government.

Dr. Terry Kupers can tell you about the mental illness we are creating in prisons through prolonged solitary confinement, torture, beatings and guard brutality. I join with Dr. King and say today that I refuse to believe that the bank of justice is broke. I refuse to believe American equal protection departments are bankrupt. You can't convince me that Schwarzenegger couldn't get Donna and Tony Mendez (retired C.I.A. agents) to look at Manning's case or the Governor of Pennsylvania can't get a retired F.B.I. Agent to look at Mumia's case and tell us they are innocent. Griffin Bell, Ramsey Clark, William Sessions, David Hicks; let's get them to look at these transcripts.

In Sherman's trial, Aubrey Davis - not a defense lawyer, but a D.A., Prosecutor Aubrey Davis called (it's on the record) Mary Hanlon Stone and Judge Robert Altman and stated 'Russell Camosky is a rapist. Russell is out on bail here in Virginia and is in California illegally. I wouldn't believe anything Russell says on a stack of Bibles.' But Altman allowed Russell to testify against Manning. Russell was White, the jury was all White and they believed Russell and used his testimony to justify sending Sherman to prison. Barry Loncke can tell you that, that was wrong, but Sherman is in prison here in California. He has not seen his family in eight years. They are all in Atlanta, Georgia. We need to loose this man and let him go.

We must enforce the principles of justice and equality outlined in the constitution. You may be able to guarantee that you won't commit a crime, but you can't guarantee that you won't ever be charged with a crime. And if you are young, male, Black, Brown or poor; chances are you will be charged, tried and convicted. And in many instances, you're actually innocent. Ladies and gentlemen of the jury . . ."

The aforementioned (beginning with Murray Janus' questioning of Gray Davis) was fiction. Yet, the facts were authentic. I suspect scholars and book critics will be debating, long after I'm dead, why I decided to intermingle fiction into a non-fiction book. They'll call it inconsistent; I'll call it innovative. One of the chief aims, which I have, is to meet the challenge to uncover the truths contained in this book. I want the American public, taxpaying citizens en masse to know where their money is going and how ineffective the judicial system is. And we will put the word out. I need you who are reading these words right now to please (and I do mean please) do your part. Maybe you don't want to become a prison rights activist. Maybe you're not inclined to play an active, public role (I wish you were) in the dismantling of the monster factory. But you can and will help (greatly) if you just tell another person to "read this book". If you are unwilling to share your book with them, just tell them to log on to Barnes & Noble, Amazon.com, or www.cafeshops.com/manning and order a copy today. Tell your personal friends, your pastor, your book club, your professor, your students and your politicians about this book. Many of you received this book gratis. Will you at least order another copy for somebody else? A great way to help would also be to order a copy for a prisoner. If you don't know someone in a juvenile facility, jail or prison, call PLN, FAMM, The Fortune Society and I assure you they know thousands who would love to receive this book. If you want to remain anonymous, I happen to know Paul at PLN, Julie at FAMM, Joanne Page at the Fortune Society will keep your address, name and telephone number confidential.

I can't overemphasize the fact that we, the people, should, can and must demand a change. When we help a troubled teen, save a child and prevent him from going to prison, the life we save may be our own. Our refusal to invest in the inner and urban city youth has resulted in an entire generation of killers and rapists. Our refusal to provide adequate head start, nursery and day care has resulted in young people joining the ranks of those on welfare and getting jail care.

We will and must pay either way. The question must become would we rather pay now or later. We have seen what paying "later" will do to a people, a society and to an economy. Paying later has resulted in a spectacular failure as is evident by the nearly $16 billion

127

deficit in California. Our absolute numbness and deep insensitivity to the plight of those in jails and prisons was caused by many factors. The television, the media, lobbyists and money-hungry politicians slowly but certainly convinced us that the solutions to crime were simple: A. Hire more police officers. B. Build more prisons and C. Lock 'em up and throw away the key. But the key, which we threw away has been found and we are being victimized and traumatized by the very system per se. It was set up to fail. It was designed to cripple minds and stifle mental growth. It was built on abuse and backed by corruption. It was designed to make an entire group of professionals rich. Most of these professionals, which we find working in the prisons, could not survive the ethical standards required to work in the private sector. We find men like Dr. Douglas Peterson (New Folsom) who was kicked out of three hospitals, yet hired in C.D.C. as the "Chief Medical Officer". We have psychiatrists working in C.D.C. who were fired by other institutions and/or suspended in civilian life. We have wardens who didn't make it through high school such as Mike Knowles and George Stratton.

It's deeper than you think. It will be a long time before we get it right, but together we must begin again. We must rebuild our youth. We cannot save the country without input, efforts, ideas and action from our youth. Bush, Ashcroft and Rumsfeld know that we can't fight terrorism in Afghanistan, Iraq or Fallujah without young soldiers. The people who pulled Saddam Hussein out of that hole were eighteen and nineteen-year-old boys. And just as they are intelligent, skilled and responsible enough to use machine guns in their teens, they are also skilled, intelligent and responsible enough to develop forums, commissions and task forces on crime and punishment, rehabilitation and public safety.

For years, we have been complaining about a lack of energy and action by our youth. But the truth is ever time we've called upon our youth to fight our wars in Vietnam, Japan, Iraq, Afghanistan, etc, they have suited up, trained strenuously and left their schools, families and friends to go fight our wars on foreign soil.

They have been strong, mature, bold and courageous. Our youth are dying over in Iraq. It is our youth dying in Fallujah and in other parts of the world. They are fighting because they too believe in America. They are fighting knowing that they might not make it back. They have found a calling bigger than themselves. They sacrifice and risk their lives for you and me. Yet, the same government which readily and rapidly deploys them to fight our wars on foreign ground won't allow them to fight the war on poverty, prisons, crime and urban suffering right here at home. We won't pay their college tuition. We won't put computers in their schools in rural Georgia, Mississippi and Idaho. We don't want them in judicial hearings in the congress, the senate or the legislature. But when it comes time to find Hussein or hunt for Osama, the lost, useless and selfish youth we so often complain about become the few, the proud and often the maimed, disabled and the dead.

I say America has the greatest youth on the planet. I say we don't and won't see their greatness 'til we call on it, look for it and respect it when we see it. That's why I'm not even calling on old stubborn politicians anymore. I look to see Clay Aiken and boy band fans waving this book and wearing "American Dream/A Search for Justice" T-shirts out at U2, Snoop Dogg, Beyonce and Aerosmith concerts. I look to see the Frat Brothers who read FHM, Rolling Stone, Vibe, Maxim, Stuff and Source magazines reading "Creating Monsters". When FHM, Stuff, Maxim, Source and King Magazine get their readers to back any product, it sells well.

And many people think FHM, Rolling Stone, Maxim and Stuff are only about pictures, but lack substance. Wrong again. Mr. Jimmy Jellinek, the writers for Stuff, Maxim, Rolling Stone and Source are some of the most talented young writers in this country. They are informative, educational and entertaining in their publications. I subscribe (FHM, Maxim, Stuff) to many of them and I get my inspiration from some of the things I read in them.

I'm convinced that Rishi and Jeff, Critical Resistance, The Justice Lobby, the ABA, 3EM and "Books Not Bars" can/will help us get this book in prisons across this country. I'm also convinced that my folks who are reading this book (right now) due to help from perhaps moveon.org, Mr. Soros, Bill Gates, Bill Cosby, Doug Banks, Mr. Hugh, Flynt and Robert Guccione. . .you guys ought to raise yourself up and change your life! You must figure out what's wrong with "you". (I'm writing to criminals, gangsters and violent predators at this juncture). You (yes you) know who you are. You know how you are. Now you gotta figure out how/why you got that way. If I shake up a root beer in a can and then pour it into a glass, you'll see foam, bubbles and suds at the top of the glass. The bubbles will run over and spill out onto the table, desk or in your lap. Well the bubbles and foamy suds you see running up and outside the glass are results not causes. The cause is deeper than the foam. The foam is produced by the soda, the root beer, down inside the bottom of the glass. Anger, rage, violence and belligerence are results. They are caused by something deep down inside of you. Your past, your hurt, your fears or repressed tears are often expressed with rage, anger and violence. I suggest you get down inside of "you" and figure out the reasons (cause) for the season (results).

Read! In prison you have time on your hands and you should use it. I am hoping these great magazines, which I mentioned earlier (FHM, Maxim, Stuff, Source, Rolling Stone) will begin to do a few stories on psychology, transformation and self-help.

Hell, most of their readers are in prison anyway. So why not drop a little science on subscribers that may end up saving lives, reducing crime and protecting the public.

I also suggest (I'm sounding soft right now) that you watch Oprah. Oprah does a lot of shows, which deal with real issues and can help you change you.

I suggest you read everything you get your hands on by Dr. Na'im Akbar, Dennis Kimbro, Zig Zigler, Wayne Dwyer and Tony Robbins. And you must read "Long Walk to Freedom" by Mr. Nelson Mandela. "Long Walk to Freedom" ought to be as mandatory (reading) as the "Art of War" is for the Northerners in prison. You'll free your mind by reading books such as "Makes Me Wanna Holler", "Prison Nation", "Long Walk to Freedom", "The Autobiography of Malcolm X", "Vernon Can Read", "The Miraculous Journey of Rubin Hurricane Carter", "Invisible Punishments", etc. If you are in prison, write to PLN and ask for a suggested reading list after you read the above books. You can tell your family to call The Fortune Society (212/691-7554), the Ella Baker Human Rights Center in San Francisco or The Youth Media Council in Oakland, CA and ask them to send you a list on suggested readings for prisoners.

We're about to start a revolution of action, transformation and education. We are going to involve our youth. I figure if they can survive at seventeen and eighteen in Iraq, they can survive in the congress, in the senate, in the legislature and even in the White House. I figure if they can survive in Afghanistan fresh out of high school, then they can survive in task forces and committees empowered to set wrongly convicted prisoners free. I figure they can shut down prisons and open up schools.

All our youth need is a chance. So I'm calling on them. I call forth every high school teen, college student, football player, cheerleader, student body, fraternity and sorority. I call forth the youth of America and I tell you what George Bush, Mr. Rumsfeld and Ashcroft won't tell you. I tell our youth that we need you to fight the war on illiteracy, war on violence, war on poverty and the war on police brutality and the war on tobacco right here at home. I salute you who have fought and are fighting in Iraq and Afghanistan. I have the highest appreciation, honor and respect for our young soldiers in our armed forces. I pray for you.

I also have the utmost respect for JROTC members, Boy Scouts, Girl Scouts and college ROTC students. And it is you the youth, you the geek, you the teen activists, you the youth that I entrust my future with. You have this book and you get it out there and you use it as a tool for action, change and warfare. If we can use you the youth to find Hussein and Osama then we can use you right at home to find a way to make prisons work, find a way to feed the hungry, educate the illiterate and put away the predators.

Let's form a special forces of Green Beret youth right here in America. We need you the youth to fight the non-violent wars of poverty and hopelessness right here at home. You must be strong; you must be brave, innovative, creative and bodacious.

With the Internet, college newspapers, letters to the editor, the telephone and concerts, etc. youth potential is unlimited.

Let's get the church to pray, parents to pay and we must lead the way to a better America. Let's get together and change things. We may not have all come over in the same ships, but we're all in the same beat today. This is our country. We are breathing the same air. There is no separate wind for Blacks, Whites, Latinos or Indians. It rains on the rich as well as the poor, the prisoner as well as the free man. This is our country. What affects us directly will affect us all indirectly. So we may as well take the country back. I call the youth forth; right now.

We don't need to ask the government to tell us how to care for Jesus. And there is some Jesus in the belly of every pregnant mother in this world. There is some Jesus in the soul of every prisoner in the prisons. We don't need Bush or Rumsfeld to tell us how to care for Jesus.

We must do justice, have mercy and walk humbly with God. We must feed the hungry, clothe the naked and visit those in prison. We must do unto others, as we would have them do unto us.

If you were in prison and you knew you were innocent, what would you want the lawyer, the doctor, and the governor to do? What would consume your spirit?

"Hate put me in prison, but love is gonna bust me outta here," said Rubin Hurricane Carter. And it will be the love, the action, the innovation, the demonstrations and the help of our youth that will change the country and make America better.

I call forth the youth to get up and get back in the fight. Don't just let them look over you. Make your voices heard. Right where you are today, whip out your lil cell phone and call a local talk show and speak out. Speak up and speak out. You don't have to mention, "Creating Monsters if you don't want to, but speak out on whatever you want. Don't be silent when your country is in trouble. Write your politicians, speak up and speak out. Get active today. Don't waster your talents. I call you forth. We need you the youth! We need you the student. We need you the jock, nerd, geek and freak. We need you. (Go to www.outlawsonline.com/shermanmanning). We need our youth . . .

Remember that (and this is for prisoners, activists, youth, lawyers as well as college students) the most creative thinkers always win. The folks with the most innovative ideas and approaches will win. I see so much you do, I hear nothing you say. I'd rather see a sermon any day than to hear one. I don't wanna hear what you can say; I wanna see what you can do. I need Marc Morrone, Aaron Goodwin and Barry Keenan to join PLN and FAMM. I need Attorney Joseph Cavallo, Ryan Swan, Robert Yau, Dr. Bruce Perry and Sarita Fluker. We are calling you forth! I call forth my students at U. C. Davis, U. C. Berkeley, Spellman, Morehouse, Clark, Howard, Harvard, Princeton and Yale. Come forth! We must rise up out of the ashes of mediocrity, defeat and devastation. I call Colfax High and Folsom High School students. Ninety-nine high school kids in New York, Archer/Harper and Northside in Atlanta. I call every student in school and college in America. Put on your uniform! Get your weapons and let's roll!

You students in JROTC, ROTC and OCS are already leaders! We need you to help us lead. Get your weapons and let's run to the battlefield. Your weapons are the telephone, the typewriter and the Internet. You, reading right this minute, begin. Begin, begin, begin now. Get on the Web and surf, e-mail, text and post. Get about ten (or twenty) names, which are mentioned in this book and find them. Then after your searches, you'll begin your seizure, i.e., "Kevin Shelton", the moneyman. Did you read "Creating Monsters"? I saw your name in the book and wanted to know if you'll join with us out at U. C. Davis who are establishing a youth moveon.org?" This is innovative and this you can do today. You must use your power and your weapons. Brenda Pearson, Vanita Gupta, Mitch Zamoff, (of Hogan and Hartson Fame) Will Harris, Rep. John Conyers, James Muscoreil, John Russell, Joel Foster, Rev. Warren Dolphus, Peter Riveiro and Tom Burkert would each be glad to advise youth on how you can help. And I would hope that powerful and wealthy men and women such as George Soros, Chris Gardner (Gardner and Rich), Joe Weider, Jeff Bezos and Master P. will help us build the movement to protect public safety.

On April 29th, I saw a woman on the show "Cops" who had been the victim of a money snatching. A young man had snatched thirty-eight dollars out of her purse and ran. The police caught the young man and a female officer was appalled that the woman didn't want to press charges. "He needs to go to a juvenile facility and then jail if he's going to get reformed," the officer told the woman. "No, jail does not reform them, it makes them worse. I just want my money back," the woman said. Unfortunately, this I what I know to be true and this woman was correct. Once a man goes to a juvenile facility he experiences what I call a touch of evil. This place is absolutely intolerable. It is a place of horror, sorrow, shame, violence and wickedness.

And sadly I admit that in California, it seems to be getting worse not better. On April 28th at Mule Creek, four Black and Mexican inmates attacked each other. It seems prison guards are taking the softness out of the few so-called soft (protective custody) yards in California. Guards are harassing, cursing, assaulting and disrespecting us more.

They are taking out their anger (because of all the bad publicity they're getting) on us. "Gloria Romero can kiss my ass. If she thinks she can fight the CCPOA, she must be crazy. She'll mess around and be on a one way flight out of town," a prison guard who works in the yard stated. And when Mr. Bill Lockyer decided not to charge the prison guards who clearly beat down the two youths at C.Y.A., I've heard comments like "we're more powerful than the mafia" and "Don't know D.A. or Attorney General mess with us". Perhaps they have a point.

In 2001, 2002 and 2003, several prison guards earned more money than the Governor of California. I've seen documents, which prove that one prison guard had a base pay of fifty-nine thousand dollars. And this same guard earned one hundred and twenty-four thousand dollars in overtime for a grand total of one hundred and eighty-three thousand dollars for the year of 2003. This is free spending. This is overtime and sick leave abuse. They have a racket going on in which some guards will tip off their buddies i.e., "I'm gonna call in sick Saturday. You work it and just give me fifty bucks".

And in early April, C.D.C. called a secret state of emergency, which nobody knew about except top administrators. Gloria Romero got a hold of the secret state of emergency and she's raising hell. It turns out that apparently the state of emergency was called so that prison officials could access a slush fund (more money in a midst of a budget crisis), which is otherwise unavailable. For a time, nobody could give a legitimate explanation for why this state of emergency was called and what they're doing with the money. We do know that Gloria has now called for another round of hearings on this budget manipulation and so-called state of emergency. We also know that C.D.C. is now triple bunking inmates, which is causing more violence. We do know that under the leadership of Rod Hickman and Jeannie Woodford things ain't changing yet. I'm not necessarily faulting them. I've made my high opinion of Mr. Hickman and Mrs. Woodford known in my last book, "American Dream/A Search for Justice". I'm not (yet) withdrawing that praise.

But I must state, I have not seen anything get better. We're still being routinely locked down arbitrarily. C.D.C. staff are still smuggling in drugs, setting up inmates, and transferring any of us they don't like. They are still arbitrarily throwing us into ad-seg and doctoring paperwork to justify it. Letters to downtown C.D.C. are still being returned to the institution unread. Letters to the Governor's Office are returned to downtown C.D.C. and C.D.C. sends them back to the prisons.

Missives to state senators are still being sabotaged, delayed, stolen and hindered. Mike Teselle, John Baird and Larry King still can't get into these prisons to interview us. Guards still own the gates and rehabilitation is still almost non-existent.

It's still a monster factory. We have bad keepers and the kept are bad. Prisons are a place of hypnosis. They hypnotize their residents into a sort of ruthlessness, wretched fear and a zombie like state of minds. If anybody could have come up with a man made recipe for raw madness, anger or mental illness, the main ingredient would be - prison.

. . . "We measured the depression level . . . of male prisoners before and after incarceration. Because suicide in prison is such a prevalent problem, we wanted to try to predict who was at most risk for becoming depressed. To our surprise, no one was seriously depressed upon entering prison. To our dismay almost everyone was depressed on leaving. Some might say this means the prisons are doing their job, but it seems to be something deeply disturbing is happening during imprisonment," stated Dr. Seligman, Psychiatrist and Author of "Learned Optimism".

Society is in trouble and it's getting worse, worse and worse. What is happening in here (prisons) is being evidenced out there. This should not be allowed or portrayed as a panacea to the ills of society. Reduced sentences and the incentives inherent in a program aimed at self-improvement and rehabilitation should be the trend and not the exception. Education rather than dehumanization must become the rule. The debilitating effects of this Orwellian program will only result in a further departure from society of those already alienated by virtue of their incarceration and economic backgrounds. I don't want Mr. Schwarzenegger nor governors across America to continue to overlook the logic that until prisons are first supervised in fairness and respect, everyone - prisoners, activists and prison administrators - sense a feeling of despair and hopelessness as far as accomplishing any of their goals. It is time for prison directors to rely on sound judgment and not their emotional feelings in making decisions, which eventually affect many lives including their own. The hurt, anger, evil, rage and repression that is constantly being invoked inside prisons cannot be contained just to the inside of these walls and shall eventually overflow into the neighborhoods in society and should be of urgent concern to society. Prisons are today's thermometers, which measure its repression tomorrow. Prisoners will spill back into society to the tune of almost seven hundred thousand this year alone. As the slain guard's wife cried out in hurt, so does the wife and loved ones of the tormented convict weep their tears as they experience his psychological and physical torture. Death and torture are no strangers to those who work and live within these cages, as every action causes a reaction. When one finds oneself chained and beaten up against the wall, one's actions and thoughts manifest into total wickedness and madness. In here, no deed is too vile, as all reason and humanity cease to exist. Repressive incarceration does not provide safety or a positive environment for staff or prisoners. When men are locked up and dehumanized, they rage and they snap and when they get back to society, our citizens become the victims of their anger and rage.

I'm excited and inspired by the courageous investigations being conducted by Gloria Romero and Jackie Speier. I'm glad Mark Leno seems to care. I think Darrell Steinberg cares. In California, I am proud that Arnold gave YACA its first Black head in the person of Rod Hickman. I'm very glad Arnold seated Jeannie Woodford over C.D.C. and under Rod Hickman. But that's not enough. What must we do to turn around the monster factory? There are many things, which must be done nationwide in order to stop creating monsters. The very first step any new governor of any state who really wants to clean up his/her prisons must do is visit the prisons. In California, Mr. Schwarzenegger must not be hoodwinked by cosmetic and superficial changes. Applying make-up to a wrinkled face may disguise the wrinkles, but make-up won't remove the wrinkles. If you put deodorant or perfume on an unclean body, it may smell good for a time, but sooner or later the stink comes back. C.D.C. is like a rotten apple. And you can paint a rotten apple red and it will shine and look good for a time, but eventually the rot will overtake the paint and it is worse than it was before you cosmetically (painted) restored it or gave it a cosmetic makeover. And after you pain that rotten apple, if someone comes along and bites down into it, they will discover an awful taste and the person or persons doing the biting, may become ill. Those prison guards at C.Y.A. who beat those youths were rotten apples! And when the youths did whatever they did (apparently one of the kids had punched a guard in the nose) they bit into that apple, which has been cosmetically disguised, painted and made up by the CCPOA. And they got the living daylights beat out of them by the guards. On a high note - the Sacramento Branch of the F.B.I. decided on April 30, 2004 to launch an investigation into civil rights violations by the guards. I believe without question that the Feds should overtake C.Y.A. and C.D.C. Many prison systems can be saved. In Georgia, Florida and some other states, we can clear those prisons up without the Feds taking them over. But in California, the Feds need to take C.Y.A. and C.D.C. under seize. Rod Hickman is a pretty good fella. Jeannie Woodford is the best C.D.C. can offer, but neither Rod nor Jeannie is crazy. And both of them fear the wrath of the CCPOA. They may never admit it on camera, but I know that they know they can do so much, but no more. If they anger the CCPOA, they can be scandalized, stigmatized, run out of office and even perhaps killed (i.e., Captain Doug Pieper?). The CCPOA has some dangerous, corrupted, wicked, money hungry thugs running it. And they reflect badly on the average Joe, Alexander Jeffries, and C.O. Cutler type guys who just come to work to do their jobs and go home. There are many C.D.C. officers who do their jobs efficiently and go home. They are not coming to work to kill, abuse, assault or conspire against inmates. They are just trying to earn a decent living. And although I mention many of the rotten apples, the monster makers, the beast creators and the corrupted guards in this book, I must state that I believe many of them are not that way. Many are not evil, racist or corrupt. But most are affected and eventually infected by the rottenness of their co-workers who are abusive, collusive and corrupt.

So I would suggest strenuously that Mrs. Romero, Mrs. Speier and Critical Resistance lobby the Justice Department to rapidly and stealthily seize C.Y.A. And then seize C.D.C. and since I am a pragmatic man, I am cognizant of the fact that chances are slim, that the Feds will take over . . . Ipso facto there are some immediate things I would suggest that Maria Shriver encourage her husband to do.

There must be an immediate paradigm shift in this state (as well as all other states in the U.S.) on how we deal with crime and punishment. It has been stated repeatedly that we're got to bring rehabilitation back into the prisons. Instead of touting were tough on crime, let us tout that we are pragmatic on crime. We must be willing to do whatever is effective and we must take into consideration price vs. cost. I'll use price vs. cost as a segue to the teachings of Mr. Zig Zigler. I learned at the age of thirteen, from listening to the tapes of Zig Zigler, the difference between price and cost. Concisely, pay fifteen hundred dollars for a car today and it can end up costing you three thousand dollars over a period. When you purchase the jalopy, which has been painted and cosmetically polished, it looks good and rides good. It's cheap and you save money in the short period. And then the tires go out, the carburetor goes out, the steering loses power, you need an alignment, etc. Within a year, you've paid out three grand in repairs. Their goes the engine, next comes the transmission now you've paid out ten grand plus the initial fifteen hundred. The "price" was only fifteen hundred, but the "cost" ends up being nearly twelve thousand. If you had been smart enough to invest seven or eight grand earlier on a well-conditioned automobile - the price would have been higher, yet the cost, less expensive.

We must be willing to invest in our children early. We must begin by actually (really, finally) leaving no child behind. We must bring fathers back home and families back together. We need a symposium in this country on the restoration and reconciliation of the American family. I know we're raising hell about Mayor Gavin Newsome allowing gays to marry. I know we oppose gays and lesbians raising children. And perhaps we're correct. Yet, you can't legislate morality. And to be candid, gays can't do much worse than we are doing in our so-called traditional families. We all know about the fact that inner and urban city kids are growing up in war zones. We know many poor White, Latino and Black kids have no father figures. Their dads are dead, dying, in jail or en route to jail. But we also need not continue to pretend that all is well in suburbia.

In many wealthy neighborhoods, kids are also growing up without their father and mothers. They have all the comforts of a plush lifestyle. They live in palatial estates. But the Columbine killers came from good families.

Inmate/youth/young White kid, Matthew Lovett, lived in the suburbs in New Jersey. His father made sure Matt had all the latest equipment in computers. But all too often these rich kids are being baby sat and raised by those computers while their parents work eighteen-hour days trying to pay for those palatial estates. There are more suicides, homicides, drug overdoses, orgies and DUIs involving teens in the suburbs than we've ever seen before. I submit that an epidemic by any other name is an epidemic. And there is an epidemic in the suburbs as well as in the ghettos across our United States. I'm extremely proud of what Bill Gates, Steve Jobs, Garrett Gruener and all the innovative geniuses of our society have done. But while we were busy building up the information, superhighway and playing the politics of race, weapons, building prisons and jails, etc., we forgot about the children and lost the American family. And when we found crime skyrocketing, drugs infiltrating our communities, we built more juvenile facilities, jails and prisons. We built no preschools, grade schools or colleges. We invested billions in incarceration and divested millions from education. In the process, we abandoned our families and lost our children, the lost children of America. It's disheartening, shameful and an ultimate disgrace to us all. Ipso facto, our youth find themselves spiraling out of control. And our politicians have hypnotized us into belief that the answer is to build more prisons, jails, and juvenile facilities; to lock 'em up and throw away the key. So we must begin to organize, galvanize, strategize and restore our families. We need a war on broken homes. A war on hopeless children . . .

And one of the biggest mistakes we made in this country was to cut back on our spending on public education in America. We need a real education czar. Bring together Toni Morrison, George Soros, Bill Cosby, Dr. Na'im Akbar, Dr. Henry Gates, Cornel West, Joe Clark and Marva Collins and restore our educational institutions in America. From daycare, head start, nursery school and kindergarten - all the way through high school, we need to bombard our kids with a blitz or self-help, inspirational and motivational programs, which will inspire kids from broken homes and encourage kids from suburbia. Unless we rethink, redirect and revise our schools, we will continue to deal with bullying, teenage pregnancy, babies out of wedlock, school massacres and basically graduating illiterate children . . .

We will find that an investment in our youth (to the tune of billions of dollars) will end up jailing money by a reduction in the need for juvenile facilities, jails and prisons in which to house them after our refusal to invest has cost us and contributed to a generation of predators, drug addicts and kids with damaged brains.

As an immediate weapon or tool to assist us in breaking the cycle of violence in the streets, we must break the cycle of violence in the prisons. In order to break the cycle of violence in the prisons, break the cycle of violence in the jails and the juvenile facilities . . . It leads back to breaking the cycle in the home. If kids are mistreated in the homes, they rage in the schools. In our knee-jerk, reactionary climate in America, we immediately place Band-Aids on their bleeding scars by locking them up for bleeding (raging) and once we lock 'em up in the current prison system, we may as well throw away the key. The culture of anger, rape, rage and violence in the havens of shame that we call prisons, they will learn how to get angrier, more violent and more skilled in the commission of crimes . . . So it is difficult for me to articulate a strategy for overcoming or halting the creation of monsters in the monster factory without detailing and specifying a methodology for the elimination of the dual or dubious creation of monsters in the schools, the streets and the homes.

However, since my focus (in this tome) purports to be on the prisons and the jails and the juvenile facilities in America and since my present status is one of a wrongly convicted prisoner, here in California; I shall scribe in the form of a direct message to Mr. Schwarzenegger a plan which I believe can save California. And my hope is that other governors, senators, congress and legislators will duplicate, emulate and model this plan in their states as well.

Arnold must strip the car, remove the primer and look meticulously, analytically and critically at the body. He'll find lots of Bondo. The Bondo is covering up holes and dents. Some body parts will be so damaged once the Bondo is removed that we will have to replace the entire part. We may need a new fender, a new windshield, new tires or a new hood, etc., but don't stop there . . . Go under the hood and check all the vital parts beginning with the engine. The mess Arnold inherited was created out of years and years of neglect, abuse, denial and disdain. "Looking out, I see the ferocious fences that keep the hopes and dreams of society's cast-a-ways at bay," states Preston Gresham in Dixon, Illinois. Arnold did not increase the divide between the prisoner and the preacher on the locked in and the locked out. Arnold inherited a mess made by others. He must take a hands on approach to an innovative style of leadership and begin to terminate, terminate and terminate even more. He's got to send hundreds of prison guards home. The scurrilous, corrupted and felonious characters who are masterminding the plot to create monsters in prisons and juvenile facilities must be fired, retired or forced to resign - period. Arnold should protect the sweetheart deal made by Gray Davis with the CCPOA. Strangely or oddly, I support the contract, which will pay guards more. I am not opposed to prison guards earning good money. I just don't want teachers and professors earning less than keepers. Yet, don't lower prison guard pay, instead raise teachers pay. When we pay guards well, we get better work. When you decrease the pay, the quality or caliber of the applicants will be lowered. But I don't want to see some of the filthy-minded, robotized, high school dropouts - presently working in the prisons - getting that pay raise. Remove the body part and bring in new blood. So step one is to terminate, terminate and terminate some more. I have confidence that if Jeannie Woodford is sent into the prisons and allowed access to prison guard misconduct files and if they stop throwing away and rubberstamping inmate's complaints of abuse by guards - Jeannie can come to Arnold over a six month period and say, "I want this one, this one and this one terminated. I want this one rehabilitated." Yes some guards need to be terminated and some guards can be rehabilitated. And just as no amount of rehabilitation will reform some killers and rapists, no amount of rehab will or can reform some renegade, rogue and corrupted guards. Those guards who rape inmates, set up inmates, smuggle in drugs, beat inmates, etc. don't deserve the opportunity to work in Schwarzenegger's prisons. Get rid of them. Those guards who have committed minor infractions etc., etc. can and must be rehabilitated. We must open up classes and bring in professors, psychologists and sociologists to help re-train the present guards and better train the future guards. We should teach ethics, diversity, sensitivity and conflict resolution skills to prison guards. Ipso facto, we must be extremely cautious and selective about the guards we allow to man the gates of the juveniles facilities. It takes a disciplined, clear-headed, pragmatic and skilled strategist to work with youth. Guards who beat wards maliciously are like a parent who never took parenting class. A good mother such as Maria Shriver knows how to handle Patrick (her son) when he acted out. It's tough to be a mother or a father. And yet Maria did not abuse, beat or abandon Patrick for acting out. She used discipline, incentives, education and motivation to raise Patrick. And some mothers shake their babies to death for crying too loudly. We would not want a mother who shook her baby to death or abused children physically or sexually to work in a daycare center! Some of the guards working in C.Y.A. are the kinds of mothers and fathers who will, would, can and do abuse, beat, molest, incite and kill babies.

When I look at the video of the guards beating the youths at C.Y.A. and I see a kid lying face down, restrained, obedient and see the guard strike, beat and punch the kid for a total of twenty-eight punches, when I saw the kick, the assault and the abuse, I can not under any circumstances imagine Arnold Schwarzenegger doing that kind of abuse! I believe it's not in Arnold's nature, upbringing and paradigm of manhood to beat up a boy. Arnold is big, Arnold is bad and Arnold is strong. He has the physical power to take a man's head off! But if Arnold was punched, kicked or spit on by a teenager, Arnold might slap him. Arnold would restrain him, but the former Mr. Olympia, so-called Terminator and present Governator would not viciously or maliciously beat down a kid!   Arnold could work at C.Y.A. and the place would be transformed. So then Arnold must become the C.Y.A. Terminator and terminate all abusive, unthinking and undisciplined prison guards working in C.Y.A. These are kids, teens and by and large, boys from broken homes. They are incarcerated because they were alienated, frustrated and devastated. We have a marvelous opportunity and a tough challenge to reach, transform and turn those youths around. We should use incarceration as a last resort and stop sending kids to juvenile facilities on a whim! And when we must send them, they should be met by professionals who are qualified to protect, secure and guard them. They should be required (mandatory) to go to class, go to workshops, seminars and to read. And when they refuse they should be punished. Punished, not tortured! Punished, not assaulted! Punished, not set up! Punished, i.e., diminished privileges, etc. No telephone, no TV and reduced recreation. (The same approach can be modified, adjusted and utilized in the prisons).

And we must employ a tactical strategy for disciplinary actions, which does not immediately resort to solitary and ad-seg placement. All too often, I've seen firsthand in the prisons how arbitrarily, capriciously and rapidly prison officials will uproot an inmate and send them (us) to ad-seg. And even if and when the ad-seg stay is brief, the little life the inmate has built is interrupted. You (automatically) lose your job, your cell and your cell partner. And upon being released from ad-seg, you have to go through hell and high water to "try" to get a job, a cell and a compatible celly. Very often an inmate just released from ad-seg will attack a guard or his new cell partner. Although there is (absolutely) no justification for a prisoner assaulting a guard or a fellow inmate (it is wrong and must be punished in the severest legal fashion). There is (often) an "explanation". The frustrated inmate who's been groomed for failure and trained to become a monster, comes out of the hole, often for a minor infraction or because some prison sergeant or lieutenant promised to teach him a lesson and when he gets out - still raging from having gone in, he is harassed and purposely removed from job, cell and program. So he goes off and attacks somebody and we have more crime, more violence and more pain.

How would a civilian feel if he/she were locked up in jail for minor traffic violations? No CHP officer is going to arrest you for running a stop sign or arrest you for jay walking. But he perhaps will arrest you for D.U.I. or driving on a suspended driver's license. Yet, in C.D.C. you get arrested for things as minor as yelling or a fistfight, etc. Now I adamantly oppose violence point blank. I want the violence in the prisons to stop. Yet, I also know that boys will be boys and guys in prisons will fight. We must redesign the discipline programs in the prisons. We don't suspend a kid in school for talking out of turn. We give the kid detention and if we are pragmatic on education, we listen to the youth and we discover that most kids would rather get suspended than get detention. If they are suspended they stay at home a few days and watch TV, play videos and get high. But if they are, instead, sentenced to in-school suspension or in-school detention, they are required to read, write essays, listen to lectures and learn.

An innovative, creative and perhaps unheard of idea for C.Y.A. and the prisons would be for Maria to demand that Arnold, and Arnold to demand that Rod, and for Rod to instruct Walter Allen and Jeannie Woodford to immediately activate and operationalize programs in the prisons and in C.Y.A. to reduce (by fifty percent) the number of inmates and wards being (suspended) sent to the hole. Jeannie and Walter must demand that these wardens begin to operate from a paradigm (shift) of rehabilitation and not solitary incarceration. Let us explain to wardens and captains that in schools there is expulsion, suspension and then there's detention. Let us be pragmatic enough to know that these fellas drunk and fighting don't have to be (expelled or suspended) sent to ad-seg. Lock them up in their cells and give them a book to read. Not a novel and not fiction. I am willing to bet Arnold that two guys sentenced to in-cell study for a week for a fight and required to read "Mandela" and to do an essay on it, will come out of suspension much better than they would come out of ad-seg with no job, no cell partner and a new cell. And when they refuse to read, study and learn or submit to in-cell suspension, etc., then we take their job and send them to the hole and when they get to ad-seg to their surprise we require them to do something there to prove they're ready to get out of there. Some would suggest that the acronym C.D.C. represents the California Department of Corruptions or the CA Department of Criminals (or even change it to C.D.O. the CA Dept. of Overtime). But I shall remind us, it is the California (or Georgia, or New York or Florida, etc., etc.) Department of Corrections. We must correct the employees in corrections and teach them to correct the inmates in corrections - correctly!

Presently there is little or no correcting taking place. We are locked down over and over behind fights. But before, during and after the fight, stabbing and lockdown, there is no correcting.

I have never seen a warden, captain, lieutenant or sergeant doing any corrective intervention while inmates are on lockdown. They only do investigation. Who started the fight? Was it racial? Was it sexual? Was it gang related? Was it drug related? But the missing ingredient is one abandoned long ago which is, "What can we do to prevent and correct it"? Prison authorities never ask that question. During these lockdowns, which should be rare, we ought to have gang counselors, drug counselors, pastors and counselors going door-to-door selling corrective tactics and skills. Hell, I don't even know why California presently calls their so-called counselors, counselors. I never see them counsel. They simply compute points and sit in committees. They're poorly trained and usually ex-prison guards. This must not be . . . I've literary met some prison guards as well as counselors who cannot even spell the word correction much less define the word correction. And we must bring volunteers into the prisons to teach self-help, motivation and communication skills. If I were Governor, I would follow the advice of Justice Kennedy and utilize my clemency and pardoning power. Very few governors are using it because they don't want Rush Limbaugh to call them soft on crime. But I would terminate the sentences of those who were wrongly convicted! The way to get at the truth and to determine who's innocent and who's guilty is to call on the many retired judges, college law professors, Ruth Jones, Laurie Levinson and assign them cases and ask them to look at the cases and tell me: A. Did he do it? B. Did he get a fair trial? And on the guys who are guilty, we can assemble a team of pastors, counselors, reformed ex-cons and psychologists to interview and analyze them and "tell me what's the chances of this guy re-offending"! And when the unbiased, collective opinion of the professionals is "Governator, he is a monster and should not be let go" we must not let him go. He should go back to his cell and be given intensive therapy until we can get the monster out of the man. And when the verdict is an opinion of an unlikelihood of re-offense, we must set the captive free. Order his release! And we cannot kid ourselves. Let's go in knowing that some of the guys we let out of prison on a clemency agreement will fail and re-offend. And the local media will play up the story! It goes with the territory! But hell, some of (eighty-two percent in California) the guys being released by the courts are re-offending anyway. So don't throw out the baby with the bathwater. I'd stake my life on the belief that if Arnold established a

143

committee on innocence and a committee on rehabilitation to determine who is innocent and who is guilty, but rehabilitated . . . If he released about ten thousand inmates in addition to the one hundred and twenty-five thousand who are already getting out this year, the recidivism rate of the folks Arnold let out would not even be half that of the ones who get out because their sentences are over. No psychologist at U. C. Davis, retired Judge Barry Loncke, Dr. Tyrone Hedblad or Pastor Goudeaux would have recommended that Ed Stokes be set free. But the courts set him free and his van with mattress and ambulance with kiddie porn proves he's a monster. It proves another un-rehabilitated, sadistic sociopath got out of prison to hunt prey.

No transformation of the prisons can be successful without involving the inmates. Kids in school change things when they are empowered with decision-making abilities. Teen, peer and student counselors are always more effective than parental counselors. Inmates know what will help them change. So Rod, Jeannie and their wardens must involve their staff as well as their inmates. Why not get suggestions and recommendations from inmates on their way out of prison. Why not interview the guy being released tomorrow and ask him what can we do to make our prison safe? This will benefit staff as well as inmates.

We must face the ultimate reality that C.D.C. has a racial segregation policy, which perpetuates and exacerbates racism amongst inmates. We must disband, undo and correct this segregation/racism/race baiting immediately. C.D.C. policy of using race as a factor in housing inmates does violate the U.S. Constitution's equal protection clause. C.D.C. hoodwinks the courts by doctoring paperwork to perpetuate a scam and a fraud. They claim (and provide the paperwork to prove it, but I know inmates who can disprove it) they only initially house inmates of the same racial designation together during their first sixty days of incarceration at a new facility. That statement has no basis in fact and is a big lie. Go interview any inmate at Pelican Bay, Corcoran, Savinas, Lancaster, Folsom, etc. on a level four mainline yard and ask them has any staff ever come to them on day sixty-one, seventy-one, or seven hundred and one and asked them would they like to cell with a person of a different racial designation. It ain't going down like that on any yard except D.C. Rod Hickman and Mrs. Woodford can tell any reporter that this does not happen. "After classification, all prisoners share dining, yard, chapel, work and educational facilities without regard to racial designation," stated C.D.C. as it appeared before the Ninth U. S. Circuit of Appeals. That was subterfuge at its best. Yes, we share dining and yard facilities, which makes the celling segregation more preposterous. And they use the fact that we dine together to prove they're not perpetuating racism. We use the fact that we can dine together and go to yard together to prove they do perpetuate racism. It's like separate, but equal. It's like the racist who says he works with Black people. I can work with you, but I wouldn't invite you to dinner at my house. I'm not a racist, but it's just against my rules. Prison authorities in California are not acting in good faith or in any particularized circumstances, nor are they taking into account racial tensions in maintaining security, discipline or good order in prisons and jails. To the contrary, they have a statewide unwritten rule against racial integration and it disrupts, exacerbates and perpetuates racial tension in the prisons. There is no valid, rational connection existing between this unconstitutional regulation and the legitimate governmental interest put forward to justify it. What it does is create racist monsters and give prison authorities more excuses to call states of emergency and access more money into their budgets. It also almost ensures that when the offender is paroled, he'll have racial hatred and go out and commit another crime. And his criminal offenses are job security for the prison guard! And the CCPOA will hold up as a statistical confirmation these inmates re-arrest and use crimes as a bargaining chip to ask for more money. For the subliminal, hypnotizing and subconscious effects of the recidivism, re-arrests and re-offense of parolees takes a heavy, numbing and dumbing toll on voting citizens. The unspoken thought becomes, "So what if the guards beat them up or attack them. They aren't gonna do anything but get out and commit more crimes anyway. Maybe we ought to lock them up forever". But on closer scrutiny, we must realize that the hidden notion that a guard beating up a pedophile or assaulting a bank robber, ain't gonna beat the proclivity to be a pervert or the inclination to be a robber out of an inmate. And we cannot lock dope smokers, addicts, alcoholics or drug dealers up forever! For each time we are reminded of the California $15 billion budget deficit, we must remember C.D.C. gets $5.7 billion every year. We must remember C.D.C. managers cannot account for $1.5 billion missing in action. We must remember prison guards abused overtime to the tune of $250 million last year alone. We must remember the prison guard who earned fifty-nine thousand dollars in base salary pay plus one hundred and twenty-four thousand in overtime pay. He logged nearly three thousand hours of time. And we should remember that a tired prison guard working three thousand hours overtime will go to sleep on the job, make bad decisions, become irritable and perhaps delusional.

We can't let guards handle high-powered weapons and supervise the transportation of inmates while they are tired, sleepy and burned out. Overworked, exhausted and fatigued prison guards are a threat to safety and security of prisons, prisoners and to the public. Let's correct it. Train guards properly and retrain guards comprehensively and pay them well to do their jobs properly and professionally. And limit overtime to eight hundred hours per year, maximum.

We must focus like a laser beam on bringing books into institutions of incarceration generally and bringing books into juvenile facilities especially. We must develop creative and innovative tactics to get our youth involved. In Elk Grove, they were having a racism problem amongst students. This racism was just stuff the kids learned at home from their parents. When the media got involved and Judge Barry Loncke chaired a meeting at the school, two hundred parents showed up and at the second meeting on ninety parents showed up. At the third meeting - no media - no interest; only six parents showed up. Yet, we are always claiming we can't keep the youth's attention! And we claim our young people have a problem with following through! Need I say more? Candidly, the parents should have their butts kicked (not literally) because it is a sin and a shame that we can't get parents to show up for P.T.A. meetings, organizational meetings and functions to help our youth unless . . . unless there is a massacre or the threat of a massacre, we don't show up. Let's begin (again) to commit ourselves to showing up. As Toni Morrison said, "There would be no bullying, tardiness or smoking in the bathroom if momma, daddy, Aunt Jane, Cousin Coster or Uncle Jimmy was at the school monitoring the halls. Parents need to go to these schools, show up and sit down. Sit down in those classrooms and restore order."

I concur and we must intervene into the social fabric of our youth before they are sentenced to juvenile facilities, after they go if they go and after they get out.

We must begin to contribute to the development rather than the delinquency of our minors. We must teach our brothers and sons in schools and in juvenile facilities the difference in a male, a boy and a man. Let us focus on teaching that maleness is determined by nothing more than an anatomical protrusion. The sex organ makes a male a male. And a male is dependent. He waits on momma to feed him, clean him, and stick a nipple or a bottle in his mouth when he cries. And we've got a lot of twenty, thirty and forty-year-old males working and living in prisons. But the transformation from a male to a boy transpires when males add discipline. And when the disciplined boy adds knowledge and consciousness to his boyness, he transmogrifies into a man. (Order "Maleness to Manhood" by Professor Na'im Akbar and play the tape for your sons, students, wards and prisoners).

Now . . . I stated earlier that I'm excited about what Gloria Romero and Jackie Speier are trying to do in C.D.C. and in C.Y.A., but it must not stop there. We can't do it the way Elk Grove parents did it. We can't have a real mass meeting and play into the media hype and then give up as soon as the story dies down. We need some of these legislators who claim Arnold is wrong when he says that they should go part time because they don't have enough to do; to go into the prisons and walk the walk. Quite frankly, I'm certain that if a state senator came to a prison once a week and hung out for eight hours, there would be several positives. Arguably they would perhaps alter some of these negative opinions of prison guards when they see what some of them have to go through. When they go to Pelican Bay and these ad-seg units and have convicts yelling at them, cussing them and attempting to throw urine on them, they might better understand some of the problems officers face. And also they can see how prison guards respond to fights, assaults and drunks. Yet, I believe they could and would also help to implement programs that would prevent, reduce and deal with the violence. But we should really bring legislators in unannounced. I'm not speaking of these guided tours performed by the public information officers in which a select group of bootlicking inmates are allowed to tell visitors how great it is to be an American prisoner. Jim Brulte, Mr. Cox, Goldberg, Wesson, come on in! I'll use Wesson and Goldberg as a segue to again talk about Patrick Schwarzenegger's dad (the Governator) . . . Maria must teach Arnold some of the things that Sergeant Shriver (Maria's loving, altruistic father who believes it is every citizen's duty to engage in public service) taught her. If Sergeant Shriver were running C.Y.A., we'd stop producing monsters. Arnold must stop surrounding himself with Peter Wilson and many of these other folks who worked for Mr. Pete . . . . Arianna Huffington is notorious for holding dinner parties in her home and bringing together people who have disparate opinion and diverse political views to discuss tackling political issues. In that same vein, Arnold ought to bring in Willie Brown (former mayor and also a lawyer) Barry Loncke, retired prosecutors, retired prison guards, ex-cons and pastors and establish a task force on C.Y.A. and a task force on C.D.C. and unlike Gray Davis who established the prestigious Little Hoover Commission to make recommendations on how to clean up C.D.C. But Mr. Davis never followed their recommendations! Dr. Martin Luther King, Jr. said, "There is a paralysis, which comes from

147

too much analysis." We don't really need more analysis; we need action. Power is the ability to take action on what you know. When the cameras no longer flash, the lights go off and the reporters are gone home, we need a program, which will be self-sustaining. I call on every Governor to follow the example, which is gonna be set by the trailblazing leadership (I hope) of Governor Arnold (Terminator) Schwartzenegger! With Arnold, Rod, Jeannie, Gloria, Jackie, the Youth Media Council, Youth NAACP, 3EM, The Fortunes Society and all of us working together, we can transform C.Y.A. from a dungeon of disaster into an oasis of hope and transmogrification . . .

Dr. Felix Dennis called me yesterday and we had a conference call with Larry Flynt, Hugh Heffner, Floyd Abrams, Gerald Uelmen, Robert Guccione and Paul Wright. All eight of us discussed free speech rights, artistic expression and the transformational power of creative writing by prisoners. Mr. Flynt told me, "I had nearly fifty thousand subscribers in California prisons. When I refused C.D.C. Director Alameida's demand for kickbacks, he called in Don Novey and Lance Corcoran. They tried to coerce me because we were making about $2 million off of subscriptions in California prisons. Corcoran told me they owned the prisons! And when I refused to give them hidden kickbacks and bonuses, they outlawed my magazines in prisons. Now they tried to justify it as a security issue. They claimed inmates seeing nudity in magazines inclined them to rape female officers. So they banned frontal nudity, but inmates can still receive anal nudity. Well every man in prison has a butt and so I think they're programming inmates to want butt. And so inmate rapes have skyrocketed since they banned my magazines. They are creating predators, homosexuals and booty bandits. I think it is obvious that whenever you won't pay, bribe and kick back money to the CCPOA, they punish you by not allowing your products into the prisons. And it was me first, it'll be Maxim, Stuff, Details, FHM and Source next. And if we're not careful, sooner or later, it'll be like South Africa was for "Mandela"; they'll ban newspapers and take the televisions. We must fight for free speech and artistic expression in this nation. Now Felix is gonna serialize your book in Maxim, Blender and Stuff. I talked with the folks out at "The New Yorker" magazine and they're doing something. Fairchild Publishing, Details, Ebony and King magazines are all promising to cover your book, 'Creating Predators'."

I responded, "Hey, Flynt, my book is 'Creating Monsters', not predators, although predators usually are monsters. But I want to thank ya'll for helping us to help prisoners. In a real sense, you're also helping yourselves. But let me also encourage all y'all rich publishers to help PLN, FAMM and "The Fortune Society". Now I'm willing to use my tomes as a fundraising mechanism or tool, I should say. Perhaps you all can work it out with Peter to do some direct selling and keep a couple of bucks per book. But I want you all to give a hundred grand to PLN, one to The Fortune Society and one to FAMM. You all can raise it amongst yourselves and that's up to you. But please know that I'm adamant about this. These organizations struggle and they are often marginalized because of a lack of funding. I need you all to give them this money - now."

Mr. Flynt stated, "Sherman, you're sounding a bit like Don Novey, Lance Corcoran and Mr. Alameida. Now don't strong-arm us, son. But, I'll agree to that. What did ya think, Hugh?"

Mr. Heffner stated, "I'm in." And then . . . Two months later we all met up at the Playboy Mansion. Pastors criticized me as a "minister who is wining and dining with pornographers". I replied on Air America by stating, "I love the Lord with all my heart and soul. God is worthy to be praised. He has all power and I love the church and I love pastors. But for those who would criticize me because of my affiliation or association with Mr. Heffner and Mr. Flynt, I will remind you that I begged the church to help me. I applauded Paul and Jan Crouch at T.B.N. and they never even sent me a thank you note. Now I'm not angry with T.B.N., I still love them and I still support them. And since they haven't returned any of my checks, I guess they love me too. But the bottom line is, I tried my best to get preachers to help me. They did not. And so I'll take the devil's money to do God's work and Hugh and Larry ain't the devil. Hugh and Larry ain't committing murders or rapes or extortion. C.D.C. is! But I'm willing to accept a check from Rush Limbaugh and the CCPOA, if they want to help. Sean Hannity? I was on Sean Hannity's show when he was a local radio host in my hometown of Atlanta, Georgia. Rev. Hosea Williams sent me to debate Sean on WIGO, WXLL and on MAOK. The Atlanta Constitution said I defeated Sean hands down. And I think Sean is a bigot. But if Sean Hannity wants to send me a check, I will accept. Sean, Rush and conservatives are also not devils. They are merely people with whom I disagree politically. So for Rush to personalize it and try to attack my character is a low blow. But I won't go there! I know we all know about Rush's recent problems. Let's pray for Rush Limbaugh. And let us continue to raise money and support Howard Dean's organization. Let's support the NAACP. Let us support Morris Dees and his Civil Rights Klan Watch in Alabama. Back in the day, I remember calling Attorney Morris Dees and disguising my voice to sound like Rev. Hosea Williams. Under the guise of being Rev. Williams, I asked Attorney Dees to loan Rev. Manning three hundred dollars. He did it! Now that was a nasty and unethical joke. But the fact that Morris Dees wrote the check shows he is an altruistic, philanthropic and caring man. He's also a brutal, giant and slugger in the courtroom. So guys like Dees, Stephen Bright, the ACLU, etc. deserve our support. And I want us to put our money where our mouth is. Let's support these groups. I met with First Lady Maria Shriver yesterday. I told her how I felt about Arnold refusing to meet with Jesse Jackson and Rubin "Hurricane" Carter when they were in town pleading for clemency for Mr. Cooper. I told her that Arnold disrespected Jesse by not even meeting with him. I also told Maria it was shameful that while in prison, Arnold refused to transfer me to Georgia so I could see my darling grandmother. I had not seen her in nine years. She's my mother. I love Dollie Manning. She won't live forever. And for Arnold not to exonerate me or at least transfer me to Georgia was shameful, hurtful and outrageous. But I also told her of the positive things I see Arnold doing. I pointed out that he placed a Black man over C.D.C. and C.Y.A. He placed an innovative woman over C.D.C. under the Black man. I pointed out how proud I was of little Patrick (Maria's son) for wanting to go into public service. When I mentioned Patrick and Sergeant Shriver, Maria lit up. .

A while later, I met with Roderick Hickman, Walter Allen and Jeannie Woodford. I got them to agree to allow us to teach creative writing, public speaking, conflict resolution, diversity skills and maleness to manhood to all C.D.C. and C.Y.A. inmates and staff. I promised to get Zig Zigler, Tony Robbins and Ms. Covey to donate books, courses and materials. I promised to get Tavis Smiley, Iyanla Vanzant and Na'im Akbar in to speak to staff and inmates. I told Rod we'd videotape the speeches and send them to all thirty-three prisons and ten C.Y.A. programs. I'd get with N.P.R. and PBS and get them to broadcast the tapes. It was actually a fruitful meeting. The next week, I began getting threatening telephone calls from the CCPOA. I had to get the fruits of Islam to guard me. I got the F.O.I to also guard and protect Hickman, Woodford and Gloria Romero because we discovered a contract was out on each of them and we'd heard it had been ordered by the heads of the infamous CCPOA. Retired FBI Agent Jimmy Mattocks is now a private detective and he's promised to do intelligence work for us anytime I'm prepared to come to California. It has become obvious that someone in the CCPOA wants me dead and it's not the guards. Most of them just pay their dues to try to get a good paycheck and benefits for their family. It is Don Novey, Lance Corcoran, Stratton, Martel and Chastain, etc. who want me dead. I called Larry Flynt and told him to get extra security for himself. And I ordered protection for Tom Mesereau, Attorney Navarro, Uelmen, Blane Berk, Tarlow and all of the lawyers in California who were working for me.

One of the scariest nights in my life was in mid-April at 8:16 p.m. when I was leaving a meeting with law professors outside of Sacramento. I was at a gas station on J. Street when Lance Corcoran and Don Novey approached me. Mr. Novey looked me in the eyes with the coldest stare I have ever seen in my lifetime. He said to me, "If you don't stop fighting the CCPOA, you will find yourself in hell. You will end up in a river and it will be ruled a suicide. Manning, you run your mouth too much, but I don't think you have any idea how powerful we are. We have ex-governors, present senators, and people in high places on our payrolls. You cannot defeat us. Now get out of town." I'd like to claim that I punched him or retorted with some sarcastic or courageous remarks, but the truth is, I froze. I froze in my boots. After getting over my terror, I called the police on my cell phone. A police sergeant arrived at the gas station in about ten minutes. When I told him who threatened me, he stated, "Off the record Mr. Manning, Don Novey and Lance Corcoran are two of the most powerful men in California. They can kill you. Please do yourself and me a favor and leave town and leave these two guys alone. Stay out of the CCPOA's business."

I then made one of the most important survival calls of my life. I called minister Louis Farrakhan. "We'll protect you, reverend. I'll have the armed F.O.I members at your hotel within an hour. And tomorrow, Ill send a special protection detail to protect you twenty-four hours per day. Believe it or not, Michael Jackson called me yesterday and indicated that if you needed the F.O.I. he'd foot the bill. Jayson Williams also called. I think the fact that this brother was acquitted of murder, in that accidental shooting out in New Jersey has brought out the humanitarian in him. Jayson said he read your book, which Billy Martin had given him. And Jayson asked me to look into guarding you. Now we won't let anything happen to you. You have my word on that."

I was already feeling better. God has a way of showing up through people whom you least expect to help you; just in the nick of time. In trying times, sometimes you have to walk alone. It gets dark and lonely, but you have to do like David and encourage yourself. When David's own people said they were gonna stone him, the Bible said David encouraged himself.

While I was in Mule Creek Prison most times I felt alone. And the few people that I liked such as Woody (Rayos) or Mikey barely spoke to me. At times, I thought of walking up to Woody and offering him a few hundred bucks to cell with me. But I didn't because although he's an excellent human being; folks in prison are guarded and we're easily offended and if we thought you were disrespecting us, we'd attack. So I basically remained alone and just kept my thoughts to myself. There were people I wanted to help, folks I knew I could help, but I stayed away.

I didn't fit in and I was not "fly" enough. I remember the first time I met Lil Woody Rayos (part pseudonym, but he'll know) I sent to have him come to my door. He was quite hesitant. He'd heard the spurious, scurrilous innuendo. Nevertheless, Woody, Lucas Andrews (a great guy who's out and I heard back in college and doing well) and Mikey were my favorites. I never told them. Especially (part pseudonym) Mikey. I joked with Mikey once that he, not Woody was the shortest guy at Mule Creek. He was, almost. And once he was looking for a handkerchief to buy and I sent him one gratis by Chaua (Ibarra), Mikey barely said "Gracias" and he never liked me again because of the spurious, scurrilous propaganda, innuendo and gossip. This is why I now tell inmates in Y.A. and C.D.C. and prisons in Georgia and New York to be independent! Especially on protective custody yards where you can live/cell with anyone you want to. And if your buddy stops speaking to you merely because of whom you cell with; he ain't a buddy anyhow. Men make up their own minds and do what is best for them. And I'm sick of seeing so-called men in these prisons in New York, Florida, Georgia, Virginia, etc. who allow peer pressure and fitting in with the clique to control, influence and/or dictate their decisions. "Think for yourself," I tell them. Drinking gambling, hanging out, gossiping and horseplaying is not going to get you out of jail. You must balance your recreation with and by mental stimulation and education. I tell them at Alto and Reidsville to turn your jail cell into a classroom. I often think of the fellas I haven't seen in a long time. James Nesmith, Spence Palmer, David Joiner, Scott Johnson, Sam Fuick, John Garvin and Billy York. I wonder did they ever get it together and transform their lives. I think of Lil Man (actual name - Daniel Job) who was only eighteen when I met him in Mule Creek Prison and he got out on Valentine's Day. I often wonder what happened to him. Daniel was the typical example of a boy who should have never, ever come to prison, but needed his ass kicked. He needed a father. He needed a man to show him how to be a man. He was gullible, vulnerable and easily persuaded by the fellas. He was running

152

around from person to person, gang to gang, clique to clique trying to find someone to endorse him. He wanted to fit in. He wanted to be somebody. He didn't need a jail cell; he needed a classroom. He didn't need handcuffs on his wrists; he needed books in his hands. He was a kid. And I remember he always bragged about getting out and getting on "The Fifth Wheel", "Blind Date" or "Elimidate". I found myself (even now) sometimes looking to see if he ever got his dream and got on to "The Fifth Wheel". But the sad fact is there is a strong likelihood that Mr. Job is back in some county jail, waiting to return to prison. He had little family, no job and very few prospects. I had thought of perhaps giving him a grand or two to help him when he got out. But he'd perhaps waste it on drugs. Jeffrey Glenn Howell . . . A great young man went home to Aunt China and Rosie in December of 2003. Perhaps back in prison by now - another C.D.C. failure. Jeff lied on me and to me. But I forgave Jeff and I still would help him if he asked. I even bought a Website for his little brother, Justin Howell, who is presently in C.Y.A. (www.ThePamperedPrisoner.com/CAHowell) and I want to help Justin. It's awful and horrible that we throw away our kids by sending them to sadistic, egregious witching circles called C.Y.A., prisons and jails. And we don't deprogram them after they get out. If we invested in preprogramming them for success, maleness to manhood, etc., we would never have to send them to prison. And for the fellas who are there and are getting out, it is our duty as Americans to deprogram them when they get out!

I flew to New York yesterday and stayed at the Waldorf Astoria. I was met there by Paul Wright and Alex Straus (from Maxim Magazine) and we discussed the fact that (credit Gary Hunter, The Hartford Courant, San Antonio Express News, Christian Science Monitor and Prison Legal News, Dec. 2003) censorship has slithered like an unseen, ubiquitous serpent into the crevices of the First Amendment and built its noxious nest in our nation's jails and prisons. Prisons across this country have singled out writers for persecution as they did me at New Folsom and even at Mule Creek as they also did Mumia. Attorney General Richard Patrick Blumenthal in Connecticut filed a lien against eight female prisoners who collaborated on an anthology, which prisoners at York Correctional Institute the tome, "Couldn't Keep It To Myself: Testimonies From Our Imprisoned Sisters", was initially not intended for publication. Highly acclaimed scribe and author Wally (Ames) Lamb, who teachers a writing workshop at the prison was asked by Harper Collins to allow them to publish it. "Imprisoned Sisters" immediately netted each contributor

153

seventy-five hundred dollars. And now the state is trying to confiscate the money. Lamb, a frequent guest on "Queen Oprah", accuses the state of harboring an insidious motive. He believes that C.D.C. pushed for prosecution against the women because the book is critical of the prison. ". . .They're worried, cause the doors are open now to what's really going on inside these prisons. It's the same fear they had of George Jackson and they killed him. It's the fear they had of Sherman Manning and they still have it of Mumia Abu Jamal," said contributor Robin Cullen. "Voices are coming out from behind the walls. Maybe like Rubin "Hurricane" Carter, David Quindt and President Mandela are putting a green light on the CCPOA, CYA, CDC and prisons right here in Connecticut." She said, "William Bryan Sorens, State Penn prisoner in Texas convicted of rape was scheduled to be released in 2005. Not anymore. Texas prison officials gave him another year in prison simply because he writes articles and gets paid. Officially his infraction is called, 'establishing and/or operating an unauthorized business enterprise within TDCJ', but really it's censorship in disguise. Sorens had an article published in 2001 in Play Boy depicting prison violence entitled "Hardcore Hate". Sorens recently sold an article to Penthouse decrying prison censorship. Peter Bloch of Penthouse Fame was livid. Sorens has a racist writing style and I don't support what he writes, but I told Alex I do support his right to write. We talked about Mumia Abu Jamal's book, "All Things Censored" and how they punished Mumia for writing. He sued and in 2002, the Third Circuit Court of Appeals in Philadelphia held that the ban on business rule was unconstitutional as applied to prisoner writers and enjoined its application.

I told the fellas at the Waldorf that Gary Hunter and Paul Wright could tell you that prison writers threaten institutionalized slavery and censorship. They threaten institutionalized isolation, devastation and dehumanization. I talked about the fact that Gary reminded me and Paul that Jack London, Dr. King, Malcolm X, Henry David Thoreau all penned their lines from behind prison walls. Paul concurred and jokingly interjected, "You talk about me as if I'm not in the room."

I apologized, "Hell, Paul, you just did seventeen years in prison. It's hard to remember you're out!" The telephone to the suite rang and it was Richard Stratton. Richard is a prison violence expert. He publishes "Prison Life" magazine. He and Michelle Zaretsky wanted to come over for dinner . . . After I hung up, Paul reminded me that on January 12, 2004, PLN filed suit in Federal District Court in Jacksonville, Florida against James Crosby, Secretary of Florida

Corrections and also against the warden of Charlotte Correctional Institution. Since February of 2003, the Florida DOC has banned issues of PLN by claiming each issue constitutes a threat to prison security (C.D.C. perhaps colluded with Crosby and ipso facto, banned Maxim and Stuff in April of 2004) based on the ads that PLN carries for discount telephone services, the only thing being threatened by these ads is the monopoly MCI has on the prison telephone system and the kickbacks it pays and rewards wardens and prison directors. Florida DOC gets $19 million in kickbacks from MCI. MCI (according to PLN) is the biggest perpetrator of corporate fraud in American history. The ban on PLN is aimed at protecting MCI and the benefactors of those $19 million kickbacks. And for a year now Florida has punished prison writers who write for PLN. PLN's lawsuit claims that the ban on PLN due to its ad content for a legal service, violates its rights under the First Amendment Right to free speech and the press. The lack of due process in the censorship denies PLN the right of due process of law guaranteed under the Fourteenth Amendment. The practice of punishing writers who submit articles to PLN has a chilling effect and violates its right to free speech and free press as well as constituting a prior restraint on the press. As we listened to Paul, I interjected the fact that when I was in prison just a month or two ago, I told Felix Dennis, Mr. Heffner, Mr. Guccione and Mr. Larry Flynt that, "I need twenty-five grand now for a lawyer. I'll see you the rights to my tome now! Or just loan me twenty-five grand. C.D.C. heard the telephone calls and called me to say, if it's a loan you can have it. If it's payment for your book, we'll confiscate it. I called Flynt, Felix and Guccione back and told them to say it's payment so they can confiscate it and Floyd Abrams and Tom Mesereau have already agreed to sue C.D.C. for me.

Paul then explained that Michael Gendler and Melissa Arias of the Seattle Law Firm, Gendler and Mann and Peter Siegel and Randall Berg of the Florida Justice Institute in Miami represent PLN in the action. Paul looked at Alex and began to talk about how the PLN lawsuit has gotten a lot of media coverage, but the media has focused on the prison phone rate racket and overlooked the free speech claims being contested in the lawsuit itself. Paul told Alex, "We need 'Details', 'Blender', 'Maxim' and 'Stuff' to do stories and deal with the free speech angle." Alex retorted, "As much money as we gave PLN last month, I'll tell you go buy an ad!" With that said, we all laughed. Alex picked up the telephone and called room service, "We need three glasses of champagne in Suite 1500." I reminded Alex that I don't drink alcohol. "I know that and that's why I only ordered three glasses. Two for me and one for Paul. I figured you could drink water."

After my meeting with Paul and Alex, I hustled downstairs for a meeting with Dennis Archer of the ABA, the ACLU chief, the NAACP legal defense fund head, Julie Stuart of FAMM, Barry Scheck, Ben Brafman and Johnnie Cochran. Johnnie, I learned was a no show. He was in the hospital with some kind of an infection. We had a couple of unexpected guests however. Murray Janus, Prosecutor David Hicks, Michael Morchower, retired D.A. Aubrey Davis, Gerry Spence, Alan Dershowitz, Anthony Porter, Rolando Cruz, HBOs Larry David, Tavis Smiley, Doug Banks, WAPZ Radio Host Roberta Franklin, Dan Rather, Marty Tankleff, Jay Salpeter, Mike Race, Ira London, Barry Tarlow, Tom Joyner, Scott Lechner, Carl Douglas and retired Judge Loncke were all in the house. We had CNN, C-SPAN, PBS, ABC, CBS, NBC and the Associated Press. Dominick Dunne and my pal, Jesse Jackson, Jr., the Congressman was here. I was scheduled to give the keynote speech:

"We have got to get our rich, powerful, brilliant and preeminent lawyers to help Barry Scheck set the wrongly convicted free. And we must force a systematic change in the judicial system. On the 13th of last month, a Federal Appellate Court ruled that Sacramento Judge Frank C. Damrell, Jr. was wrong to order a new trial for two men convicted of growing marijuana without a motion from defense lawyers. Judge Damrell tossed out a jury's 2002 guilty verdict and ordered a new trial stating, 'A serious miscarriage of justice has occurred.' The D.A. appealed. 'The district court's logic and sentiment are understandable, especially in light of its evaluation of the evidence . . . Nonetheless, we conclude the language and structure of the rules (governing criminal procedure) preclude Damrell's actions", said the three judges panel of the Ninth U. S. Circuit Court of Appeals. Now if the situation was reversed, etc. and the tables turned, all of you in here knows there are men in prison whom courts have said they're probably innocent, but the appeal only shows a few errors and they were harmless. 'It sickens me that the system will not allow something good to survive,' said Attorney Caro Marks, the Federal Public Defender representing one of the men. "This leaves me really bitter," said Marks. Marks promised that the fight is not over, adding her client Miguel Navallo Viayra 'will be vindicated'. She said, 'He'll get ten years over my dead body.' She vowed in a reference to the mandatory minimum federal sentencing guidelines, which Julie Stewart works so indefatigably to change. In granting a new trial on his own motion, Judge Damrell said, 'circumstances of these two young, virtually penniless, likely illiterate and illegal (immigrants) who were found abandoned in a remote camp in the wilderness with apparently no idea where they were.' His ruling was hailed by defense lawyers as a breakthrough and Marks said, 'The appellate ruling robs district judges of discretion. Judge Damrell is a trial judge. His job is to assess the evidence. If he can't do this, what can he do? Do they just want a conviction machine?'

I call on each of you lawyers here today to support Caro Marks. You know public defenders ain't go no money. And you ought to rally around this judge. It is extremely difficult to find judges willing to make discretionary rulings in favor of the defense to secure even an innocent defender's freedom. So when we find one, let's elassate and celebrate him! You know the CCPOA and politicians on the right will campaign that he's soft on crime and use ploys to try to get rid of him. But we must bring in twenty-four-year-old Eli Pariser, the brilliant campaign director for "Move On". Let's get Al Franken, Michael Moore, Wes Boyd and Joan Blades to help us with a national media blitz. We can get my friends Rishi and Jeff and Cyril out at the Youth Media Council in Oakland to get the youth on board. And let there be no doubt, we need the youth. FAMM, Prison Focus and all of these fledgling organizations, which are operating on shoestring budgets, are marginalized and looked over by the mainstream media; they need the youth. We've got to be pragmatic and exacting. If we get Mike Rafter, Tim Goebbels, Clay Aiken, R. J. Helton, Josh Gracin, Kirk Franklin, R. Kelly and Ricky Martin, they will pull in Zachary Amendt and Vanessa Stumpf out at American River College. And these college students will write about wrongful convictions, unfair sentencing, mandatory minimums, prison corruption, etc. in their school papers. Then we go to the Yale Law Review, Professor Eskridge, Laurie Levinson, etc. We get professor, student, student, professor, youth, activist and eventually the mainstream American.

We can't let hope die in our people. We can't continue to allow innocent men to die in prison for crimes they did not commit. We need money, muscle (lawyers) and the media. I'm calling my friends, Sergey Brin and Larry Page out at Google tonight and asking them for money! Sergey is already paying for a full page ad in the New York Times for my book "Creating Monsters" and I'm gonna tell him and Larry, I need a little more help. My wife Sabine lunches with Edwina Beaus up in the Googleplex and Peter Andrist and I are planning to go biking with Sergey and Larry up in Mountain View in a few weeks. Steve Berkowitz out at Ask Jeeves, Inc. is getting Bill Gates and Jeff Bezos to donate us about fifty thousand used, motivational books so we can get them into our jails, juvenile facilities and prisons project. Mike out at FoodandFamilyLive.com, Gerry Kohring, Ben Hinman out at Perdue University, etc. Are all helping us . . .

I moved on to challenge the ABA, NACDL, etc. to put muscle into fighting prison conditions, stay in the media and to fight wrongful convictions like never before.

This and the previous few pages (beginning with Dr. Felix Dennis calling me) was "Fiction". It was fiction! I cannot receive telephone calls in prison. And it was based on facts, true-to-life, etc. But most of it could not have taken place yet because I am (as of 5/13/04) still trapped in prison for crimes I did not commit. And I must also note that (to my personal knowledge) neither Don Novey or Lance Corcoran is a murderer! That scenario was also "fiction" born out of situational facts. I have taken the liberty to utilize fiction sporadically in this tome, but have always informed the reader (you) when I was exercising that creativity. But FAMM, PLN and all of the above mentioned organizations are real groups and they deserve your support. The lawyers' names, case data, lawsuit data and Caro Mark's comments, etc. were real and authentic.

I guess I'll take this moment to thank Patricia Lee for her typing expertise, patience and her uncanny, ability to decipher my doctor's handwriting and horrible penmanship. (Any professionals interested in working with Patricia Lee ought to look her up in Kissimmee, Florida). I also want to thank my mother/grandmother and the first lady of my life, Dollie Manning a/k/a "Cat". I love her and I miss her so very much. I love my lil sisters, Shanteeka and Shateecia Smith. My biological mother, Brenda Smith, Reggie, Gerald, Norris, Aunt Annette, Aunt Mauderee and my father/grandfather James Scott Manning. James Manning is a great man and I don't think he even knows how solid, stable and instructive he was/is as a father. None of the mistakes I've made and certainly not this wrongful conviction can be blamed on me not having a good man, a great father and a man with the best work ethic I've ever seen in my life. James Manning taught me how to be a man. I respect him. I honor him and "Cat". I miss them so very much. My prayer is that God won't let them leave this earth without me making it back home to see their faces. I rarely cry at all and the few times that I do cry it is usually for my family. I miss them. I also thank Sabine, my stealth supporter. I thank my best Christian friend on the planet, Peter Andrist and his wife Kathryn. I thank Alwyn and Margrit for raising him the way they did. Peter has a spirit, an aura and a peace that just lights up a room. Peter is a brilliant, intelligent and analytical young Swiss man. I also am proud of that person whom I still love dearly. I met her on Broad Street while getting my jewelry cleaned in Richmond, Virginia. She still loves me. No matter what she does or where she goes, she'll never stop loving me. And I love her too. Her name? Boo Ban!

And the late, great Rev. Hosea Williams, former Ambassador and Mayor Andrew Young. I honor them (Andy and Hosea) for teaching me to entertain diverse ideas to balance activism with pragmatic realism. To express myself, believe in me and to courageously challenge discrimination and racism wherever they raise their ugly heads. I thank Michael Jackson's present lawyer, Attorney Tom Mesereau. If Tom had tried my case, I would not be sitting in prison right now. Tom represented me for a period and then my so-called friend Conrad Gamble extorted and exploited the capital set aside to compensate Mr. Mesereau. Nevertheless, Tom still called the CA county jail and utilized his clout to have me removed from a dangerous and volatile situation. Michael Jackson's lawyer probably saved my life! I thank God for Tom and I think with him, Michael is in good hands. I still remember Tom telling me, "I always make a long, methodical, exacting record at preliminary hearings. Cases are sometimes won at the preliminary hearing just on the record." I remember Arsen Serafin recommending Tom to me. Arsen was a unique person. I think Robert Blake made a big mistake by firing Tom. And I also applaud Tom for "giving". Tom Mesereau is perhaps being paid a million dollars right now by Michael Jackson. And Tom deserves it. Not only because he is a brilliant, low-key, meat and potatoes type lawyer, but also because he "cares". Tom does pro bono work when a case moves him or turns his stomach. And I've been tempted on numerous occasions to send Tom my trial transcripts to let him see the injustice I got. But in fact, I sent Tom a gratis copy of "American Dream/A Search For Justice" and C.D.C. stole it. Mr. Goldsmith and the folks in the mailroom at New Folsom stole the book. Nevertheless, if we could get other great men and brilliant lawyers like Stanley Greenberg, Barry Tarlow and Dennis Riordin to do pro bono appeals and work like Tom does; the system would improve. I assure you that with the dogged arguments of Tom Mesereau and the legal brilliance of a Laura Levinson or Professor Chenerinsky; I'd be home in six months!!

I also thank Tom's pastor, Rev. Cecil Murray of the Fame Church in LA. Dr. Murray is a great pastor, leader and businessman.

In 1994, Dr. Murray and Fame sent a check to I-May in Richmond, Virginia at the bequest of Rev. Hosea Williams. Thank

God for Rev. Cecil Murray, John Johnson and Ebony magazine and Earl Graves at Black Enterprise magazine. I'm praying for Michael Jackson (see my book "American Dream/A Search For Justice" 2004 . . . Amazon.com/Barnes & Noble or www.cafeshops.com/Manning). I want him to get justice, whatever that is. And I thank God that Dr. Firpo Carr and Johnnie Cochran, etc are standing with him. I think Michael would be wise to have the trial moved to LA. But he'd be wise to follow the strategy set forth by Tom.

Billy Martin succeeded for Jayson Williams. I am waiting to hear from Billy Martin and Vernon Jordan. "The greatest thing that can happen for a criminal defense lawyer is to walk out of a courtroom with his client after a manslaughter trial," stated Billy Martin after he mounted a successive defense for basketball great Jayson Williams. Maybe now Jayson will use some of his wealth to help some other innocent trapped in prison who could not afford a Billy Martin, Johnnie Cochran or a Gerry Spence. I hope Jayson will bow down on his knees (see "American Dream/A Search For Justice" and I hope, you reading, will e-mail Jayson Williams, Billy Martin and Michael and tell them to help us get this book into the juvenile facilities to save our youth) and thank Almighty God and the Divine Grace of Jesus Christ for allowing him to walk out of that courtroom. He got the victory and to God be all the glory.

I also thank Patricia Kennedy who is now a counselor at New Folsom Prison. If every officer or counselor were like Mrs. Kennedy, we wouldn't have a cesspool of sin; nor would we keep creating monsters. Rod Hickman would be wise to tap Pat Kennedy and promote her to CCII or Captain. She is a caring, bright and an unbiased professional.

I thank Paul Comiskey and all of his legal advice and critiques . . . There is a C.D.C. Lieutenant at Mule Creek who perhaps does not even like me. But she is professional, intelligent and she has great people skills. I shan't divulge her name here, but let's just say that a part of her name involves a car. So I'll call her Lieutenant Ford. It perhaps seems ridiculous for me to praise a lieutenant who found me guilty of an R.V.R. and whom I've only conversed with on three occasions, but that's okay. My desire has never been to find folks who like me or agree with me all the time. My concern is that you can actually dislike or disagree with me and still remain professional. Lieutenant Ford represents C.D.C. well.

I've met a lot of good people in the prisons and I even admire some of them who hate me. When I know you hate me, I can wisely avoid you. It is the duplicitous, deceptive and manipulative staff who specializes in disarming you with their charm; smiling in your face, yet trying to kill you. Those who pretend to like me and secretly wish I was dead; those are the dangerous people. But as I continue to publicize and scrutinize the misconduct, corruption and sadistic ways of some of those working in corrections, law enforcement and in our courts, I must also readily admit that (again) law enforcement is dangerous, tough and scary work. I am reminded of a "Cops" program I watched (I rarely watch Cops!) in which police responded to a call at a liquor store and found two people shot. One (a woman) was seriously injured. The other was a gentleman who they had to put in a body bag. Witnesses said the perpetrator walked in and grabbed the cash register. After he got the cash register, he just opened fire on the man and woman. He just shot and shot and shot.

I felt hurt for the victims and their families and I thought to myself (even though it still could not justify the shooting) that the murderer must have been on crack, speed or PCP. People abusing drugs tend to do some sick and shameful things. Cops went to a commercial break and when they returned they went into a video store (I hope this was the right culprit and not another false arrest) and arrested the murderer. I seethed. This guy was not high. This guy was just low, wicked, cold and cruel. He apparently needed money to rent videos (and perhaps go buy drugs later) and went into a liquor store and committed robbery, assault and took a life. There are some cold-blooded, wicked, evil, sadistic and shameful excuses for human beings in this world. And they need to be arrested, prosecuted to the full extent of the law, convicted, sent to prison and given long prison sentences. That's justice! I do not advocate leniency for murderers, rapists or molesters. Never! What I do advocate is that we become pragmatic on crime and pragmatic on criminals. Make darn sure we arrest the "right guy". Because when we arrest the wrong person, we leave a real killer, rapist or molester on the streets to continue their lawlessness! When we put the wrong guy in prison, chances are very likely that the system as it is will turn him into a monster, a maniac, a killer, a rapist and a pervert. We need a judicial system, which is transparent, unbiased and realistic. Judge Jane Ure (see "American Dream/A Search For Justice") sentenced me for a crime that pragmatically she could and should have dismissed. But even though she did not exercise that judicial power, I like and respect Judge Jane Ure. She didn't know all of the facts to be true; Paul Comiskey didn't know all the facts. Only Michael Sajatovich and myself have ever known . . . I can truly tell you (first time ever and yes, I know prosecutors are reading this book) that I had been threatened by numerous staff persons at New Folsom such as D. Fidel, Captain Schievelbein, Brody, Mayfield, etc. that they were going to transfer me to Corcoran! This was when the gladiator beatings were going on. They were racially charged threats against me because Lt. Trujillo, Sgt. R. N. Saunders, Sgt. Scarcella and C.O. M. Nielson hated me for celling with Mexican and Whites. So flatly they told me I'd be transferred, raped and killed. They had already orchestrated a successful plan, which had thrown me into ad-seg for writing a book. They successfully got Susan Hubbard, Rosario and downtown C.D.C. to order my transfer to Corcoran. The only way to halt, hinder and/or delay a transfer at that time was to secure, obtain a D.A. Referral. And I was off meds, depressed, in fear, stressed and angry that these people were actually going to get me raped or killed. So in a moment of total panic, I sat down and scribbled a senseless missive to Clayton, a county sheriff and a threat to the D.A.'s office in LA. And it worked. I received a D.A. Referral and my transfer to Corcoran, to be raped, stabbed and maybe killed, was cancelled. A few days after I got my D.A. Referral, inmate Sajatovich moved into the cell with me. He informed me that he was scheduled to transfer to Corcoran. I told him about my D.A. Referral. He said, "So if I write a threatening letter to the D.A., it will keep me here?" I replied, "It would be too coincidental if you, all of a sudden, wrote a threat to the D.A. right after you move with me." Michael said, "What if I threaten the Governor? I already spit on that bastard Rosario and that didn't work. What if I threaten Davis?" So that night Michael Sajatovich sat down and wrote a threatening letter to Gray Davis. Michael only wrote it to save his life. Michael was not and is not a violent person. It worked. He received a D.A. Referral and his transfer to Corcoran was stopped.

It is sinful and shameful to have inmates so afraid that they (we) are willing to write out a threat, which we have no way and no intention of carrying out. And in the process our fears mean nothing to them. Yes, I had tried everything to halt the transfer. Nobody did anything, so due to Michael's letter, he's doing more time for a crime of necessity.

Due to me, those letters, Prosecutor Mary Hanlon Stone and John Pezone are still trying to get me seventy-five years to life in prison.

So I thank Judge Ure and I also thank Michael Sajatovich. He never, ever deceived me or sold me out. I'm not selling him out. His case is over and they can't retry him. He did not appeal and pragmatically my truthful, honest and factual words herein won't hurt him. If Jan Scully had a heart, she'd loose Michael and let him go.

162

They say the truth shall set you free. I want to thank the Honorable President Nelson Mandela. If they told me that I would have to give up my right hand (literally) in order to get a ten minute visit from Mr. Mandela, I'd cry, ask God to forgive me and then I'd let them amputate my right hand. Mr. Mandela, Oprah, Iyanla Vanzant, Tony Robbins and a few others have served as unknowing angels of inspiration. I love them. And I really, really wish Mr. Bush (as well as John Kerry) Arnold Schwarzenegger and Rod Hickman would consult with Mr. Mandela and ask him to advise them. It would be hilarious if it was not so sad that Mr. Hickman had proposed to assist this state in overcoming our huge budget deficit by sending a memo to all forty-nine thousand two hundred and forty-seven corrections employees announcing a "Dollar-A-Day" initiative. Rod told employees to find excess clothing, monitor the feeding of inmates (has he forgotten that staff eats the inmate's food at the taxpayers' expense?) and to keep track of handcuffs. Rod's memo stated, "A-Dollar-A-Day is only a beginning to this agency becoming known as the greatest correctional agency on earth." Jeannie one upped Rod with her own memo to cut costs with ideas like, "reducing duplication costs by making fewer copies of documents, turning off lights when not in use and . . . Well, this is where you fill in the blank with your ideas"! Remember that this is the same agency which overspent its $5.7 billion budget by more than $500 million this year - and which has been over budget every year since 1998. Now I respect the Governator (he ain't gonna set me free. His handlers would tell him it was/is political suicide, but . . . I still like him and I believe he means well) and I like Hickman, I know him and I have great praise for Jeannie Woodford. But these ideas are elementary, ludicrous and preposterous.

I want (and I mean this) John Kerry and Arnold to do themselves a favor and call Mr. Mandela. They don't have to publicize it. But ten minutes of his advice on government, on prisons or on national leadership is like ten days being trained in business by Donald Trump. I'll betcha Oprah got some advice from Phil Donahue; especially after Phil retired. I want my country to get better. No matter what Arnold, Bush, Kerry, etc. think of me as a person and no matter how unfair they are to me, I still love America. We have a great country with a great people. Attorney Brian Landsberg, Ruth Jones, Steve Stanzak, Paul Sherrin, Atty. Theodore Boutrous, Zach Liptak, Kate Allen, Alex Cayley, Daniel Peres, Jeff Gordinier, Anthony Swofford and Patrick McCarthy: I love yall!

If I were given face to face with Arnold Schwarzenegger and allowed to make suggestions to him on how to make "Caleefornia" better, I'd tell him this: a real leader (John F. Kennedy, Dr. King, etc.) must often do things which are unpopular or whose effects shall not be seen for years to come. There are successes whose glory lies only in the fact that they are known to the people who win them. Leaders should find consolation in being authentic to their ideals, even if no one else knows about it. Leaders do not shape their policies in response to public opinion polls. Leaders massage and mold public opinion. I'd tell Arnold that Mr. Mandela says, "A leader must . . . tend his garden, he too, plants seeds and then watches, cultivates, and harvests the results. A leader must be a promoter of unity, an honest broker, a peacemaker, etc." I'd tell Arnold, a leader does what it takes to know his people for if you don't know them, you won't understand them. I would tell Mr. Schwarzenegger to always be open to new ideas, disparate opinions and to make fair decisions.

Attorney John Rogers calls himself "the people's lawyer". I want the Terminator to become the "people's governor".

If I were talking to Gerry Spence, Gerry Uelmen, Johnnie Cochran, Floyd Abrams or Willie Gary right this moment . . . Instead of begging them to get me out of prison (I'm not being arrogant, but they could and if they were inclined to they would) or begging for sympathy; I'd tell them that I respect them. I love what they have done for clients across our nation and I'd suggest that each of them read "Long Walk To Freedom" and "Mandela". Mr. Mandela said, "I always know that deep down in every human being, there is mercy and generosity. No one is born hating another person because of . . . color, background or religion. People must learn to hate, as if they can learn to hate, they can be taught to love, for love comes more naturally to the human heart than its opposite. Even in the grimmest times in prison, when my comrades and I were pushed to our limits, I would see a glimmer of humanity in one of the guards, perhaps just for a second, but it was enough to reassure me and keep me going. Man's goodness is a flame that can be hidden, but never extinguished."

Re-read that and read it to every American child. (Dr. Christine McFadden whose husband killed her two sons and then himself . . . Oprah told her that I know America will be praying for you tonight. I just want to tell you I'm praying for you too. Please don't give up. God loves you). Although I have so much more to say in this book and I'm experiencing the fear, the rush, the anxiety and the labor pains every author can relate to, I've got to seal this deal and close this one out. I'll ask each person reading for four things: A. Pray for me. B. Please share this book with friends and troubled teens. C. Write me a letter here in Mule Creek and get involved with helping to correct corrections. D. ??? D. Would be, please read the forthcoming paragraph at least four times. If you forget "Sherman Manning", it's okay, but don't forget this:

Nkosi Sikelel' Iafrika! "I found that I could not . . .enjoy . . . freedom. I was allowed when I knew my people were not free. Freedom is indivisible; the chains on any one of my people were the chains on all of them, the chains on all of my people were the chains on me. A man who takes away another man's freedom is a prisoner of hatred; he is locked behind the bars of prejudice and narrow-mindedness. The oppressed and the oppressor alike are robbed of their humanity". The Honorable Nelson Mandela . . .

The End: June 2004

Editors Note:
A&M requests that each person who has received this tome gratis, please send eighteen dollars (or as much as you'd like) to:

> Sherman D. Manning - J98796
> M.C.S.P.
> A-2-240
> P.O. Box 409099
> Ione, CA 95640

We also strenuously request that readers use the Internet and telephone to be certain that each person mentioned by the author in this book, finds out about this book. www.cafeshops.com/manning. The following pages appeared in the prologue of "American Dream/A Search For Justice".

Prison Update:
In spite of a $15 billion budget deficit, which has been thrown onto the backs of California taxpayers - in spite of the fact that the C.D.C. has squandered hundreds of millions of dollars in the aforementioned overtime pay scandals - in spite of the fact that the C.D.C. has overspent its budget and kept taxpayers in the red every year since 1998, the C.D.C. is building an $800 million prison called Delano II. This prison will cost taxpayers over $100 million per year to run and will require the C.D.C. to hire more than twelve hundred new employees. This prison will house and bed five thousand

prisoners, in spite of the fact that the inmate population in California has declined! Senator Gloria Romero and Attorney Rose Braz indicated, "This appears to have been negotiated by Gray Davis as a thank you note to the CCPOA".

Now it would appear to me that by now there should be a taxpayer revolt. We have young kids dropping out of universities and opting for community college because their tuitions are being raised in an effort to deal with the budget crisis. We have kids now dropping out of community colleges because their tuitions are being raised to offset the budget crisis. We are building no new colleges, schools or libraries even though more kids (than ever) want to go to school. Yet the C.D.C. is exempt and elite or special. We have police departments laying off officers and buying fewer patrol cars. Yet, with a lessening prisoner population, C.D.C. guards got a pay raise and will build a brand new, state of the art monster factory. Citizens should be livid, outraged and shocked. But we are lullabied to sleep by a dazing, hypnotic trance while the CCPOA continues to bankrupt the state. Arnold should demand that all C.D.C. employees earning more than seventy thousand dollars per year accept a ten percent pay cut. Arnold should demand that the plan to build Delano II be halted. Arnold should demand that a finance wizard come in and audit the C.D.C. and reduce its budget by a billion dollars. Pragmatically, it is ludicrous to assume that a prison guard captain (barely out of high school with a so-called Associates Degree in Criminal Justice, which was obtained through a correspondence course) is financially literate enough to control a $100 million budget. Arnold can meticulously inspect the educational credentials of wardens such as Mike Knowles and shall perhaps discover fraud, deceit and a duplicitous past. But Mr. Knowles directs and controls more than $90 million per year. Terry L. Rosario was basically an illiterate, deceptive, brutal prison lieutenant with a racist past who conned and connived his way to the top (C.D.W.) and was allowed to also control nearly $100 million per year in taxpayers' dollars. Terry was untouchable and nicknamed "Teflon Don" because for thirty years, he dodged the knives and shanks of inmates while also dodging the long arm of the law.

Mr. Schwarzenegger must get the taxpayers' money, budgeting and funding out of the hands of prison staff, up from underneath the influence of the CCPOA and totally into the hands of financial planners. We must have people who specialize in handling money, in charge of the C.D.C. budget; not prison administrators.

I will use the budget mess as a segue to talk about my passion, wrongful convictions and how these catastrophes also take money out

166

of the taxpayers' pockets. Ricky Daye spent ten years in Folsom prison and Leonard McSherry spent thirteen years in prison. Daye was convicted of rape . . . Exonerated by D.N.A. He now gets (only) $389,000 of taxpayers' money because some prosecutor, judge and jury convicted an innocent man of a horrible rape. The victim was cheated, the system was unjust, an innocent man had ten years taken from his life, taxpayers paid three hundred and fifty thousand dollars to keep him in prison, fifty grand to prosecute him and now almost four hundred grand to correct the system's error. Dwight Ritter was his lawyer. McSherry got $481,000 for his wrongful conviction of kidnapping and molesting a six-year-old girl. DNA proved he did not do it. It cost taxpayers nearly six hundred thousand dollars to wrongly prosecute and incarcerate this man. He was vilified and scandalized in prison and he was innocent. Now we pay another half million and the person who committed this horrendous and awful crime is still walking the streets. Kevin Greene spent sixteen years in a California prison cell for a crime that was proven he did not commit. He was awarded $620,000 under special compensation, legislation. In New York, Anthony Faison and Charles Shepherd spent fourteen years behind bars for a murder that Mike Race proved they didn't commit. They will split $3.3 million for the fourteen years we took off their lives. They were represented by Ronald L. Kuby and Daniel M. Perez. "The state treats these cases like lawyers for the sleaziest insurance companies treat their cases," said Kuby. Vincent H. Jenkins spent seventeen years in prison for rape (there's a pattern by prosecutors). Attorney Roy Black says, "Rape is the easiest charge to make, the hardest to prove and yet juries send men to prison everyday based on he said, she said." Jenkins was sixty years old when DNA proved him innocent. Taxpayers in New York paid $2 million for this mistake. Ray Krone was put on death row convicted of rape and murder in prison. He spent ten years on death row and he was innocent . . . Gary Gauger was falsely convicted of killing his own mother. Chicago Lawyer Larry Marshall got him out and proved his innocence . . . Robert Miranda spent fourteen years on death row for murder . . . Peter Limone spent thirty-three years on death row and one day a judge tapped his gavel and said in essence, "Oops. Never mind. Our mistake! You're free to go". Peter Limone didn't come home for thirty-three years. A mafia hit man (no - this is not a fiction anecdote in this tome, it is fact. Facts!) turned FBI informant fingered Peter and three other men (see my book "American Dream/A Search For Justice", Joe Salvatti) for the 1965 murder of gangster Edward Deegan, shot six times in an alley in Chelsea, Massachusetts. Peter, who had a minor criminal record, but did not know the informant, surrendered to cops, certain that no jurors would buy the word of a killer! (In my trial, I'll remind you - Russell Shannon Kamosky was flown in by Mary Hanlon Stone. Russell was out of jail, on bail for rape and molestation. Prosecutor Aubrey Davis told Judge Robert Altman, "I wouldn't trust Russell on a stack of Bibles. He should not even be in California. He left Virginia illegally." And Altman still allowed Russell to testify! I was convicted! Post jury interviews stated, "Without Russell's testimony, we could not have convicted Mr. Manning"). But twelve did and the Judge called for the electric chair. In 2000 John Cavicchi, a lawyer for one of those men (the others wrongly convicted) took on Limone's case and uncovered old FBI reports which proved he had not been involved with the murder and that the Feds had known about his wrongful conviction - part of a pattern of corruption among Boston FBI agents. "It was a bad case, just treachery all around," said Cavicchi, who worked for free. On January 5, 2001, a Judge set aside Limone's conviction. He's suing for $375 million. I applaud John Cavicchi, Ron Kuby, Victor Garrows, Jay Salpeter, Edwin Spencer Matthews, Jr., all great, dedicated lawyers, private detectives and soldiers who fight for truth and justice.

I've told Joey Greco (of Cheaters Fame) he ought to get his private investigators to take a case or two pro bono and free some innocent prisoners. "The Practice" is about to end. It is my favorite show in the world. I love the writing of David E. Kelly. He takes his stories right out of the headlines. I've often contemplated writing him. On May 2, 2004, "Eugene Young" was in a confirmation hearing to become a judge. I won't replay the episode, but you ought to call ABC and get it on video. Every judge ought to watch that episode. It is a fact that more than ten thousand men and women (that we know about and have been able to prove) were wrongly convicted right here in America last year alone. And one of the problems is that we have too many ex-prosecutors sitting on the bench as judges. Their entire paradigms are pro prosecution and anti-defendant. More than eight-nine percent of America's judges are ex-prosecutors. Not to mention 92.6 percent of them are White. Most of them would sell their souls for the power they obtained with the robes they wear. And those rushes to judgment, wrongful convictions and expensive prison housing are contributing to the financial crisis right here in America. Oprah is building schools in South Africa. God bless her. But with the way these states are bankrupting our economy by building state of the art prisons and three striking dope smokers in efforts to fill those prisons, we might have to ask Oprah, Gates, Bezos, Soros and Cosby to build us some schools in California!!!

On May 3, 2004 that great woman, First Lady of California, Maria Shriver spoke at a memorial service for one of our American soldiers who lost his life fighting in Iraq. Queen Maria quoted her uncle (one of America's greatest presidents) President John F. Kennedy. She quoted, "Ask not what your country can do for you, but ask what you can do for your country." On this same day, her husband, Arnold met with Palestinian officials. Arnold said, "I'm always willing to meet with anybody if I can learn something or if it is educational. I'll meet with them and listen to them no matter who the group is." Well, I am asking (here and now) for a meeting with the Governor. His office never answers our mail. So I want every reader to call, write and e-mail the State Capitol in Sacramento and tell the Governor I would like to meet with him. I'm not certain why he refused to meet with Mike Farrell, Rubin "Hurricane" Carter and Rev. Jesse Jackson??? But I would like to meet with him. I want to talk about sadistic, wanton, blatant criminal prisoner abuse, wrongful convictions and what can be done to turn around the system. And on a personal note - I would like to tell my Governor that my mother has not seen my face in nine years. She's getting very old. I'm getting scared. Governor: I want to see my mother . . .

* * *

. . . On May 4, 2004 C.D.C. Director Jeannie Woodford and Deputy Director Richard Rimmer were grilled in a senate hearing on the "State of Emergency", which was called in secret and apparently unjustified. When asked what is the protocol on notifying the Senate and Governor when there is a state of emergency, both Mrs. Woodford and Mr. Rimmer appeared lost. "I'm not sure if we are supposed to notify them or not. Ah," stated Director Woodford as she looked to Mr. Rimmer for help. Mr. Rimmer pulled his microphone up close as if he were about to clear this up with a definitive, clear and direct answer. Upon clearing his throat, he stated, "At this time, we do not know the answer to that question."

Critics have stated C.D.C. is in trouble when the two top dogs don't even know whether or not rules require them to tell the Governor when they call an expensive state of emergency. I am trying to look at the upside and thank God that Mrs. Woodford (at least) didn't follow the precedents of her predecessors (Gomez, Tristan and Alameida) and simply lie to the senators. But it is also appalling to note that C.D.C. has already overspent its budget by $300 million this year and we still have six more months remaining in the fiscal year. They are triple

169

bunking inmates (as I stated earlier) and transferring inmates without notice. This is un-American, a threat to safety and potentially explosive. It was a manipulative ploy to access more money, justify the building of Delano II and to try to protect the sweetheart contract Gray Davis promised the mafia (oops - union not mafia?) bosses. I will reiterate (especially since this could be my last tome) to date C.D.C. still won't allow me a single copy of my book "American Dream/A Search For Justice". They manipulate, lie and play games. I appealed and they gave me a decision deadline. After the deadline passed, they sent me a new notice indicating they gave themselves an extension. Those are delaying tactics designed to punish me for daring write about C.D.C. What is next? They could pretend my safety is threatened and transfer me to a SHU program or Pelican Bay, etc. And any missive I try to send to Gloria Romero, the NAACP, media, lawyers etc. usually comes up missing. I encourage my readers to call Mr. Schwarzenegger's office! E-mail him and ask him to check up on me. Find out if I'm in ad-seg and why. Did they transfer me again and why? My request is that you all get involved with saving your states and one of the ways you can create a safe society to ensure the fair treatment, rehabilitation and education of those behind bars who will get out one day. I encourage you to become active. We need Josh Nieto, Garo Bechirian, Zachary Amendt, Vanessa Stumpf and Attorney Bert Fields to ally with Josh A. Kreuitt, Christopher J. Cox, Joan Blades, Wes Boyd and Eli Pariser and rock the media! We've got to get the Dan Rathers, Tavises, Tom Brokaws and Ted Koppers to talk about this mass incarceration and exploitation.

You the reader have got to find (activist) William Upski Wimsatt, Andrew Sorkin Ross, Michael Moore, Ed Schultz and Al Franken and ask them to help you. I assure you that if thousands of you call, write, fax and e-mail AirAmerica radio, ABC, NBC and CBS, they will cover it . . . John Stoll was released after twenty years in prison for fourteen counts of child molestation and his lawyers (unfortunately at publishing time, I don't have the lawyer's names. If you know them, drop me a line and I will put them in a revised edition if C.D.C. allows me) proved he was innocent. Twenty years in prison for a crime he did not commit. My Lord and my God. He probably wrote Davis, Wilson, Deukmejian, Arnold, etc. and nobody wrote back. They rarely read prisoners' mail. But as I stated, Mr. Schwarzenegger agrees to "meet with anybody no matter what group it is, if it is educational or he can learn something". Perhaps the folks out at KSTE Radio (Paul and Phil?) maybe Adam Lietzke or Amanda Griscom will let Mr. Stutzman or Margita Thomson know that I humbly request a meeting. I'd like to talk to the Governator in an unprecedented, educational and learning experience. I'll be courteous, respectful and concise. I would love to make the Bible come alive here in California. I won't call Arnold, King Pharaoh, but I am in Joseph's predicament . . .

Sherman D. Manning
June 2004

Editor's Note: If you are a lawyer, journalist or reporter and know of wrongful convictions, please inform Mr. Manning of those cases . . .

Now read "Rush to Judgment" from "American Dream/A Search For Justice". . .

Rush (to judgment?) Limbaugh

Is Rush Limbaugh really a big fat liar? Is Rush really a drug addict and hypocrite? Does he really know "the way things ought to be"? Perhaps it would be pragmatic to advise you (the reader) to refer to the book by Al Franken in order to form an opinion concerning Mr. Limbaugh. Possibly I should not risk potentially frustrating or alienating some of my core readers by taking any position on the Limbaugh fiasco. A large majority of my advisors have expressed to me, in no uncertain terms, their negative and potent critiques of this talk show mogul. Many people think that Mr. Limbaugh has "talent on loan from the devil"!

Rush was born in Cape Girardeau, Missouri, a mid-western small town. He became a top forty deejay in the mid-1960s and held numerous other jobs prior to discovering his "true" calling as a radio talk show host in Sacramento. In 1980 his radio show went national and it is now heard in more than five hundred and twenty markets across America. Rush is definitely a media celebrity with a strong, sound following. The vast majority of Mr. Limbaugh's listeners are God-fearing, decent, successful and hardworking Americans. Many of his fans and supporters believe (as I do) in the basic idea that the "American Dream" is still a possible dream. They believe that if you give a man a fish, you'll feed him for a day but if you teach him how to fish you'll feed him for a lifetime. Quite frankly, I take issue with anyone who can't find logic, truth and reality in the aforementioned adage. Studying, schooling, hard work and self-reliance are (in my humble opinion) necessary ingredients for success and accomplishment in this great country.

Some of Rush's rhetoric is used as a divisive tool by liberals including civil rights leaders, pastors and politicians. My guess is that Rush uses sensational and (sporadically) explosive monologue as shock factors and attention grabbers. I think Rush is perhaps a brilliant talk show host. It is also obvious that Rush is an avid, omnivorous reader. He prepares well and definitely knows how to stir up a debate. Mr. Limbaugh comes across as insensitive, arrogant, pompous and a "liar, liar, big fat liar" if one does not take the time to really analyze his political positions.

Arguably, there are some people in the world who specialize in *excuse making*. When it comes to failure, they always have an *excuse*. They blame these failures on their skin color, their parents or their poverty. Yet, one cannot dispute the fact that many people have been able to overcome seemingly insurmountable obstacles and climbed over humongous hurdles to succeed and grow rich in America. Many of those minorities who have achieved success in America are profiled in my book, "Dream and Grow Rich".

Some people just don't seem to understand Rush. They allege that he is racist and a bigot. There are some of us who are tired of hearing every failure, in minority America, being blamed on racism and (to me) it is obvious that a portion of the so-called leaders on the left have become wealthy by capitalizing on so-called racism in America. Please understand that Rush admits there is still racism in America. Mr. Limbaugh has made it crystal clear that slavery was wrong. Slavery was a sin; a crime against humanity and Blacks will continue to suffer the after effects of slavery for a long, long time. Slavery was absolutely horrible. A brilliant psychologist by the name of Dr. Na'im Akbar explains many of the psychological effects of this tragedy in his book, "Breaking the Chains of Psychological Slavery".

My opinion is that Rush is not a racist. I believe he has biases as we all do. He may be prejudiced and possibly a classicist. But I'm pretty much convinced that one needs to not worry about Mr. Limbaugh burning a cross on anybody's lawn. I guess what I enjoy most about Rush is that he seems to genuinely believe what he preaches. I think that he thinks he's right and, of course, I concur with Rush on many, many issues. I am ridiculously impressed with the personal success (es) of many of his callers/listeners. Rush has energy, passion and confidence. He's a self-made multi-millionaire. But, Mr. Limbaugh needs to dig a lot deeper, study a lot longer and explore the ideas of scholars who also proved to be brilliant and credible.

The problem I have with Rush is that I think he's sort of a zealot at times and he seemingly refuses to study or entertain any school of thought or pool of knowledge, which does not corroborate his views. I have learned to read books I don't like, study other languages, cultures and philosophies, which doesn't always support or bolster my political paradigms. I have come to understand that sometimes one need not only study the writings, thoughts and ideas of great men, it is also advisable to study the books that scholars studied in order to try to understand the ingredients, which were utilized in order to cause these scholars to think what they thought and know what they know.

In some instances, when I've read the tomes, which writers read, I've ended up questioning some of the positions which they took after having read what they read. "How could she have gotten this out of that?" I've sometimes ended up asking. One needs to go beyond or beneath this surface level of pseudo intellectualism if one desires to gain a solid and well-rounded set of core beliefs.

If a Black kid likes the speeches and oratory of Malcolm X, I have no problem with that. I do have a major problem with anyone deciding that all White people are blue-eyed devils or all republicans/conservatives are racist and bigoted. But an authentic student of Malcolm X needs to do more than read an article or two about Malcolm in some magazine or newspaper. One may be mesmerized when one discovers that Malcolm read the entire dictionary and hand copied it while sitting in a cold jail/prison cell. Malcolm read books about the Jewish people, masonry, legal law, science, politics, and racism. If I wish to know him, I need to know what books he read, etc. in order to more adequately comprehend why he believed as he believed and did the things that he did.

Maybe Mr. Limbaugh ought to read a book or two by Cheikh Anta Diop, Dr. Cornel West or Andrew Young. Maybe he ought to read some of the writings of Langston Hughes, James Baldwin and Marcus Garvey.

It seems only logical (to me) that Phil Jackson should do more than study the Lakers' film footage from their last game. If Mr. Jackson plans to win the prize, it would be advisable or should I say we would expect Mr. Jackson to study film from the opponent's games. Show me what you *eat* and I'll understand why you weigh what you weigh and how your body became the body (size, shape and weight) which it is.

"Has Limbaugh read a single book by a Black author in the past few years?" an activist asked me. Mr. Randall Robinson could elucidate some issues, which Rush discussed from time to time.

Obviously none of us agree on everything and diverse opinions, differing views and beliefs make for a greater America. I started listening to Rush years ago just because it was entertainment to me and I wanted to debate him. I thought I would disagree with him on almost every single issue; I was wrong. I thought he was an airhead and full of hot air; I was incorrect. Rush knows exactly what he's doing (on the radio) and he is one of the best.

So far as drugs are concerned, I think a man must be presumed innocent. Yet Rush need not request this entitlement or right because he admits to being addicted. Being addicted to any kind of drug is sad and terrifying. Since Rush has been so hard on drug addicts, etc. on his show, it's obviously embarrassing and hypocritical for him to abuse drugs. It's quite disturbing to learn he was obviously using a poor maid to buy the drugs. Mr. Limbaugh ought to be ashamed of himself. He lacks discipline and no matter how much some of us may like listening to his show or concur with his belief in

174

self-reliance, we must stand up and announce Rush was wrong, wrong, wrong.

We must not be afraid to debate Mr. Limbaugh on critical issues if we disagree with him. This is America and Rush has an intelligent, intellectual and mostly well-educated audience. None of Mr. Limbaugh's fans are going to hate, fight or kill because someone disagrees. His listeners are above that. So I admit that Rush disappointed me with this drug addiction. This is not some plot or just left wing conspiracy at work here. He is or was addicted to drugs, plain and simple. A drug addict by any other name is still a drug addict. Rush knows "the way things ought to be" so he must take responsibility, get treatment and then he ought to go on a speaking tour to help other drug addicts by telling them his story.

I'm also disappointed with Mr. Limbaugh's lack of accurate information and obvious ill preparation on the subject of multiculturalism. On this issue, it seems that Mr. Limbaugh just does not really get it. Rush says a series of things that seem to be accurate and sensible on the surface. Yet, it appears he needs to dig a bit deeper and study more meticulously some of the issues, which he chooses to elaborate upon. One of the closest associates to me in North America stated, "I find it disturbing to know that you agree with Rush on so many issues. Rush Limbaugh is a narrow-minded, fat, pseudo intellectual. He's racist, classicist and a bigot."

I strenuously disagree with that critique and I respect each person's right to believe whatever he or she wants to believe. I am also cognizant of the fact that Mr. Limbaugh makes it easy for some to dislike him. If I were a poor minority living in the slums and I heard Rush discussing multiculturalism (for example) I'd become disenchanted.

At this juncture, I want to elucidate a few points on which I tend to disagree with Mr. Limbaugh. Rush believes that most advocates and/or spokesmen for multiculturalism are attempting to revise history. In fact, they are simply attempting to correct history. Rush said, "Some kids are being taught the ideas of the American Constitution were really borrowed from the Iroquois Indians and that Africans discovered America by crossing the Atlantic on rafts hundreds of years before Columbus . . . and made all sorts of other scientific discoveries and inventions that were later stolen from them . . . Ancient Greeks and Romans stole all of these ideas from the Egyptians and that the Egyptians were Black Africans."

Anyone who implies that the Ancient Greeks and Romans stole "all" of their ideas (I believe) is incorrect. Yet, there is much empirical and credible data, which clearly proves many ideas were indeed stolen. I will not attempt to utilize this tome to dispute in any expansive manner the details or the facts on which I think Rush is partially incorrect. I will, however, suggest that Rush needs to become more open-minded and to broaden his own mental horizons by studying historical data (which is indisputable) written by and about Cheikh Anta Diop, Dr. Al Mansour, Dr. Cornell West and many others. Quite often it has been my personal experience that we tend to limit ourselves by studying one school of thought and subconsciously deciding that this school is right and everybody else is wrong. If we decide not to even entertain the possibility that one group of scholars or historians could be wrong on a particular point, we limit our own understanding and our potential for growth and development. Rush said that there is a fallacious premise out there that minority children suffer low self-esteem because they don't have any roots. Rush does not think it is necessary to teach Black kids the origins of their history and the facts that many of them are in the lineage of kings and queens. Basically Rush believes that if you want to get a job at IBM or Xerox, you need to acquire the skills necessary to compete and to work in those companies. I agree with the latter but take issue with the former. Any psychologist or specialist in human behavior will tell us that before you learn skills, which are adequate to compete on any level, etc., you must have a basic, fundamental and elemental belief in yourself. You must believe that you are somebody and it is absolutely absurd to assume that kids in school (i.e. minorities) who are taught with history books that never mentions the factual, credible and successful contributions, which have been made by their ancestors . . . will indeed stunt the mental growth of those children. If you study books written by people who don't look like you, with stories about the roots, origins and contributions of everybody except you, it will contribute to low self-esteem. I'm not going to argue the Hippocratic oath and Imhotep or who built the pyramids or who designed the city of our nation's capitol, etc. Yet, I will suggest that no child should have their history robbed or stolen from them.

Rush said, "And if kids have been taught learning these things means compromising themselves and conforming to White values, how on earth can they be expected to succeed?" Mr. Limbaugh goes on to point out that, "If they want to prosper in America, if they want access to opportunity in America, they must be able to assimilate - to become part of the American culture." Quite frankly, on the surface, Rush is making a valid point. Yet, from a psychological aspect, it's deeper than this surface statement. Perhaps Rush actually means well and maybe his intentions are positive. Yet, without an in-depth knowledge of what it means and how it is to be Black in America or Brown or Indian, etc., Rush does not seem to fully appreciate the improbability of properly assimilating into a culture which routinely discriminates against you. To think that one should not place major importance on one's roots, beginnings and history is not sensible. Simplistically, people need to know where they came from and how/why they got where they are. If all they've been taught is their slave history and about the traumas and tragedies of their blackness or brownness and not about the kings and queens in Africa, etc., their ability to assimilate and prosper in a culture will be extremely difficult. If you don't know who you are, you won't know what you're capable of accomplishing. Blacks, Browns and all other minorities definitely need to assimilate into the American culture. Rush is absolutely correct on that. Yet, there must absolutely be an inclusion (not necessarily a revision) to their cultures, contributions and past in that history. Mr. Limbaugh is an extremely intelligent man and I don't believe that Rush is incapable of comprehending the effects of the psychological torture, physical abuse, kidnapping and lynching that Blacks have suffered here in North America. To imply that one should merely "forget it" and move on may be (indeed) the way things ought to be. But it is "not" the way things are. Gumption tells us that the poverty, crime and hopelessness, which is running rampart in epidemic proportions in many Black (Latino and White) ghettos in North America has a cause. What we see in those communities is a direct result of what was done to the people in this country. I agree that they, which know not their history, are destined to repeat it. Yet, they who dwell on their history are also destined to remain stuck. I want Blacks to *get over it*. That is "the way things ought to be". I understand that merely sitting around talking about slavery in a redundant fashion will not pull minorities out of poverty or put food on the table. I also know we must deal with our past in order to understand our present and improve our future. Rush wants us all to strive for self-reliance. So do I! That is "the way things ought to be". We should all fend for ourselves.

I'm not interested in seeing people who are depending on welfare checks forever. I am cognizant of the fact that there are many trapped in our slums that pay more for their red party lights than they do for their white reading lights. They pay more for their liquor and reefer than they do for their books. This must be changed if we are to ever eliminate poverty and failure in this country. I also agree that many Blacks in this country have been able to pull themselves up by their own bootstraps and achieve remarkable success. Yet, one can't pull oneself up by the bootstraps if one has no boots. We must deal with facts and not just dream about "the way things ought to be". When the dream is over, we are still faced with the way things are.

If you hold a man back for four hundred miles of an eight hundred mile run, you can't just decide, oh well, that was then and this is now. "The way things ought to be" is you fend for yourself. You are now allowed to participate (equally) in the race, that's the way it ought to be and we are not going to do you any favors. This is America and we are all equal.

"Sir, may I ask you what do I do to catch up? How am I equal when you've got four hundred laps or four hundred miles on me?"

I know many of us who have moderate and conservative views don't like to hear things like "leveling the playing field". We don't want to give a hand out but what about a hand up? When you methodically kick a man down, should you not be decent enough to help him to get up? Can we totally pretend that racism is over in America? Do we really, really believe that things are equal? Do we believe that there is equality, liberty and justice for all? Since we know that's not true, what must we do about it? Overlook it? Rush and I both know better.

Blacks "will" be able to make it when playing by the same rules. But those rules must be applied equally and where there is bias and prejudice, there is no equality. If there were a rule stating - a man had to weigh at least two hundred pounds in order to play basketball - I would want that rule applied equally. It would not be right to allow one or two White guys who only weighed one hundred and eighty-five pounds to play just because of their skin color. This would be reverse discrimination! But on closer scrutiny, if it were proven that Blacks systematically and strategically stunted the growth and physical development of Whites (i.e. by withholding food, vitamins and nutritionally robbing them) I would have no problem making allowances and modifying the rules for Whites. The entrance rules must be modified in order to let them in. Yet, in order to stay in, those Whites who weighed only one hundred and eighty-five pounds would need to play the game of basketball by the same rules as everybody else in the game. There should and could be no acceptable excuses for not showing up for practice or not staying and learning the variety of plays. The White player should not be allowed to use the fact that food was withheld to justify a turnover or fumble in the game. I believe (adamantly) he should and can play by the same rules. But we must all be given equal access to the throne of opportunity.

178

Many claim to wonder how boatloads of Vietnamese came to this country and have assimilated and accomplished success in America. This is an example of the fact that Blacks can make it in America!

Mr. Limbaugh titled his tome, "The Way Things Ought To Be". Yet in the book, he admits you must deal with things the way they are. Ditto! I want Rush to know that the way things are in this country is not equal, not just and the Vietnamese, how/why and when they came to America is an entirely different thing. It's like mixing apples with oranges. Mr. Limbaugh failed to mention the special (rule modification) tax breaks given to these Vietnamese business upstarts, which is not given to Blacks in America who wish to start businesses.

There are various other things, which have been done and are being done to especially accommodate foreigners who come to America and open new businesses. Blacks are not given these special accommodations. So we don't only need to dwell on the forty acres and a mule, which Blacks were cheated out of. We can focus on the special tax breaks and incentives given (daily) to Vietnamese and Korean entrepreneurs yet withheld from Blacks entering businesses. So then it is quite easy and simplistic to speak comparatively about the accomplishments of various groups who arrived here in America with nothing and point out what Blacks have not achieved. It is quite easy to paint everything with a broad stroke; to speak in nebulous and ambiguous terms or generalities, etc. but one must deal in the reality of how things are! I don't know many people claiming we should "punish the wealthy" and reward the poor. Nor do I hear Reverend Jesse Jackson or others claiming that equality means everybody in America ought to have the exact size house or the exact amount of insurance, etc. Yet, Mr. Limbaugh takes pains to imply that "all liberals" want everybody to have the exact same amount of money, insurance and even food.

Quite frankly, that smacks of pandering and sensationalism. The very bottom line is Rush has a lot of good points and he's a smart guy. But on many issues, Rush is flat wrong. That does not make him a bad guy.

In my humble opinion, it is absolutely wrong to penalize the wealthy and/or punish the rich. It is also appropriate to teach self-help, self-reliance and self-worth to the poor. One of the ways you teach self-worth to anybody is to empower him or her with the detailed specifics of their authentic history.

Mr. Limbaugh also takes pains in his tome, "The Way Things Ought To Be", to explain how our country was founded on faith in

God, the Ten Commandments and the power of the Holy Bible. I concur. Without engaging in any controversies involving denominational or theological diversities, etc., I suggest that Mr. Limbaugh re-read the entire Book of Isaiah in the Bible. He will clearly see that if we, the church, we America or we the people wish to continue prospering and being blessed, it is our Christian duty to feed the hungry, clothe the naked and take care of the least of these our brethren. Then, perhaps, Mr. Limbaugh should consider perusing the 25th Chapter of St. Matthew in our Holy Bible. We must strive to be open-minded and not zealots. It is absolutely ridiculous to engage in fanaticism or to subscribe to an idea whose time has not come merely because a republican has initiated the idea. Likewise, those who support any and everything advocated by liberals are also pragmatically unsound.

One of the dangers of lifting groups or individuals up as heroes or heroines and supporting any and every idea, which comes out of their mouths, is that when and if those superstars fall from grace, our spirits and very often our political beliefs are shattered.

We cannot ignore the fact that Mr. Limbaugh has lambasted drug addicts and even "prescription" drug addicts for years. He's called them immoral, crazy and spoiled. Now we discover that the man with "talent on loan from God" has (for years and years) articulated many of his extreme ideas while high, stimulated an inebriated by drugs. That's not "the way things ought to be". I'm praying for Mr. Limbaugh and I would hope he would pray for himself.

I am also praying for Michael Jackson. Michael Jackson has been charged with molestation, lewd acts on a child and giving alcohol to a minor. He too is presumed innocent. In the eyes of the law, he is absolutely innocent until proven guilty beyond a reasonable doubt. Mike is eccentric. Michael should not be sleeping with children. In my opinion, he needs help. "If" he is a pedophile he needs help and prison, period. Even if he's innocent (which a part of me really believes he's not a pedophile) he needs help. I believe it would do Mr. Jackson well to obtain therapeutic counseling from the likes of Dr. Na'im Akbar and Tony Robbins.

Michael is one of the most brilliant and skilled entertainers the world has ever seen. He is the king of pop and we hate to see his legacy tarnished by the implications of his eccentricities. We cannot legislate eccentricity and I would hope, believe and pray that Michael is found to be innocent of the crimes. Perhaps, maybe and hopefully after Michael is exonerated and vindicated, he will be persuaded to help others who are in similar situations.

Michael said he was mistreated, manhandled and roughed up by Santa Barbara Sheriff's authorities. (Author's note: The Santa Barbara Sheriff has unequivocally denied these accusations). Well, if this is true, I feel sorry for Michael. I want Michael to remember the pain, injustice and trauma he felt and to do something to help somebody else. Michael has always expressed a desire to "heal the world" and I think that is laudable and applaudable. But we must now recognize the fact that prisoners (too) are a part of the world. There are many wrongly convicted, indigent, innocent inmates trapped in the bowels of prisons across this great nation. Guys such as Mr. Limbaugh, Mr. Bryant, P. Diddy, Mr. Jackson, etc. could help these guys with lawyers. I know it sounds like a pipe dream but I still believe in the milk of human kindness.

At some point (why not now?) we must come together (as people) since we are sharing the planet and breathing the same air. We need to feel good about each other and not a single one of us should feel good about an innocent man or woman languishing in a cold jail or prison cell for a crime he or she did not commit.

We should demand law and order. We should be extremely tough on crime and it's time (also) for a pragmatic toughness on crime. We need to rid our streets of rapists, murderers and violent predators. We must protect the safety of the public. Our senior citizens and our children must be safe and secure. We won't accomplish either of those goals by putting the wrong men in jails or letting the wrong guys out of prisons.

Someone should remind Mr. Jackson, Mr. Bryant, Rolando Cruz and Geronimo Pratt that the universe sometimes allows horrible things to happen (to us) so that we will never let it happen to somebody else!

The wealthy, educated and prominent very rarely go to prison and we have empirical data that proves it's not just because rich folk don't commit crimes. Often true crime takes place in corporate suites, not in the streets. But poor folks get poor lawyers and inadequate legal representation. Very, very often they go to prisons for crimes of which they are clearly innocent.

For much of the short time that I've been on the planet, I have thought that all the guys in jails and prisons were violent, vicious predators. Yet, experience has shown me that many in prisons are nonviolent, petty violators who are taking up space and wasting taxpayers' money. We are on the verge of bankrupting our economy by incarcerating petty thieves, weed smokers and bad check writers. America must begin to demand a more pragmatic spending of her tax

181

dollars. With the enormously high rate of recidivism in this country, she must also demand a better return on her investment. To say the system is not working is an understatement.

Brilliant, well-versed and learned men such as Tony Brown are cognizant of these facts. Yet, Tony Brown gets only thirty minutes airtime on Sunday mornings and most of the guys in jails and prisons are watching cartoons at that time. It is inexcusable to not get behind Tony Brown and help him educate the public concerning the sham of a system, which we call crime and punishment here in North America.

The public ought to know that despite empty promises, reform has eluded prisons across America. Let us take California for example: Five years ago, after state prison scandals gripped California with tales of officers conspiring against and setting up prisoners in human cockfights and then shooting them dead, the Department of Corrections vowed to transform its ways. They claimed whistleblowers would be protected, not punished. Internal investigations were to be encouraged to pursue corrupted guards. The correctional officers union no longer would have a hand in dictating policy. This new day never came. C.D.C. remains riddled with allegations that rogue cops still go unpunished, union bosses continue to exercise strong power and the wardens still thwart whistleblowers. It is a sad fact that "corrections" in California need "correcting".

Senator Gloria Romero (D - Los Angeles) who heads the prison oversight committee said, "We intend to start the New Year off with a bang and take a hard look at everything. We have a great opportunity with the new administration to make some real changes." One would expect that a guy such as Rush Limbaugh would be willing to add his voice and influence to the call to clean up C.D.C. Especially since Rush worked in Sacramento for a number of years. Since Rush's hypocrisy is obvious by his admitted addiction to drugs, etc. he could redeem himself by helping expose the evils of C.D.C. The brilliant entertainer, Michael Jackson, who is arguably one of the most philanthropic artists alive, should also join the fight.

Michael said the deputies at Santa Barbara abused him physically. He said they bruised his arm and locked him in a bathroom with human feces all over the walls. If this actually occurred, it is sick, illegal and immoral. If this transpired, then Michael should have no problem believing that inmates, trapped in prisons across America, are set up, beat, abused and attacked on a daily basis in these prisons. Michael has lived an insulated, pampered and upscale life for the past thirty plus years. I am a personal witness that when one lives a life of opulence and has limited or no contact with the police, prisons, etc., it is quite easy to become disconnected by ***those*** people who are trapped in jails and prisons. The atmosphere and subculture inside prison walls is foreign, unique, terror-filled and horrendous. It is quite easy to assume that tales of abuse at the hands of authorities, etc. are spurious and mendacious.

But experience is the best teacher and I would hope Mr. Jackson's abuse at the hands of jail and law enforcement authorities will cause the fire of justice and equality to burn in his belly. I was moved to tears when Michael declared years ago his desire to "heal the world". Prisoners would suggest to Michael that, "we (too) are the world". I would hope Michael is now propelled to help "heal the world" of guys trapped in jails and prisons. Michael is smart enough to know that just as he claims he's innocent and falsely accused of this horrible crime, there are others. These people did/do not have the wealth of Michael Jackson. If one of the most famous citizens in this world can be wrongly accused, who can't be? The authorities "know" that Michael has the money to hire a "dream team" of defense lawyers. They are cognizant of the fact that (to many) he is considered an untouchable celebrity and famous, opulent and influential in every sense of the word. Yet, they charged him! According to Michael, he is innocent.

Donald Trump stated, "Michael is a wonderful person. I believe he is innocent and they're just looking for a ***payday***. People always take advantage of Michael."

It would be fantastic to win the interest of someone as brilliant as Mr. Trump in the fight to correct wrongful convictions and prison corruption in this country. If America is ever to adequately right these wrongs and truly correct the evils of a judicial system which is apparently out of control, we need to bring forth a pragmatic mindset such as that which is utilized by Donald Trump in the business world.

Prisons are big business! Prisons cost an enormous amount of money to run. Entire communities are built off the backs of prisoners. One of the difficulties is that we have wardens who barely read and write overseeing ninety million dollar budgets.

I don't envy the "governator" in California (Schwarzenegger). Arnold has a mess on his hands. He has been catapulted into the midst of a cesspool of sin, shame, torture and corruption. I have confidence that Arnold is basically a good human being who means well and intends to do no harm. But if he is going to clean up the California "department of corruption", he may need to appoint a prison czar. Unfortunately, protests, marches and emotionalism won't correct C.D.C. It needs a catharsis.

As much as I admire Rod Q. Hickman, I must state that I don't think Rod can/will clean up C.D.C. Rod has been in the system for twenty-five years. He certainly knows the system. But is he willing to risk everything including the wrath of the CCPOA by doing what it takes to put the system in check?

I hope that one day soon a Don King, Donald Trump, Jackson, Bryant or P. Diddy Combs will come forward and take an interest in corrections in California.

Michael Jackson fired Frank Dileo years ago in a "power" struggle. Yet, even though Michael *fired* Frank, Frank calls Michael the most giving and altruistic person he knows. "I don't believe Michael would molest a child," Frank said. Frank explains how insulated and isolated superstars like Michael are. He said the staff is afraid to speak out or criticize anything their boss (the superstar) says or does. Ipso facto nobody had the gall to tell Michael, "It's kinda weird to sleep with eleven-year-old boys." To be fair, Michael now claims he would sleep on the floor. I'm not so sure this is true (but I'm not a judge. I was not there).

I do believe Donald Trump, perhaps, has it right. These people are looking for a *payday*. I shall reiterate that it is sick and shameful to molest a child. Child molesters should be (while being treated for their sickness and perversion) put away for a very, very long time. It's unthinkable and unspeakable to harm a child!

It is also unthinkable to falsely accuse a man (Michael or anyone else) of child molestation. Calling Michael "Jacko" and "whacko", etc. is also mean, foolish and unfair. Michael deserves justice!

Mike Tyson did not get justice! Tyson (I'm convinced from reading the actual transcripts and from the writings of brilliant Attorney Alan Dershowitz) was wrongly and falsely convicted of rape. No matter how troubled (mentally speaking) Tyson may be, he was mistreated by the judicial system! Wrong! Wrong! Wrong!

It would appear that superstar Kobe Bryant may be headed in the same direction as Mr. Tyson (more on Kobe in other sections of this tome). We need to clear our minds as Americans. After the media hype has cleared the air and after we negate all of the sensationalism and perhaps yellow journalism, it is extremely difficult to believe Kobe committed rape.

The evidence (says insiders closely familiar with the facts) does not support the charge. Kobe was foolish. Kobe is young, gifted and Black. Kobe should probably have his butt kicked for numerous reasons. I love Kobe's basketball skills. I am a Laker fan! I love the brilliance and wizardry of Phil Jackson. I am also rooting for Mr. Mailman Malone to finally get that ring. Setting aside all fan loyalty, I am livid that Kobe allowed *any* situation to seemingly turn him at odds with his parents. I adamantly oppose that foolishness. I also oppose adultery from a Christian paradigm. I am also critical of the fact that Mr. Bryant, Tim Duncan, Michael Jordan and many, many, other rich sports superstars don't give a damn or a dime for the least of these/those in prisons who are wrongly convicted, poor, busted, broke and disgusted. Shame on them!!

But Kobe probably did *not* commit rape. Something in the milk is not clean. Was/is the sheriff a friend of the alleged victim's family? The alleged victim has a checkered past. She has been a drug abuser? Suicidal? Had semen on her panties, which did not belong to Kobe? Kobe seems to be factually and actually innocent. I've not heard Mr. Limbaugh speaking out against the Kobe prosecution. There is something inconsistent about Mr. Limbaugh believing that he (himself) is supposedly being singled out by a left wing conspiracy and a witch-hunt. Yet, he simultaneously refuses to believe that a Kobe or a Jackson could also be innocent. Rush wants us to believe that although he has admitted to being a drug addict, etc., he did not shop for doctors and pay his housekeeper to buy drugs, etc. Yet, Rush refuses to believe that although Michael admits to sharing his bed with kids, he is innocent of molestation. Likewise, Rush does not believe that Kobe is authentic when he admits to adultery but denies rape.

There appears to be a pattern here. Rush seems to assume that he is the only celebrity who can be a victim of embellished, exaggerated and blown out of proportion criminal accusations.

Rush is blessed to have Roy Black, a brilliant lawyer, as his attorney. I suggest Rush ask Roy how often men are falsely accused of rape.

I'm tired of people who think, "It's only me"! They will lambaste, criticize and ridicule others when others are accused or charged with a crime. They will imply that the judicial system is perfect and never errs. Yet, the moment their (prescription) drug addiction is uncovered or their personal crimes come to light, (all of a sudden) they want the public to believe that the accusations are embellished . . . "Everybody else is guilty! R. Kelly? Guilty! Absolutely no way anyone would fabricate these kinds of allegations against an innocent man. Kobe? Of course, he's guilty and so is Michael Jackson. We ought to lock the three of them away and never allow them to see the light of day. They are predators, thugs, vicious miscreants and they cannot be allowed to play the race card either.

Lock 'em up and throw away the key." That's what Rush would say. It is what many of us say when we have never been charged with or accused of a crime. Yet, what is seriously disturbing is to see a person accused who dares to look straight into a camera and claim, "I'm wrongly accused but they're not." That smacks of elitism and perhaps delusional thinking.

Not a single person who is perusing this tome at this juncture was there with Mr. R. Kelly, Mr. Michael Jackson, Mr. Kobe Bryant or Mr. Michael Tyson (with the exception of the victims or alleged victims who may be reading this). So no one is capable of stating what transpired to a degree of certainty. We may speculate, assume and surmise but whenever we get finished; we just don't know.

We routinely destroy people's lives, careers and families by jumping the gun and spreading journalistic accusations around the world as if they were fact. The old folks say that a lie will travel all over the world before the truth even gets out of the bed in the morning.

The mere thought of sending people to dangerous prisons across this country for crimes of which they are innocent is frightening. As a matter of fact, when one of our kids has one beer too many and accidentally kills somebody and goes to prison; now what? This teenager, kid or youngster will be (and you can believe it does happen everyday) catapulted into one of these cold and violent prisons and once he gets there; life will never, ever be the same for him again.

Imagine what it would be like in prison for smoking or dealing weed and you are housed with violent sexual predators or you find yourself in a small cell with a killer, pervert or lunatic. Society, in general, would have us assume that you'd be okay because prison authorities will ensure your safety and security. You're in good hands. *Good hands*? If Americans still believe that prisons are safe havens, which rehabilitate humans or correct criminal behavior, etc., one would need to ask - what planet have they been living on? One needs to only peruse California newspapers (in a cursory fashion) such as the L.A. Times to discover how wicked, evil, violent and corrupted the California prison system is. (C.D.C. is not an aberration . . . It is indicative of the conditions of prison across the nation including New York's Riker's Island, Lorton, Reidsville in Georgia, Angola, etc., etc.).

In the last year, for example, the California Department of Corrections has reversed its demotions of two sergeants working at Ironwood Prison in Blythe, California. After a lengthy internal probe, C.D.C. initially decided to terminate Jesse Lara and Glenn Barr for tying up a fellow officer, spray painting him with obscenities and displaying photos of the dastardly hazing. Yet, after both admitted to the misconduct, C.D.C. agreed to demote them instead.

Afterwards, in a move that stunned the Internal Affairs Unit, both officers were given back their sergeant stripes and full back pay. According to C.D.C. spokesman, Ruis Heimerich, the decision to restore Barr and Lara nearly fifteen months of their demotions was made by wardens at their respective prisons. "The promotions send the absolute wrong message that even when you do wrong, it doesn't matter in the Department of Corrections. You'll be quickly forgiven," stated Monroe Mabon, council for the Internal Affairs Unit.

C.D.C. flip-flopped on the Orozco killing at the hands of Officer Bruce Brumana. Twenty-three-year-old Orozco was serving nine years for dealing drugs when he was gunned down by C.O. Brumana during a fistfight at Pleasant Valley Prison. A few months latter C.D.C.'s Shooting Review Board ruled the killing unjustified. It was a murder by a correctional cop. "The fight posed no imminent danger or threat to inmates or staff", stated the report. "The fight could have been stopped without a gunshot".

C.D.C. suspended Brumana for ninety days. He was clearly a murderer. In civilian life, had he not been a C.D.C. officer, he would have been charged with murder! But under the color of authority and hiding behind badges of power, officers are often allowed to cut down inmates like a hunter kills rabbits.

This was the first time a Shooting Review Board had ever ruled against a prison guard. Union representatives were livid, but then C.D.C. Director Cal Terhune stood firm assembling an Executive Review Committee that ratified the finding. Supposedly the case was over and Brumana agreed to his punishment before the State Personnel Board.

Attorney Bob Navarro said, "It was signed, sealed and delivered, (Bob was co-counsel for the Orozco family) it went all the way up to the director."

Yet, late last year, Robert Borg, former warden and longtime corrections analyst, took it upon himself to dig back into the well-worn case. Borg read the case files and decided that the shooting was justified. Borg took his findings to C.D.C. Deputy David Tristan. In an amazing unilateral ruling outside C.D.C. policy, Tristan assigned an internal investigator to re-review the shooting. Five months ago, Tristan reversed the finding. Brumana was awarded back pay. Tristan, not surprisingly, is a friend of the union bosses.

Any careful and pragmatic observer has to admit that the "prison guards own the gates" and they control everything that goes on inside those gates and one major difficulty in correcting corrections is the fact that the guards union spend heavily on wining and dining state legislators and politicians. Basically, the guards union has many powerful state politicians in their hip pockets. So when there is a need for oversight, reprimand or termination, politicians turn a blind eye to prison officials' corruption. For example: powerful State Senator Jim Brulte, (R-Rancho Cucamonga), who is the senate republican leader, has been showered with vacations, trips and more than one hundred and fifteen thousand dollars in campaign contributions. Ipso facto, Brulte is trying to persuade the governor to close the state's last five private prisons - nonunion prisons that the guards union views as a jobs threat. "The guards own the gates". The guards union opposes the training, education and counseling programs that keep communities safer by reducing inmates relapse into criminal activity after their release from prison.   Last year, then Governor Gray Davis, who had received $3.4 million from the guards union since 1998, persuaded legislators to shut down four of the state's nine private prisons and cut prison vocational programs. These cuts left more money to raise prison guard's salaries by 37.3 percent over three years, to $73,428 by 2006. That is more than twice the average salary in the next highest paying state. By contrast, the average California teacher's salary is less than fifty-four thousand dollars. The union also undermined oversight by successfully pushing for a large cut in the inspector general's budget. Presently, the union is trying to eliminate college and voc-ed programs statewide. The "governator" must question why the union wants to close all private prisons when the best of them provide drug treatment, counseling and moral education for fifty-five dollars a day - a bargain compared with the eighty-seven dollars a day for only a bed at a minimum security public (union run) prison. Some private prisons provide laboratories for transformation for reforms which public prisons shun.

The ultimate victims of this feudal control of prisons are law-abiding citizens who live and work in the neighborhoods into which prisoners are released, full of hate, anger, devoid of skills and *programmed* to *fail.*

I will not "rush" to judgment but the jury is *not out* (as it is in Limbaugh's situation, R. Kelly, Michael Jackson and Kobe Bryant) on the status of our judicial system nationwide and on the need for corrections in corrections across this country.

Inmates trapped in prisons in Alabama, Texas, Florida and many other states in North America will never be the same again.

The biggest mistake we made in America was to snatch rehabilitation out of the prisons. We would be foolish to coddle prisoners. We don't need to make prisons country clubs or glamorous. Nevertheless, we must do away with the knee-jerk decision to make them rough and tough. Obviously, we have empirical data, which proves conclusively that warehousing inmates does not work. We have empirical data from Reidsville State Prison in Georgia, Pelican Bay in California, Rikers Island in New York and Lorton Penitentiary (to name a few) that locking them down, denying them privileges, incentives, education, etc. does not solve crime, correct behavior or lessen recidivism upon their release. It does not take a rocket scientist, penologist or psychiatrist to know that the prisons as they are - don't work. It's broken and needs to be fixed.

Public outcry, publicity and a taxpayer revolt against prison corruption are a must if we're going to protect safety and security. Small-minded, petty and uneducated thugs out of the woods must no longer be allowed to keep the kept and guard the gates. You can take a man out of the country but you can't take the country out of him is *more* than a cliché.

How can we justify prison guards who rise to the rank of captain, associate warden, chief deputy and warden who can't read, write or spell? It's called the good ole boy (country as it sounds) network. It's called nepotism, bias and prejudice.

Captain Martel, who is at New Folsom State Prison is basically, functionally illiterate. New Folsom Chief Deputy Warden George Stratton reads at a seventh grade level, yet earns ninety-four thousand dollars per year.

At this very moment, I am a living, breathing victim of the combined effects of corruption and retaliation of Mr. Stratton and Mr. Martel. They got rid of me. They coerced Lt. Moreno to lie about a R.V.R. hearing. Lt. Moreno clearly indicated to me, "I'm finding you guilty of this '115' and I'm dismissing the other '115'". He dismissed it. Yet, lo and behold, when I got the paperwork, it stated that I was found guilty of both "115s". Shortly after, Captain Martel took over as the general population captain in New Folsom. He told me that he was going to get rid of me one way or another. Martel pitted an inmate against me - J. G. H. of whom I still have concern for. They manipulated him and at heart he's not a bad guy. They locked me in ad-seg, refused to allow me to call my attorney, withheld all of my incoming and outgoing mail, persuaded Corey McKay to lie to Attorney Comiskey and orchestrated a transfer to Mule Creek Prison. "Oh no, Paul. Sherman is not being transferred."

I'm here! They got me. Mr. Stratton's son works at New Folsom State Prison's A-facility. This young man is described by his co-workers as lazy, arrogant, egotistical and vindictive.

The blood of Gilbert Salazar is on Stratton's hands. Stratton was in the control booth playing dominoes (I've been able to verify) when Salazar was murdered by Frank Christian. Christian had killed a celly before and should have been in single cell status. Since C.D.C. erred, C.D.W. Stratton covered up the murder and coerced New Folsom's investigative unit to rule the homicide as a suicide. The Federal Bureau of Investigations should investigate this cover-up.

My vindictive transfer on December 9, 2003 was clearly retaliation by Captain Martel. He (seriously) claims I'm his enemy. The fact that I mentioned him in a book makes me a threat to him and vice versa. Well, since the C.D.C. director is corrupted and I'm writing it, will they now transfer me out of C.D.C. and send me home to Georgia to finish out my wrongful conviction? I would be glad to go home since I have no family or friends in California. (Any reader interested in true justice is encouraged to contact the F.B.I, the media, politicians, etc. about the Salazar murder/cover-up and/or any other data contained in this tome).

California's prison and parole systems are horrible, miserable and colossal failures that shackle the state with debt and crime, including repeat-offender rates, which are the highest in the nation.

Many prison inmates tell me, "I hate people" and they admit they're on a road to self-destruction. There are more drugs in prisons than there are in most ghettos. Guards smuggle them in and so do visitors. There is a cycle of despair in prison, which feeds violent offenders back into the streets. Experts have warned us that we can't incarcerate ourselves out of crime. Yet, we constantly build more jails and prisons and no schools and colleges.

Ex-inmate, Mike Brady, who was in prison himself three years ago on drug- related offenses, envisioned a treatment centers plan. He prepares the release of fifteen thousand low-risk inmates to centers, which are cost-effective, and reduces addictions. Mike is now deputy secretary of the State of California's Prison Management Agency. Mike knows better than most that success depends not on whether the inmates go to public or private prisons but on whether they end up able to function in society.

Initially, however, California state leaders should utilize some of the $277 million in projected savings from release/transfer to adequately fund treatment. If they fail to do this, the "for profit prisons" will get out of the rehab business and county facilities will end

190

up as glorified drunk tanks, which are respites for crashing a few days after stealing the public's cars and wallets.

Missouri pioneered a no-jargon program called the "Buns Out of Bed" initiative, which requires inmates to participate in school full time, therapy or work. Work is mandatory. Between 1994 and 1999, the amount of Missouri parolees returning to prison on new felony charges dropped from thirty-three percent to twenty percent, the sixth lowest recidivism rate in the nation. California is sixty-nine percent. How could Georgia, California, New York, Alabama or any state argue with these results? Perhaps Mr. Limbaugh will advocate for reform on his radio show?

It is perhaps unthinkable for some to believe that some sworn peace officers are violent, vicious and predatory. Yet, there is an associate warden (Max Lemon) at Folsom State Prison who can attest to the fact that many of them are indeed thugs in uniform.

Max Lemon told KCRA News (in Sacramento) on January 9, 2004, "The cover-up (at Folsom) continues. Chief Deputy Warden Michael Bunnell should not be allowed anywhere near inmates."

On April 8, 2002 there was a riot between Hispanic inmates at Folsom. Captain Pieper had warned Warden Butler not to allow the Hispanics off lockdown. Mr. Pieper stated he feared a riot would break out. Mr. Pieper carried his concerns to C.D.C. Director Alameida and several state senators. No one listened to him and allegedly C.D.W. (Chief Deputy Warden) Bunnell stated to Captain Pieper, "Shut the fu . . up and do as I say. Let them off lockdown." Bunnell and Butler got their wish and as Pieper and A.W. (Associate Warden) Max Lemon had warned; a riot broke out . . . Captain Pieper took the incident so seriously that he shot himself. Yes, (absolutely, not a joke and yes, this book is **non**fiction). Captain Pieper committed suicide. It turns out he even left a suicide note concerning C.D.C. corruption, G. Stratton, Mr. Martel, Billy Mayfield and Director Alameida. He also wrote about Mr. Bunnell. Captain Pieper's widow, Evette Pieper, demands an investigation and wants to know why C.D.C. withheld the missive from her.

Reportedly, Mike Bunnell was fired from Tracy State Prison in 1993 for having personal contacts with inmates. Bunnell allegedly was actually calling "hits" for Hispanic gangs and revealing confidential information to inmates. C.D.C. has telephonic recordings to prove that inmates, while in state prison, were calling Bunnell at home via collect telephone calls. He was apparently involved with perhaps the Mexican mafia. They fired him. Now comes the powerful California prison guards union, which assisted Bunnell in an appeal of his dismissal. They won!! Bunnell was given his job back and moved up the ladder of promotion.

"It is inexcusable that he's still in C.D.C. This creates the image that peace officers are not bound by the same laws as others. No one is above the law," stated Max Lemon.

Ten years and two promotions later, M. Bunnell is (indeed) the Chief Deputy Warden at Folsom and apparently as corrupted as ever. On January 14, 2004 Max Lemon and several other Folsom employees asked the governor and Rod Hickman for protection for their *families*. Max fears that Bunnell may order an attack on his family or himself. One would think that perhaps I'm writing about the mob instead of C.D.C. Yet, this is the California Department of Corrections.

"Lemon will be viewed as some type of plague. Nobody will talk to him anymore. He broke the code. There is nowhere for him (now) in C.D.C.," stated a veteran C.D.C. officer. How strange and unique that a person sworn to "protect and to serve" would feel that Lemon screwed up by blowing the whistle and have no concern about the viciousness, corruption and immorality of the actions of Bunnell.

Captain Pieper was "a punk and went out like a sucker" for killing himself. This statement was made by an inmate? Wrong! An ex-con? Wrong! This foul, vicious statement was made by a C.D.C. staff member. I will repeat (at the risk of tautology) that Associate Warden Max Lemon is presently seeking armed guards to protect him from fellow correctional officers who are also sworn peace officers.

Is it still so difficult to believe tales of abuse, violence, killings, etc., by inmates? If a top administrator at Folsom State Prison is in fear for his life even though he is free, how must an inmate trapped in prison feel? Please understand that officers control every (Remember: The Guards Own the Gates!) moment, action and activity of an inmate. The officers can place an inmate into the hole on a whim and read, withhold, destroy and/or delay his/her mail, etc., deny telephone calls and even lie to lawyers. If they will threaten to kill the family of an associate warden, what will they do to me? I am well cognizant of the fact that Pelican Bay is a place I may visit soon. I've always known there are some who would love to see me in a Shu or full lockdown situation. A counselor recently authorized a chrono (memorandum) stating that I may need to be transferred to a Shu or lockdown program because I filed a grievance!!!

They specialize in doctoring paperwork and utilizing write-ups - C-file data, etc. to portray certain inmates in certain lights. The C-file of President Nelson Mandela, while he was in prison states that

Mr. Mandela was highly manipulative! Ipso facto, when I read in my C-file that I am "highly manipulative" I feel I am in good company. Yet, there are also some statements, writings and claims in my C-file, which are alarming, cruel, spurious and preposterous. However, on any given day, any staff member can document any chrono, which they want to document and place it into the prisoner's file. This data will be utilized at a future time to justify transfers, ad-seg placement, etc., etc.

On any given day, a staff member who is angry with an inmate for filing a grievance or verbally arguing, etc, etc. can pay another inmate to claim "I was raped by inmate so and so" or "I was threatened by inmate so and so". That inmate, so and so, will be placed in the hole. C.D.W. Stratton and Captain Martel did it to me.

I'm just thankful that the inmate did not claim I raped him. I thank God that he didn't stoop low enough to make any sexual allegations. My experiences in dealing with C.O. Ferris, (New Folsom R & R) C.O. Zamudio, Macias, Ed Brody have taught me to never underestimate their wrath, vindictiveness or ability to retaliate. C.O. Mansky (for example) is a consummate control freak. He attempts to intimidate inmates by his build, size and gesticulations. Mansky is hated by most of his own co-workers. He is racist, vindictive and anti-inmate.

Sgt. Elsberry did so. She saw Sgt. R. N. Saunders and Sgt. Scarcella beating an inmate viciously and she reported it. Sgt. Scarcella was fired (but knowing C.D.C. Scarcella will probably be back and promoted to Lieutenant) and Sgt. Saunders is on administrative leave. Scarcella and Saunders both threatened and lied on me back in 1998. When I grieved and appealed, they were both cleared. "Mr. Manning's allegations are unfounded and unsubstantiated," stated the reply. Having read this data and being cognizant of the fact that taxpayers are paying Bunnell (a known crook), paying Max Lemon's (a whistleblower) salary and paying to protect Max and his family from Bunnell, Stratton, Martel, Mansky, G. Wolfe, etc., etc., it becomes crystal clear that "governator/terminator" has his work cut out for him.

I like Arnold and I respect him. He's not a Gray Davis but I pray to God that Arnold will clean up this mess. C.D.C. needs a catharsis. It needs to be cleansed from the director's office all the way down to the ground. Arnold must be firm, he must be fair, pragmatic and he must be courageous. (As an aside, I suggest Arnold get extra security around Maria and his children. And *if* Rod Hickman is really going to clean up C.D.C., he too would be wise to get armed guards for himself and his family). Cleaning up C.D.C. is a job for a tough guy.

I shall remind you that if you have convinced yourself that prisons and prisoners don't affect you, think again. California alone releases one hundred and twenty-five thousand inmates per year. The State's prison and parole cost - $409 million in 1980, bloated to $5.2 billion this year. California's miserable failure is rooted in its erroneous decision, decades ago, to pour money into bricks and mortar and not into the community, prison-based jobs and educational and treatment programs which (in other states) kept inmates from returning to jails and prisons.

A few courageous jail/prison leaders are fighting amidst a culture, which resists inmate rehabilitation. One such leader is Jeannie Woodford, warden of California's oldest penitentiary, San Quentin. Warden Woodford is intent on correcting, not coddling, abusing, pampering or warehousing convicts. She has persuaded volunteers from the community, business groups, motivators, church leaders, etc. to come and tutor her prisoners. She has more volunteers than any prison in California.

Woodford says her goal is to "help inmates change their lives so that we don't create more victims out there. When you ask people whether prisons should have more programs, the knee-jerk reaction is no. But when you explain that the purpose is to hold inmates accountable for their behavior, there's a great deal of support".

This warden should be applauded and emulated. Instead, her efforts are threatened by the prison guards' union.

California has abandoned basic literacy and vocational training as I've pointed out. Even though the Bureau of Prisons reports that inmates who attend school are substantially less likely to re-offend after released. State law requires prisons to provide literacy programs to anyone reading below the ninth grade level. There is widespread condoning of drug sales and abuse in prisons in Texas, California, New York, Florida and many other states. Almost ninety percent of California inmates are incarcerated for substance abuse connected crimes. Yet, less than six percent of inmates in California are in drug treatment programs. Drugs are smuggled in by prison guards and by visitors.

Recently the State Assembly in California began contemplating taking tobacco out of all California prisons. The reasons are supposedly to save taxpayers money on smoking related illnesses.

On the surface, it seems sensible. Pragmatically it is ludicrous. Drugs are illegal on the streets and in prison! Yet, C.D.C. is full of drugs and thousands of inmates have contracted (i.e. The California inmate hepatitis epidemic) diseases from illegal prison drug use. Tattooing is illegal in prison yet cells are full of tattoo guns and inmates get new tattoos every single day of the week. They catch diseases from this illegal tattooing. Taxpayers pay for the treatment of these diseases. How difficult could it be to stop tattooing in prisons? They strip inmates down to the nude on a regular basis. "Inmate Sanchez has no tattoos", an officer could document on December 1, 2003. Well if Sanchez goes to a visit on February 1, 2004 and (all inmates are strip searched before and after visits) he now has a tiger tattooed on his arm, is it safe to assume somebody tattooed him in prison?

But inmates actually share their newly obtained tattoos with staff. Point being? If it's about saving money for taxpayers, we could save hundreds of millions by merely enforcing the rules already in place. Stop the tattooing, alcohol and drugs in prisons and we'd save (arguably) a half billion dollars.

Three California prisons have already eliminated cigarette smoking for inmates. One such prison is the New Folsom State Prison. I just left (as you well know) New Folsom one month ago. Tobacco was outlawed in New Folsom two years ago and I can report to you with integrity and probity that cigarette smoking is still taking place by inmates in New Folsom right now. New Folsom is filled with tobacco! Prison guards smuggle tobacco in to inmates daily and one can of Bugler ($11.40 at Wal-mart) now costs up to two hundred dollars at New Folsom. I have direct, detailed and specific knowledge of numerous tobacco salesmen (inmate salesmen) at New Folsom. I know numerous New Folsom staff members who bring it in to inmates.

I've also watched inmates become assaultive, combative and suicidal when they didn't have the money to buy tobacco.

So the bottom line is that removing the tobacco from New Folsom was a complete failure and created a new avenue for extortion, assaults and violence. Perhaps the CCPOA should fight against the ban because officers are being tempted into committing more crimes by smuggling in tobacco.

Scientific studies have shown nicotine addiction is more powerful than heroin addiction. New Folsom offered *no* assistance to inmates desiring to stop smoking. Not even nicotine patches or gum. So a man who has been smoking twenty years is all of a sudden (supposedly) told, "You can't smoke anymore. No more tobacco!" Yet, he watches an officer walk right up to him blowing cigarette smoke in his face. It is my opinion that this creates a potential threat to staff's safety and security. It's like telling a crack addict, "No more crack for you beginning at 9:00 a.m. tomorrow." Yet at 9:15 a.m., you walk up to the crack addict and wave crack in his face. The guards at New Folsom absolutely refuse to stop smoking. They also refuse to stop smoking in the presence of inmates. Am I crazy or is there something wrong with this strategy? This is a recipe for extortion, violence and rage. It is clear John Burton and Gloria Romero don't know the specifics of the so-called no smoking for prisoners plan. It is obvious that assembly members have been hoodwinked and shammed. Something is wrong! Something is really wrong!

If Mr. Schwarzenegger or Mr. Hickman would like the names of officers bringing in tobacco at New Folsom State Prison, now they can feel free to contact me. However, since experience has taught me that if a captain such as Martel, does not like what I write in a tome, he will transfer me capriciously, etc. Perhaps they'll need to transfer me to another state. I have no objection to going home to Georgia to serve out my illegal and wrongful conviction.

In January of 2004, C.D.C. ordered its agents who investigate wrongdoing in state prisons *not* to disclose information to legislators, the media or the governor's office. They were told to sign a pledge committing to follow the confidentiality rules or face punishment.

This strange directive was issued as Senators Gloria Romero and Jackie Speier were preparing to hold hearings on cover-ups and misconduct within the corrections department. Senators are also investigating a "code of silence" that often protects rogue guards. "I am deeply concerned that the wording . . .could create a chilling affect on employees who seek to report wrongdoing, waste, corruption or illegal activities," stated Mrs. Romero.

It was "in-artfully written and, from my read, violated individuals' civil rights and the whistleblower statute in this state," said Mrs. Speier.

The memorandum was written by Martin Hoshino, Chief of the department's Office of Investigative Services. At least two agents - both of whom spoke on the condition of anonymity for fear of reprisals - said they viewed the policy as an attempt to silence them at a time of intense scrutiny of the department.

"This obviously is an effort to quiet us down and keep us from coming forward. The hearings are coming up and they want to muzzle us," stated an agent. The hearings were prompted by agents who divulged stories about the code of silence among prison guards and pressure by the guards union to stymie investigations of brutality in California prisons and jails.

"The timing suggests that the department is interested in managing information by suppressing it," stated Attorney Steve Fama of the prison law office.

Former New Folsom Prison Guard Robert Flores stated he was fired for refusing to cooperate with a cover-up and the code of silence. "Keys were smuggled into an inmate and I had to do a report on it. Zamudio and Martel changed my reports and when I demanded they be corrected, I was fired," he said.

Former prison guard Sallie Brooks (ex-New Folsom office) states, "I've seen staff commit sexual assault on inmates and fellow staff right on the prison grounds. Staff (to me) is more dangerous than the convicts we were guarding."

One can imagine what would happen to Michael Jackson if he is convicted and sent to the California prison system. Even though my wrongful conviction is bad, I thank God that my conviction does not involve a child. Child molesters are treated as scum of the earth in prison. Staff refuses to believe an inmate can be wrongfully convicted. Michael did well by hiring Carl Douglas and Ben Brafman (two excellent trial lawyers) to join his dream team. I would hope (if he's innocent and the evidence is beginning to look like Michael may indeed be innocent) Carl, Ben and Mark are successful at vindicating his rights. Michael had a *caravan of love* to show up at his arraignment on January 16, 2004 to show support.

As I rode down the highway, exiting the prison at Ione en route to Sacramento, I almost cried. Out of the windows of the sedan, I looked up at the hills. I saw horses and cows. I saw lots of open land. Ione is like the country. My mind went back to those dusty and country roads that I traveled (with my loving grandmother, Dollie Manning, her sister Annette, Lorrie, Terry and Chico) down in the country as a boy preacher. We were going to churches in McDonough, Georgia, Monroe, Winder, Macon and Griffin. I wondered (to myself) what would have happened if I had Ben Brafman, Johnnie Cochran, Carl Douglas or Donald Marks defending me at trial time. "I would not be here." I mumbled to myself.

I thought, "Here I am going to Sacramento Supreme Court to see a woman (Mary Hanlon Stone) who knows I'm innocent. I'm going to watch her lie, fabricate, exaggerate and embellish to try to see to it that I "never, ever" see my family again. I'm not in Russia. I'm not in South Africa but I'm in America. How can this be?" We arrived at Sacramento Court and Hanlon Stone, Deputy D.A. John Pezone and Jan Scully orchestrated a strategic, passionate and sophisticated plan to try to persuade Judge Jane Ure into abolishing the six-year sentence she had given me for the so-called threatening letter, which was supposedly mailed to Mary Hanlon. Mary, John and the entire D.A.'s office demanded a thirty-five years to life sentence in prison for me. I was horrified. So many times, I've watched judges abuse their power and mete out life sentences as if they were giving out water. The enormous pressure, which was on Jane Ure, is unfathomable. I owe Jane Ure an apology. Yes, I believe she should have dismissed the entire case for several reasons and she could have. Yet, in spite of Mary Hanlon Stone's melodramatics and prosecutorial demands, Judge Ure was fair. All any citizen, who is charged with a crime can ask for is fair. Fairness is justice, which is tempered with mercy.

Attorney Comiskey is not an eloquent man but he did his job - finally. "This alleged threatening letter was written after Mr. Manning had been in solitary confinement for more than ten months, Your Honor. Prison authorities had thrown Mr. Manning into ad-seg because they were retaliating against him for writing a book, which named some of them. It was an angry letter by an angry, despondent, wrongly convicted Black man in prison. I urge the court to reinstate the six-year sentence imposed which is more than enough punishment for an idle threat," stated Paul Comiskey.

I cannot repeat all of the vicious statements made by Prosecutor Hanlon Stone and John Pezone demanding a twenty-five or thirty-five year to life sentence. It was horrible.

"I cannot in good conscience send Mr. Manning to prison for twenty-five years to life for a piece of paper," stated Judge Ure. "If a higher court thinks I'm incorrect, they'll have to overturn my sentence. But I think I'm right. Twenty-five years to life would be cruel and unusual under these circumstances. I have the power by law to strike a strike and I am exercising that power within the law and by the law. Mrs. Stone stated in the newspaper today that if I gave Manning six years, he would be getting away with it. I disagree. I must mete out justice. I must follow the law. I've done that to the best of my ability as an officer of the court. I'll sleep well tonight. This court is adjourned," so stated the Honorable Judge Jane Ure.

I unsuccessfully fought my tears. Fortunately, Mr. Comiskey, Pezone and Judge Jane Ure did not notice the tears trickling down my cheeks. Judge Jane Ure is fair, honest, just and the universe will be kind to this woman. I was humbled. All along, I thought she was going to cave in and just go through the motions like many other judges do. "This is a great woman," I thought.

"You should get down on your knees, thank your lucky stars and thank the man upstairs (God)," stated Officer Coleman aka "Juice".

I whispered to Comiskey and inquired, "What newspaper is Mrs. Ure speaking of? Am I in the paper today?"

"Mary Stone planted a vicious article in the Sacramento Bee today to try to sway Judge Ure. It is biased, embellished and one-sided. We should sue reporter Laura MeCoy. MeCoy did not have the decency and ethics to even contact me for comment," he told me.

I shook Paul's hand. "Thank you for a tremendous job. God bless you," was all I could say. "Thank you, Your Honor," I stated as I shuffled out of the courtroom.

Downstairs, I persuaded C.O. Coleman to let me read his newspaper. I read Laura McCoy's story and was amazed and mesmerized. Not one word from our side. Everything written here came from Prosecutor Hanlon Stone. Is this what reporting has come to? Ken Auletta, Helen Thomas and Ed Bradley would call this "biased, one-sided and inadequate" reporting. I decided to send Laura "back story" a book by Mr. Auletta. Mary Hanlon Stone is a *wicked* woman. I am afraid of people like her. If the D.A., who is prosecuting Michael Jackson, is half as vindictive, evil, dishonest and corrupted as Mary Hanlon Stone (as I've heard is true), I fear for Mr. Jackson.

Prior to my contact with Mary, I basically believed that most prosecutors were by the book, honest and fair. But Mary Hanlon Stone proved (to me) conclusively that neither F. Lee Bailey, Johnnie Cochran nor Gerry Spence is lying about the so-called myriad of corrupted prosecutors. Judge Robert Altman proved that judges often lie, cheat and coerce even witnesses into lying or not testifying at all. (Refer to my book, "If It Doesn't Fit, You Must Acquit").

If we could get a federal judge, the F.B.I. or a special prosecutor to take a look at Altman's and Hanlon Stone's actions (on and off the record), I believe Arnold would "terminate" my sentence. And send me back home to Georgia.

It turns out that Attorney Robert T. Burns and Private Investigator Curtis Waite were having secret, in chambers, meetings with Judge Altman. There was judicial misconduct, witness tampering and evidence planting during my trial and it was all done in the name of justice. Believe me, I needed that blessed experience from Judge Jane Ure. It has reminded me that God can still say yes. God can still inspire a Johnnie Cochran, Anthony Brooklier, Barry Scheck, Jimmy Mattocks or even Schwarzenegger to set me free from prison. I don't belong here. I did not commit this crime.

So Jayson Williams' words resonated with this author (me) when he stated, "I'm terrified, horrified and I want to be here with my family," he said this on the possibility of going to prison for a death (of his limousine driver) which Jayson says was "an accident". By the time you're holding this tome in your hands, Jayson's trial will be over. Some would assume that I hope he gets off! Absolutely incorrect. I hope Jayson gets justice! Justice is "innocent" until proven guilty beyond a reasonable doubt to a moral certainty. If this intelligent young man didn't do the crime, he shouldn't do any time and his wish to "come home and hug his wife and children and thank God for everyday with his family", should be granted.

Jayson's wife said, "I have tremendous faith in the will of God." She believes he'll be exonerated. His wife reminds me of Cookie Johnson (Magic Johnson's wife) with her outstanding, unshakeable faith in the divine "creator" of the universe.

I want to tell (write) you as you sit on the airplane, in the car, on the bus, train, on your yacht, boat, in your office or living room reading my words that it is absolutely unconscionable and tremendously painful to live in prison knowing you didn't do the crime. I would not wish a wrongful conviction on even my worst enemy. This prison life can break your spirit, bust your dreams and it has the potential to ruin your entire life.

Quite candidly, I don't think the public has any perception about the mentality (much less the brutality) of the prison subculture. There is an odd, unique and unnatural group mentality which runs rampart in prisons that destroys almost anybody who comes here.

Sigmund Freud explained an aspect of the collective (foolish) mentality of which I'm speaking by stating: "The prison mentality goes directly to extremes; if a suspicion is expressed, it is instantly changed into an incontrovertible certainty. A trace of antipathy is turned into furious hatred".

In prison there are what is called "cars". A car means a clique or group you associate closely with. "I'm in the Bronx car" or "I'm in the San Jose car", etc. One does well to find himself a car to get in so that when one has a problem one can call on the members of one's car to bail one out.

The leaders of these cars often specialize in an elementary (keep in mind that many prisoners are not well-educated) form of psychological warfare or prison "Hitlerism." The big lie. Time after time, I've watched guys who were a bit eccentric or odd and who didn't fit in so the group leaders would invent a "jacket" for him. A "jacket" is a representation or an allegation. An "R" in his "jacket" means he has a rape conviction in his file. Fool is a "Chester" means he has a child molestation charge in his "jacket". So if he's disliked, one can simply claim, Dude is a "Chester" and within hours this unsubstantiated, uncorroborated rumor will be all over the prison. Officers will reply by stating, "I heard that too but don't quote me on it." So the rumormonger has now manipulated the entire mindset of hundreds or even thousands of so-called grown men. We are now isolating ourselves and alienating ourselves from this person because we "heard" he was a child molester. But we can know (for a fact) that he's a fratricidal murderer. We can know he/she emptied a shotgun into the heads of his mother and father. We can know that he laughed as he stood over the bullet-riddled bodies of his own kith and kin. Instead of *isolating* him we end up *celebrating* him.

Dr. Freud went on to state that since a group is in no doubt as to what constitutes truth or error, and it's conscious, moreover, of it's own great power, it's as intolerant as it is obedient to authority. It respects force and can only be slightly influenced by kindness, which it regards merely as a form of weakness. It wants to be ruled and oppressed and to fear its masters.

My inside experience with prison has taught me to treat prison as a snake, a dragon and a monster factory - to never get too comfortable because I'm misplaced, wrongly convicted and this is not my home. I've had to psychoanalyze myself over and over and remain free from the group(s). In prison, the mere fact that a man becomes a part of an organized group or gang, he descends several levels down the ladder of civilization. Isolated, he could/can be a polished, cultivated human being; in a prison crowd/group, he is barbaric, brutal, unthinking - that is, a creature acting by instinct. Neither his left/right brain hemisphere, nor his frontal lobe is of any use to him. He is a raging idiot. A damn fool. He utilizes the spontaneity, the violence, viciousness, the ferocity and also the enthusiasm and heroin of primitive beings. He dwells, lives and operates within the lowered intellectual disability, which individuals experience when their mentality is merged into a group. Most prisoners who are in these cars, cliques or groups are impulsive, changeable and irritable. The impulses that these groups obey may (according to the circumstances) be generous or cruel, courageous or cowardly, yet they are always too imperious that one personal ambition, not even self-preservation, can make itself felt. The masters, the guards, the keepers of the prisoners are like convicts in uniform or prisoners with badges. Most of them (too) are in cars. They promote and demote according to the dictates of the driver or leader of those cars. Ipso facto (i.e.) Lieutenant Jimmy Gaton, Lt. Percy Massey would or could never promote to Captain at New Folsom State Prison because of the bias and perhaps racism of group leader.

201

Revisiting the subject of Folsom State Prison: Last evening - January 17, 2004 - there was a prayer vigil held at Folsom State Prison for the late Captain Doug Pieper. My level of respect for Associate Warden Max Lemon increased twofold as I watched him speak with power, conviction, emotion and with tears rolling down his cheeks. For a time, I had suspected that perhaps some of Max's anger with C.D.C. was suspect. "I know he's not lying about the corruption and cover-ups but still he may be trying to get a promotion or something. Why speak out now?" I had thought. Not anymore. I am fully persuaded and totally convinced that Max Lemon is absolutely authentic, selfless and true to his convictions. He stood there at the podium, braving the cold winds and said, "On January 15, 2002 Doug Pieper called me and said Max, I've been called by the Investigative Services Unit and they want to talk to me about the Folsom riots. Later that day, I got a call from David Tristan telling me Douglas had taken his life. It's deeper than we know and it is a shame that not *one* uniformed officer is here at this vigil. Their absence speaks volumes about how afraid they are to get involved."

They're afraid for their lives and livelihoods. At this vigil: George Stratton? - Absent! Captain Martel, Lt. Baughman, Kimbrell, Lance Corcoran and David Tristan? - All Absent! How could they not show up?

Doug Pieper's son said, "It was not in my Dad's character to commit suicide." Doug's widow, Evette Pieper said, "Everything has not come out yet. It's deeper than we know."

A prison officer (on the condition of anonymity) alleges that maybe Doug was murdered by an angry officer.

It's chilling to think that these guys are responsible for protecting public safety, charged to serve and to protect the public but their co-workers are so afraid of them that they need armed federal agents to guard their families from fellow officers. I say to Arnold Schwarzenegger, Gloria Romero, Jackie Speier, John Burton, etc., etc., it is time! From C.D.C.'s headquarters downtown all the way to Calapatria, we must clean up the department. Starting at the top we must rid C.D.C. of these vindictive, angry, uneducated supervisors such as Mr. Schievelbein, Stratton, Duane Fidel, M. Todd, Martel, Bunnell. They must be fired! If we are to clean up C.D.C., we must bring in new blood.

We need a brand new start. Let's start grading wardens on lessening recidivism. Grade them! "How many inmates got out of Chino or Folsom last year and stayed out?" - is the question. If we adjust warden's paychecks by the success or failure of their inmates, they'd have an incentive to ***correct***.

The senate hearings on the corrections cover-up begin this week. I am tempted to delay finishing this update and "Rush to Judgment" Chapter until the hearings are over but my best friend, Peter and numerous others in the publishing field are absolutely insisting that I finish and finish today. Rest assured that I shall begin another book this month and if all goes well, we can have it in your hands by June of this year. I suggest readers begin to e-mail Amazon.com, Barnes & Nobel, B. Dalton Books and CafePress in May of this year to reserve your copies of the upcoming book.

I must reiterate the fact that ***you the people*** must insist on the governors of these states and our senators clean up these prisons. Almost a million prisoners will get out this year. They will be living in your neighborhoods, shopping in your stores and working (if they're lucky) at your places of employment. The more humane, corrective, sane and rehabilitative their places of incarceration are, the less likely they are to kill, steal, rob, rape and maim when they re-join you in society. Groups such as Critical Resistance in California, CA Prison Focus, FAMM and I-May are making a difference and you should support them. I would hope that Frank Dileo, Donald Trump, Michael Jackson, Rush, Jayson Williams, R. Kelly, P. Diddy and others who have felt the sting and imagined the horrors of an unfair judicial system will join us in the struggle. We all need to pool our resources, give of our money, time and talents to get innocent men out of prison and clean up the corruption in these prisons. I continue to salute, applaud and recognize the tenacious efforts of Barry Scheck, Peter Neufeld and other lawyers who work pro bono on behalf of innocents in prison.

I would hope that sooner rather than later; Ben Brafman, Johnnie, Roy Black, Gerry Spence, Carl Douglas, Dershowitz, Ephraim Margolin, Dennis Riordin and thousands of wealthy and powerful lawyers will step up and help the innocent, indigent and wrongfully convicted who are trapped in the bowels of evil prisons all over America.

Preachers ought to preach about it, teachers ought to teach about it, singers ought to sing about it and mothers ought to pray about those who are here doing the time but did not commit the crime.

I want to make a special appeal here to the former President of the United States of America, The Honorable Jimmy Carter. If President Carter is reading, I need his (your) help. Mr. Carter is my homeboy (he's from Plaines, GA and I'm from Atlanta) and I have the utmost respect for him. I've often stated that the main problem Mr.

Carter had was his honesty. The man embodies the authentic definition of Christianity. Politics today require compromise, dishonesty, saying what people want to hear and having few strong convictions. If President Carter had sold out, he would have been re-elected. My only (if I were a politician, I'd delete this because you're only supposed to say what you think people want to hear) disagreement with Mr. Carter was his asking Uncle Andy (Ambassador Andrew Young) to resign as U.N. Ambassador. I think that was a bad decision!

No former president has worked more vigorously for the poor, homeless and the downtrodden than Mr. Jimmy Carter - i.e. Habitat for Humanity, etc. He's not running for office. He's not trying to lobby on behalf of billion dollar corporations. He's not looking for a photo op. The only explanation for Carter's altruism and struggle for the poor is he "loves those people".

When I think of Harriet Tubman and ask myself why did she continue to risk her life going back and forth to free other slaves? She "loved those people". Honorable Martin Luther King, Jr. sacrificed his life as the Black Moses; he "loved those people". My personal mentor, leader, advisor, hero, the late, great Rev. Dr. Hosea Williams - kept on feeding the hungry, clothing the naked and fighting for justice; Hosea "loved those people". Glory to God.

Jimmy Carter, the man who walked all the way from a peanut factory in a country Georgia town to the White House in D.C. He "loves those people".

I'm asking Mr. Carter for two things:

A. Pray for me. Pray for my justice!

B. Come and visit me so I can tell you what happened to me.

I need to see Jimmy Carter. If he looks me in my eyes and I tell him that I'm innocent; that I did *not commit this crime*, he will feel my integrity and he'll help me to get my freedom.

If Aaron Goodwin in Oakland, California, Lt. Colonel Samuel Harris, Chris Gardner, President Mandela, Bruce Cutler and Anthony Brooklier get behind me, I'll win my exoneration, soon . . .

They claim I'm one of the best public speakers since Dr. Martin Luther King, Jr. and I hope they're correct. Ipso facto, I'm afraid every time I write a book. My books are arguments! Arguments for justice and about injustice. I'm concerned that my arguments, which have proven to be successful when presented in person and received by the eyes and ears of the people, will appear inadequate and amateurish on the written page. When I speak, I don't try to speak as if what I say will be literally transcribed. When one thinks the linear thoughts of a written speech, one which proceeds from left to right as it takes place, word by word, on a page, the magic is lost, and the raw power which drags from the pit of the soul all the elixir of the oratory dries up.

Although this book is filled with empirical data, which has been carefully researched about a variety of "searches for justice". I really wish I could converse with you right now. I want to talk to you. I need to talk to Mr. Jimmy Carter, Jesse Jackson, Rod Hickman and Governor Arnold. I need to talk to Gloria Romero and John Ashcroft. Because regardless of how well the written (i.e. this tome) argument is delivered, it shall never move the listener, it can't transform a person's mind, it can't win and succeed like something born spontaneously from the soul. But (at present) the only tool I have (this argument) for its exposition is the black words printed linearly by machinery on empty white paper. It isn't easy to explain multi-dimensional magic on mere two-dimensional pages. I would, therefore ask you to (as you read this) imagine Dr. Martin Luther King, Jr. preaching this book to you. Use your imaginative ear and hear Martin saying every word in this book to you.

Hear King telling you that they need to let Marcus Dixon out of prison. Marcus Dixon? He was an "A" student in Rome, Georgia on his way to Vanderbilt University. Marcus is Black and he had consensual sex with a White classmate. When her parents discovered she was messing around with a Black boy, she screamed, "He raped me!" (Kobe Bryant??) But a mostly White jury found Marcus "not guilty" of rape. Jurors believed it was definitely consensual sex. No question. But District Attorney Lee Patterson added a charge of aggravated child molestation and implied to the jury that this was a misdemeanor. Lee persuaded the jury to believe by saying, "If you do believe the evidence proved it was consensual and not rape; well, you ought to send a message about sex between minors so let's slap him on the wrist with this minor charge." He told the jury that even if it was consensual; if a minor receives an injury during consensual sex, then that is aggravated child molestation. The *injury* (he convinced them) was the fact that she lost her virginity!! Gerry Spence would not have lost this trial! Willie Gary, M. Gerald Schwartzbach, Roy Black and Ben Brafman would have won the case out right. But in these little rural towns, quite often juries are hoodwinked and the public defenders are poorly trained and ill prepared. Marcus received a ten-year prison term! Marcus was adopted as a kid by White parents. His adoptive dad (Ken Jones) stated, "When he told me he had sex with a White girl

- I just sat down and cried like a baby. Cause (sic) I know what they was going to do to him."

Juror K. Tippet told Dan Rather, "We were sure he was going to go home that day. We were deceived by the prosecutor. Marcus needs to come home."

Think of it, en route to Vanderbilt University an "A" student. Has consensual sex and now he sits in prison serving ten years. Prosecutors deceive jurors everyday of the week. "Prosecutors are not concerned about *justice*. They are concerned about *winning*," said Gerry Spence. Remember, Mr. Spence himself was once a prosecutor.

"Their need for a conviction helps them to look innocence straight in the face and pretend not to see it," stated F. Lee Bailey.

Peter lost the argument! I'm still writing. Still trying to transform my verbal argument into a written argument. Max Lemon testified yesterday before Gloria Romero. Max had tears in his eyes.

"There is corruption and cover-ups at the highest levels of C.D.C.," Associate Warden Lemon testified. "There is a 'code of silence' among C.D.C. employees. I've had to have twenty-four hour protection from the state police since I began speaking out." This testimony was powerful and gut wrenching.

Sgt. Sam Cox testified that he had been ordered to go into the media room and dub out all the audio from the videotape of the Folsom riot so Bunnell couldn't be heard giving orders to let the riot proceed. Mr. Cox refused and has been demoted twice. Bunnell was scheduled to testify but refused to show up.

An audit has shown that C.D.C. overspent its budget by $1.4 billion in the last three years. Much of the money is unaccounted for. Rod Hickman testified and to his credit he admitted that there are problems in C.D.C. - "I'm working aggressively to rectify those problems," he said. I don't envy him and if Rod is really, really going to clean up C.D.C., I encourage (and I'm not being melodramatic) him to get twenty-four hour personal protection. If the CCPOA can run Senator Richard Polanco out of town, if they can threaten the higher ups to keep Associate Warden Chastain on the job (without a demotion) after he was accused of sexual misconduct, if they got Bunnell's job back . . . what can they do to the first Black corrections chief if he does not tap dance? Rod, if you're reading - get protection.

I don't understand the lack of public outcry and outrage. California is flat broke! When it is proven that C.D.C. has squandered a billion and a half dollars yet they want to cut cigarette smoking in the prisons to save taxpayers a few million dollars, the public should rise up.

I demand that preachers get the heck out of the pulpit and get involved. We all sing the praises of Martin Luther King, Jr. but we don't want to work as he worked.

One (I'm digressing but it's the preacher in me so y'all stay with me) Easter Sunday, Dr. King's dad (Daddy King) was calling Birmingham and urging King, Jr. to come back to Atlanta. He needed to be at Ebenezer for the most important Sunday service (Easter Sunday) of the year. King told his staff, "I've got to go and pray about it." He returned to the room in blue jeans instead of a suit. It was obvious King was bypassing anthems, flowers and ceremonies and would not be in church that Easter Sunday. "I'm going to jail," he told his staff. King continued, "Unmerited suffering is always redemptive." He chose to walk right into the teeth of suffering. The media eviscerates Dr. King's platform. Joe Lowery tells us how . . . "Now that he's safely dead, let us praise him. Because dead men cannot rise up and challenge the images we fashion of them, let us make a monument. It is easier to build a monument than it is to build a movement."

The media's favorite line is "I have a dream". But what of the other parts of that speech? America has written poor people a check or promissory note and the check has come back stamped insufficient funds. But I refuse to believe that the bank of justice is bankrupt. Let us hear that part of the "I have a dream" speech. God has not chosen America to be a messianic messenger or a world police. God has a way of rising up and saying, don't play with me; America you're too arrogant. But I will rise up and break the very backbone of your power and nation. I will put a nation in charge that doesn't even know my name. God will tell America to be still and know I'm God."

John Ashcroft and Mr. Rumsfeld ought to listen to that entire speech. Shortly before King was cut down, he said, "Let me be clear. Integrating lunch counters did not cost America one penny. Giving Black people the right to vote did not cost America one penny. But now America needs to spend billions of dollars and undergo a radical redistribution of wealth and power." I've never seen that speech on ABC, CBS or NBC. Contractor Peter Gaeth, mailroom clerk David Dasky and J. Ashcroft probably never heard it either.

In lieu of all of these wrongful convictions, prison brutality and corruption within the judiciary *somebody* (Eddie Long, Jesse Jackson, T. D. Jakes, Billy Graham?) must rise up and take a stand even if it is an unpopular stand. When Martin spoke out and fought against the war in Vietnam, he was criticized by even his own supporters. "Other preachers, leaders and politicians can choose not to speak out. They may feel, for various reasons that they can't speak out. That's their business! But I must say today that justice is indivisible. Injustice anywhere is a threat to justice everywhere," King said.

Yes, they fought him. During some of his marches, the police and politicians orchestrated planned disruptions. They paid youngsters to disrupt the march to try to make it appear that King's nonviolent methods was not working. Then that good ole boy Senator Robert Byrd asked the public to look at Dr. King in a different light and to not follow him. Police officer cover-ups, corruption and the orchestration of trumped up charges, etc. has been going on forever.

The only time and the only way it can change is when we rise up and fight corruption. The senate hearings on C.D.C. corruption are still going on but what will happen when they end? This is not the first time C.D.C. has been in the media for their corruption, setups and brutality. But what happened the last time? There was great focus for a few weeks, heads rolled, butt was kicked but as Judge Steve White testified before the senate, "In ninety days C.D.C. will be back to normal. The higher ups will continue to obstruct justice and prison guard brutality will march on." Judge White was the inspector general of C.D.C. so he ought to know. He just became a judge (Superior Court) recently. I'm trying (desperately not to be redundant but I've got to repeat (re-write?) that Max Lemon - an associate warden in command at Folsom State Prison, has had to obtain twenty-four hour protection for his family. He's being guarded by the state police at home! He walks amongst convicted murderers and rapists all day long in prison. But he's unsafe (he feels) in the quiet comforts of his own home. When we come to a place where a warden is more afraid of sworn peace officers than he is of convicted killers, the prisons are out of control. This tome is not all about *me*, but I'm gonna reiterate to Jimmy Carter, Chris Gardner, M. L. King, III, Jesse, Sharpton, Dershowitz and Cochran: I need y'all to come get me out of here.

I am misplaced! I don't belong in prison. If you can't exonerate me rapidly, at least (Mr. Carter) call Rod Q. Hickman and Mr. Schwarzenegger and ask them to send me to Georgia's prison system, while we fight this wrongful conviction. It is inhumane, cruel and unusual to keep my mother, grandmother and entire family from seeing me. I have nobody in California - no family and no friends in California at all. Get me out! Please get me home! There are many Rolando Cruzes, Hurricane Carters and Anthony Porters trapped right here.

If Dr. Goudeaux, Charles Blake, Eddie Long and T. D. Jakes were to organize, galvanize and mobilize their congregations, if they committed money toward cleaning up corruption (corrections?) and weeding/seeding the wrongly convicted in prisons, what would happen?

What would happen if they engaged in sustained, organized and publicized efforts on behalf of the least of these? Need I remind you that it's awfully dark and lonely in these prisons? It is a horrible and awful place to be. Especially if you're innocent. We need help. We need to transform these dungeons of despair into havens of hope. We must immediately begin to restore rehabilitations into these prisons. Otherwise, we can't complain about the *monsters* we keep creating. We will either clean up the prisons, save the people together or we will continue to witness the destruction and annihilation of the community at large! Those one hundred and twenty-five thousand California inmates who will get out of prison in California *are coming to get you*! Those seven hundred thousand prisoners leaving prisons (in Georgia, Alabama, Mississippi, New York, Illinois, etc.) this year are coming to your neighborhood!

They will work, reside, deal (drugs), kill, stab, rape and molest right where you are. You cannot keep them in prison forever. With George Bush, John Ashcroft and Rumsfeld in office, we are locking up more and more crack addicts and dope dealers than ever before. Where will we house them? What will we do with them when their time is served?

I hope governors, senators and our congress will overhaul the system at once. We cannot incarcerate ourselves out of poverty! We cannot arrest our way out of crime. Now is the time for pragmatic action. We must fight for real change. We need to fight poverty just as we fight crime. We must fight hunger, homelessness and illiteracy in North America. If we put in one-tenth of the money we put into ousting Saddam Hussein, we will win. Money is power. "The only thing the power structure understands and responds to is money! White folks will listen to you if you bring them some money!" Rev. Hosea Williams stated to me in late 1994.

Money is power! There are many inequities, etc. There is tremendous poverty in the urban cities but there is also wealth. If ten churches combined their wealth, we're talking hundreds of millions of dollars. Everybody wants to call Oprah. Hell, Oprah can't save the world. She is one person (only) and she can't support everybody. Often times, we just want a "hand-out" not a "hand-up". But if we would take the time to come up with real pragmatic plans that we can show Oprah, Donald Trump, Don King, Bill Gates, Warren Buffett or Chris Gardner, then they would help us.

We can't go begging, "Give us some money, so we can fight poverty." Fight poverty how? Fight poverty with what?

We must have strategic plans, which we can implement at once. To be sure, (on the prisons issue) the more volunteers from the civil community, pastors and church workers, etc. we have working in the prisons, the less likely officers are to abuse and brutalize prisoners.

Presidential candidate Dennis Kucinich (D-Ohio) told me, "We must look at the broader context of the criminal justice in America and the journey that takes people into repeated offense. We need to understand there is a direct link between the hopelessness and despair that causes people to repeatedly break the law and the fact that people don't have jobs, people don't have housing, there is not adequate education - the society fails. Forty-three hundred individuals (in California) mostly people of color are serving this 'three strikes' and you're out law and basically their whole lives have been sacrificed to it. Three strikes and you're out has been a form of capital punishment." Presidential candidate Kucinich went on to explain, "Incarceration can go as high as fifty thousand dollars a year. There are many other charges, depending on where you're housed and at what level, and then the Shu . . . we must let the taxpayers know what's going on. As people become aware that the transfer of wealth also includes the building of new prisons, the building of the criminal justice system that locks people up without any hope of recovery. I think people can understand that they can't separate themselves from what's happening in the criminal justice system."

I concur with those assessments. One way to inform the nation about what's going on is to get them this book. Y'all need to e-mail every congress member, every senator, every governor, mayor, etc. and tell them to log on to the Internet (CafePress.com/Sherman Manning or Amazon.com or HalloPeter@freesurf.ch) and order this book!

Since we know our system is not working and we know politicians (with the exception of a few, i.e. Romero, Speier, Hickman and perhaps the "terminator") are not trying to fix it, we must begin to organize in the communities.

A.   Lets do all we can to stop people from ever going to prison. (I shall discuss solutions in the next tome but for now - you develop programs).

B.   We must shake up and clean up the prisons. We can't allow officers and wardens to set up fights, riots and killings. When guys come to prison nowadays its like entering into a war zone (literally)! Hell, when they get out on parole we ought to tie a yellow ribbon around them and help them get jobs and to stay out of prison.

C.   We have got to convince Rod Hickman and prison directors across the nation to bring rehabilitation back into the penal system. Let's have self-help, motivational seminars and programs to develop the inner man inside out. Let's start "turn around" programs and stop warehousing and creating "monsters" in prison.

I had gotten the famed motivator, Zig Zigler, to agree to provide the prison *free* materials and to collaborate with me on teaching his "I can" course in prison. Director Alameda said, "Hell no." We're talking about a free program! No cost to C.D.C. and they disallowed it. I had convinced famed author Stephen Covey to work with me and develop the "Seven Habits of Highly Effective People/Prisoners". Again free - Alameida? No way! Gloria Romero ought to call Mr. Covey and Zigler and arrange to allow the materials in the prison!

On January 23rd, I spoke with Peter Andrist: "Marc (Peter calls me Marc) I had a dream the other night that you were out preaching and speaking. I believe God was telling me we are on the brink of your miracle." It was an exciting and inspiring conversation. Peter is without a doubt the best friend that I have in this country. He's getting married in September of this year and you all can e-mail wedding congratulations to him at hallopeter@freesurf.ch. Peter went on to state, "What is wrong with the judicial system in America? One thing I know is you do not belong in prison. Should we send Mr. Coronado, (reporter at Sacramento Bee) Dan Rather, Jesse Jackson and Arianna Huffington your book?   Do you think we can persuade Michael Jackson to buy twenty thousand copies of this book and donate them to prisons and juveniles across the country? We must get this book to movers and shakers. We need help! We must get you out! And not only that, this book will help many, many people. It will help young men to not go to prison. It will help men in prison to get out."

I concurred with Brother Andrist as he concluded, "Can't Gloria Romero and Jackie Speier get you out? Is there any way possible to get Mrs. Romero or Jackie to merely read your trial transcripts?   Because pragmatically, if they would read just Mr. Calvario's testimony they would know that you are innocent all over the world - we in Switzerland, Japan, Spain and France, etc. are usually so impressed with America. Everybody wants to at least visit the land of the free and home of the brave. I'm not criticizing America as a whole; it is a great country but something needs to be done to fix the justice system. It is unthinkable and unimaginable that a country as great as America would allow wrongful convictions to stand up in the face of innocence and keep people incarcerated based upon technicalities, trumped up profiles and propaganda.

Peter went on to state, "Why is it so difficult for many Americans to believe they falsely accuse and wrongly convict men! And that they establish, create and utilize profiles to substantiate their convictions. If the former head of the Federal Bureau of Investigations Chief (F.B.I. Director J. Edgar Hoover) could and would lie on the world famous Martin Luther King, Jr., what won't they do to a normal citizen? Mr. Hoover used propaganda, disinformation and misinformation against Dr. King. He stooped so low as to accuse King of being a homosexual! So prosecutors stand up in court and declare eloquently to jurors that there is a pattern of crime in this man's life. In 1988 he was arrested for this. In 1992 he went to jail for that. In 1996 a woman accused him of this and in 1999 a man accused him of that. But they never tell the whole story, Marc. They will not explain that in many instances once you have been accused of any type of crime you are marked for life. So innocent or guilty, the police will now focus on you for any similar type case. They will tell that woman who is a victim of an assault or rape; that well, you know this guy probably did it because he's done it before and got away with it. Take a hard look at him. Did the assailant look anything like him? There goes his life. He will be arrested and re-arrested. So when he gets in prison and attempts to reach out for help, people look at his criminal record and assume he's guilty or if he didn't commit this crime he still deserves to be in prison for the other crimes. Marc, we must fight! The battle begins with getting you out of there. Should I call Floyd Abrams, Mr. Uelman, Gerry Spence, and Johnnie? Should we ask Mrs. Romero, Speier or Hickman to read your trial transcripts? What must we do?"

I had to calm Peter down. It appears that his dream about me being at home preaching had lit and ignited a fire in his belly. We strategize and I **believe** that we cannot forget the spiritual elements, which are also at work. We won't leave God out of the battle. I am asking every believer who is reading this tome at this juncture, wherever you are today, "pray for me". I'm serious. I want people who know there is a God to pray for my safety and for my freedom. Then, after you pray, get on your telephone and call another believer and tell them to get this book and to also pray! I want you to send e-mails (i.e. to Bishop T. D. Jakes, Eddie Long, Gloria Romero, P. Diddy, Stevie Wonder and Oprah) and announce this book and my need for prayer to them. Do it! Just do it!

If we could get churches to have shut-ins for prisoners and even for prison staff, we'd transform the nation! Many, many guys in prisons need prayer! Guys like Chava, (inmate Ibarra) Johnnie Willie, Mumia Abu Jamal and many others need your prayer and your support.

And let's get the word out to prisoners that true change comes from the inside out. Guys in prisons have a helluva fight if they're going to get out in one piece. It requires discipline, stick-to-it-tiveness and drive to study, plan, dream and visualize while you're incarcerated. But you can't get out until you start seeing out! While you're still in trouble you must have a vision that you're going to get out. You must dream, hope, yearn, visualize and have faith in your God and in yourself. God is not going to do for you what you can do for yourself. Get some nonfiction books and read! Your oppressor can't stop you from reading! Read books by Na'im Akbar, Nathan MeCoy, Malcolm, Dennis Kimbro, Tony Robbins, etc. You ought to turn your prison cell into a classroom! I tell y'all if Mexicans stop fighting these petty butt wars against each other in prisons, if Caucasian brothers turn to each other and not on each other, if the Black on Black prison wars would cease and if we put down our arms and pick up our books, Bibles and Korans . . . if each one would reach and teach one, we could begin to shut down prisons! Let me be clear! There are hundreds of billions of dollars being earned on the backs of prisoners. It's a numbers game as quiet as it's kept; they want you to come to prison. But if prisons became learning centers and universities, etc., they'd start letting folks out of prison. Can you imagine if the guys in jails came out educated, rehabilitated and ready to live, work and succeed? What would happen? We've got to try something different because this prison thing isn't working anymore. Of the one hundred and twenty-five thousand who got out of the California prison system last year; eighty percent of them went in illiterate and came out scholars. They're not committing any more crimes. Let's pump more crack, heroin and acid into their communities. Arrest them and give them fines instead of (prison) time! Do anything except send them to prison, is what they'd say. I'm tired of these cry babies in prison walking around waiting on the man to change a law and let them out of prison. They drink pruno, smoke dope, shoot heroin and gamble (their lives away) while they wait! Think! Plan! Get a strategy! Let's think our way out of this monster factory!

Candidly, if you can't read, write and count and you've got all this time in prison and aren't trying to learn, I don't want to talk to you. You ought to kick your own butt! Let's call a moratorium on violence and stickings. To all prisoners nationwide, I say beginning June 15,

2004, let us stop all prison violence for six months! No stabbings, no assaults, no violence! Let's ask Gloria Romero, Governor Schwarzenegger, Rod Hickman, the Sacramento Bee, New York Times, L.A. Times, Atlanta Constitution, African American Newspapers, Doug Banks, Larry King, Snoop Dogg, Michael Jackson, Kobe, Arianna Huffington, Dennis Kucinich, T. D. Jakes and Eddie Long to put the word out about this moratorium. Are y'all down? Put your money where your mouth is. You claim to be a warrior so out think, out smart, out strategize your opponents and right now your opponents are corrupted government officials who have you oppressed. Fight! Fight the power! Fight physical force with soul force! Fight with the weapons of pen and paper. Call you momma, daddy and your girlfriend. Call your male lover or that woman you're playing out of money and packages and tell them to contact the media, contact their pastor, their fraternity and sorority and tell them to put the word out about this national moratorium. Call, write and e-mail Bishop T. D. Jakes and ask him to send "Bad Boys And The God Who Loves Them" and "A Prince In Egypt". Ask Eddie Long to send "Passion For Life" to your Chaplain. Ask Na'im Akbar to send "Morehouse A Hall Of Transportation" and play these videos on April 15th to prisoners.

We've tried gangs and we're still in prison. We have fought and killed fellow prisoners for years and we're still here! What we have been doing is not working so lets try something new. Call Jesse Jackson, Al Sharpton, Steve Harvey, and Oprah and tell them to put the word out! No violence for six months. Ask Michael Jackson, Magic Johnson, Bill Gates, Donald Trump, Aaron Goodwin, Willie Gary, lawyers, pastors and professors to send this book around the country. We want this announcement, this book, in all thirty-three prisons in California. We want the inmates in Reidsville, Georgia, Alto, Georgia, Valdesta, Georgia, Rikers and every prison in every state in North America to have at least two copies of this book. You all pass it around and you know how to copy it.

It's time for the non-violent revolution to take place. If you e-mail Michael Jackson, he will help! Tell him his dad, Joe Jackson knows me! When I worked with Rev. Hosea Williams, I met Mr. Jackson. Michael has a heart. If you get this book to him (however you need to do it, i.e., via his kid's nanny, his ex-wife, Brian Oxman in L.A., etc.) he will help! We are asking Mr. Jackson to purchase at least twenty thousand copies of this book (or more if possible) and let's arrange to "heal the world" by sending two copies to ten thousand prisons nationwide.

I'm ready to go to war! I am ready to do war! War with our heads and hearts and not our bodies and blood. Write to President Nelson Mandela in South Africa and ask for his support. Ask him to give a press statement to CNN, C-Span, ABC, NBC and CBS supporting our moratorium on prison violence. I know for a fact that President Mandela will do it. He is a compassionate, altruistic, authentic modern day Moses.

You people reading my words who are free must get on your computers, the internet and the telephones to contact Mr. Mandela and ask the Honorable President Mandela to announce our moratorium and pledge his support. If you reach him, he will support it!

I believe Mr. Mandela is one of the greatest men to have ever walked the planet. "Long Walk To Freedom" ought to be required reading for every prisoner in America.

In a perfect world we could/would get Rod Hickman, Schwarzenegger and governors across America to provide inmates incentives to read! Shave six months off the sentences of any inmate who reads (and is capable of proving he or she read it) "Long Walk To Freedom" and "Makes Me Wanna Holler" by Nathan McCall. Actually, just as judges sometimes sentence people to "community service", etc. Granting inmates incentives to read nonfiction books would be a community service per se because books build character, discipline and self-growth! I know I'm correct.

But pragmatism says most politicians are not going to give prisoners a sentence reduction for reading. They want to be hard and tough on crime! It's the only way to get elected! "I'll be tough on crime". Translation? "I'll lock 'em up and throw away the key" and "I'll give them twenty-five years to life for stealing four cartons of cigarettes". I'm not going to waste another page explaining politicians to you. If you don't know them by now, you'll never know them. If we want change, then it shall begin with the "Man In The Mirror"! Though millions of civilians will end up perusing this tome, the plan (goal) is for every one of you out there to reach in here with a book! I'm not going to beg you! I'm not going to speak (write) in tongues or prophesy, etc. to get you to do it. The bottom line is either you want to make a difference or you don't. If you do, it will help to "heal the world". Our world! When guys find out a book is written by a guy presently in prison they are more inclined to peruse it. If we only get *one* out of ten to "turn around" and get it together, etc. that's one *less* to come out an animal and wreak havoc in your community. One less to get out and shoot, kill, rob and rape.

My pen is a tool and it is a weapon being used to fight corruption, violence and rage. It is a tool being used to educate, elevate, inspire and encourage others.

I've done my part, now it's up to you to call John Burton, the governor's office, reporters and radio stations and ask them have they gotten this book. You must tell them to go on to CafePress and get it.

You get a copy and take it to your pastor. You make sure Rev. Henry B. Lyons, Rubin "Hurricane" Carter and Bruce Cutler get this book. Prisoners need it! Preachers need it. Law professors, law students and politicians need it. Snoop Dogg needs to read this book.

Congressman Janklow was drunk, ran a stop sign, hit a telephone pole and killed a man. The judge sentenced him to one hundred days in prison. Basically three months for recklessly taking a life under the influence of alcohol. But Mike Tyson did not take a life and probably didn't rape anybody and yet served more than three years in state prison!

Hanlon/Stone wanted Judge Jane Ure to give this author twenty-five or thirty-five years to life in prison for a six year old irrational letter! But only one hundred days to the congressman for taking a life! Mr. Bush, Ashcroft, governors, senators are you reading this?

Something Is Wrong! Something about our sentencing laws is unequal. Somebody on the judicial oversight committee needs to examine this one hundred day vehicular homicide sentence. If Michael Jackson is convicted of fondling this kid (and certainly child molestation is a shameful, horrible, dastardly and unspeakable crime! But when you take a life it is the ultimate and final crime! A homicide victim can't go get counseling and psychotherapy. Yet, I don't believe Michael will be convicted. If he's innocent, he should not be convicted) I'll betcha Michael won't be let off with a one hundred day sentence! Where is the equity, fairness and equal justice under the law?

I suggest you contact Professor Charles Ogletree at Harvard Law School and Professor David Cole at Georgetown and request their research data on (so called) equality in the justice system.

Let me tell you again that prison is awful, horrible and a dirty place. It took God through (my homeboy) Bishop Eddie Long to remind me that "I am a seed". In case you missed it, I'll repeat it, "I am a seed"! You've never seen a seed grow unless it was in a whole lot of dirt. Sometimes God realizes and recognizes that a *prince* doesn't know he's a *prince*. The *prince* is running around trying to be president of the "willing to fry chicken committee". He's running around wasting his talents and not recognizing his power. God will take a Joseph and snatch him up and throw him in prison. God will let Joseph (and Sherman, Henry B. Lyons, Hurricane Carter, Anthony Porter, Geronimo Pratt?) get charged and convicted of a sex crime. Now Joseph is abandoned because church folks and even preachers don't want to have anything to do with a sex offender. We're too high up to stoop down (that) low and visit a sex offender. Now Joseph is trapped in prison and he spent (you know the Bible and if you don't, go read the Book of Genesis) almost fourteen years in prison isolated and alone. How could he be one of the fellas when they all thought he was a sex offender? Joseph had an "R" in his jacket but God willed it to be, so Joseph would have to talk to God and not men. Some of you reading right now have been abandoned by your family and friends. But get up and stop being sad. Start praising God for your alone time because some things God won't reveal to you until you are alone.

You're down in the dirt but you have to be because you're a seed. Folks on the top (of the ground) think it's all just dirt. But it's hard to understand on top what's going on underground. While you're still in prison, in trouble and in that dirt, God is raising you up!!

Many of you are not wrongly convicted. You did the crime for which you're serving time. But you can still change. You can still transform. Just because you "did it" does not mean you "are it". If I go into a garage it does not make me a car. You may have committed a crime but don't define your future by your past. Don't let your history hinder you from your destiny. You can change who you are and how you are by changing what goes into your mind.

I see a lot of physical workouts and exercising in jail. I see push-ups, sit-ups and burpees but you need to exercise your mind daily. Exercise your vision. You can't be it until you're able to see it. Visualize, imagine, dream and see your future in your mind. What grows in your mind grows (into and with) in time. But I don't see a lot of *vision* in prison.

If you want to leave prison in a body bag with a tag on your toe, just put this book down and keep on doing what you're doing. Smoke that dope, drink that hooch, play cards and watch sports all day long. Prison is and forever shall be your home. But for the guys who are ready to get out, for the few of you who want God, Allah, Buddha (or whoever you believe in) to make a way out of no way, for the few folks who know that what we have been doing ain't working, I say, "Lets break the cycle of despair and choose to go another way!"

I am so glad that God has delivered me from people. Did you miss it? He delivered me from people! I have no desire to be popular.

217

I'm not attempting to get anybody (in here or out there) to "endorse me". I don't need your approval. I know me! I don't give a hoot about what you "think" about me. I know me. So the reason people run from drug to drug, from gang to gang, from man to man, woman to woman trying to get a "Mr. Feel Good" high and to be popular is because they don't know who they are. "Jacob - what is your name?" "My name is trickster. My name is conman. My name is crook. I am who people say I am. They named me so I'm just living up (down) to my name." But God told Jacob (which means trickster) "Your name is not Jacob . . . your name is Israel and Israel means *prince.* You've been a trickster but now you're a *prince.*"

Brothers be careful who you allow to name you! You may be in the hood, in the slums or in the prison but the hood, the slums and prisons are not in "you". Get up! You are a *prince*!

Call Ruthie Bolton. She's a star basketball player for the Sacramento Monarchs. Her brother is Rev. L. W. Bolton. I love Rev. Bolton. I met him at Leroy's church (New Greater St. John) in Chicago. You tell Ruthie we want her entire team praying for our moratorium.

I believe it's time for a miracle! It's time to transform these prisons and make the public safer. Listen to me! God can rearrange governments if he has to, to get you out of this. I want some brothers who are trapped in prison right now to reach over and grab your cellmate's hand and tell him "I'm a Prince". He's going to think you're going crazy but it will probably make him curious enough to want to *read this book* when you finish. That is a good thing and every few hours I want you to look up at your celly and tell him something that sounds crazy. Tell him, "I'm getting ready to get up out of here." Since he knows you got a twenty-year sentence, twenty-five to life, etc. he's gonna ask you, "How you gonna get out of here?" I want to you look at your cell partner and tell him, "My *gift* is gonna get me out of here." So the Bible says that your *gift* will make room for you! Joseph got out of prison because of his *gift*! And you have a *gift*. No matter who you are or where you are, you do have a *gift*. My, my, my, I wish you all could get my point. I know I'm talking crazy but it seems crazy because I'm talking like a man. You can't ever become a man until and unless you meet your daddy!

The vast majority of guys in jails and prisons had limited contact (if any) with their fathers. You can't become the success you were supposed to be until your father lays his hands on you and identifies you as a *prince*. I want to let you know that even though you never met your natural daddy and/or even though you met him and he abandoned you, etc., don't worry about "him" right now. Instead, go to your spiritual daddy (God) and ask Him, "Who am I?" God will identify you as a ***prince***. You'll have to understand that everybody can't talk to God because God talks crazy! He'll call a poor man rich and a bound man loosed! God calls things that are not as though they already were. If you hadn't gone to prison, you would have never talked to God. God had to let you go to prison in order to "save your life" and now it's time to find out who you are. The reason your fleshly father left you was simply that God didn't trust him. God trusted him to carry (you) the seed. But God knew he was not qualified to nurture (you) the seed. So now that your daddy is gone, get over it. Pick yourself up. You've been running too long. You've played every game you knew how to play. You've manipulated everybody you knew how to manipulate. You've wasted time and farted in the wind too long. You need to "pull yourself together". I want my law professors who are reading this book right now to tell you students "pull yourself together". I want mothers who are at home in Atlanta, New York, Chicago and Los Angeles to put your thumb right here in the book and go tell your husband, son and daughter to "pull yourself together." You guys in juvenile, jails and prisons - go tell your buddy, "Dude you need to pull yourself together." Those of you at home who have a computer, I want you to put your thumb here and log on to the Internet and e-mail T. D. Jakes, Eddie Long and Creflo Dollar and tell them to, "Pray for me Bishop because it's time for me to pull myself together."

It's February 2004 and I'm so excited I can hardly see straight. I'm having trouble sleeping at night because I'm so anxious to wake up and see what God is going to do next. I believe you who are reading are on the brink of a miracle.

I believe you are about to break the curse, which has been spoken over your life. Generational bondages are being loosed as you read this. The spirit of failure is being broken right now.

That's why we must get this book into the prisons because we've got to tell those Brothers that it's not over. It is not over! Your life is not over. These mean, wicked, corrupted and often racist judges are not going to tell prisoners it's time to change. Prison guards depend on those prisoners for job security, so they won't/don't tell them. Prosecutors don't give a darn about them changing their lives.

You must tell them they can, will and must change. You must help them to pull themselves together. You on the outside ought to take a break right now and write a little note to your nephew, son, daughter or cousin in prison and tell them, "Pull yourself together."

A Brother was telling me the other day that when we see Jesus we shall be rich and then we will rule. I had to mess up his theory. I told the brother this - Jesus Christ is Lord. The Bible says, "It does not yet appear what we **shall** be but when He appeared we **shall** be like him". But Brother when you read the Holy Bible you need to really study and pray and ask God for revelation. There were certain words added into the translation and it kind of altered it a bit. There is absolutely no **shall** in there; it was added to make it flow and to sound good. To be candid, it was put in there to sort of keep people in bondage. Just get a Strong's Concordance and you'll see there is no **shall** in it. So we've been singing for years that when Jesus comes back, we **shall** rule and reign but we should be ruling and reigning right now. Read it and eliminate the word **shall**. It does not yet appear what we "be" but when He appeared we "be" like Him. Your prayer ought to be, "God let me see Jesus in the spirit."

I was talking to a young man the other night (Whisper is what we call him) and I dropped a bomb on him. I told him he was a phony. I explained that even his closest buddies didn't know him. His candor and probity in his reply shocked me.

"I've been let down and hurt so many times that I had to develop a façade to keep people from knowing me. I don't let anybody in. To be honest, I don't even know how to be me. I've forgotten how to be me."

Damn! We need to begin to understand why people do what they do and we need to begin to address the cause of crime, racism, anger and rage in order to transform the effect . . .

I shall remind you that politicians aren't going to do it. They make money off of crime. Gloria Romero and Jackie Speier types come far and few between.

It's going to take Deion Sanders, Michael Irving, Eddie Long, etc. to come together and build programs for prisoners such as the Joseph project for prisoners (contact Creflo Dollar in Atlanta, Georgia to find out what the Joseph project is all about). If we want to protect public safety (with tautology, I shall reiterate) we must create an atmosphere of change in the prisons. Otherwise, prisoners will continue to lash out. Eventually they will begin to (I fear; God forbid) lash out at prison guards. They'll riot, hold guards hostage and take over prisons.

Bottled rage and caged loneliness is a recipe for violence. Ipso facto crime continues to skyrocket.

I'm cognizant of the fact that perhaps more civilians are perusing this tome than prisoners are. My advice to you is to do something on the outside to change those on the inside. Order some tapes by Bishop Eddie Long, Noel Jones, Gilbert Patterson, Billy Graham, Na'im Akbar and Malcolm and send them to somebody in prison. What are you waiting on?

Pre-order "Creating Monsters", my next book by logging on to CafePress.com.

More to come . . .

Publishers Note: Some of the following pages appeared in the first edition of this best-selling book . . . Join the national call for a moratorium on prison violence beginning June 15, 2004.

E-mail every pastor, politician, radio station and newspaper which you can think of and ask them to announce the "truce" which is being advanced. Tell the Mexican mafia, northerners, southerners, bloods, crips, bulldogs, 415, nazi low riders, Aryan Brotherhood, etc. to stop all prison violence on June 15, 2004. Encourage prisoners to have their family or chaplain or lawyer to e-mail hallopeter@freesurf.ch and let us know that their gang, their prison is in the truce and will join the moratorium. We challenge Rush Limbaugh to debate prison issues with Ed Schultz. These kinds of debates can help Sherman to reach guys like Woody Rayos, Barney and Chano....

What will happen to Michael?

Media pundits who have never seen the inside of a jail cell are all speculating about what will happen to Michael Jackson if he goes to prison. Their predictions are speculative at best. I am here and I know what goes on and who is treated in what way. You cannot simply read one book on prisons and consider yourself an authority. Most especially if the book is not written by a person in prison. If Michael went to prison in the state of Georgia, he'd be okay. The Georgia prison system has some problems. It is not an ideal department of corrections. However, some of the horrible, terrifying and violent rage Michael could face in the California prison system are problems, which are not rampant in the Georgia prison system. And there are various reasons, which can be disputed as to why Michael would not face certain problems in Georgia. I would surmise that the best explanation for a lack of certain types of abuses in the Georgia prison system is the fact that the media are allowed a much greater access to prisoners in Georgia. And folks like Andy Young, State Representative Tyrone Brooks and Rev. C. T. Vivian will and do respond to prisoner's gripes and complaints in their prisons. Here in California there is a virtual ban on media interviews with inmates. And Gray Davis stripped inmates of the right to correspond confidentially with members of the press. So when inmates do write to the media, all of the letters are read. And if the staff member does not like what is written, they steal and destroy the letter(s). How does an inmate prove that a sworn peace officer stole outgoing mail? If you send out ten letters on Monday and one is going to your mom, you call mom on Thursday in Atlanta and she received your missive, you have someone to e-mail the nine politicians, lawyers and media folk on Friday and none has received your letter. So you follow up by having someone to telephone each of the nine a few days later and none got your mail; it's safe to assume the C.D.C. staff stole them. They are fairly sophisticated in their mail thefts. They usually don't steal mail to people they know you can/will and do call collect routinely. But the Governor's Office ain't gonna accept a collect call. Ipso facto, although mail theft is a federal crime, the U.S. Postal Office refuses to prosecute mail theft in U.S. Prisons. Sources indicate to me that the CCPOA influenced, manipulated and coerced postal officials not to prosecute these cases. And there were so many complaints that perhaps the U.S. Postal Office was inundated. This Carte Blanche power, which the C.D.C. exercises over its prisons, gives C.D.C. the ability to operate with a code of silence and in an atmosphere of secrecy. This kind of secrecy is usually not widespread in Georgia . . .

Michael would be housed in solitary confinement in the Santa Barbara County jail. Initially the media would be all over the jail snooping and trying to get snippets of what Mike's life is like in county jail. A few officials and jail guards would simply make up things to tell the media, off the record. Inmates who are being discharged after having been arrested on petty crimes would contact the media claiming to have information on how Michael is living in jail. Most of these stories would also be embellished and some would constitute outright lies. The real truth is, Michael will have absolutely no physical contact with other general population inmates in county jail. He will eat in his cell. He will shower alone. He will get about an hour per day recreation on a jail SHU type yard. He will be allowed to just walk around, shoot basketball with himself or play ping-pong with himself. He will get two telephone calls per day, which will be on collect call telephones only and these calls will be monitored and recorded.

The official reason for Michael's isolation will be for his own safety. Yet, this isolation will be torture to Michael. The lack of human contact makes hours seem like weeks. The first couple of days in jail for Michael will be surreal. He'll feel like he's floating or in some type of a nightmare. Michael will keep telling himself that he's going to wake up and be out of jail. He'll lay in bed (which will be a steel cot smaller than a bunk bed with a two inch thick mattress on it) for hours but get little sleep. He will hold on to the hope that an appeal, a judge or a governor is gonna let him out of jail. And then comes the reality. It could happen his second week or his second month. But at some point, Michael will say to himself, "This is real and I'm here to stay." By the time he adapts and adjusts to the jail, it will be time to go. One morning early, Michael will be awakened at five or six and placed into a sheriff's (regular non high profile inmates are jam packed into a large bus) sedan and transported to C.D.C. He will probably go to Delano. Delano serves as a reception center and all California inmates entering state prison must go to a reception center for approximately ninety days. At Delano, Michael will be stripped naked and a California prison guard will (unofficially; officially they don't do this anymore) put on a rubber glove and stick two fingers up Michael's anus to check for drugs or weapons. Michael will then be sprayed (they spray all incoming inmates much like an exterminator sprays roaches) with a chemical, which supposedly kills crabs and scabies. Michael will then be placed into an open shower while guards look on and crack jokes about his genitals. After the shower, he will be given a prison jumpsuit to put on and a bedroll. The bedroll consists of a blanket, a sheet and a towel rolled up together. Michael will then be given a haircut at which time all of his hair will be shaved off! Then he'll get a fish kit. A fish kit is a brown paper bag containing a cheap toothbrush, tooth cleansing powder and one bar of soap. Michael will then be placed into a 6x12 foot cell with two bunks in it. Since he's Michael Jackson, he'll initially be placed on single cell status. During this time, he'll be fed in his cell, segregated and isolated. Michael will receive a cursory psychological evaluation and a medical check up. For ninety days, he will basically not have much activity with the exception of going to see doctors, nurses and psychologists, etc. He'll get no telephone calls and he'll have no television or radio.

Eventually Michael will be transferred to one of California's thirty-three cold and vicious prisons. However, I believe Michael will be placed on one of the few (there are only three) protective custody or sensitive needs yard (i.e., Mule Creek, New Folsom Facility A) or he will be placed in PHU (Protective Housing Unit) which is at Corcoran and is basically solitary confinement. He will lose his single cell status because he has not (yet) been raped in prison and has not raped anybody in prison. Michael would not last ten minutes on most yards in California's prisons. Inmates and guards would eat him alive. If he were sent to Pelican Bay, Jan Quentin, Lancaster, Old Folsom, etc., his only chance of survival would be to hire a "daddy". He'd have to get the biggest, most brutal guy on the yard and cell up with him. This "war daddy" would protect Michael for a fee, which could include money, drugs, packages and sex. The drugs would be easily arranged through one of C.D.C.'s finest prison guards.

But my genuine belief is that Mr. Jackson will be placed on a sensitive needs yard. And this will still be very difficult for Michael. Privacy? Nonexistent. On a daily basis Michael will get inmates begging for money, guards begging for money and autographs, etc., etc. then there will be the professional predators who will offer themselves as veteran convicts usually beginning with the opening spiel of, "I've been down for fifteen years and I don't want nothing you got. But I'm gonna give you some good advice. You see that guy over there; don't talk to him. And watch that guard over there and . . ." This person will try to manipulate and insinuate himself into Michael's mind, cell, world, pants and into his wallet. There will be some guys who just hate and despise him because generally speaking child molesters are scum of the earth. There will also be prison guards who despise him. Some will spit in this food, set him up, plant drugs in his cell and attempt to invent reasons to throw him into the hole. There will also be a few guards, psychologists, administrators, etc. who identify themselves as veteran officials and who offer (in a very duplicitous manner) to stand up for Michael against all others. Michael will have extreme difficulties with the race problems in C.D.C. prison authorities as well as inmates will oppose his interracial dealings, views and they will despise him if he desired to cell with a White or Mexican inmate. After a time the media will lose interest in Michael and he'll be just another rich molester in prison. But jail is hell and Michael will always create controversy. Some guards go out of their way to mistreat him only because they don't want to be accused of sucking up to a child predator. Others will discreetly offer him drugs, food and other perks. In a case such as Michael's, C.D.C. would be wise (but it is highly unlikely and unheard of) to transfer Michael to another state to serve his sentence. He'll be a hot potato in California and unless he goes bankrupt, he'll probably be able to survive with few fights, hopefully no rapes and no stabbings.

This is an inside view of what will happen to Michael if he comes to prison. I would hope that if he is innocent (see my book "American Dream/A Search For Justice") he gets a fair trial and a fair judge. Because if the jury is fair, I have every confidence in the skilled representation of Thomas Mesereau. Tom can keep Michael out of prison.

And with all the abuse, corruption and sadistic behavior the C.D.C. prison guards are involved in every day this is not a place I'd wish on my worst enemy. The prison abuse which was/is being perpetrated on Iraq's prisoners is not an aberration in the C.D.C.

Don Rumsfeld knew about it in January. He failed to tell Mr. Bush about it until May! He called CBS and asked them not to air the photos for two weeks and used soldier safety as a manipulative ploy. In a similar manner many times C.D.C. wardens, etc. are aware of the beatings and killings of prisoners and they don't tell the director. And sometimes the director knows but does not tell the governor. And the small time media people in these hick towns where the prisons are located are very often manipulated by C.D.C. and the CCPOA. Very often they keep our stories out of the media to protect the guards. On May 7, as Don Rumsfeld was telling the congress that there is more to come, more photos and videos, which the media has not aired yet Californians were being notified that there is (also) more to come. There is a hidden video, which shows a C.Y.A. prison guard abusing a youth inmate by having a canine to bite him. The inmate was not resisting and in the typical reactionary manner C.Y.A. has not suspended the use of canines in the prisons. It has come to light that

C.Y.A. knew about this instance of abuse as early as December of 2003, but the story was kept out of the media and out of the state senate. There is a striking resemblance between Rumsfeld's cover up and secrecy and C.D.C.'s cover up and secrecy.

Unfortunately most California inmates saw nothing strange or unusual about nude inmates. Being chained together, etc. we see that every day of the week. We see violence, abuse, rapes and beatings. We see cell extractions in which inmates are brutalized and occasionally killed. We've been desensitized to the abuse and programmed to believe it just comes with the territory. But we are waiting on Amnesty International, Human Rights Watch and the American Red Cross to come save these inmates who are being burned at the cross in California's monster factory.

I understand more clearly than ever before why sadistic abuse and wanton criminal assaults are allowed in California's prison system: Because the people are desensitized and they don't know, don't show or don't care about what's happening inside their prisons. And also because the media rarely cover the real issues involving prisons. And when they do, you never hear inmate quotes. You only get quotes from the keepers, because the kept are prevented access to the media. Armstrong and Getty ain't gonna discuss C.D.C. and Rush Limbaugh is not going to discuss prison issues. But our hope is that Larry King, Air America, Tavis and Doug Banks will put our story back into the headlines. We need to tell our congress, tell Carl Levin, John McCain, Ted Kennedy and Mr. Bush that there is vicious, sadistic and criminal abuse of inmates transpiring right here, right now, at home in the California Prison System. And if Mr. Bush won't address it, then perhaps John Kerry will. And maybe we need to send Mr. Bush back to Texas. And send Dick Cheney back to Halliburton (Imclone, MCI or Enron)!

If Michael Jackson is innocent, I want him to get justice. I don't want to see him come to prison. I'm cognizant of the fact that there are forces working behind the scenes with ulterior, hidden and biased motives who want to see Michael fall! Mike is eccentric and unique and I don't think he should be sleeping with children in his bed - period. But I also don't want folk giving children scripts to act out in efforts to extort a charitable, decent and God loving humanitarian and sources very close to the DA's office have indicated to me that there is a lot we don't know about involving past lies, spurious and scurrilous accusations, which this boy has allegedly been led to make at the urging of his mother. I would urge Dr. Firpo Carr, Randy and Frank Tyson to advise Michael to: A. Follow all the advice given by Tom

Mesereau. Tom is a brilliant, low key, philanthropic and a Christian. All of which make up the key ingredients for a top lawyer. B. Michael must pay any price and I do mean any price to lessen the chances for him ever seeing the inside of a prison. He should retain the best experts in every profession relating to the defense of a criminal defendant in a high profile case. Hire Jo Ellen Demetrius (jury consultant), get the best publicist, top trial consultants, private detectives etc., to challenge the prosecutor's case in every way, shape, fashion and form allowed by the law. C. I would challenge Michael to use his status, power and finances to help expose the human rights violations transpiring in American prisons, juvenile facilities and jails. It would be a preemptive strike, a strategic (but genuine and altruistic) move for Michael and anybody close to him to begin to bring America's torture factories to the American media now. I applaud Seymour Hersh for his vigorous reporting on the criminal torture of those prisoners in Iraq. And I want Seymour, Graham Messick, Chuck D., Oprah and Dan Rather to know that systemic and deliberate abuse of inmates is transpiring everyday in prisons right here on American soil. Roderick Johnson was raped in front of guards on a daily basis nearly ever time he stepped out of his cell in a Texas prison. "Stop Prisoner Rape", in Los Angeles, can attest to the fact that inmates in prisons across America are sodomized, abused and tortured routinely. The Black hoods we were all so appalled to see Iraq's prisoners wearing? California and Texas (to name a few) inmates are being forced to wear Black net hoods on a routine and daily basis. Where is the public outrage? If we are waiting on a photo, we will be waiting. Neither California nor Texas will allow cameras in the prisons. But I declare under penalty of perjury that I have seen and been required to wear a Black, net hood over my head in ad-seg right at New Folsom prison. It makes you feel like an animal. Karen Gotsch, Rose Braz and Paul Wright can testify that it happens. As a matter of fact, California justifies it by claiming the hoods will prevent us from spitting on them. The torture we saw at the prisons in Iraq appears to be us exporting American prison abuse abroad. It is not an aberration in America. Let us remember that the soldier who provided these pictures to "60 Minutes" had written congress members. He wrote seventeen congress members two months prior to contacting "60 Minutes" and none of them did a darned thing about it. So yes, Mr. Rumsfeld knew about it and failed to tell the President. And I'm certainly not a Rumsfeld fan! Yet, there is enough blame to go around and it reaches around all seventeen of those congress members who failed to respond to his letters.

To be true, when Mr. Bush was Governor of the great state of Texas, hundreds of inmates wrote to him about abuse, rapes and torture transpiring in his prison system. And Governor Bush (present President Bush) ignored them. This is one of the reasons this inmate I mentioned earlier (whom I think is somewhat delusional and probably should not be let out) wants to get out and do harm to him. Wanting to hurt a president, governor or anybody is wrong. There is no legal justification (and I am totally opposed to anybody doing physical harm to anybody else) for hurting anybody, but there is an explanation. It is a reflex response to humiliation. And when a person is tortured, abused, raped and disregarded, he or she will become a monster. The reason Mr. Rumsfeld has apologized is only because the media expected it. And the only reason inmates in California, Texas, Arizona, Washington, etc. will ever get justice and perhaps an apology is if the media expose it. Mr. Bush ignored (see "American Dream/A Search For Justice") the cries of innocence from inmate Chris Ochoa while he was Governor of Texas. He also ignored a missive/confession from another inmate stating, "I committed the rape and murder Mr. Ochoa is innocent." And it took Barry Scheck and DNA to get Chris out of prison. I would hope and I would pray that Al Franken, Larry King, Tavis Smiley, Chuck D., Jeff Vonkaenel, Jill Stewart, Shannon Savage, Chris Doherty, Brian Dixon and Attorney James Blatt will help tell the world about the abuse, systemic monster creation and the torture transpiring every day right here in America's prison system.

Wally Lamb, Pen American Center, the Center for Constitutional Rights, Critical Resistance, etc. are willing to help create programs inside the prisons to rehabilitate inmates. But the prison bureaucracies fight them. When Wally Lamb got inmate Barbara Parsons Lane a twenty-five thousand dollar Pen American Award for writing and exercising her free speech; the prison responded by confiscating all her writing material, stealing her writings and immediately suspending the rehabilitative writing program in the prison! This was a program that best-selling author Wally Lamb volunteered to teach. And the prison director's excuse was, "We needed to bring everybody back together to talk about communicating." That was a ridiculous non statement. When a reporter pressed on, "We wanted to make sure Barbara would not be pressured by other inmates for money," stated the prison director.

I hope Professor Gates, Cornel West, Toni Morrison, Grisham and Berholtz will begin to volunteer to do seminars on writing in the prisons. Writing is a release and a positive form of expression which can reduce stress levels, transmogrify your soul and heal a broken heart. So Mr. Jackson can and should help raise money for these type programs, which will interrupt and prevent the creation of monsters and in the process prevent some of the thousands of wrongly convicted prisoners from getting killed in these angry prisons.

I shall close by saying Michael has said he's innocent. And no matter how bad it looks; according to the law of the land, he is presumed innocent. So if Mr. Jackson is innocent, I say to him in the words of Oprah, "Sometimes God allows horrible things to happen so we will never let it happen to somebody else."

Afterword

Mr. Michael Berg has indicated that his son Nick Berg's blood is on the hands of Mr. Bush and his administration. Mr. Berg is hurt, angry, frustrated and he's in tremendous pain. He went on to say that America has no business being over in Iraq. He mentioned that this is the first war in which America began the fighting against a country, which had done nothing to us. Mr. Bush calls it a preemptive strike against terror and the build up of weapons of mass destruction. The costs of this so-called preemptive strike to obtain weapons of mass destruction has been the blood, lives and limbs of America's patriotic soldiers who are fighting an un-winnable and unnecessary war. Mr. Bert, his wife Suzanne, son David and daughter, Sarah, deserve to know that our hearts ache and our heads are bowed in memory of Nicholas Berg. Nick's friend, Aaron Spool said that Nick used "his God given ability to help others. What more could you ask of a human being"? Nick's atrocious, sadistic murder was retaliation and revenge for the torture and abuse of prisoners in Iraq. This torture, abuse and sodomy are now being called "only hazing" by an Iowa congressman and Rush Limbaugh. Rush's protégé, Sean Hannity, played all the screams, the entire unedited decapitation of Nick over his radio show. I unequivocally and categorically believe in Sean's absolute right as an American to air those screams. Also, morally I categorically and unequivocally believe Sean was wrong. I believe it takes a constipated mind and distorted thinking to have a desire to air that audio just to get ratings. And for every person who wanted to hear those screams, it speaks volumes about what we have become as a people. The F.C.C. fined and scorned Howard Stern for profanity and vulgarity. Yet, they are silent on Sean airing real life, actual death screams. The F.C.C. was distraught and livid over Janet Jackson's breast at halftime, but silent on Sean's murderous ratings scheme. What will we air next? If a woman is raped or a child is molested and it's caught on tape, are Sean and Rush going to air it so that the whole world can know the sound of rape and molestation? Where do we draw the line? I'm not anti-republican and I'm no zealot. I am supportive of the platforms and policies of many republicans. I believe in an open and free society. But candidly, I have a problem with the lack of moral outrage at Sean's plot. It is sickening . . . "America is ushering in a new responsibility era where each of us understands we're responsible for the decisions we make in life," President Bush said on a stump speech prior to America learning about the abuse and torture in Iraqi prisons. While speaking about bad CFO's he says, "You're beginning to see the consequences of people making irresponsible decisions. They need to pay a price for their responsibility." On the torture, rapes and beatings of prisoners in Iraq, "I take full responsibility," said Mr. Donald Rumsfeld in his testimony before congress. What is the price, Mr. Bush was talking about? Seemingly taking responsibility in the Bush Gate White House merely means nothing more than saying the magic words, "I take responsibility". Need I remind you that after the vicious 9/11 attacks, no one was asked to resign and the Bush Gate White House refused to even launch a serious investigation into it. The 9/11 commission was created only after months of refusals because some of the victims' families pursued it aggressively and refused to give up. After we discovered no weapons of mass destruction in Iraq, not one person resigned or even got reassigned. The only people fired in Bush Gate's "responsibility" White House are people like General Eric Shinseki, Paul O'Neill and Larry Lindsey, who spoke embarrassing and inconvenient truths. Americans ought to remember that (at minimum) Rumsfeld and Bush created the climate for this abuse and torture of Iraqi prisoners. Rumsfeld is the guy who attacked the Geneva conventions and tried persistently to keep prisoners out of the reach of either American courts or international law. Mr. Rumsfeld initially forgot Colin Powell, who urged that prisoners in Guantanimo be accorded rights under the conventions. Eventually Powell gave in . . .

The Bush Gate war mongering is responsible for the creation of a poisonous atmosphere of anti-Americanism around the globe and Bush has single-handedly dismantled, negated and destroyed the credibility of America on the international scene. Seymour Herish has uncovered the fact that Donald Rumsfeld authorized ultra secret intelligence covert operations in Iraq. He apparently authorized the use of commandos whose motto was grab who you must and do what you want. Mr. Rumsfeld reportedly authorized military intelligence operations managers to treat prisoners roughly and expose them to sexual humiliation. This Bush Gate terror operation set the stage for the abuse and torture we saw in those photos. And this torture gave the true monsters the ammunition, which they felt they needed to decapitate Nick Berg. Nick's murder was awful, evil and cannot be justified under any circumstances whatsoever. And for Mr. Rumsfeld to authorize or even turn a blind eye to torture by military prison guards in Iraq cannot be justified under any circumstances. Put a piece of tape over the names George Bush and Don Rumsfeld. Forget about Democrats and Republicans. If John Kerry, Jesse Jackson, Bill Clinton, Griffin Bell or anyone calling themselves an American had

231

authorized this torture, I'd want them to resign. We in America seem to have been sucked into a vacuum of fools and fanatics. Some of us will support or approve of anything with the name Democrat on it. And some will support it only with the name Republican on it. We have those who are the party faithful. Yet it is time to become more faithful to humanity and morals than we are to parties and partisanship. We have fallen victim and prey to sound bite politics and slick politicians. I don't even find John Kerry all that pleasing. I think he'd do better than Bush. I don't think Kerry is a warmonger or corrupted. But Kerry is afraid of the word liberal. He's afraid to define himself and speak from his heart. If Kerry will stand up with the candor, consistently and boldness that his wife, Teresa, has, he can win. And we all know that if Kerry is not aggressive, consistent and candid - the Bush Gate scandal will proceed for another five years. We in America even on regional and local levels are seeing the effects of slick politicians who play on words and manipulate the press and continue to weave a tangled web of deception. California (for example) is nearly $16 billion in debt. And Mr. Schwarzenegger promised to clean house and to be proactive and independent. Yet, it appears there is a possibility that Mr. Schwarzenegger is falling into the footsteps of his predecessors such as Pete Wilson. The Governator appears to be backing off of his earlier demand of the renegotiation of the raise contract of C.D.C. employees. (I've stated for the record that I'm not really opposed to the raise in salary as long as teachers get a raise and professors get raises). It appears union bosses Mike Jiminez, Lance Corcoran and Don Novey are causing the Governator to soften his language in recent days as the budget deadline grows closer. In an idiotic, inhumane, cruel and unusual move, the Governator has decided to cutback on inmate meals in California prisons to help save the budget. In his $103 billion budget, his decision to take lunches away from inmates adds up to 0.001 percent cut. He's making the least sum pathetic. Citizens feel the pain (literally) of budget wars. The new food reduction plan appeared in the Sacramento Bee in a story written by Clea Benson. Benson claims Rod Hickman indicated that California's 162,000 inmates are fed three hot meals per day every weekday and two hot meals and a lunch sack on weekends. Perhaps Mr. Hickman needs to come inside these gates with a hands-on approach so that he can learn his information is incorrect. California's state prisoners are never fed three hot meals per day seven days per week. Inmates are served two hot meals per day and a lunch sack, period. And if Mr. Hickman gave Clea this incorrect data, he also gave Mr. Schwarzenegger this incorrect data. And this is an excellent example of local, regional and national leaders making decisions based on erroneous data. It is sad and incompetent for Mr. Hickman to not know what is being served and done in his prisons. The only way you can really cut prison spending is to reduce the number of people being sentenced to prison. Rose Biaz of the Coalition for Effective Public Safety states, "For Arnold to resort to cutting a sack lunch as an operational efficiency is incredibly dismaying." This food cutback is the brainchild of prisons, Chief Rod Hickman. Rod plans to serve a late breakfast (brunch?) and dinner on weekends and holidays. This plan will delay yard releases and result in hungry, frustrated inmates getting less recreational (yard) time. The savings from lunch cutback are expected to be a meager $1.2 million! Hickman called this "a good operational idea. I think the inmates' rights groups will accept it and I think the inmates will accept it". He also said, "It will give inmates an opportunity to sleep in a little later on the weekend."

First, I'd like to know has Rod asked a single inmate if we will "accept it"? And again, I'll renew my request to speak to the Governor who says he's always willing to meet with any person or group, "no matter who they are as long as it is educational or I can learn something". I can educate Arnold to the fact that Rod's data (about three hot meals) is totally incorrect. And I can explain to Mr. Schwarzenegger (who believes in health and fitness) that eliminating the lunch sack will be a threat to safety and security. Violent, hungry and frustrated inmates will assault more prison guards and the state will lose money as they pay the guards hospital and funeral bills and as they prosecute inmates for the additional assaults and killings. And we don't get enough food as it is. Mr. Schwarzenegger has never been in prison. He definitely has never sat in a confined space the size of a prison cell for twenty-four hours per day. Not without any exaggeration, I will readily admit I have not personally been hungry in a long time. This is due to canteen and food packages sent to me by my family. There are many inmates unable to buy canteen and they have no one to send them a package. Couple that with the fact that authorities are now taking half of any meager money earned by prisoners and half of any monies inmate's families send in; and couple that with the extortion via the exorbitant, astronomical amount of money charged by MCI for a prisoner to call home (and MCI gave C.D.C. kickbacks to the tune of tens of millions of dollars last year) and it becomes clear inmates are not faring well. I only weigh 160 pounds and it does not take a lot of food to fill me up. And I can truly write that each time I've been thrown in the hole (ad-seg) where I had no access to canteen or packages (a ludicrous rule Rod needs to change; especially since he's taking the lunch sacks). C.D.C. policy is when an inmate is put in the hole; he can't take any canteen with him. Even it he has food, which must be eaten by a certain date, etc., which his family sent him. Oops, too bad. If you go to ad-seg, you take no food with you. I have been hungry. I find myself (in ad-seg) literally praying that the meals, lunch sacks, etc. will hurry up and get there. You get hungrier (period) when you are confined twenty-four hours per day. And add to that no canteen and believe me, you need that lunch sack seven days per week. And if I'm 160 pounds and hungry with the lunch sack, how about the guy who's 360 pounds? We could argue he needs to go on a diet. He could argue he can't get Jenny or Benny Craig in prison. The bottom line is this arbitrary and capricious decision ought to be reversed by Arnold merely based on the fact that Rod gave him misinformation. I can think of ten ways (off the top of my head) for the Governator to save ten million dollars off the prison budget; none of which needs to include taking food. That is inhumane and inmates will suffer physically. I suggest Arnold call former President Nelson Mandela and ask (I'm serious, Mr. Mandela could teach the Governor a lot about prisons), Mr. Mandela what being in isolation, ad-seg, etc. does to a man psychologically, physically and what happens to his appetite . . . I'm beginning to lose faith in Hickman. I've got to be candid. I'm beginning to wonder whom he's listening to, consulting with and what is on Hickman's mind. He raised his hand and claimed there would be a new day in C.D.C. and he would clean up corruption. Thus far, all I've seen him do is clean out lunch sacks and ask prison employees to look out for extra laundry. It's time to get real. If Rod would walk through these prisons and stop the violence, end the corruption and stop the beatings that would save the taxpayers money. The $1.2 million he plans to save by making inmates go hungry; he could have saved double that if he had prevented those two prison guards from using extensive force and beating those two kids at C.Y.A. in Stockton. Davey Turner is suing C.D.C./C.Y.A. for the videotaped beating. He will win. It's clear-cut abuse and excessive force. Jurors award judgments every day in courts to the tune of million dollar judgments against prison guards for beatings, rapes and torture. Those ethics classes Mrs. Woodford claimed every C.D.C. officer needed to undergo have not been mentioned since she gave the interview. That fraudulent state of emergency, which C.D.C. secretly called on April 1st, cost the state millions and the lawsuits, which will spring out of triple bunking violent men, will also cost taxpayers tens of millions to litigate. Ask Rod how many millions (upon millions) of dollars C.D.C. paid out to settle lawsuits out of court last year alone (see my book "American Dream/A Search For Justice"). In just one case in which prison guards set up an inmate to be raped by an inmate nicknamed "the Booty Bandit", C.D.C. paid the family a reported $650 thousand to not go to trial. There goes the lunch sacks . . .

The ultra secret meetings Mr. Rumsfeld held authorizing the abuse of inmates in Iraq are the same kinds of ultra secret meeting held by prison wardens authorizing rape, torture and beatings right here in America and yes right here in California. Ask Max Lemon, Steve Rigg or Yvette Pieper. Those terrorists doubling as prison guards and military police in Iraq are home grown i.e. U. S. Army Corporal Charles A. Graner, Jr. Corporal Graner is being court-martialed for abusing Iraqi prisoners. Guess what Mr. Graner's U.S. job was on the home front? He was an America, state prison guard in several prisons. Recently he worked at state correctional institution, Greene, a Pennsylvania Maximum-Security prison. He was fired from that job for reasons the army refused to disclose! Why? Why allow a prison guard, fired from his job as a prison guard go guard prisons in Iraq? I'll leave the answer to you. But my point is, if Graner were a decent, non-abusive prison guard in America, he would have been the same in Iraq. Many of our soldiers are decent, good and law-abiding soldiers. They're not a problem at home. And they are not a problem in Iraq. But the abuse we saw was professional abuse done under the color of authority with the blessings of higher-ups in America. The game is played the same. These places like Riker's, Reidsville, Pelican Bay, Corcoran, Folsom, etc. Where inmates are beat, abused, raped and set up to be raped, etc. This is professional abuse taught to prison guards by higher-ups. So we can argue all day long that it is only a few bad apples. But to the man being sodomized by a guard or being sodomized by an inmate, who was paid to do so by a guard; that few bad applies argument is irrelevant. To that mother who is being called by the prison chaplain and told she must bury her son because he was shot by a drunken prison guard; the few a bad apples argument is meaningless. What is a few? Ten percent? Ten percent in California would mean nearly five thousand few bad apples! And just as it takes a village to raise a child, it also only takes a village to destroy a child and an enormous amount of damage can be done by a few. "The few, the proud, the marines!" C.D.C.'s finest few bad apples?

Mr. Hickman needs to talk to me. Mr. Hickman needs to give us a chance to prove that we (too) can think and we have opinions. And just because they don't speak to us, does not give them a right to speak for us. And I'm seeing a lot of misinformation and propaganda in the media about what inmates do or don't think, will or won't like, etc. Yet nobody is talking to us . . . And I'm sick of Rumsfeld and Bush and Colin (Sorry Colin, I still like you and I know you tried) hypnotizing the public and crying about how isolated this abuse was and how it's only the few (The proud? The marines?) bad apples. We are only as strong as the weakest link in the chain. And leadership at the top sets the tone for behavior at the bottom. And if you got Bush yelling "wanted dead or alive", Colin talking about "mushroom clouds" and Rumsfeld yelling "grab who you must, do what you want", they are not protected by the Geneva conventions, etc., you create the climate for abuse and all Rumsfeld does is look every American, in the face and say "it happened on my watch". I take full responsibility. Well when a defendant takes responsibility and pleads guilty in a courtroom he still goes to prison. They want to put Martha (Stewart) in prison for a few thousand dollars but Bush thinks taking responsibility for murders, torture and rape needs not be punished. Not a reprimand, no suspension, no reduction in rank, nothing! After all it's "only a few". And likewise, I'm sick of prison guards crying and complaining that, "it's only a few bad cops". Most of us don't smuggle drugs, foment violence or beat down inmates. "It's only a few"! It only takes one hole to sink the titanic. And if we ignore that hole, don't report and repair it, the ship will sink. These crybaby union officials need to get rid of the code of silence and stop defending the few (good men?) bad apples and fighting to keep their jobs. Prison guards need to stop turning their heads when they see abuse, excessive force and let it be known that, "if I see it, I'm going to report it" and the abuse would stop and the state would save money. Inmates don't cry when some pervert gets released from jail and goes out and rapes babies. We disown him and distance ourselves from him. But the Rumsfelds and the wardens and the prison guards want to embrace corrupted brother guards on the down low and cry about their image in the public view.

Prisons just need to get real and get genuine and clean up or shut up. We need to rethink it, correct it and get it right. We need to open up on prisons to the public via the media. And the public must demand a change now. C.D.C. officers' files need to be opened for public scrutiny. Yet, the CCPOA guards their guard's personnel records in a more secretive fashion than the F.B.I. You can't find out when, if or why a prison guard was disciplined or suspended. It ought to be public record.

Prison guards claim they can't, won't and don't tell an inmate what another inmate is in prison for. They claim it is policy to protect safety and security. So if Bill Doc is in prison for child molestation, no prison guard (supposedly) can tell me about it. But if you (right now) call this prison or any prison in California and ask what I or any inmate in prison is charged with or convicted of, they will tell you. And the news media will air it on TV on the evening news. And that safety the guards claim to be protecting just went out the window because a C.D.C. administrator just told the media (as well as every inmate watching the news) what Joe Blow is in prison for. And no media outlet is going to give the inmate equal time to explain, "I didn't do it" or "they set me up" or "I did it, but I've change" etc. It's ridiculous, but it's just the way prison authorities operate. And this foolishness has been allowed because our pastors, teachers, students and every day citizens have allowed it. But people can wake up. And with Al Franken, Ed Schultz, Randi Rhodes, Tavis and the alternative press, etc. we can wake up America and get people back to thinking again. The public ought to think about "Where is my money going"? and "if I allow them to treat this guy like that for nine years what kind of monster thug or animal will he be when he gets out of prison"?

We must think! A thinking America is a patriotic America. A thinking America is a successful America. A thinking America doesn't just take it to the bank or take it to heart because Sean Hannity or Rush said it. A thinking man or woman reads, studies, questions, investigates and analyzes. And too many of us have been out to lunch (not if Rod Hickman has his way; you can sleep in) too long. I say wake up! You need not believe in me. If you never support my efforts or believe in my innocence, okay. But believe in something other than what Bush, Rumsfeld, Rush and Sean tell you. You gotta think my brother and my sister. Life is a thinking persons game.

And at times, we are all cynical and jaded. It is easy to give up and not vote, thinking you can't make a difference.   But the key to reviving America is going to be bringing folks together who have disparate or diverse backgrounds and viewpoints. We've got to find ways to get people's willingness to work together on issues in which they have common interests regardless of their background, i.e., "Creating Monsters" affects every American; the rich, the poor, the Black and the White. Regardless of age, race, color or creed, all of us have a vested interest in crime and punishment. So we need to develop think tanks, which include input from our youth and develop strategies for creating citizens who give a damn and who are willing to get involved. Code Pink Women for Peace is a powerful organization headed by Jody Evans in Venice, California. And I must say on a personal note that Jody is one of the most gregarious, affable and articulate women I've ever spoken with. She cares about people and

237

she cares about America. Her organization disrupted Mr. Rumsfeld as he was testifying (testilying?) before congress in May. They were escorted out while the whole nation watched over television. Jody told me (personally at 1:05 p.m. on May 13, 2004) that the guy who was escorted out is from Iraq and he owns a few restaurants in D.C. and has worked with her over the years. Jody expressed to me a strong, interest in this book and informed me that her friends, Leslie Neale and John Densmore have made a film about "Creating Monsters". She wanted me to - "Be certain to send your book to them. John was a drummer for the band 'Doors' and I know they will talk about your book. Write Tom Hayden etc., etc., and we can publicize it," she said. And on May 15, I called my agent who had already received an optimistic e-mail from Jody indicating that she was "blessed to speak with Sherman Manning" and "quite impressed with him". Jody provided addresses to folks we should contact and seemingly wants to help us. It is as if my calling Jody was divine order, divine timing and the beginning of a powerful coalition. I suggest every civilian log on to BadBabes.com and Code Pink Women For Peace and get involved. I suggest that each of you will help Leslie Neale and John Densmore put the word out about their film, which I'll now call (thanks to Jody) the sister to this tome. I hope Jody, Tom Hayden, Arianna Huffington and Tavis Smiley can get this book into schools, churches and juvenile facilities. And that some young man or young woman will read this book and decide to change her/his life. We must bring Gayle Murphy, Attorney Joe Morris, David Berg, Aaron Spool and Clay Aiken into the movement. And if Jody, Gayle and Leslie will coordinate telethons, call-a-thons, etc. and mobilize folks to call, write and e-mail, Radionation in New York, Air America, Celebrity Justice, Inside Edition and Larry King, etc., we can get columnists to write about the issue of "Creating Monsters" and we can get talk show hosts to talk about it. Randi Rhodes said on her show the other day, "I love to read", to a caller. Ipso facto, you need to be certain that Randi gets this book. You can e-mail her and ask if she has it. And if she doesn't, log on to cafeshops.com/manning or call Jody Evans or your bookstore or Amazon.com and get a copy and mail it to her. In the process of inundating the alternative media, schools, churches and juvenile facilities with this book and with Leslie's film, we will begin to expose the human rights violations, which are taking place in America's Youth Prisons as well as the adult prisons. We will reiterate the fact to our citizens that there are a few men in prison who should never be let out of prison. And by the same token, there are some prison guards who should never be let in prison. Because they go in the prisons and juvenile facilities under the color of authority and they arrest the mental development of our young men and young women. They abuse, confuse, rape, torture, traumatize and brutalize our young people. And they create monsters. They are creating monsters. They are specialists at creating monsters. But the monsters they create will affect our society. Let us break the cycle together. I spoke with a highly intelligent young man today whom I'll call Paya (pseudonym) and to my utter surprise, he knew I was a scribe. As I looked into this young man's eyes, I saw hurt, pain, rage, confusion, and anger. At the same time, I saw hope, inspiration and the desire for a better life. "I been in and out of jail since I was fifteen," he told me. "I like to read about real people and to try to better myself," he went on to say. I wanted to offer to help him. I wanted to say, "move in with me today and lets write a book about your life to prevent some other young Brown, White and Black kids from coming in here when they're fifteen. Paya we can save our youth. You can make a difference. Your story can help somebody else." But in all honesty, I said none of that. I find that when I'm pulled toward an individual behind these walls, although in many instances I know I can help them or that I have some platonic or social affinity toward them, I resist telling them because the subculture of the prison factory causes propaganda, innuendo and suspicions to keep good people away from good people. The stage was set a long time ago to keep the races separate and keep divisions amongst us. And our minds have been so narrowed and programmed that we would rather miss a blessing just to prevent our homies from thinking we are soft or we are race mixing, etc. Paya is a good guy and he is one of the guys who should not be in prison. Playboy is another one. Playboy is a dude I wish I could lecture for two hours per day. So are Justin, Chuckie, Youngster and Ronnie. But some are so lost that you could offer them a thousand dollars to get out of the cell with that alcoholic, that gangbanger or that guy who pays more attention to rolling up his mattress than he does to rolling up his sleeves and de-institutionalizing his mind. But they are stuck and the only way to save them is to work, to pray, to write, to tear down these walls. Tear down these walls!!

On May 16th, I was paged for a telephone call with Mr. Kanipes who is the Litigation Coordinator for Mule Creek Prison. He called to tell me he has jury duty and is on prison grounds to deny my appeal. Bottom line is I cannot receive or have or even view a copy of my book, "American Dream/A Search For Justice". I have absolutely nothing against Mr. Kanipes. In fact, there are a lot of good staff at Mule Creek. However, I do expect another arbitrary, vindictive and retaliatory transfer and/or ad-seg placement soon. Once you're on their radar system as a published scribe, they get rid of you by any means necessary. Disallowing me access to my book is unconstitutional and violates the spirit of the First Amendment. This is an invisible punishment much like Marc Mauer, Peter Sussman and Mumia Abu Jamal write about. C.D.C. uses intimidation factors! They "win" their arguments, not by persuasion or logic but by stifling dissent. They don't encourage open discussions about the problems within C.D.C., instead they prefer swagger to shut down opposition voices. I would hope Joe Morris, Mike Farrell, Denzel Washington, Jody, Tom and the Youth Media Council will tell Dan Rather, tell Randi Rhodes, tell Doug Banks and tell the world about C.D.C.'s finest engaging in taliban justice to the tune of raping constitutional rights to free speech and artistic expression. Once the light is shined consistently in the monster factories across our nation, then and only then will our nation rise up and demand a change. Again I say tear down these walls! Stay tuned. There is more to come . . .

Write to me at:

Sherman D. Manning, J98796
CSP SAC A8-226
P. O. Box 290066
Represa CA 95671

Call C.D.C. Director Jeannie Woodford, YACA General Secretary Roderick Q. Hickman and inundate Governor Arnold Schwarzenegger and politicians across America and tell them, "You must read 'Creating Monsters' by Sherman Manning . . .

I want to thank Kevin Shelton, Julian Bond, Aaron Goodwin, Chris Webber, Bishop Eddie Long, T. D. Jakes, Noel Jones, Tommy Goss, Roberta Franklin, Paul Wright, Allan Rafferty, Nick Bentley, Little Caesars Pizza in Turlock, etc. and all those who are already telling politicians, professors, lawmakers and lawyers about this book.

Thank you!

How You Can Help

1. Call 1-800-Bishop2 and order tapes and video's by Bishop Jakes.

2. Log on to www.outlawsonline.com/ShermanManning.htm and www.thepamperedprisoner.com/smanningca.htm, e-mail to hallopeter@freesurf.ch and pledge $100.00 or more to help exonerate Sherman Manning. (We pray that the La Van Hawkins, Cathy Hughes, P. Diddy and John Johnson's will *help*)

3. Call in to the Doug Banks Radio Show, Larry King, Radio One, Tommy Goss and Tom Joyner and discuss this book.

4. Call C.D.C. (Headquarters in Downtown Sacramento Ca.) and Warden Pliler and check (916-985-8610) up on Sherman.

5. Read and support Justice Denied Magazine.

6. Tell every lawyer, politician and pastor you know to get this book.

7. Order a copy of this book for a prisoner.

8. Discuss this tome on the internet and in debates.

9. Support Barry Scheck and the Innocence project in New York City.

10. Write to Sherman Manning at CSP Sacramento, Ca.
    J. Albert Emslander ? John Densmore ? And Randi Rhodes ? Stay tuned . . .

To order more copies of this and other books, t-shirts, mugs, caps, hats, cards etc. visit *www.cafeshops.com/manning* or *www.cafeshops.com/creating* or call *877-809-1659*. If you received this tome *gratis* please forward twenty five dollars to Sherman Manning at the Mule Creek address in One California.

"If you really want to become *great*; you must be willing to make another man great. If you have not been motivated to help me achieve justice, (for *me*) so be it. But I pray that *you* will help make other men (and women) great. You police officers, prison guards, lawyers and judges who have just finished reading this book need to make men great. I call on you to reach out to that bad boy (or girl) in your neighborhood and help them. Don't walk away from them. Look them in the eyes and tell them "I see *greatness* inside *you*." Take them under your wings and build them up. They need to know that you *care*. Take them to manpower and let them see T. D. Jakes, Eddie Long, Noel Jones and Paula White. Take them to the movies, a ballgame or to a concert.... Become innovative and creative and just *save our youth*. We can't give up on them. I love you and God be with you"....

Sherman Manning
Bestselling Author, Motivator, Peak Performance Coach, expert in the psychology of change, Entrepreneur, consultant, President, founder and CEO of G.B.G.

June 2004 / 2010

243